RED DRAGON

Also by Thomas Harris

Black Sunday

The Silence of the Lambs

Hannibal

RED DRAGON

by

Thomas Harris

A DUTTON BOOK

DUTTON
Published by the Penguin Group
Penguin Putnam Inc., 375 Hudson Street, New York, New York 10014, U.S.A.
Penguin Books Ltd, 27 Wrights Lane, London W8 5TZ, England
Penguin Books Australia Ltd, Ringwood, Victoria, Australia
Penguin Books Canada Ltd, 10 Alcorn Avenue, Toronto, Ontario, Canada M4V 3B2
Penguin Books (N.Z.) Ltd, 182–190 Wairau Road, Auckland 10, New Zealand

Penguin Books Ltd, Registered Offices: Harmondsworth, Middlesex, England

Published by Dutton, a member of Penguin Putnam Inc.
Previously published by G. P. Putnam's Sons.

First Dutton Printing, June 2000
10 9 8 7 6 5 4

Frontispiece: "The Red Dragon and the Woman Clothed with the Sun"
by William Blake (1757-1827), courtesy of The Brooklyn Museum,
gift of William Augustus White.

Ⓟ REGISTERED TRADEMARK—MARCA REGISTRADA

LIBRARY OF CONGRESS CATALOGING-IN-PUBLICATION DATA

Harris, Thomas.
   Red dragon / by Thomas Harris.
      p.   cm.
   ISBN 0-525-94556-3
   1. Serial murders—Fiction. 2. Government investigators—Fiction. I. Title.
   PS3558.A6558 R4 2000
   813'.54—dc21   00-022500

Printed in the United States of America

PUBLISHER'S NOTE
This book is a work of fiction. Names, characters, places, and incidents are either the
product of the author's imagination or are used fictitiously, and any resemblance to
actual persons, living or dead, business establishments, events, or locales is entirely
coincidental.

This book is printed on acid-free paper. ∞

FOREWORD TO A
FATAL INTERVIEW

I WANT TO TELL you the circumstances in which I first encountered
Hannibal Lecter, M.D.

In the fall of 1979, owing to an illness in my family, I returned
home to the Mississippi Delta and remained there eighteen months.
I was working on *Red Dragon*. My neighbor in the village of Rich
kindly gave me the use of a shotgun house in the center of a vast cotton field, and there I worked, often at night.

To write a novel, you begin with what you can see and then you
add what came before and what came after. Here in the village of
Rich, Mississippi, working under difficult circumstances, I could see
the investigator Will Graham in the home of the victim family, in the
house where they all died, watching the dead family's home movies.
I did not know at the time who was committing the crimes. I pushed
to find out, to see what came before and what came after. I went
through the home, the crime scene, in the dark with Will and could
see no more and no less than he could see.

Sometimes at night I would leave the lights on in my little house
and walk across the flat fields. When I looked back from a distance,
the house looked like a boat at sea, and all around me the vast Delta
night.

I soon became acquainted with the semi-feral dogs who roamed
free across the fields in what was more or less a pack. Some of them
had casual arrangements with the families of farm workers, but much
of the time they had to forage for themselves. In the hard winter
months with the ground frozen and dry, I started giving them dog

food and soon they were going through fifty pounds of dog food a week. They followed me around, and they were a lot of company— tall dogs, short ones, relatively friendly dogs and big rough dogs you could not touch. They walked with me in the fields at night and when I couldn't see them, I could hear them all around me, breathing and snuffling along in the dark. When I was working in the cabin, they waited on the front porch, and when the moon was full they would sing.

➤

Standing baffled in the vast fields outside my cabin in the heart of the night, the sound of breathing all around me, my vision still clouded with the desk lamp, I tried to see what had happened at the crime scene. All that came to my dim sight were loomings, intimations, the occasional glow when a retina not human reflected the moon. There was no question that *something* had happened. You must understand that when you are writing a novel you are not making anything up. It's all there and you just have to find it.

Will Graham had to ask somebody, he needed some help and he knew it. He knew where he had to go, long before he let himself think about it. I knew Graham had been severely damaged in a previous case. I knew he was terribly reluctant to consult the best source he had. At the time, I myself was accruing painful memories every day, and in my evening's work I felt for Graham.

So it was with some trepidation that I accompanied him to the Baltimore State Hospital for the Criminally Insane, and there, maddeningly, before we could get down to business, we encountered the kind of fool you know from conducting your own daily business, Dr. Frederick Chilton, who delayed us for two or three interminable days.

I found that I could leave Chilton in the cabin with the lights on and look back at him from the dark, surrounded by my friends the dogs. I was invisible then, out there in the dark, the way I am invisible to my characters when I'm in a room with them and they are deciding their fates with little or no help from me.

Finished with the tedious Chilton at last, Graham and I went on to the Violent Ward and the steel door slammed shut behind us with a terrific noise.

Will Graham and I, approaching Dr. Lecter's cell. Graham was tense and I could smell fear on him. I thought Dr. Lecter was asleep and I jumped when he recognized Will Graham by scent without opening his eyes.

I was enjoying my usual immunity while working, my invisibility to Chilton and Graham and the staff, but I was not comfortable in the presence of Dr. Lecter, not sure at all that the doctor could not see me.

Like Graham, I found, and find, the scrutiny of Dr. Lecter uncomfortable, intrusive, like the humming in your thoughts when they X-ray your head. Graham's interview with Dr. Lecter went quickly, in real time at the speed of swordplay, me following it, my frantic notes spilling into the margin and over whatever surface was uppermost on my table. I was worn out when it was over—the incidental clashes and howls of an asylum rang on in my head, and on the front porch of my cabin in Rich thirteen dogs were singing, seated with their eyes closed, faces upturned to the full moon. Most of them crooned their single vowel between O and U, a few just hummed along.

I had to revisit Graham's interview with Dr. Lecter a hundred times to understand it and to get rid of the superfluous static, the jail noises, the screaming of the damned that had made some of the words hard to hear.

I still didn't know who was committing the crimes, but I knew for the first time that we would find out, and that we would arrive at him. I also knew the knowledge would be terribly, perhaps tragically, expensive to others in the book. And so it turned out.

Years later when I started *The Silence of the Lambs*, I did not know that Dr. Lecter would return. I had always liked the character of Dahlia Iyad in *Black Sunday* and wanted to do a novel with a strong woman as the central character. So I began with Clarice Starling and, not two pages into the novel, I found she had to go visit the doctor. I admired Clarice Starling enormously and I think I suffered some feelings of jealousy at the ease with which Dr. Lecter saw into her, when it was so difficult for me.

By the time I undertook to record the events in *Hannibal*, the doctor, to my surprise, had taken on a life of his own. You seemed to find him as oddly engaging as I did.

I dreaded doing *Hannibal*, dreaded the personal wear and tear, dreaded the choices I would have to watch, feared for Starling. In the end I let them go, as you must let characters go, let Dr. Lecter and

Clarice Starling decide events according to their natures. There is a certain amount of courtesy involved.

As a sultan once said: I do not *keep* falcons—they live with me.

When in the winter of 1979 I entered the Baltimore State Hospital for the Criminally Insane and the great metal door crashed closed behind me, little did I know what waited at the end of the corridor; how seldom we recognize the sound when the bolt of our fate slides home.

T.H.
Miami, January 2000

One can only see what one observes, and one observes
only things which are already in the mind.
                    —ALPHONSE BERTILLON

➢

. . . For Mercy has a human heart,
Pity a human face,
And Love, the human form divine,
And Peace, the human dress.
                    —WILLIAM BLAKE, *Songs of Innocence*
                    (The Divine Image)

Cruelty has a Human Heart,
and Jealousy a Human Face,
Terror the Human Form Divine,
and Secrecy the Human Dress.

The Human Dress is forged Iron,
The Human Form a fiery Forge,
The Human Face a Furnace seal'd,
The Human Heart its hungry Gorge.
                    —WILLIAM BLAKE, *Songs of Experience*
                    (A Divine Image)*

* After Blake's death, this poem was found with prints from the plates
of *Songs of Experience*. It appears only in posthumous editions.

RED DRAGON

CHAPTER 1

WILL GRAHAM sat Crawford down at a picnic table between the house and the ocean and gave him a glass of iced tea.

Jack Crawford looked at the pleasant old house, salt-silvered wood in the clear light. "I should have caught you in Marathon when you got off work," he said. "You don't want to talk about it here."

"I don't want to talk about it anywhere, Jack. You've got to talk about it, so let's have it. Just don't get out any pictures. If you brought pictures, leave them in the briefcase—Molly and Willy will be back soon."

"How much do you know?"

"What was in the Miami *Herald* and the *Times*," Graham said. "Two families killed in their houses a month apart. Birmingham and Atlanta. The circumstances were similar."

"Not similar. The same."

"How many confessions so far?"

"Eighty-six when I called in this afternoon," Crawford said. "Cranks. None of them knew details. He smashes the mirrors and uses the pieces. None of them knew that."

"What else did you keep out of the papers?"

"He's blond, right-handed and really strong, wears a size-eleven shoe. He can tie a bowline. The prints are all smooth gloves."

"You said that in public."

"He's not too comfortable with locks," Crawford said. "Used a glass cutter and a suction cup to get in the house last time. Oh, and his blood's AB positive."

13

"Somebody hurt him?"

"Not that we know of. We typed him from semen and saliva. He's a secretor." Crawford looked out at the flat sea. "Will, I want to ask you something. You saw this in the papers. The second one was all over the TV. Did you ever think about giving me a call?"

"No."

"Why not?"

"There weren't many details at first on the one in Birmingham. It could have been anything—revenge, a relative."

"But after the second one, you knew what it was."

"Yeah. A psychopath. I didn't call you because I didn't want to. I know who you have already to work on this. You've got the best lab. You'd have Heimlich at Harvard, Bloom at the University of Chicago—"

"And I've got you down here fixing fucking boat motors."

"I don't think I'd be all that useful to you, Jack. I never think about it anymore."

"Really? You caught two. The last two we had, you caught."

"How? By doing the same things you and the rest of them are doing."

"That's not entirely true, Will. It's the way you think."

"I think there's been a lot of bullshit about the way I think."

"You made some jumps you never explained."

"The evidence was there," Graham said.

"Sure. Sure there was. Plenty of it—afterward. Before the collar there was so damn little we couldn't get probable cause to go in."

"You have the people you need, Jack. I don't think I'd be an improvement. I came down here to get away from that."

"I know it. You got hurt last time. Now you look all right."

"I'm all right. It's not getting cut. You've been cut."

"I've been cut, but not like that."

"It's not getting cut. I just decided to stop. I don't think I can explain it."

"If you couldn't look at it anymore, God knows I'd understand that."

"No. You know—having to look. It's always bad, but you get so you can function anyway, as long as they're dead. The hospital, interviews, that's worse. You have to shake it off and keep on thinking. I don't believe I could do it now. I could make myself look, but I'd shut down the thinking."

"These are all dead, Will," Crawford said as kindly as he could.

Jack Crawford heard the rhythm and syntax of his own speech in Graham's voice. He had heard Graham do that before, with other people. Often in intense conversation Graham took on the other person's speech patterns. At first, Crawford had thought he was doing it deliberately, that it was a gimmick to get the back-and-forth rhythm going.

Later Crawford realized that Graham did it involuntarily, that sometimes he tried to stop and couldn't.

Crawford dipped into his jacket pocket with two fingers. He flipped two photographs across the table, face up.

"All dead," he said.

Graham stared at him a moment before picking up the pictures.

They were only snapshots: A woman, followed by three children and a duck, carried picnic items up the bank of a pond. A family stood behind a cake.

After half a minute he put the photographs down again. He pushed them into a stack with his finger and looked far down the beach where the boy hunkered, examining something in the sand. The woman stood watching, hand on her hip, spent waves creaming around her ankles. She leaned inland to swing her wet hair off her shoulders.

Graham, ignoring his guest, watched Molly and the boy for as long as he had looked at the pictures.

Crawford was pleased. He kept the satisfaction out of his face with the same care he had used to choose the site of this conversation. He thought he had Graham. Let it cook.

Three remarkably ugly dogs wandered up and flopped to the ground around the table.

"My God," Crawford said.

"These are probably dogs," Graham explained. "People dump small ones here all the time. I can give away the cute ones. The rest stay around and get to be big ones."

"They're fat enough."

"Molly's a sucker for strays."

"You've got a nice life here, Will. Molly and the boy. How old is he?"

"Eleven."

"Good-looking kid. He's going to be taller than you."

Graham nodded. "His father was. I'm lucky here. I know that."

"I wanted to bring Phyllis down here. Florida. Get a place when I retire, and stop living like a cave fish. She says all her friends are in Arlington."

"I meant to thank her for the books she brought me in the hospital, but I never did. Tell her for me."

"I'll tell her."

Two small bright birds lit on the table, hoping to find jelly. Crawford watched them hop around until they flew away.

"Will, this freak seems to be in phase with the moon. He killed the Jacobis in Birmingham on Saturday night, June 28, full moon. He killed the Leeds family in Atlanta night before last, July 26. That's one day short of a lunar month. So if we're lucky we may have a little over three weeks before he does it again."

"I don't think you want to wait here in the Keys and read about the next one in your Miami *Herald.* Hell, I'm not the pope, I'm not saying what you ought to do, but I want to ask you, do you respect my judgment, Will?"

"Yes."

"I think we have a better chance to get him fast if you help. Hell, Will, saddle up and help us. Go to Atlanta and Birmingham and look, then come on to Washington. Just TDY."

Graham did not reply.

Crawford waited while five waves lapped the beach. Then he got up and slung his suit coat over his shoulder. "Let's talk after dinner."

"Stay and eat."

Crawford shook his head. "I'll come back later. There'll be messages at the Holiday Inn and I'll be a while on the phone. Tell Molly thanks, though."

Crawford's rented car raised thin dust that settled on the bushes beside the shell road.

Graham returned to the table. He was afraid that this was how he would remember the end of Sugarloaf Key—ice melting in two tea glasses and paper napkins fluttering off the redwood table in the breeze and Molly and Willy far down the beach.

➤

Sunset on Sugarloaf, the herons still and the red sun swelling.

Will Graham and Molly Foster Graham sat on a bleached drift log, their faces orange in the sunset, backs in violet shadow. She picked up his hand.

"Crawford stopped by to see me at the shop before he came out here," she said. "He asked directions to the house. I tried to call you. You really ought to answer the phone once in a while. We saw the car when we got home and went around to the beach."

"What else did he ask you?"

"How you are."

"And you said?"

"I said you're fine and he should leave you the hell alone. What does he want you to do?"

"Look at evidence. I'm a forensic specialist, Molly. You've seen my diploma."

"You mended a crack in the ceiling paper with your diploma, I saw that." She straddled the log to face him. "If you missed your other life, what you used to do, I think you'd talk about it. You never do. You're open and calm and easy now . . . I love that."

"We have a good time, don't we?"

Her single styptic blink told him he should have said something better. Before he could fix it, she went on.

"What you did for Crawford was bad for you. He has a lot of other people—the whole damn government I guess—why can't he leave us alone?"

"Didn't Crawford tell you that? He was my supervisor the two times I left the FBI Academy to go back to the field. Those two cases were the only ones like this he ever had, and Jack's been working a long time. Now he's got a new one. This kind of psychopath is very rare. He knows I've had . . . experience."

"Yes, you have," Molly said. His shirt was unbuttoned and she could see the looping scar across his stomach. It was finger width and raised, and it never tanned. It ran down from his left hipbone and turned up to notch his rib cage on the other side.

Dr. Hannibal Lecter did that with a linoleum knife. It happened a year before Molly met Graham, and it very nearly killed him. Dr. Lecter, known in the tabloids as "Hannibal the Cannibal," was the second psychopath Graham had caught.

When he finally got out of the hospital, Graham resigned from the

Federal Bureau of Investigation, left Washington and found a job as a diesel mechanic in the boatyard at Marathon in the Florida Keys. It was a trade he grew up with. He slept in a trailer at the boatyard until Molly and her good ramshackle house on Sugarloaf Key.

Now he straddled the drift log and held both her hands. Her feet burrowed under his.

"All right, Molly. Crawford thinks I have a knack for the monsters. It's like a superstition with him."

"Do you believe it?"

Graham watched three pelicans fly in line across the tidal flats. "Molly, an intelligent psychopath—particularly a sadist—is hard to catch for several reasons. First, there's no traceable motive. So you can't go that way. And most of the time you won't have any help from informants. See, there's a lot more stooling than sleuthing behind most arrests, but in a case like this there won't *be* any informants. *He* may not even know that he's doing it. So you have to take whatever evidence you have and extrapolate. You try to reconstruct his thinking. You try to find patterns."

"And follow him and find him," Molly said. "I'm afraid if you go after this maniac, or whatever he is—I'm afraid he'll do you like the last one did. That's it. That's what scares me."

"He'll never see me or know my name, Molly. The police, they'll have to take him down if they can find him, not me. Crawford just wants another point of view."

She watched the red sun spread over the sea. High cirrus glowed above it.

Graham loved the way she turned her head, artlessly giving him her less perfect profile. He could see the pulse in her throat, and remembered suddenly and completely the taste of salt on her skin. He swallowed and said, "What the hell can I do?"

"What you've already decided. If you stay here and there's more killing, maybe it would sour this place for you. *High Noon* and all that crap. If it's that way, you weren't really asking."

"If I *were* asking, what would you say?"

"Stay here with me. Me. Me. Me. And Willy, I'd drag him in if it would do any good. I'm supposed to dry my eyes and wave my hanky. If things don't go so well, I'll have the satisfaction that you did the right thing. That'll last about as long as taps. Then I can go home and switch one side of the blanket on."

OCEAN CITY
FREE PUBLIC
LIBRARY

07-07-2022 06:27PM
Item(s) checked out to Davison, Reagan.

TITLE: Red dragon
BARCODE: 2001896
DUE DATE: 07-21-22

TITLE: Hannibal
BARCODE: 634588
DUE DATE: 07-21-22

YOU SAVED
$54.95
Value of Materials Checked out!

Ocean City Free Public Library
1735 Simpson Ave.
Ocean City, NJ 08226
(609) 399-2434
http://www.oceancitylibrary.org

"I'd be at the back of the pack."

"Never in your life. I'm selfish, huh?"

"I don't care."

"Neither do I. It's keen and sweet here. All the things that happen to you before make you know it. Value it, I mean."

He nodded.

"Don't want to lose it either way," she said.

"Nope. We won't, either."

Darkness fell quickly and Jupiter appeared, low in the southwest. They walked back to the house beside the rising gibbous moon. Far out past the tidal flats, bait fish leaped for their lives.

➤

Crawford came back after dinner. He had taken off his coat and tie and rolled up his sleeves for the casual effect. Molly thought Crawford's thick pale forearms were repulsive. To her he looked like a damnably wise ape. She served him coffee under the porch fan and sat with him while Graham and Willy went out to feed dogs. She said nothing. Moths batted softly at the screens.

"He looks good, Molly," Crawford said. "You both do—skinny and brown."

"Whatever I say, you'll take him anyway, won't you?"

"Yeah. I have to. I have to do it. But I swear to God, Molly, I'll make it as easy on him as I can. He's changed. It's great you got married."

"He's better and better. He doesn't dream so often now. He was really obsessed with the dogs for a while. Now he just takes care of them; he doesn't talk about them all the time. You're his friend, Jack. Why can't you leave him alone?"

"Because it's his bad luck to be the best. Because he doesn't think like other people. Somehow he never got in a rut."

"He thinks you want him to look at evidence."

"I do want him to look at evidence. There's nobody better with evidence. But he has the other thing too. Imagination, projection, whatever. He doesn't like that part of it."

"You wouldn't like it either if you had it. Promise me something,

Jack. Promise me you'll see to it he doesn't get too close. I think it would kill him to have to fight."

"He won't have to fight. I can promise you that."

When Graham finished with the dogs, Molly helped him pack.

CHAPTER 2

WILL GRAHAM drove slowly past the house where the Charles Leeds family had lived and died. The windows were dark. One yard light burned. He parked two blocks away and walked back through the warm night, carrying the Atlanta police detectives' report in a cardboard box.

Graham had insisted on coming alone. Anyone else in the house would distract him—that was the reason he gave Crawford. He had another, private reason: he was not sure how he would act. He didn't want a face aimed at him all the time.

He had been all right at the morgue.

The two-story brick home was set back from the street on a wooded lot. Graham stood under the trees for a long time looking at it. He tried to be still inside. In his mind a silver pendulum swung in darkness. He waited until the pendulum was still.

A few neighbors drove by, looking at the house quickly and looking away. A murder house is ugly to the neighbors, like the face of someone who betrayed them. Only outsiders and children stare.

The shades were up. Graham was glad. That meant no relatives had been inside. Relatives always lower the shades.

He walked around the side of the house, moving carefully, not using his flashlight. He stopped twice to listen. The Atlanta police knew he was here, but the neighbors did not. They would be jumpy. They might shoot.

Looking in a rear window, he could see all the way through to the light in the front yard, past silhouettes of furniture. The scent of Cape jasmine was heavy in the air. A latticed porch ran across most of the back. On the porch door was the seal of the Atlanta police department. Graham removed the seal and went in.

The door from the porch into the kitchen was patched with plywood where the police had taken out the glass. By flashlight he unlocked it with the key the police had given him. He wanted to turn on lights. He wanted to put on his shiny badge and make some official noises to justify himself to the silent house where five people had died. He did none of that. He went into the dark kitchen and sat down at the breakfast table.

Two pilot lights on the kitchen range glowed blue in the dark. He smelled furniture polish and apples.

The thermostat clicked and the air conditioning came on. Graham started at the noise, felt a trickle of fear. He was an old hand at fear. He could manage this one. He simply was afraid, and he could go on anyway.

He could see and hear better afraid; he could not speak as concisely, and fear sometimes made him rude. Here, there was nobody left to speak to, there was nobody to offend anymore.

Madness came into this house through that door into this kitchen, moving on size-eleven feet. Sitting in the dark, he sensed madness like a bloodhound sniffs a shirt.

Graham had studied the detectives' report at Atlanta Homicide for most of the day and early evening. He remembered that the light on the vent hood over the stove had been on when the police arrived. He turned it on now.

Two framed samplers hung on the wall beside the stove. One said "Kissin' don't last, cookin' do." The other was "It's always to the kitchen that our friends best like to come, to hear the heartbeat of the house, take comfort in its hum."

Graham looked at his watch. Eleven-thirty P.M. According to the pathologist, the deaths occurred between eleven P.M. and one A.M.

First there was the entry. He thought about that . . .

The madman slipped the hook on the outside screen door. Stood in the darkness of the porch and took something from his pocket. A suction cup, maybe the base of a pencil sharpener designed to stick to a desktop.

Crouched against the wooden lower half of the kitchen door, the madman raised his head to peer through the glass. He put out his tongue and licked the cup, pressed it to the glass and flicked the lever to make it stick. A small glass cutter was attached to the cup with string so that he could cut a circle.

Tiny squeal of the glass cutter and one solid tap to break the glass. One hand to tap, one hand to hold the suction cup. The glass must not fall. The loose piece of glass is slightly egg-shaped because the string wrapped around the shaft of the suction cup as he cut. A little grating noise as he pulls the piece of glass back outside. He does not care that he leaves AB saliva on the glass.

His hand in the tight glove snakes in through the hole, finds the lock. The door opens silently. He is inside. In the light of the vent hood he can see his body in this strange kitchen. It is pleasantly cool in the house.

Will Graham ate two Di-Gels. The crackle of the cellophane irritated him as he stuffed it in his pocket. He walked through the living room, holding his flashlight well away from him by habit. Though he had studied the floor plan, he made one wrong turn before he found the stairs. They did not creak.

Now he stood in the doorway of the master bedroom. He could see faintly without the flashlight. A digital clock on a nightstand projected the time on the ceiling and an orange night light burned above the baseboard by the bathroom. The coppery smell of blood was strong.

Eyes accustomed to the dark could see well enough. The madman could distinguish Mr. Leeds from his wife. There was enough light for him to cross the room, grab Leeds's hair and cut his throat. What then? Back to the wall switch, a greeting to Mrs. Leeds and then the gunshot that disabled her?

Graham switched on the lights and bloodstains shouted at him from the walls, from the mattress and the floor. The very air had screams smeared on it. He flinched from the noise in this silent room full of dark stains drying.

Graham sat on the floor until his head was quiet. Still, still, be still.

The number and variety of the bloodstains had puzzled Atlanta detectives trying to reconstruct the crime. All the victims were found slain in their beds. This was not consistent with the locations of the stains.

At first they believed Charles Leeds was attacked in his daughter's room and his body dragged to the master bedroom. Close examination of the splash patterns made them reconsider.

The killer's exact movements in the rooms were not yet determined.

Now, with the advantage of the autopsy and lab reports, Will Graham began to see how it had happened.

The intruder cut Charles Leeds's throat as he lay asleep beside his wife, went back to the wall switch and turned on the light—hairs and oil from Mr. Leeds's head were left on the switchplate by a smooth glove. He shot Mrs. Leeds as she was rising, then went toward the children's rooms.

Leeds rose with his cut throat and tried to protect the children, losing great gouts of blood and an unmistakable arterial spray as he tried to fight. He was shoved away, fell and died with his daughter in her room.

One of the two boys was shot in bed. The other boy was also found in bed, but he had dust balls in his hair. Police believed he was dragged out from under his bed to be shot.

When all of them were dead, except possibly Mrs. Leeds, the smashing of mirrors began, the selection of shards, the further attention to Mrs. Leeds.

Graham had full copies of all the autopsy protocols in his box. Here was the one on Mrs. Leeds. The bullet entered to the right of her navel and lodged in her lumbar spine, but she died of strangulation.

The increase in serotonin and free histamine levels in the gunshot wound indicated she had lived at least five minutes after she was shot. The histamine was much higher than the serotonin, so she had not lived more than fifteen minutes. Most of her other injuries were probably, but not conclusively, postmortem.

If the other injuries were postmortem, what was the killer doing in the interval while Mrs. Leeds waited to die? Graham wondered. Struggling with Leeds and killing the others, yes, but that would have taken less than a minute. Smashing the mirrors. But what else?

The Atlanta detectives were thorough. They had measured and photographed exhaustively, had vacuumed and grid-searched and taken the traps from the drains. Still, Graham looked for himself.

From the police photographs and taped outlines on the mattresses, Graham could see where the bodies had been found. The evidence—nitrate traces on bedclothes in the case of the gunshot wounds—indicated that they were found in positions approximating those in which they died.

But the profusion of bloodstains and matted sliding marks on the hall carpet remained unexplained. One detective had theorized that some of the victims tried to crawl away from the killer. Graham did not believe it—clearly the killer moved them after they were dead and then put them back the way they were when he killed them.

What he did with Mrs. Leeds was obvious. But what about the others? He had not disfigured them further, as he did Mrs. Leeds. The children each suffered a single gunshot wound in the head. Charles Leeds bled to death, with aspirated blood contributing. The only additional mark on him was a superficial ligature mark around his chest, believed to be postmortem. What did the killer do with them after they were dead?

From his box Graham took the police photographs, lab reports on the individual blood and organic stains in the room and standard comparison plates of blood-drop trajectories.

He went over the upstairs rooms minutely, trying to match injuries to stains, trying to work backward. He plotted each splash on a measured field sketch of the master bedroom, using the standard comparison plates to estimate the direction and velocity of the bloodfall. In this way he hoped to learn the positions the bodies were in at different times.

Here was a row of three bloodstains slanting up and around a corner of the bedroom wall. Here were three faint stains on the carpet beneath them. The wall above the headboard on Charles Leeds's side of the bed was bloodstained, and there were swipes along the baseboards. Graham's field sketch began to look like a join-the-dots puzzle with no numbers. He stared at it, looked up at the room and back to the sketch until his head ached.

He went into the bathroom and took his last two Bufferin, scooping up water in his hand from the faucet in the sink. He splashed water on his face and dried it with his shirttail. Water spilled on the floor. He had forgotten that the trap was gone from the drain. Otherwise the bathroom was undisturbed, except for the broken mirror and traces of the red fingerprint powder called Dragon's Blood. Toothbrushes, facial cream, razor, were all in place.

The bathroom looked as though a family still used it. Mrs. Leeds's panty hose hung on the towel racks where she had left them to dry. He saw that she cut the leg off a pair when it had a runner so she could match two one-legged pairs, wear them at the same time, and save money. Mrs. Leeds's small, homey economy pierced him; Molly did the same thing.

Graham climbed out a window onto the porch roof and sat on the gritty shingles. He hugged his knees, his damp shirt pressed cold across his back, and snorted the smell of slaughter out of his nose.

The lights of Atlanta rusted the night sky and the stars were hard to see. The night would be clear in the Keys. He could be watching shooting stars with Molly and Willy, listening for the whoosh they solemnly agreed a shooting star must make. The Delta Aquarid meteor shower was at its maximum, and Willy was up for it.

He shivered and snorted again. He did not want to think of Molly now. To do so was tasteless as well as distracting.

Graham had a lot of trouble with taste. Often his thoughts were not tasty. There were no effective partitions in his mind. What he saw and learned touched everything else he knew. Some of the combinations were hard to live with. But he could not anticipate them, could not block and repress. His learned values of decency and propriety tagged along, shocked at his associations, appalled at his dreams; sorry that in the bone arena of his skull there were no forts for what he loved. His associations came at the speed of light. His value judgments were at the pace of a responsive reading. They could never keep up and direct his thinking.

He viewed his own mentality as grotesque but useful, like a chair made of antlers. There was nothing he could do about it.

Graham turned off the lights in the Leeds house and went out through the kitchen. At the far end of the back porch, his flashlight revealed a bicycle and a wicker dog bed. There was a doghouse in the backyard, a dog bowl by the steps.

The evidence indicated the Leedses were surprised in their sleep.

Holding the flashlight between his chin and chest, he wrote a memo: *Jack—where was the dog?*

Graham drove back to his hotel. He had to concentrate on his driving, though there was little traffic at four-thirty A.M. His head still ached and he watched for an all-night pharmacy.

He found one on Peachtree. A slovenly rent-a-cop dozed near the door. A pharmacist in a jacket dingy enough to highlight his dandruff sold Graham Bufferin. The glare in the place was painful. Graham disliked young pharmacists. They had a middle-of-the-litter look about them. They were often smug and he suspected that they were unpleasant at home.

"What else?" the pharmacist said, his fingers poised above the cash register keys. "What else?"

The Atlanta FBI office had booked him into an absurd hotel near the city's new Peachtree Center. It had glass elevators shaped like milkweed pods to let him know he was really in town now.

Graham rode up to his room with two conventioneers wearing name tags with the printed greeting "Hi!" They held to the rail and looked over the lobby as they ascended.

"Looka yonder by the desk—that's Wilma and them just now coming in," the larger one said. "God damn, I'd love to tear off a piece of that."

"Fuck her till her nose bleeds," the other one said.

Fear and rut, and anger at the fear.

"Say, you know why a woman has legs?"

"Why?"

"So she won't leave a trail like a snail."

The elevator doors opened.

"Is this it? This is it," the larger one said. He lurched against the facing as he got off.

"This is the blind leading the blind," the other one said.

Graham put his cardboard box on the dresser in his room. Then he put it in a drawer where he could not see it. He had had enough of the wide-eyed dead. He wanted to call Molly, but it was too early.

A meeting was scheduled for eight A.M. at the Atlanta police headquarters. He'd have little enough to tell them.

He would try to sleep. His mind was a busy rooming house with arguments all around him, and they were fighting somewhere down the hall. He was numb and empty and he drank two fingers of whiskey from his bathroom glass before he lay down. The darkness pressed too closely on him. He turned on the bathroom light and went back to bed. He pretended Molly was in the bathroom brushing her hair.

Lines from the autopsy protocols sounded in his own voice, though he had never read them aloud: ". . . the feces was formed . . . a trace of talcum on the lower right leg. Fracture of the medial orbit wall owing to insertion of mirror shard . . ."

Graham tried to think about the beach at Sugarloaf Key, he tried to hear the waves. He pictured his workbench in his mind and thought about the escapement for the water clock he and Willy were building. He sang "Whiskey River" under his breath and tried to run "Black Mountain Rag" through his head from one end to the other. Molly's

music. Doc Watson's guitar part was all right, but he always lost it in
the fiddle break. Molly had tried to teach him clog dancing in the
backyard and she was bouncing . . . and finally he dozed.

He woke in an hour, rigid and sweating, seeing the other pillow
silhouetted against the bathroom light and it was Mrs. Leeds lying
beside him bitten and torn, mirrored eyes and blood like the legs of
spectacles over her temples and ears. He could not turn his head to
face her. Brain screaming like a smoke alarm, he put his hand over
there and touched dry cloth.

Having acted, he felt some immediate relief. He rose, his heart
pounding, and put on a dry T-shirt. He threw the wet one into the
bathtub. He could not move over to the dry side of the bed. Instead he
put a towel on the side where he had sweated and lay down on it,
propped against the headboard with a stiff drink in his hand. He
swallowed a third of it.

He reached for something to think about, anything. The pharmacy
where he bought the Bufferin, then; perhaps because it was his only
experience all day that was not related to death.

He could remember old drugstores with soda fountains. As a boy,
he thought old drugstores had a slightly furtive air. When you went
in, you always thought about buying rubbers whether you needed any
or not. There were things on the shelves you shouldn't look at too
long.

In the pharmacy where he bought the Bufferin, the contraceptives
with their illustrated wrappings were in a lucite case on the wall
behind the cash register, framed like art.

He preferred the drugstore and sundry of his childhood. Graham
was nearly forty and just beginning to feel the tug of the way the world
was then; it was a sea anchor streamed behind him in heavy weather.

He thought about Smoot. Old Smoot had been the soda jerk and
manager for the pharmacist who owned the local drugstore when
Graham was a child. Smoot, who drank on the job, forgot to unroll
the awning and the sneakers melted in the window. Smoot forgot to
unplug the coffeepot, and the fire department was summoned. Smoot
sold ice cream cones to children on credit.

His principal outrage was ordering fifty Kewpie dolls from a detail
man while the store owner was on vacation. On his return, the owner
fired Smoot for a week. Then they held a Kewpie doll sale. Fifty of the
Kewpie dolls were arranged in a semicircle in the front window so that
they all stared at whoever was looking in.

They had wide eyes of cornflower blue. It was a striking display and Graham had looked at it for some time. He knew they were only Kewpie dolls, but he could feel the focus of their attention. So many of them looking. A number of people stopped to look at them. Plaster dolls, all with the same silly spit curl, yet their concentrated gaze had made his face tingle.

Graham began to relax a little on the bed. Kewpie dolls staring. He started to take a drink, gasped, and choked it onto his chest. He fumbled for the bedside lamp and fetched his box from the dresser drawer. He took out the autopsy protocols of the three Leeds children and his measured field sketches of the master bedroom and spread them on the bed.

Here were the three bloodstains slanting up the corner, and here were the matching stains on the carpet. Here were the dimensions of the three children. Brother, sister, big brother. Match. Match. Match.

They had been in a row, seated along the wall facing the bed. An audience. A dead audience. And Leeds. Tied around the chest to the headboard. Composed to look as though he were sitting up in bed. Getting the ligature mark, staining the wall above the headboard.

What were they watching? Nothing; they were all dead. But their eyes were open. They were watching a performance starring the madman and the body of Mrs. Leeds, beside Mr. Leeds in the bed. An audience. The crazy could look around at their faces.

Graham wondered if he had lit a candle. The flickering light would simulate expression on their faces. No candle was found. Maybe he would think to do that next time . . .

This first small bond to the killer itched and stung like a leech. Graham bit the sheet, thinking.

Why did you move them again? Why didn't you leave them that way? Graham asked. *There's something you don't want me to know about you. Why, there's something you're ashamed of. Or is it something you can't afford for me to know?*

Did you open their eyes?

Mrs. Leeds was lovely, wasn't she? You turned on the light after you cut his throat so Mrs. Leeds could watch him flop, didn't you? It was maddening to have to wear gloves when you touched her, wasn't it?

There was talcum on her leg.

There was no talcum in the bathroom.

Someone else seemed to speak those two facts in a flat voice.

You took off your gloves, didn't you? The powder came out of a rubber glove as you pulled it off to touch her, DIDN'T IT, YOU SON OF A BITCH? You touched her with your bare hands and then you put the gloves back on and you wiped her down. But while the gloves were off, DID YOU OPEN THEIR EYES?

Jack Crawford answered his telephone on the fifth ring. He had answered the telephone in the night many times and he was not confused.

"Jack, this is Will."

"Yes, Will."

"Is Price still in Latent Prints?"

"Yeah. He doesn't go out much anymore. He's working on the single-print index."

"I think he ought to come to Atlanta."

"Why? You said yourself the guy down here is good."

"He *is* good, but not as good as Price."

"What do you want him to do? Where would he look?"

"Mrs. Leeds's fingernails and toenails. They're painted, it's a slick surface. And the corneas of all their eyes. I think he took his gloves off, Jack."

"Jesus, Price'll have to gun it," Crawford said. "The funeral's this afternoon."

CHAPTER 3

"I THINK he had to touch her," Graham said in greeting.

Crawford handed him a Coke from the machine in Atlanta police headquarters. It was seven-fifty A.M.

"Sure, he moved her around," Crawford said. "There were grip marks on her wrists and behind her knees. But every print in the place is from nonporous gloves. Don't worry, Price is here. Grouchy old bastard. He's on his way to the funeral home now. The morgue released the bodies last night, but the funeral home's not doing anything yet. You look bushed. Did you get any sleep?"

"Maybe an hour. I think he had to touch her with his hands."

"I hope you're right, but the Atlanta lab swears he wore like surgeon's gloves the whole time," Crawford said. "The mirror pieces had those smooth prints. Forefinger on the back of the piece wedged in the labia, smudged thumb on the front."

"He polished it after he placed it, so he could see his damn face in there probably," Graham said.

"The one in her mouth was obscured with blood. Same with the eyes. He never took the gloves off."

"Mrs. Leeds was a good-looking woman," Graham said. "You've seen the family pictures, right? I'd want to touch her skin in an intimate situation, wouldn't you?"

"*Intimate?*" Distaste sounded in Crawford's voice before he could stop it. Suddenly he was busy rummaging in his pockets for change.

"Intimate—they had privacy. Everybody else was dead. He could have their eyes open or shut, however he liked."

"Any way he liked," Crawford said. "They tried her skin for prints, of course. Nothing. They did get a hand spread off her neck."

"The report didn't say anything about dusting nails."

"I expect her fingernails were smudged when they took scrapings. The scrapings were just where she cut her palms with them. She never scratched him."

"She had pretty feet," Graham said.

"Umm-hmm. Let's head upstairs," Crawford said. "The troops are about to muster."

➤

Jimmy Price had a lot of equipment—two heavy cases plus his camera bag and tripod. He made a clatter coming through the front door of the Lombard Funeral Home in Atlanta. He was a frail old man and his humor had not been improved by a long taxi ride from the airport in the morning rush.

An officious young fellow with styled hair hustled him into an office decorated in apricot and cream. The desk was bare except for a sculpture called *The Praying Hands*.

Price was examining the fingertips of the praying hands when Mr. Lombard himself came in. Lombard checked Price's credentials with extreme care.

"Your Atlanta office or agency or whatever called me, of course, Mr. Price. But last night we had to get the police to remove an obnoxious fellow who was trying to take pictures for *The National Tattler*, so I'm being very careful. I'm sure you understand. Mr. Price, the bodies were only released to us about one o'clock this morning, and the funeral is this afternoon at five. We simply can't delay it."

"This won't take a lot of time," Price said. "I need one reasonably intelligent assistant, if you have one. Have you touched the bodies, Mr. Lombard?"

"No."

"Find out who has. I'll have to print them all."

➤

The morning briefing of police detectives on the Leeds case was concerned mostly with teeth.

Atlanta Chief of Detectives R. J. (Buddy) Springfield, a burly man in shirtsleeves, stood by the door with Dr. Dominic Princi as the twenty-three detectives filed in.

"All right, boys, let's have the big grin as you come by," Springfield said. "Show Dr. Princi your teeth. That's right, let's see 'em all. Christ, Sparks, is that your tongue or are you swallowing a squirrel? Keep moving."

A large frontal view of a set of teeth, upper and lower, was tacked to the bulletin board at the front of the squad room. It reminded Graham of the celluloid strip of printed teeth in a dime-store jack-o'-lantern. He and Crawford sat down at the back of the room while the detectives took their places at schoolroom desks.

Atlanta Public Safety Commissioner Gilbert Lewis and his public-relations officer sat apart from them in folding chairs. Lewis had to face a news conference in an hour.

Chief of Detectives Springfield took charge.

"All right. Let's cease fire with the bullshit. If you read up this morning, you saw zero progress.

"House-to-house interviews will continue for a radius of four additional blocks around the scene. R & I has loaned us two clerks to help cross-matching airline reservations and car rentals in Birmingham and Atlanta.

"Airport and hotel details will make the rounds again today. Yes, again to*day*. Catch every maid and attendant as well as the desk people. He had to clean up somewhere and he may have left a mess. If you find somebody who cleaned up a mess, roust out whoever's in the room, seal it, and get on the horn to the laundry double quick. This time we've got something for you to show around. Dr. Princi?"

Dr. Dominic Princi, chief medical examiner for Fulton County, walked to the front and stood under the drawing of the teeth. He held up a dental cast.

"Gentlemen, this is what the subject's teeth look like. The Smithsonian in Washington reconstructed them from the impressions we took of bite marks on Mrs. Leeds and a clear bite mark in a piece of cheese from the Leedses' refrigerator," Princi said.

"As you can see, he has pegged lateral incisors—the teeth here and here." Princi pointed to the cast in his hand, then to the chart above him. "The teeth are crooked in alignment and a corner is missing from this central incisor. The other incisor is grooved, here. It looks like a 'tailor's notch,' the kind of wear you get biting thread."

"Snaggletoothed son of a bitch," somebody mumbled.

"How do you know for sure it was the perpetrator that bit the cheese, Doc?" a tall detective in the front row asked.

Princi disliked being called "Doc," but he swallowed it. "Saliva washes from the cheese and from the bite wounds matched for blood type," he said. "The victims' teeth and blood type didn't match."

"Fine, Doctor," Springfield said. "We'll pass out pictures of the teeth to show around."

"What about giving it to the papers?" The public-relations officer, Simpkins, was speaking. "A 'have-you-seen-these-teeth' sort of thing."

"I see no objection to that," Springfield said. "What about it, Commissioner?"

Lewis nodded.

Simpkins was not through. "Dr. Princi, the press is going to ask why it took four days to get this dental representation you have here. And why it all had to be done in Washington."

Special Agent Crawford studied the button on his ball-point pen.

Princi reddened but his voice was calm. "Bite marks on flesh are distorted when a body is moved, Mr. Simpson—"

"Simpkins."

"Simpkins, then. We couldn't make this using only the bite marks on the victims. That is the importance of the cheese. Cheese is relatively solid, but tricky to cast. You have to oil it first to keep the moisture out of the casting medium. Usually you get one shot at it. The Smithsonian has done it for the FBI crime lab before. They're better equipped to do a face bow registration and they have an anatomical articulator. They have a consulting forensic odontologist. We don't. Anything else?"

"Would it be fair to say that the delay was caused by the FBI lab and not here?"

Princi turned on him. "What it would be fair to say, Mr. Simpkins, is that a federal investigator, Special Agent Crawford, found the cheese in the refrigerator two days ago—after your people had been through the place. He expedited the lab work at my request. It would be fair to say I'm relieved that it wasn't one of you that bit the goddamned thing."

Commissioner Lewis broke in, his heavy voice booming in the squad room. "Nobody's questioning your judgment, Dr. Princi.

Simpkins, the last thing we need is to start a pissing contest with the FBI. Let's get on with it."

"We're all after the same thing," Springfield said. "Jack, do you fellows want to add anything?"

Crawford took the floor. The faces he saw were not entirely friendly. He had to do something about that.

"I just want to clear the air, Chief. Years ago there was a lot of rivalry about who got the collar. Each side, federal and local, held out on the other. It made a gap that crooks slipped through. That's not Bureau policy now, and it's not my policy. I don't give a damn who gets the collar. Neither does Investigator Graham. That's him sitting back there, if some of you are wondering. If the man who did this is run over by a garbage truck, it would suit me just fine as long as it puts him off the street. I think you feel the same way."

Crawford looked over the detectives and hoped they were mollified. He hoped they wouldn't hoard leads. Commissioner Lewis was talking to him.

"Investigator Graham has worked on this kind of thing before."

"Yes, sir."

"Can you add anything, Mr. Graham, suggest anything?"

Crawford raised his eyebrows at Graham.

"Would you come up to the front?" Springfield said.

Graham wished he had been given the chance to talk to Springfield in private. He didn't want to go to the front. He went, though.

Rumpled and sun-blasted, Graham didn't look like a federal investigator. Springfield thought he looked more like a house painter who had put on a suit to appear in court.

The detectives shifted from one buttock to the other.

When Graham turned to face the room, the ice-blue eyes were startling in his brown face.

"Just a couple of things," he said. "We can't assume he's a former mental patient or somebody with a record of sex offenses. There's a high probability that he doesn't have any kind of record. If he does, it's more likely to be breaking and entering than a minor sex offense.

"He may have a history of biting in lesser assaults—bar fights or child abuse. The biggest help we'll have on that will come from emergency-room personnel and the child-welfare people.

"Any bad bite they can remember is worth checking, regardless of who was bitten or how they said it happened. That's all I have."

The tall detective on the front row raised his hand and spoke at the same time.

"But he only bit women so far, right?"

"That's all we know about. He bites a lot, though. Six bad ones in Mrs. Leeds, eight in Mrs. Jacobi. That's way above average."

"What's average?"

"In a sex murder, three. He likes to bite."

"Women."

"Most of the time in sex assaults the bite mark has a livid spot in the center, a suck mark. These don't. Dr. Princi mentioned it in his autopsy report, and I saw it at the morgue. No suck marks. For him biting may be a fighting pattern as much as sexual behavior."

"Pretty thin," the detective said.

"It's worth checking," Graham said. "Any bite is worth checking. People lie about how it happened. Parents of a bitten child will claim an animal did it and let the child take rabies shots to cover for a snapper in the family—you've all seen that. It's worth asking at the hospitals—who's been referred for rabies shots."

"That's all I have." Graham's thigh muscles fluttered with fatigue when he sat down.

"It's worth asking, and we'll ask," Chief of Detectives Springfield said. "Now. The Safe and Loft Squad works the neighborhood along with Larceny. Work the dog angle. You'll see the update and the picture in the file. Find out if any stranger was seen with the dog. Vice and Narcotics, take the K-Y cowboys and the leather bars after you finish the day tour. Marcus and Whitman—heads up at the funeral. Do you have relatives, friends of the family, lined up to spot for you? Good. What about the photographer? All right. Turn in the funeral guest book to R & I. They've got the one from Birmingham already. The rest of the assignments are on the sheet. Let's go."

"One other thing," Commissioner Lewis said. The detectives sank back in their seats. "I have heard officers in this command referring to the killer as the 'Tooth Fairy.' I don't care what you call him among yourselves, I realize you have to call him something. But I had better not hear any police officer refer to him as the Tooth Fairy in public. It sounds flippant. Neither will you use that name on any internal memoranda.

"That's all."

Crawford and Graham followed Springfield back to his office. The chief of detectives gave them coffee while Crawford checked in with the switchboard and jotted down his messages.

"I didn't get a chance to talk to you when you got here yesterday," Springfield said to Graham. "This place has been a fucking madhouse. It's Will, right? Did the boys give you everything you need?"

"Yeah, they were fine."

"We don't have shit and we know it," Springfield said. "Oh, we developed a walking picture from the footprints in the flowerbed. He was walking around bushes and stuff, so you can't tell much more than his shoe size, maybe his height. The left print's a little deeper, so he may have been carrying something. It's busywork. We did get a burglar, though, a couple of years ago, off a walking picture. Showed Parkinson's disease. Princi picked it up. No luck this time."

"You have a good crew," Graham said.

"They are. But this kind of thing is out of our usual line, thank God. Let me get it straight, do you fellows work together all the time—you and Jack and Dr. Bloom—or do you just get together for one of these?"

"Just for these," Graham said.

"Some reunion. The commissioner was saying you were the one who nailed Lecter three years ago."

"We were all there with the Maryland police," Graham said. "The Maryland state troopers arrested him."

Springfield was bluff, not stupid. He could see that Graham was uncomfortable. He swiveled in his chair and picked up some notes.

"You asked about the dog. Here's the sheet on it. Last night a vet here called Leeds's brother. He had the dog. Leeds and his oldest boy brought it in to the vet the afternoon before they were killed. It had a puncture wound in the abdomen. The vet operated and it's all right. He thought it was shot at first, but he didn't find a bullet. He thinks it was stabbed with something like an ice pick or an awl. We're asking the neighbors if they saw anybody fooling with the dog, and we're working the phones today checking local vets for other animal mutilations."

"Was the dog wearing a collar with the Leeds name on it?"

"No."

"Did the Jacobis in Birmingham have a dog?" Graham asked.

"We're supposed to be finding that out," Springfield said. "Hold on, let me see." He dialed an inside number. "Lieutenant Flatt is our liaison with Birmingham . . . yeah, Flatt. What about the Jacobis' dog? Uh-huh . . . uh-huh. Just a minute." He put his hand over the phone. "No dog. They found a litter box in the downstairs bathroom with cat droppings in it. They didn't find any cat. The neighbors are watching for it."

"Could you ask Birmingham to check around in the yard and behind any outbuildings," Graham said. "If the cat was hurt, the children might not have found it in time and they might have buried it. You know how cats do. They hide to die. Dogs come home. And would you ask if it's wearing a collar?"

"Tell them if they need a methane probe, we'll send one," Crawford said. "Save a lot of digging."

Springfield relayed the request. The telephone rang as soon as he hung it up. The call was for Jack Crawford. It was Jimmy Price at the Lombard Funeral Home. Crawford punched on from the other phone.

"Jack, I got a partial that's probably a thumb and a fragment of a palm."

"Jimmy, you're the light of my life."

"I know. The partial's a tented arch, but it's smudged. I'll have to see what I can do with it when I get back. Came off the oldest kid's left eye. I never did that before. Never would have seen it, but it stood out against an eight-ball hemorrhage from the gunshot wound."

"Can you make an identification off it?"

"It's a very long shot, Jack. If he's in the single-print index, maybe, but that's like the Irish Sweepstakes, you know that. The palm came off the nail of Mrs. Leeds's left big toe. It's only good for comparison. We'll be lucky to get six points off it. The assistant SAC witnessed, and so did Lombard. He's a notary. I've got pictures *in situ*. Will that do it?"

"What about elimination prints on the funeral-home employees?"

"I inked up Lombard and all his Merry Men, major case prints whether they said they had touched her or not. They're scrubbing their hands and bitching now. Let me go home, Jack. I want to work these up in my own darkroom. Who knows what's in the water here—turtles—who knows?

"I can catch a plane to Washington in an hour and fax the prints down to you by early afternoon."

Crawford thought a moment. "Okay, Jimmy, but step on it. Copies to Atlanta and Birmingham PD's and Bureau offices."

"You got it. Now, something else we've got to get straight on your end."

Crawford rolled his eyes to the ceiling. "Gonna piss in my ear about the per diem, aren't you?"

"Right."

"Today, Jimmy my lad, nothing's too good for you."

Graham stared out the window while Crawford told them about the prints.

"That's by God remarkable," was all Springfield said.

Graham's face was blank; closed like a lifer's face, Springfield thought.

He watched Graham all the way to the door.

➤

The public-safety commissioner's news conference was breaking up in the foyer as Crawford and Graham left Springfield's office. The print reporters headed for the phones. Television reporters were doing "cutaways," standing alone before their cameras asking the best questions they had heard at the news conference and extending their microphones to thin air for a reply that would be spliced in later from film of the commissioner.

Crawford and Graham had started down the front steps when a small man darted ahead of them, spun and took a picture. His face popped up behind his camera.

"Will Graham!" he said. "Remember me—Freddy Lounds? I covered the Lecter case for the *Tattler*. I did the paperback."

"I remember," Graham said. He and Crawford continued down the steps, Lounds walking sideways ahead of them.

"When did they call you in, Will? What have you got?"

"I won't talk to you, Lounds."

"How does this guy compare with Lecter? Does he do them—?"

"Lounds." Graham's voice was loud and Crawford got in front of him fast. "Lounds, you write lying shit and *The National Tattler* is an asswipe. Keep away from me."

Crawford gripped Graham's arm. "Get away, Lounds. *Go on.* Will, let's get some breakfast. Come on, Will." They rounded the corner, walking swiftly.

"I'm sorry, Jack. I can't stand that bastard. When I was in the hospital, he came in and—"

"I know it," Crawford said. "I reamed him out, much good it did." Crawford remembered the picture in *The National Tattler* at the end of the Lecter case. Lounds had come into the hospital room while Graham was asleep. He flipped back the sheet and shot a picture of Graham's temporary colostomy. The paper ran it retouched with a black square covering Graham's groin. The caption said "Crazy Guts Cop."

The diner was bright and clean. Graham's hands trembled and he slopped coffee in his saucer.

He saw Crawford's cigarette smoke bothering a couple in the next booth. The couple ate in a peptic silence, their resentment hanging in the smoke.

Two women, apparently mother and daughter, argued at a table near the door. They spoke in low voices, anger ugly in their faces. Graham could feel their anger on his face and neck.

Crawford was griping about having to testify at a trial in Washington in the morning. He was afraid the trial could tie him up for several days. As he lit another cigarette, he peered across the flame at Graham's hands and his color.

"Atlanta and Birmingham can run the thumbprint against their known sex offenders," Crawford said. "So can we. And Price has dug a single print out of the files before. He'll program the FINDER with it—we've come a long way with that just since you left."

FINDER, the FBI's automated fingerprint reader and processor, might recognize the thumbprint on an incoming fingerprint card from some unrelated case.

"When we get him, that print and his teeth will put him away," Crawford said. "What we have to do, we have to figure on what he *could* be. We have to swing a wide loop. Indulge me, now. Say we've arrested a good suspect. You walk in and see him. What is there about him that doesn't surprise you?"

"I don't know, Jack. Goddammit, he's got no face for me. We could spend a lot of time looking for people we've invented. Have you talked to Bloom?"

"On the phone last night. Bloom doubts he's suicidal, and so does Heimlich. Bloom was only here a couple of hours the first day, but he and Heimlich have the whole file. Bloom's examining Ph.D.

candidates this week. He said tell you hello. Do you have his number in Chicago?"

"I have it."

Graham liked Dr. Alan Bloom, a small round man with sad eyes, a good forensic psychiatrist—maybe the best. Graham appreciated the fact that Dr. Bloom had never displayed professional interest in him. That was not always the case with psychiatrists.

"Bloom says he wouldn't be surprised if we heard from the Tooth Fairy. He might write us a note," Crawford said.

"On a bedroom wall."

"Bloom thinks he might be disfigured or he may believe he's disfigured. He told me not to give that a lot of weight. 'I won't set up a straw man to chase, Jack,' is what he told me. 'That would be a distraction and would diffuse the effort.' Said they taught him to talk like that in graduate school."

"He's right," Graham said.

"You could tell something about him or you wouldn't have found that fingerprint," Crawford said.

"That was the evidence on the damn wall, Jack. Don't put this on me. Look, don't expect too much from me all right?"

"Oh, we'll get him. You know we'll get him, don't you?"

"I know it. One way or the other."

"What's one way?"

"We'll find evidence we've overlooked."

"What's the other?"

"He'll do it and do it until one night he makes too much noise going in and the husband gets to a gun in time."

"No other possibilities?"

"You think I'm going to spot him across a crowded room? No, that's Ezio Pinza you're thinking about, does that. The Tooth Fairy will go on and on until we get smart or get lucky. He won't stop."

"Why?"

"Because he's got a genuine taste for it."

"See, you do know something about him," Crawford said.

Graham did not speak again until they were on the sidewalk. "Wait until the next full moon," he told Crawford. "Then tell me how much I know about him."

Graham went back to his hotel and slept for two and a half hours. He woke at noon, showered, and ordered a pot of coffee and a sandwich. It was time to make a close study of the Jacobi file from Birmingham. He scrubbed his reading glasses with hotel soap and settled in by the window with the file. For the first few minutes he looked up at every sound, footsteps in the hall, the distant thud of the elevator door. Then he knew nothing but the file.

The waiter with the tray knocked and waited, knocked and waited. Finally he left the lunch on the floor outside the door and signed the bill himself.

CHAPTER 4

HOYT LEWIS, meter reader for Georgia Power Company, parked his truck under a big tree in the alley and settled back with his lunch box. It was no fun opening his lunch now that he packed it himself. No little notes in there anymore, no surprise Twinkie.

He was halfway through his sandwich when a loud voice at his ear made him jump.

"I guess I used a thousand dollars' worth of electricity this month, is that right?"

Lewis turned and saw at the truck window the red face of H. G. Parsons. Parsons wore Bermuda shorts and carried a yard broom.

"I didn't understand what you said."

"I guess you'll say I used a thousand dollars' worth of electricity this month. Did you hear me that time?"

"I don't know what you've used because I haven't read your meter yet, Mr. Parsons. When I do read it, I'll put it down on this piece of paper right here."

Parsons was bitter about the size of the bill. He had complained to the power company that he was being prorated.

"I'm keeping up with what I use," Parsons said. "I'm going to the Public Service Commission with it, too."

"You want to read your meter with me? Let's go over there right now and —"

"I know how to read a meter. I guess you could read one too if it wasn't so much trouble."

"Just be quiet a minute, Parsons." Lewis got out of his truck. "Just

43

be quiet a minute now, dammit. Last year you put a magnet on your meter. Your wife said you was in the hospital, so I just took it off and didn't say anything. When you poured molasses in it last winter, I reported it. I notice you paid up when we charged you for it.

"Your bill went up after you did all that wiring yourself. I've told you until I'm blue in the face: something in that house is draining off current. Do you hire an electrician to find it? No, you call down to the office and bitch about me. I've about got a bait of you." Lewis was pale with anger.

"I'll get to the bottom of this," Parsons said, retreating down the alley toward his yard. "They're checking up on you, Mr. Lewis. I saw somebody reading your route ahead of you," he said across the fence. "Pretty soon you'll have to go to work like everybody else."

Lewis cranked his truck and drove on down the alley. Now he would have to find another place to finish his lunch. He was sorry. The big shade tree had been a good lunch place for years.

It was directly behind Charles Leeds's house.

➤

At five-thirty P.M. Hoyt Lewis drove in his own automobile to the Cloud Nine Lounge, where he had several boilermakers to ease his mind.

When he called his estranged wife, all he could think of to say was "I wish you was still fixing my lunch."

"You ought to have thought about that, Mr. Smarty," she said, and hung up.

He played a gloomy game of shuffleboard with some linemen and a dispatcher from Georgia Power and looked over the crowd. God-damned airline clerks had started coming in the Cloud Nine. All had the same little mustache and pinkie ring. Pretty soon they'd be fixing the Cloud Nine English with a damned dart board. You can't depend on nothing.

"Hey, Hoyt. I'll match you for a bottle of beer." It was his supervisor, Billy Meeks.

"Say, Billy, I need to talk to you."

"What's up?"

"You know that old son of a bitch Parsons that's all the time calling up?"

"Called me last week, as a matter of fact," Meeks said. "What about him?"

"He said somebody was reading my route ahead of me, like maybe somebody thought I wasn't making the rounds. You don't think I'm reading meters at home, do you?"

"Nope."

"You don't think that, do you? I mean, if I'm on a man's shit list I want him to come right out and say it."

"If you was on my shit list, you think I'd be scared to say so to your face?"

"No."

"All right, then. If anybody was checking your route, I'd know it. Your executives is always aware of a situation like that. Nobody's checking up on you, Hoyt. You can't pay any attention to Parsons, he's just old and contrary. He called me up last week and said, 'Congratulations on getting wise to that Hoyt Lewis.' I didn't pay him any mind."

"I wish we'd put the law on him about that meter," Lewis said. "I was just setting back there in the alley under a tree trying to eat my lunch today and he jumped me. What he needs is a good ass-kicking."

"I used to set back there myself when I had the route," Meeks said. "Boy, I tell you one time I seen Mrs. Leeds—well, it don't seem right to talk about it now she's dead—but one or two times she was out there sunning herself in the backyard in her swimming suit. Whooee. Had a cute little peter belly. That was a damn shame about them. She was a nice lady."

"Did they catch anybody yet?"

"Naw."

"Too bad he got the Leedses when old Parsons was right down the street convenient," Lewis observed.

"I'll tell you what, I don't let my old lady lay around out in the yard in no swimming suit. She goes 'Silly Billy, who's gonna see me?' I told her, I said you can't tell what kind of a insane bastard might jump over that hedge with his private out. Did the cops talk to you? Ast you had you seen anybody?"

"Yeah, I think they got everybody that has a route out there. Mailmen, everybody. I was working Laurelwood on the other side of Betty Jane Drive the whole week until today, though." Lewis picked at the label on his beer. "You say Parsons called you up last week?"

"Yep."

"Then he must have saw somebody reading his meter. He wouldn't have called in if he'd just made it up today to bother me. You say you didn't send nobody, and it sure wasn't me he saw."

"Might have been Southeastern Bell checking something."

"Might have been."

"We don't share poles out there, though."

"Reckon I ought to call the cops?"

"Wouldn't hurt nothing," Meeks said.

"Naw, it might do Parsons some good, talk with the law. Scare the shit out of him when they drive up, anyhow."

CHAPTER 5

GRAHAM WENT BACK to the Leeds house in the late afternoon. He entered through the front door and tried not to look at the ruin the killer had left. So far he had seen files, a killing floor and meat—all aftermath. He knew a fair amount about how they died. How they lived was on his mind today.

A survey, then. The garage contained a good ski boat, well used and well maintained, and a station wagon. Golf clubs were there, and a trail bike. The power tools were almost unused. Adult toys.

Graham took a wedge from the golf bag and had to choke up on the long shaft as he made a jerky swing. The bag puffed a smell of leather at him as he leaned it back against the wall. Charles Leeds's things.

Graham pursued Charles Leeds through the house. His hunting prints hung in the den. His set of the Great Books were all in a row. Sewanee annuals. H. Allen Smith and Perelman and Max Shulman on the bookshelves. Vonnegut and Evelyn Waugh. C. S. Forrester's *Beat to Quarters* was open on a table.

In the den closet a good skeet gun, a Nikon camera, a Bolex Super Eight movie camera and projector.

Graham, who owned almost nothing except basic fishing equipment, a third-hand Volkswagen, and two cases of Montrachet, felt a mild animosity toward the adult toys and wondered why.

Who was Leeds? A successful tax attorney, a Sewanee footballer, a rangy man who liked to laugh, a man who got up and fought with his throat cut.

Graham followed him through the house out of an odd sense of obligation. Learning about him first was a way of asking permission to look at his wife.

Graham felt that it was she who drew the monster, as surely as a singing cricket attracts death from the red-eyed fly.

Mrs. Leeds, then.

She had a small dressing room upstairs. Graham managed to reach it without looking around the bedroom. The room was yellow and appeared undisturbed except for the smashed mirror above the dressing table. A pair of L. L. Bean moccasins was on the floor in front of the closet, as though she had just stepped out of them. Her dressing gown appeared to have been flung on its peg, and the closet revealed the mild disorder of a woman who has many other closets to organize.

Mrs. Leeds's diary was in a plum velvet box on the dressing table. The key was taped to the lid along with a check tag from the police property room.

Graham sat on a spindly white chair and opened the diary at random:

December 23rd, Tuesday, Mama's house. The children are still asleep. When Mama glassed in the sun porch, I hated the way it changed the looks of the house, but it's very pleasant and I can sit here warm looking out at the snow. How many more Christmases can she manage a houseful of grandchildren? A lot, I hope.

A hard drive yesterday up from Atlanta, snowing after Raleigh. We had to creep. I was tired anyway from getting everyone ready. Outside Chapel Hill, Charlie stopped the car and got out. He snapped some icicles off a branch to make me a martini. He came back to the car, long legs lifting high in the snow, and there was snow in his hair and on his eyelashes and I remembered that I love him. It felt like something breaking with a little pain and spilling warm.

I hope the parka fits him. If he got me that tacky dinner ring, I'll die. I could kick Madelyn's big cellulite behind for showing hers and carrying on. Four ridiculously big diamonds the color of dirty ice. Icicle ice is so clear. The sun came through the car window and where the icicle was broken off it stuck up out of the glass and made a little prism. It made a spot of red and green on my hand holding the glass. I could feel the colors on my hand.

He asked me what I want for Christmas and I cupped my hands

*around his ear and whispered: Your big prick, silly, in as far as it will
go.*

*The bald spot on the back of his head turned red. He's always afraid
the children will hear. Men have no confidence in whispers.*

The page was flecked with detective's cigar ash.

Graham read on as the light faded, through the daughter's
tonsillectomy, and a scare in June when Mrs. Leeds found a small
lump in her breast. *(Dear God, the children are so small.)*

Three pages later the lump was a small benign cyst, easily removed.

*Dr. Janovich turned me loose this afternoon. We left the hospital
and drove to the pond. We hadn't been there in a long while. There
never seems to be enough time. Charlie had two bottles of champagne
on ice and we drank them and fed the ducks while the sun went
down. He stood at edge of the water with his back to me for a while
and I think he cried a little.*

*Susan said she was afraid we were coming home from the hospital
with another brother for her. Home!*

Graham heard the telephone ring in the bedroom. A click and the
hum of an answering machine. "Hello, this is Valerie Leeds. I'm
sorry I can't come to the phone right now, but if you'll leave your
name and number after the tone, we'll get back to you. Thank you."

Graham half-expected to hear Crawford's voice after the beep, but
there was only the dial tone. The caller had hung up.

He had heard her voice; now he wanted to see her. He went down
to the den.

➤

He had in his pocket a reel of Super Eight movie film belonging to
Charles Leeds. Three weeks before his death, Leeds had left the film
with a druggist who sent it away for processing. He never picked it up.
Police found the receipt in Leeds's wallet and got the film from the
druggist. Detectives viewed the home movie along with family
snapshots developed at the same time and found nothing of interest.

Graham wanted to see the Leedses alive. At the police station, the
detectives had offered Graham their projector. He wanted to watch

the movie at the house. Reluctantly they let him check it out of the property room.

Graham found the screen and projector in the den closet, set them up, and sat down in Charles Leeds's big leather armchair to watch. He felt something tacky on the chair arm under his palm—a child's sticky fingerprints fuzzed with lint. Graham's hand smelled like candy.

It was a pleasant little silent home movie, more imaginative than most. It opened with a dog, a gray Scotty, asleep on the den rug. The dog was disturbed momentarily by the moviemaking and raised his head to look at the camera. Then he went to sleep again. A jumpy cut to the dog still asleep. Then the Scotty's ears perked up. He rose and barked, and the camera followed him into the kitchen as he ran to the door and stood expectantly, shivering and wagging his stumpy tail.

Graham bit his lower lip and waited too. On the screen, the door opened and Mrs. Leeds came in carrying groceries. She blinked and laughed in surprise and touched her tousled hair with her free hand. Her lips moved as she walked out of the picture, and the children came in behind her carrying smaller sacks. The girl was six, the boys eight and ten.

The younger boy, apparently a veteran of home movies, pointed to his ears and wiggled them. The camera was positioned fairly high. Leeds was seventy-five inches tall, according to the coroner's report.

Graham believed that this part of the movie must have been made in the early spring. The children wore windbreakers and Mrs. Leeds appeared pale. At the morgue she had a good tan and bathing-suit marks.

Brief scenes followed of the boys playing Ping-Pong in the basement and the girl, Susan, wrapping a present in her room, tongue curled over her upper lip in concentration and a wisp of hair down over her forehead. She brushed her hair back with her plump hand, as her mother had done in the kitchen.

A subsequent scene showed Susan in a bubble bath, crouched like a small frog. She wore a large shower cap. The camera angle was lower and the focus uncertain, clearly the work of a brother. The scene ended with her shouting soundlessly at the camera and covering her six-year-old chest as her shower cap slipped down over her eyes.

Not to be outdone, Leeds had surprised Mrs. Leeds in the shower. The shower curtain bumped and bulged as the curtain does before a grade-school theatrical. Mrs. Leeds's arm appeared around the curtain. In her hand was a large bath sponge. The scene closed with the lens obscured in soapsuds.

The film ended with a shot of Norman Vincent Peale speaking on television and a pan to Charles Leeds snoring in the chair where Graham now sat.

Graham stared at the blank square of light on the screen. He liked the Leedses. He was sorry that he had been to the morgue. He thought the madman who visited them might have liked them too. But the madman would like them better the way they were now.

➤

Graham's head felt stuffed and stupid. He swam in the pool at his hotel until he was rubber-legged, and came out of the water thinking of two things at once—a Tanqueray martini and the taste of Molly's mouth.

He made the martini himself in a plastic glass and telephoned Molly.

"Hello, hotshot."

"Hey, baby! Where are you?"

"In this damned hotel in Atlanta."

"Doing some good?"

"None you'd notice. I'm lonesome."

"Me too."

"Horny."

"Me too."

"Tell me about yourself."

"Well, I had a run-in with Mrs. Holper today. She wanted to return a dress with a huge big whiskey stain on the seat. I mean, obviously she had worn it to the Jaycee thing."

"And what did *you* say?"

"I told her I didn't sell it to her like that."

"And what did *she* say?"

"She said she never had any trouble returning dresses before, which was one reason she shopped at my place rather than some others that she knew about."

"And then what did *you* say?"

"Oh, I said I was upset because Will talks like a jackass on the phone."

"I see."

"Willy's fine. He's covering some turtle eggs the dogs dug up. Tell me what you're doing."

"Reading reports. Eating junk food."

"Thinking a good bit, I expect."

"Yep."

"Can I help you?"

"I just don't have a lock on anything, Molly. There's not enough information. Well, there's a lot of information, but I haven't done enough with it."

"Will you be in Atlanta for a while? I'm not bugging you about coming home, I just wonder."

"I don't know. I'll be here a few more days at least. I miss you."

"Want to talk about fucking?"

"I don't think I could stand it. I think maybe we better not do that."

"Do what?"

"Talk about fucking."

"Okay. You don't mind if I think about it, though?"

"Absolutely not."

"We've got a new dog."

"Oh hell."

"Looks like a cross between a basset hound and a Pekingese."

"Lovely."

"He's got big balls."

"Never mind about his balls."

"They almost drag the ground. He has to retract them when he runs."

"He can't do that."

"Yes he can. *You* don't know."

"Yes I do know."

"Can you retract yours?"

"I thought we were coming to that."

"Well?"

"If you must know, I retracted them once."

"When was that?"

"In my youth. I had to clear a barbed-wire fence in a hurry."

"Why?"

"I was carrying this watermelon that I had not cultivated."

"You were fleeing? From whom?"

"A swineherd of my acquaintance. Alerted by his dogs, he burst from his dwelling in his BVD's, waving a fowling piece. Fortunately, he tripped over a butterbean trellis and gave me a running start."

"Did he shoot at you?"

"I thought so at the time, yes. But the reports I heard might have issued from my behind. I've never been entirely clear on that."

"Did you clear the fence?"

"Handily."

"A criminal mind, even at that age."

"I don't have a criminal mind."

"Of course you don't. I'm thinking about painting the kitchen. What color do you like? Will? What color do you like? Are you there?"

"Yeah, uh, yellow. Let's paint it yellow."

"Yellow is a bad color for me. I'll look green at breakfast."

"Blue, then."

"Blue is cold."

"Well goddammit, paint it baby-shit tan for all I care. . . . No, look, I'll probably be home before long and we'll go to the paint store and get some chips and stuff, okay? And maybe some new handles and that."

"Let's do, let's get some handles. I don't know why I'm talking about this stuff. Look, I love you and I miss you and you're doing the right thing. It's costing you too, I know that. I'm here and I'll be here whenever you come home, or I'll meet you anywhere, anytime. That's what."

"Dear Molly. Dear Molly. Go to bed now."

"All right."

"Good night."

Graham lay with his hands behind his head and conjured dinners with Molly. Stone crab and Sancerre, the salt breeze mixed with the wine.

But it was his curse to pick at conversations, and he began to do it now. He had snapped at her after a harmless remark about his "criminal mind." Stupid.

Graham found Molly's interest in him largely inexplicable.

He called police headquarters and left word for Springfield that he wanted to start helping with the legwork in the morning. There was nothing else to do.

The gin helped him sleep.

CHAPTER 6

FLIMSY COPIES of the notes on all calls about the Leeds case were placed on Buddy Springfield's desk. Tuesday morning at seven o'clock when Springfield arrived at his office, there were sixty-three of them. The top one was red-flagged.

It said Birmingham police had found a cat buried in a shoebox behind the Jacobis' garage. The cat had a flower between its paws and was wrapped in a dish towel. The cat's name was written on the lid in a childish hand. It wore no collar. A string tied in a granny knot held the lid on.

The Birmingham medical examiner said the cat was strangled. He had shaved it and found no puncture wound.

Springfield tapped the earpiece of his glasses against his teeth.

They had found soft ground and dug it up with a shovel. Didn't need any damned methane probe. Still, Graham had been right.

The chief of detectives licked his thumb and started through the rest of the stack of flimsies. Most were reports of suspicious vehicles in the neighborhood during the past week, vague descriptions giving only vehicle type or color. Four anonymous telephone callers had told Atlanta residents: "I'm gonna do you like the Leedses."

Hoyt Lewis' report was in the middle of the pile.

Springfield called the overnight watch commander.

"What about the meter reader's report on this Parsons? Number forty-eight."

"We tried to check with the utilities last night, Chief, to see if they had anybody in that alley," the watch commander said. "They'll have to get back to us this morning."

"You have somebody get back to *them* now," Springfield said. "Check sanitation, the city engineer, check for construction permits along the alley and catch me in my car."

He dialed Will Graham's number. "Will? Meet me in front of your hotel in ten minutes and let's take a little ride."

At 7:45 A.M. Springfield parked near the end of the alley. He and Graham walked abreast in wheel tracks pressed in the gravel. Even this early the sun was hot.

"You need to get you a hat," Springfield said. His own snappy straw was tilted down over his eyes.

The chain-link fence at the rear of the Leeds property was covered with vines. They paused by the light meter on the pole.

"If he came down this way, he could see the whole back end of the house," Springfield said.

In only five days the Leeds property had begun to look neglected. The lawn was uneven, and wild onions sprouted above the grass. Small branches had fallen in the yard. Graham wanted to pick them up. The house seemed asleep, the latticed porch striped and dappled with the long morning shadows of the trees. Standing with Springfield in the alley, Graham could see himself looking in the back window, opening the porch door. Oddly, his reconstruction of the entry by the killer seemed to elude him now, in the sunlight. He watched a child's swing move gently in the breeze.

"That looks like Parsons," Springfield said.

H. G. Parsons was out early, grubbing in a flowerbed in his backyard, two houses down. Springfield and Graham went to Parsons' back gate and stood beside his garbage cans. The lids were chained to the fence.

Springfield measured the height of the light meter with a tape.

He had notes on all the Leedses' neighbors. His notes said Parsons had taken early retirement from the post office at his supervisor's request. The supervisor had reported Parsons to be "increasingly absentminded."

Springfield's notes contained gossip, too. The neighbors said Parsons' wife stayed with her sister in Macon as much as she could, and that his son never called him anymore.

"Mr. Parsons. Mr. Parsons," Springfield called.

Parsons leaned his tilling fork against the house and came to the fence. He wore sandals and white socks. Dirt and grass had stained the toes of his socks. His face was shiny pink.

Arteriosclerosis, Graham thought. He's taken his pill.

"Yes?"

"Mr. Parsons, could we talk to you for a minute? We were hoping you could help us," Springfield said.

"Are you from the power company?"

"No, I'm Buddy Springfield from the police department."

"It's about the murder, then. My wife and I were in Macon, as I told the officer—"

"I know, Mr. Parsons. We wanted to ask about your light meter. Did—"

"If that . . . meter reader said I did anything improper, he's just—"

"No, no. Mr. Parsons, did you see a stranger reading your meter last week?"

"No."

"Are you sure? I believe you told Hoyt Lewis that someone else read your meter ahead of him."

"I did. And it's about time. I'm keeping up with this, and the Public Service Commission will get a full report from me."

"Yes, sir. I'm sure they'll take care of it. Who did you see reading your meter?"

"It wasn't a stranger, it was somebody from Georgia Power."

"How do you know?"

"Well, he looked like a meter reader."

"What was he wearing?"

"What they all wear, I guess. What is it? A brown outfit and the cap."

"Did you see his face?"

"I can't remember if I did. I was looking out the kitchen window when I saw him. I wanted to talk to him, but I had to put on my robe, and by the time I got outside, he was gone."

"Did he have a truck?"

"I don't remember seeing one. What's going on? Why do you want to know?"

"We're checking everybody who was in this neighborhood last week. It's really important, Mr. Parsons. Try hard to remember."

"So it is about the murder. You haven't arrested anybody yet, have you?"

"No."

"I watched the street last night, and *fifteen minutes* went by without a single squad car passing. It was horrible, what happened to the Leedses. My wife has been beside herself. I wonder who'll buy their house. I saw some Negroes looking at it the other day. You know, I had to speak to Leeds a few times about his children, but they were all right. Of course, he wouldn't do anything I suggested about his lawn. The Department of Agriculture has some *excellent* pamphlets on the control of nuisance grasses. Finally I just put them in his mailbox. Honestly, when he mowed the wild onions were suffocating."

"Mr. Parsons, exactly when did you see this fellow in the alley?" Springfield asked.

"I'm not sure, I was trying to think."

"Do you recall the time of day? Morning? Noon? Afternoon?"

"I know the times of day, you don't have to name them. Afternoon, maybe. I don't remember."

Springfield rubbed the back of his neck. "Excuse me, Mr. Parsons, but I have to get this just right. Could we go in your kitchen and you show us just where you saw him from?"

"Let me see your credentials. Both of you."

In the house, silence, shiny surfaces, and dead air. Neat. Neat. The desperate order of an aging couple who see their lives begin to blur.

Graham wished he had stayed outside. He was sure the drawers held polished silver with egg between the tines.

Stop it and let's pump the old fart.

The window over the kitchen sink gave a good view of the backyard.

"There. Are you satisfied?" Parsons asked. "You *can* see out there from here. I never talked to him, I don't remember what he looked like. If that's all, I have a lot to do."

Graham spoke for the first time. "You said you went to get your robe, and when you came back he was gone. You weren't dressed, then?"

"No."

"In the middle of the afternoon? Were you not feeling well, Mr. Parsons?"

"What I do in my own house is my business. I can wear a kangaroo suit in here if I want to. Why aren't you out looking for the killer? Probably because it's cool in here."

"I understand you're retired, Mr. Parsons, so I guess it doesn't matter if you put on your clothes every day or not. A lot of days you just don't get dressed at all, am I right?"

Veins stood out in Parsons' temples. "Just because I'm retired doesn't mean I don't put my clothes on and get busy every day. I just got hot and I came in and took a shower. I was working. I was mulching, and I had done a day's work by afternoon, which is more than you'll do today."

"You were what?"

"Mulching."

"What day did you mulch?"

"Friday. It was last Friday. They delivered it in the morning, a big load, and I had . . . I had it all spread by afternoon. You can ask at the Garden Center how much it was."

"And you got hot and came in and took a shower. What were you doing in the kitchen?"

"Fixing a glass of iced tea."

"And you got out some ice? But the refrigerator is over there, away from the window."

Parsons looked from the window to the refrigerator, lost and confused. His eyes were dull, like the eyes of a fish in the market toward the end of the day. Then they brightened in triumph. He went to the cabinet by the sink.

"I was right here, getting some Sweet 'N Low when I saw him. That's it. That's all. Now, if you're through prying . . ."

"I think he saw Hoyt Lewis," Graham said.

"So do I," Springfield said.

"It was *not* Hoyt Lewis. It was *not.*" Parsons' eyes were watering.

"How do you know?" Springfield said. "It might have been Hoyt Lewis, and you just *thought—*"

"Lewis is brown from the sun. He's got old greasy hair and those peckerwood sideburns." Parsons' voice had risen and he was talking so fast it was hard to understand him. "That's how I knew. Of course it wasn't Lewis. This fellow was paler and his hair was blond. He turned to write on his clipboard and I could see under the back of his hat. Blond. Cut off square on the back of his neck."

Springfield stood absolutely still and when he spoke his voice was still skeptical. "What about his face?"

"I don't know. He may have had a mustache."

"Like Lewis?"

"Lewis doesn't have a mustache."

"Oh," Springfield said. "Was he at eye level with the meter? Did he have to look up at it?"

"Eye level, I guess."

"Would you know him if you saw him again?"

"No."

"What age was he?"

"Not old. I don't know."

"Did you see the Leedses' dog anywhere around him?"

"No."

"Look, Mr. Parsons, I can see I was wrong," Springfield said. "You're a real big help to us. If you don't mind, I'm going to send our artist out here, and if you'd just let him sit right here at your kitchen table, maybe you could give him an idea of what this fellow looked like. It sure wasn't Lewis."

"I don't want my name in any newspapers."

"It won't be."

Parsons followed them outside.

"You've done a hell of a fine job on this yard, Mr. Parsons," Springfield said. "It ought to win some kind of a prize."

Parsons said nothing. His face was red and working, his eyes wet. He stood there in his baggy shorts and sandals and glared at them. As they left the yard, he grabbed his fork and began to grub furiously in the ground, hacking blindly through the flowers, scattering mulch on the grass.

➤

Springfield checked in on his car radio. None of the utilities or city agencies could account for the man in the alley on the day before the murders. Springfield reported Parsons' description and gave instructions for the artist. "Tell him to draw the pole and the meter first and go from there. He'll have to ease the witness along.

"Our artist doesn't much like to make house calls," the chief of detectives told Graham as he slid the stripline Ford through the traffic. "He likes for the secretaries to see him work, with the witness standing on one foot and then the other, looking over his shoulder. A police station is a damn poor place to question anybody that you don't need to scare. Soon as we get the picture, we'll door-to-door the neighborhood with it.

"I feel like we just got a whiff, Will. Just faint, but a whiff, don't you? Look, we did it to the poor old devil and he came through. Now let's do something with it."

"If the man in the alley is the one we want, it's the best news yet," Graham said. He was sick of himself.

"Right. It means he's not just getting off a bus and going whichever way his peter points. He's got a plan. He stayed in town overnight. He knows where he's going a day or two ahead. He's got some kind of an idea. Case the place, kill the pet, then the family. What the hell kind of an idea is that?" Springfield paused. "That's kind of your territory, isn't it?"

"It is, yes. If it's anybody's, I suppose it's mine."

"I know you've seen this kind of thing before. You didn't like it the other day when I asked you about Lecter, but I need to talk to you about it."

"All right."

"He killed nine people, didn't he, in all?"

"Nine that we know of. Two others didn't die."

"What happened to them?"

"One is on a respirator at a hospital in Baltimore. The other is in a private mental hospital in Denver."

"What made him do it, how was he crazy?"

Graham looked out the car window at the people on the sidewalk. His voice sounded detached, as though he were dictating a letter.

"He did it because he liked it. Still does. Dr. Lecter is not crazy, in any common way we think of being crazy. He did some hideous things because he enjoyed them. But he can function perfectly when he wants to."

"What did the psychologists call it—what was wrong with him."

"They say he's a sociopath, because they don't know what else to call him. He has some of the characteristics of what they call a sociopath. He has no remorse or guilt at all. And he had the first and worst sign—sadism to animals as a child."

Springfield grunted.

"But he doesn't have any of the other marks," Graham said. "He wasn't a drifter, he had no history of trouble with the law. He wasn't shallow and exploitive in small things, like most sociopaths are. He's not insensitive. They don't know what to call him. His electroencephalograms show some odd patterns, but they haven't been able to tell much from them."

"What would you call him?" Springfield asked.

Graham hesitated.

"Just to yourself, what do you call him?"

"He's a monster. I think of him as one of those pitiful things that are born in hospitals from time to time. They feed it, and keep it warm, but they don't put it on the machines and it dies. Lecter is the same way in his head, but he looks normal and nobody could tell."

"A couple of friends of mine in the chiefs' association are from Baltimore. I asked them how you spotted Lecter. They said they didn't know. How did you do it? What was the first indication, the first thing you felt?"

"It was a coincidence," Graham said. "The sixth victim was killed in his workshop. He had woodworking equipment and he kept his hunting stuff out there. He was laced to a pegboard where the tools hung, and he was really torn up, cut and stabbed, and he had arrows in him. The wounds reminded me of something. I couldn't think what it was."

"And you had to go on to the next ones."

"Yes. Lecter was very hot—he did the next three in nine days. But this sixth one, he had two old scars on his thigh. The pathologist checked with the local hospital and found he had fallen out of a tree blind five years before while he was bow hunting and stuck an arrow through his leg.

"The doctor of record was a resident surgeon, but Lecter had treated him first—he was on duty in the emergency room. His name was on the admissions log. It had been a long time since the accident, but I thought Lecter might remember if anything had seemed fishy about the arrow wound, so I went to his office to see him. We were grabbing at anything then.

"He was practicing psychiatry by that time. He had a nice office. Antiques. He said he didn't remember much about the arrow wound, that one of the victim's hunting buddies had brought him in, and that was it.

"Something bothered me, though. I thought it was something Lecter said, or something in the office. Crawford and I hashed it over. We checked the files, and Lecter had no record. I wanted some time in his office by myself, but we couldn't get a warrant. We had nothing to show. So I went back to see him.

"It was Sunday, he saw patients on Sunday. The building was empty except for a couple of people in his waiting room. He saw me right away. We were talking and he was making this polite effort to help me and I looked up at some very old medical books on the shelf above his head. And I knew it was him.

"When I looked at him again, maybe my face changed, I don't know. I knew it and *he knew* I knew it. I still couldn't think of the reason, though. I didn't trust it. I had to figure it out. So I mumbled something and got out of there, into the hall. There was a pay phone in the hall. I didn't want to stir him up until I had some help. I was talking to the police switchboard when he came out a service door behind me in his socks. I never heard him coming. I felt his breath was all, and then . . . there was the rest of it."

"How did you know, though?"

"I think it was maybe a week later in the hospital I finally figured it out. It was *Wound Man*—an illustration they used in a lot of the early medical books like the ones Lecter had. It shows different kinds of battle injuries, all in one figure. I had seen it in a survey course a pathologist was teaching at GWU. The sixth victim's position and his injuries were a close match to *Wound Man*."

"*Wound Man*, you say? That's all you had?"

"Well, yeah. It was a coincidence that I had seen it. A piece of luck."

"That's some luck."

"If you don't believe me, what the fuck did you ask me for?"

"I didn't hear that."

"Good. I didn't mean to say it. That's the way it happened, though."

"Okay," Springfield said. "Okay. Thank you for telling me. I need to know things like that."

➤

Parsons' description of the man in the alley and the information on the cat and the dog were possible indications of the killer's methods: it seemed likely that he scouted as a meter reader and felt compelled to hurt the victims' pets before he came to kill the family.

The immediate problem the police faced was whether or not to publicize their theory.

With the public aware of the danger signals and watching, police might get advance warning of the killer's next attack— but the killer probably followed the news too.

He might change his habits.

There was strong feeling in the police department that the slender leads should be kept secret except for a special bulletin to veterinarians and animal shelters throughout the Southeast asking for immediate reports on pet mutilations.

That meant not giving the public the best possible warning. It was a moral question, and the police were not comfortable with it.

They consulted Dr. Alan Bloom in Chicago. Dr. Bloom said that if the killer read a warning in the newspapers, he would probably change his method of casing a house. Dr. Bloom doubted that the man could stop attacking the pets, regardless of the risk. The psychiatrist told the police that they should by no means assume they had twenty-five days to work—the period before the next full moon on August 25.

On the morning of July 31, three hours after Parsons gave his description, a decision was reached in a telephone conference among Birmingham and Atlanta police and Crawford in Washington: they would send the private bulletin to veterinarians, canvass for three days in the neighborhood with the artist's sketch, then release the information to the news media.

For those three days Graham and the Atlanta detectives pounded the sidewalks showing the sketch to householders in the area of the

Leeds home. There was only a suggestion of a face in the sketch, but they hoped to find someone who could improve it.

Graham's copy of the sketch grew soft around the edges from the sweat of his hands. Often it was difficult to get residents to answer the door. At night he lay in his room with powder on his heat rash, his mind circling the problem as though it were a hologram. He courted the feeling that precedes an idea. It would not come.

Meanwhile, there were four accidental injuries and one fatality in Atlanta as householders shot at relatives coming home late. Prowler calls multiplied and useless tips stacked up in the In baskets at police headquarters. Despair went around like the flu.

Crawford returned from Washington at the end of the third day and dropped in on Graham as he sat peeling off his wet socks.

"Hot work?"

"Grab a sketch in the morning and see," Graham said.

"No, it'll all be on the news tonight. Did you walk all day?"

"I can't drive through their yards."

"I didn't think anything would come of this canvass," Crawford said.

"Well, what the hell did you expect me to do?"

"The best you can, that's all." Crawford rose to leave. "Busywork's been a narcotic for me sometimes, especially after I quit the booze. For you too, I think."

Graham was angry. Crawford was right, of course.

Graham was a natural procrastinator, and he knew it. Long ago in school he had made up for it with speed. He was not in school now.

There was something else he could do, and he had known it for days. He could wait until he was driven to it by desperation in the last days before the full moon. Or he could do it now, while it might be of some use.

There was an opinion he wanted. A very strange view he needed to share; a mindset he had to recover after his warm round years in the Keys.

The reasons clacked like roller-coaster cogs pulling up to the first long plunge, and at the top, unaware that he clutched his belly, Graham said it aloud.

"I have to see Lecter."

CHAPTER 7

DR. FREDERICK CHILTON, chief of staff at the Baltimore State Hospital for the Criminally Insane, came around his desk to shake Will Graham's hand.

"Dr. Bloom called me yesterday, Mr. Graham—or should I call you Dr. Graham?"

"I'm not a doctor."

"I was delighted to hear from Dr. Bloom, we've known each other for *years*. Take that chair."

"We appreciate your help, Dr. Chilton."

"Frankly, I sometimes feel like Lecter's secretary rather than his keeper," Chilton said. "The volume of his mail alone is a nuisance. I think among some researchers it's considered chic to correspond with him—I've seen his letters *framed* in psychology departments—and for a while it seemed that every Ph.D. candidate in the field wanted to interview him. Glad to cooperate with *you*, of course, and Dr. Bloom."

"I need to see Dr. Lecter in as much privacy as possible," Graham said. "I may need to see him again or telephone him after today."

Chilton nodded. "To begin with, Dr. Lecter will stay in his room. That is absolutely the only place where he is not put in restraints. One wall of his room is a double barrier which opens on the hall. I'll have a chair put there, and screens if you like.

"I must ask you not to pass him any objects whatever, other than paper free of clips or staples. No ring binders, pencils, or pens. He has his own felt-tipped pens."

"I might have to show him some material that could stimulate him," Graham said.

"You can show him what you like as long as it's on soft paper. Pass him documents through the sliding food tray. Don't hand anything through the barrier and do not accept anything he might extend through the barrier. He can return papers in the food tray. I insist on that. Dr. Bloom and Mr. Crawford assured me that you would cooperate on procedure."

"I will," Graham said. He started to rise.

"I know you're anxious to get on with it, Mr. Graham, but I want to tell you something first. This will interest you.

"It may seem gratuitous to warn *you*, of all people, about Lecter. But he's very disarming. For a year after he was brought here, he behaved perfectly and gave the appearance of cooperating with attempts at therapy. As a result—this was under the previous administrator—security around him was slightly relaxed.

"On the afternoon of July 8, 1976, he complained of chest pain. His restraints were removed in the examining room to make it easier to give him an electrocardiogram. One of his attendants left the room to smoke, and the other turned away for a second. The nurse was very quick and strong. She managed to save one of her eyes.

"You may find this curious." Chilton took a strip of EKG tape from a drawer and unrolled it on his desk. He traced the spiky line with his forefinger. "Here, he's resting on the examining table. Pulse seventy-two. Here, he grabs the nurse's head and pulls her down to him. Here, he is subdued by the attendant. He didn't resist, by the way, though the attendant dislocated his shoulder. Do you notice the strange thing? His pulse never got over eighty-five. Even when he tore out her tongue."

Chilton could read nothing in Graham's face. He leaned back in his chair and steepled his fingers under his chin. His hands were dry and shiny.

"You know, when Lecter was first captured we thought he might provide us with a singular opportunity to study a pure sociopath," Chilton said. "It's so rare to get one alive. Lecter is so lucid, so perceptive; he's trained in psychiatry . . . and he's a mass murderer.

He seemed cooperative, and we thought that he could be a window on this kind of aberration. We thought we'd be like Beaumont studying digestion through the opening in St. Martin's stomach.

"As it turned out, I don't think we're any closer to understanding him now than the day he came in. Have you ever talked with Lecter for any length of time?"

"No. I just saw him when . . . I saw him mainly in court. Dr. Bloom showed me his articles in the journals," Graham said.

"He's very familiar with *you*. He's given you a lot of thought."

"You had some sessions with him?"

"Yes. Twelve. He's impenetrable. Too sophisticated about the tests for them to register anything. Edwards, Fabré, even Dr. Bloom himself had a crack at him. I have their notes. He was an enigma to them too. It's impossible, of course, to tell what he's holding back or whether he understands more than he'll say. Oh, since his commitment he's done some brilliant pieces for *The American Journal of Psychiatry* and *The General Archives*. But they're always about problems he doesn't have. I think he's afraid that if we 'solve' him, nobody will be interested in him anymore and he'll be stuck in a back ward somewhere for the rest of his life."

Chilton paused. He had practiced using his peripheral vision to watch his subject in interviews. He believed that he could watch Graham this way undetected.

"The consensus around here is that the only person who has demonstrated any practical understanding of Hannibal Lecter is you, Mr. Graham. Can you tell me anything about him?"

"No."

"Some of the staff are curious about this: when you saw Dr. Lecter's murders, their 'style,' so to speak, were you able perhaps to reconstruct his fantasies? And did that help you identify him?"

Graham did not answer.

"We're woefully short of material on that sort of thing. There's one single piece in *The Journal of Abnormal Psychology*. Would you mind talking with some of the staff—no, no, not this trip—Dr. Bloom was very severe with me on that point. We're to leave you alone. Next trip, perhaps."

Dr. Chilton had seen a lot of hostility. He was seeing some at the moment.

Graham stood up. "Thank you, doctor. I want to see Lecter now."

➤

The steel door of the maximum-security section closed behind Graham. He heard the bolt slide home.

Graham knew that Lecter slept most of the morning. He looked down the corridor. At that angle he could not see into Lecter's cell, but he could tell that the lights inside were dimmed.

Graham wanted to see Dr. Lecter asleep. He wanted time to brace himself. If he felt Lecter's madness in his head, he had to contain it quickly, like a spill.

To cover the sound of his footsteps, he followed an orderly pushing a linen cart. Dr. Lecter is very difficult to slip up on.

Graham paused partway down the hall. Steel bars covered the entire front of the cell. Behind the bars, farther than arm's reach, was a stout nylon net stretched ceiling to floor and wall to wall. Through the barrier, Graham could see a table and chair bolted to the floor. The table was stacked with softcover books and correspondence. He walked up to the bars, put his hands on them, took his hands away.

Dr. Hannibal Lecter lay on his cot asleep, his head propped on a pillow against the wall. Alexandre Dumas' *Le Grand Dictionnaire de Cuisine* was open on his chest.

Graham had stared through the bars for about five seconds when Lecter opened his eyes and said, "That's the same atrocious aftershave you wore in court."

"I keep getting it for Christmas."

Dr. Lecter's eyes are maroon and they reflect the light redly in tiny points. Graham felt each hair bristle on his nape. He put his hand on the back of his neck.

"Christmas, yes," Lecter said. "Did you get my card?"

"I got it. Thank you."

Dr. Lecter's Christmas card had been forwarded to Graham from the FBI crime laboratory in Washington. He took it into the backyard, burned it, and washed his hands before touching Molly.

Lecter rose and walked over to his table. He is a small, lithe man. Very neat. "Why don't you have a seat, Will? I think there are some folding chairs in a closet just down that way. At least, that's where it sounds like they come from."

"The orderly's bringing one."

Lecter stood until Graham was seated in the hall. "And how is Officer Stewart?" he asked.

"Stewart's fine." Officer Stewart left law enforcement after he saw Dr. Lecter's basement. He managed a motel now. Graham did not mention this. He didn't think Stewart would appreciate any mail from Lecter.

"Unfortunate that his emotional problems got the better of him. I thought he was a very promising young officer. Do you ever have any problems, Will?"

"No."

"Of course you don't."

Graham felt that Lecter was looking through to the back of his skull. His attention felt like a fly walking around in there.

"I'm glad you came. It's been what now, three years? My callers are all professional. Banal clinical psychiatrists and grasping second-rate *doctors* of psychology from silo colleges somewhere. Pencil lickers trying to protect their tenure with pieces in the journals."

"Dr. Bloom showed me your article on surgical addiction in *The Journal of Clinical Psychiatry*."

"And?"

"Very interesting, even to a layman."

"A layman . . . layman—layman. Interesting term," Lecter said. "So many learned fellows going about. So many *experts* on government grants. And you say you're a layman. But it was you who caught me, wasn't it, Will? Do you know how you did it?"

"I'm sure you've read the transcript. It's all in there."

"No it's not. Do you know how you did it, Will?"

"It's in the transcript. What does it matter now?"

"It doesn't matter to *me,* Will."

"I want you to help me, Dr. Lecter."

"Yes, I thought so."

"It's about Atlanta and Birmingham."

"Yes."

"You read about it, I'm sure."

"I've read the papers. I can't clip them. They won't let me have scissors, of course. Sometimes they threaten me with loss of books, you know. I wouldn't want them to think I was dwelling on anything morbid." He laughed. Dr. Lecter has small white teeth. "You want to know how he's choosing them, don't you?"

"I thought you would have some ideas. I'm asking you to tell me what they are."

"Why should I?"

Graham had anticipated the question. A reason to stop multiple murders would not occur readily to Dr. Lecter.

"There are things you don't have," Graham said. "Research materials, filmstrips even. I'd speak to the chief of staff."

"Chilton. You must have seen him when you came in. Gruesome, isn't it? Tell me the truth, he fumbles at your head like a freshman pulling at a panty girdle, doesn't he? Watched you out of the corner of his eye. Picked *that* up, didn't you? You may not believe this, but he actually tried to give *me* a Thematic Apperception Test. He was sitting there just like the Cheshire cat waiting for Mf 13 to come up. Ha. Forgive me, I forget that you're not among the anointed. It's a card with a woman in bed and a man in the foreground. I was supposed to avoid a sexual interpretation. I laughed. He puffed up and told everybody I avoided prison with a Ganser syndrome—never mind, it's boring."

"You'd have access to the AMA filmstrip library."

"I don't think you'd get me the things I want."

"Try me."

"I have quite enough to read as it is."

"You'd get to see the file on this case. There's another reason."

"Pray."

"I thought you might be curious to find out if you're smarter than the person I'm looking for."

"Then, by implication, you think you are smarter than I am, since you caught me."

"No. I know I'm not smarter than you are."

"Then how did you catch me, Will?"

"You had disadvantages."

"What disadvantages?"

"Passion. And you're insane."

"You're very tan, Will."

Graham did not answer.

"Your hands are rough. They don't look like a cop's hands anymore. That shaving lotion is something a child would select. It has a ship on the bottle, doesn't it?" Dr. Lecter seldom holds his head upright. He tilts it as he asks a question, as though he were screwing an auger of curiosity into your face. Another silence, and Lecter said, "Don't think you can persuade me with appeals to my intellectual vanity."

"I don't think I'll persuade you. You'll do it or you won't. Dr. Bloom is working on it anyway, and he's the most—"

"Do you have the file with you?"

"Yes."

"And pictures?"

"Yes."

"Let me have them, and I might consider it."

"No."

"Do you dream much, Will?"

"Good-bye, Dr. Lecter."

"You haven't threatened to take away my books yet."

Graham walked away.

"Let me have the file, then. I'll tell you what I think."

Graham had to pack the abridged file tightly into the sliding tray. Lecter pulled it through.

"There's a summary on top. You can read that now," Graham said.

"Do you mind if I do it privately? Give me an hour."

Graham waited on a tired plastic couch in a grim lounge. Orderlies came in for coffee. He did not speak to them. He stared at small objects in the room and was glad they held still in his vision. He had to go to the rest room twice. He was numb.

The turnkey admitted him to the maximum-security section again.

Lecter sat at his table, his eyes filmed with thought. Graham knew he had spent most of the hour with the pictures.

"This is a very shy boy, Will. I'd love to meet him. . . . Have you considered the possibility that he's disfigured? Or that he may believe he's disfigured?"

"The mirrors."

"Yes. You notice he smashed all the mirrors in the houses, not just enough to get the pieces he wanted. He doesn't just put the shards in place for the damage they cause. They're set so he can see himself. In their eyes—Mrs. Jacobi and . . . What was the other name?"

"Mrs. Leeds."

"Yes."

"That's interesting," Graham said.

"It's not 'interesting.' You'd thought of that before."

"I had considered it."

"You just came here to look at me. Just to get the old scent again, didn't you? Why don't you just smell yourself?"

"I want your opinion."

"I don't have one right now."

"When you do have one, I'd like to hear it."

"May I keep the file?"

"I haven't decided yet," Graham said.

"Why are there no descriptions of the grounds? Here we have frontal views of the houses, floor plans, diagrams of the rooms where the deaths occurred, and little mention of the grounds. What were the yards like?"

"Big backyards, fenced, with some hedges. Why?"

"Because, my dear Will, if this pilgrim feels a special relationship with the moon, he might like to go outside and look at it. Before he tidies himself up, you understand. Have you seen blood in the moonlight, Will? It appears quite black. Of course, it keeps the distinctive sheen. If one were nude, say, it would be better to have outdoor privacy for that sort of thing. One must show some consideration for the neighbors, hmmmm?"

"You think the yard might be a factor when he selects victims?"

"Oh yes. And there will be more victims, of course. Let me keep the file, Will. I'll study it. When you get more files, I'd like to see them, too. You can call me. On the rare occasions when my lawyer calls, they bring me a telephone. They used to patch him through on the intercom, but everyone listened of course. Would you like to give me your home number?"

"No."

"Do you know how you caught me, Will?"

"Good-bye, Dr. Lecter. You can leave messages for me at the number on the file." Graham walked away.

"Do you know how you caught me?"

Graham was out of Lecter's sight now, and he walked faster toward the far steel door.

"The reason you caught me is that we're *just alike*" was the last thing Graham heard as the steel door closed behind him.

He was numb except for dreading the loss of numbness. Walking with his head down, speaking to no one, he could hear his blood like a hollow drumming of wings. It seemed a very short distance to the outside. This was only a building; there were only five doors between Lecter and the outside. He had the absurd feeling that Lecter had walked out with him. He stopped outside the entrance and looked around him, assuring himself that he was alone.

From a car across the street, his long lens propped on the window sill, Freddy Lounds got a nice profile shot of Graham in the doorway and the words in stone above him: "Baltimore State Hospital for the Criminally Insane."

As it turned out, *The National Tattler* cropped the picture to just Graham's face and the last two words in the stone.

CHAPTER 8

Dr. Hannibal Lecter lay on his cot with the cell lights down after Graham left him. Several hours passed.

For a while he had textures; the weave of the pillowcase against his hands clasped behind his head, the smooth membrane that lined his cheek.

Then he had odors and let his mind play over them. Some were real, some were not. They had put Clorox in the drains; semen. They were serving chili down the hall; sweat-stiffened khaki. Graham would not give him his home telephone number; the bitter green smell of cut cocklebur and teaweed.

Lecter sat up. The man might have been civil. His thoughts had the warm brass smell of an electric clock.

Lecter blinked several times, and his eyebrows rose. He turned up the lights and wrote a note to Chilton asking for a telephone to call his counsel.

Lecter was entitled by law to speak with his lawyer in privacy and he hadn't abused the right. Since Chilton would never allow him to go to the telephone, the telephone was brought to him.

Two guards brought it, unrolling a long cord from the telephone jack at their desk. One of the guards had the keys. The other held a can of Mace.

"Go to the back of the cell, Dr. Lecter. Face the wall. If you turn

75

around or approach the barrier before you hear the lock snap, I'll Mace you in the face. Understand?"

"Yes indeed," Lecter said. "Thank you so much for bringing the telephone."

He had to reach through the nylon net to dial. Chicago information gave him numbers for the University of Chicago Department of Psychiatry and Dr. Alan Bloom's office number. He dialed the psychiatry department switchboard.

"I'm trying to reach Dr. Alan Bloom."

"I'm not sure he's in today, but I'll connect you."

"Just a second, I'm supposed to know his secretary's name and I'm embarrassed to say I've forgotten it."

"Linda King. Just a moment."

"Thank you."

The telephone rang eight times before it was picked up.

"Linda King's desk."

"Hi, Linda?"

"Linda doesn't come in on Saturday."

Dr. Lecter had counted on that. "Maybe you could help me, if you don't mind. This is Bob Greer at Blaine and Edwards Publishing Company. Dr. Bloom asked me to send a copy of the Overholser book, *The Psychiatrist and the Law*, to Will Graham, and Linda was supposed to send me the address and phone number, but she never did."

"I'm just a graduate assistant, she'll be in on Mon—"

"I have to catch Federal Express with it in about five minutes, and I hate to bother Dr. Bloom about it at home because he told Linda to send it and I don't want to get her in hot water. It's right there in her Rolodex or whatever. I'll dance at your wedding if you'll read it to me."

"She doesn't have a Rolodex."

"How about a Call Caddy with the slide on the side?"

"Yes."

"Be a darling and slide that rascal and I won't take up any more of your time."

"What was the name?"

"Graham. Will Graham."

"All right, his home number is 305 JL5-7002."

"I'm supposed to mail it to his house."

"It doesn't give the address of his house."

"What does it have?"

"Federal Bureau of Investigation, Tenth and Pennsylvania, Washington, D.C. Oh, and Post Office Box 3680, Marathon, Florida."

"That's fine, you're an angel."

"You're welcome."

Lecter felt much better. He thought he might surprise Graham with a call sometime, or if the man couldn't be civil, he might have a hospital-supply house mail Graham a colostomy bag for old times' sake.

CHAPTER 9

SEVEN HUNDRED MILES to the southwest, in the cafeteria at Gateway Film Laboratory of St. Louis, Francis Dolarhyde was waiting for a hamburger. The entrées offered in the steam table were filmed over. He stood beside the cash register and sipped coffee from a paper cup.

A red-haired young woman wearing a laboratory smock came into the cafeteria and studied the candy machine. She looked at Francis Dolarhyde's back several times and pursed her lips. Finally she walked over to him and said, "Mr. D.?"

Dolarhyde turned. He always wore red goggles outside the darkroom. She kept her eyes on the nosepiece of the goggles.

"Will you sit down with me a minute? I want to tell you something."

"What can you tell me, Eileen?"

"That I'm really sorry. Bob was just really drunk and, you know, clowning around. He didn't mean anything. Please come sit down. Just for a minute. Will you do that?"

"Mmmm-hmmm." Dolarhyde never said "yes," as he had trouble with the sibilant /s/.

They sat. She twisted a napkin in her hands.

"Everybody was having a good time at the party and we were glad you came by," she said. "Real glad, and surprised, too. You know how Bob is, he does voices all the time—he ought to be on the radio. He did two or three accents, telling jokes and all—he can talk just like a Negro. When he did that other voice, he didn't mean to make you feel bad. He was too drunk to know who was there."

"They were all laughing and then they . . . didn't laugh." Dolarhyde never said "stopped" because of the fricative /s/.

"That's when Bob realized what he had done."

"He went on, though."

"I know it," she said, managing to look from her napkin to his goggles without lingering on the way. "I got on his case about it, too. He said he didn't mean anything, he just saw he was into it and tried to keep up the joke. You saw how red his face got."

"He invited me to . . . perform a duct with him."

"He hugged you and tried to put his arm around you. He wanted you to laugh it off, Mr. D."

"I've laughed it off, Eileen."

"Bob feels terrible."

"Well, I don't want him to feel terrible. I don't want that. Tell him for me. And it won't make it any different here at the plant. Golly, if I had talent like Bob I'd make jo . . . a joke all the time." Dolarhyde avoided plurals whenever he could. "We'll all get together before long and he'll know how I feel."

"Good, Mr. D. You know he's really, under all the fun, he's a sensitive guy."

"I'll bet. Tender, I imagine." Dolarhyde's voice was muffled by his hand. When seated, he always pressed the knuckle of his forefinger under his nose.

"Pardon?"

"I think you're good for him, Eileen."

"I think so, I really do. He's not drinking but just on weekends. He just starts to relax and his wife calls the house. He makes faces while I talk to her, but I can tell he's upset after. A woman knows." She tapped Dolarhyde on the wrist and, despite the goggles, saw the touch register in his eyes. "Take it easy, Mr. D. I'm glad we had this talk."

"I am too, Eileen."

Dolarhyde watched her walk away. She had a suck mark on the back of her knee. He thought, correctly, that Eileen did not appreciate him. No one did, actually.

The great darkroom was cool and smelled of chemicals. Francis Dolarhyde checked the developer in the A tank. Hundreds of feet of home-movie film from all over the country moved through the tank hourly. Temperature and freshness of the chemicals were critical. This was his responsibility, along with all the other operations until the film had passed through the dryer. Many times a day he lifted samples of film from the tank and checked them frame by frame. The darkroom was quiet. Dolarhyde discouraged chatter among his assistants and communicated with them largely in gestures.

When the evening shift ended, he remained alone in the darkroom to develop, dry, and splice some film of his own.

➤

Dolarhyde got home about ten P.M. He lived alone in a big house his grandparents had left him. It stood at the end of a gravel drive that runs through an apple orchard north of St. Charles, Missouri, across the Missouri River from St. Louis. The orchard's absentee owner did not take care of it. Dead and twisted trees stood among the green ones. Now, in late July, the smell of rotting apples hung over the orchard. There were many bees in the daytime. The nearest neighbor was a half-mile away.

Dolarhyde always made an inspection tour of the house as soon as he got home; there had been an abortive burglary attempt some years before. He flicked on the lights in each room and looked around. A visitor would not think he lived alone. His grandparents' clothes still hung in the closets, his grandmother's brushes were on her dresser with combings of hair in them. Her teeth were in a glass on the bedside table. The water had long since evaporated. His grandmother had been dead for ten years.

(The funeral director had asked him, "Mr. Dolarhyde, wouldn't you like to bring me your grandmother's teeth?" He replied, "Just drop the lid.")

Satisfied that he was alone in the house, Dolarhyde went upstairs, took a long shower, and washed his hair.

He put on a kimono of a synthetic material that felt like silk and lay down on his narrow bed in the room he had occupied since childhood. His grandmother's hair dryer had a plastic cap and hose.

He put on the cap and, while he dried, he thumbed through a new high-fashion magazine. The hatred and brutishness in some of the photographs were remarkable.

He began to feel excited. He swiveled the metal shade of his reading lamp to light a print on the wall at the foot of the bed. It was William Blake's *The Great Red Dragon and the Woman Clothed with the Sun.*

The picture had stunned him the first time he saw it. Never before had he seen anything that approached his graphic thought. He felt that Blake must have peeked in his ear and seen the Red Dragon. For weeks Dolarhyde had worried that his thoughts might glow out his ears, might be visible in the darkroom, might fog the film. He put cotton balls in his ears. Then, fearing that cotton was too flammable, he tried steel wool. That made his ears bleed. Finally he cut small pieces of asbestos cloth from an ironing-board cover and rolled them into little pills that would fit in his ears.

The Red Dragon was all he had for a long time. It was not all he had now. He felt the beginnings of an erection.

He had wanted to go through this slowly, but now he could not wait.

Dolarhyde closed the heavy draperies over windows in the downstairs parlor. He set up his screen and projector. His grandfather had put a La-Z-Boy recliner in the parlor, over his grandmother's objections. (She had put a doily on the headrest.) Now Dolarhyde was glad. It was very comfortable. He draped a towel over the arm of the chair.

He turned out the lamps. Lying back in the dark room, he might have been anywhere. Over the ceiling fixture he had a good light machine which rotated, making varicolored dots of light crawl over the walls, the floor, his skin. He might have been reclining on the acceleration couch of a space vehicle, in a glass bubble out among the stars. When he closed his eyes he thought he could feel the points of light move over him, and when he opened them, those might be the lights of cities above or beneath him. There was no more down or up. The light machine turned faster as it got warm, and the dots swarmed over him, flowed over furniture in angular streams, fell in meteor showers down the walls. He might have been a comet plunging through the Crab Nebula.

There was one place shielded from the light. He had placed a piece of cardboard near the machine, and it cast a shadow over the movie screen.

Sometimes, in the future, he would smoke first to heighten the effect, but he did not need it now, this time.

He thumbed the drop switch at his side to start the projector. A white rectangle sprang on the screen, grayed and streaked as the leader moved past the lens, and then the gray Scotty perked up his ears and ran to the kitchen door, shivering and wagging his stump of a tail. A cut to the Scotty running beside a curb, turning to snap at his side as he ran.

Now Mrs. Leeds came into the kitchen carrying groceries. She laughed and touched her hair. The children came in behind her.

A cut to a badly lit shot in Dolarhyde's own bedroom upstairs. He is standing nude before the print of *The Great Red Dragon and the Woman Clothed with the Sun*. He is wearing "combat glasses," the close-fitting wraparound plastic glasses favored by hockey players. He has an erection, which he improves with his hand.

The focus blurs as he approaches the camera with stylized movements, hand reaching to change the focus as his face fills the frame. The picture quivers and sharpens suddenly to a close-up of his mouth, his disfigured upper lip rolled back, tongue out through the teeth, one rolling eye still in the frame. The mouth fills the screen, writhing lips pulled back from jagged teeth and darkness as his mouth engulfs the lens.

The difficulty of the next part was evident.

A bouncing blur in a harsh movie light became a bed and Charles Leeds thrashing, Mrs. Leeds sitting up, shielding her eyes, turning to Leeds and putting her hands on him, rolling toward the edge of the bed, legs tangled in the covers, trying to rise. The camera jerked toward the ceiling, molding whipping across the screen like a stave, and then the picture steadied, Mrs. Leeds back down on the mattress, a dark spot on her nightdress spreading and Leeds, hands to his neck and eyes wild rising. The screen went black for five beats, then the tic of a splice.

The camera was steady now, on a tripod. They were all dead now. Arranged. Two children seated against the wall facing the bed, one seated across the corner from them facing the camera. Mr. and Mrs.

Leeds in bed with the covers over them. Mr. Leeds propped up against the headboard, the sheet covering the rope around his chest and his head lolled to the side.

Dolarhyde came into the picture from the left with the stylized movements of a Balinese dancer. Blood-smeared and naked except for his glasses and gloves, he mugged and capered among the dead. He approached the far side of the bed, Mrs. Leeds's side, took the corner of the covers, whipped them off the bed and held the pose as though he had executed a veronica.

Now, watching in the parlor of his grandparents' house, Dolarhyde was covered with a sheen of sweat. His thick tongue ran out constantly, the scar on his upper lip wet and shiny and he moaned as he stimulated himself.

Even at the height of his pleasure he was sorry to see that in the film's ensuing scene he lost all his grace and elegance of motion, rooting piglike with his bottom turned carelessly to the camera. There were no dramatic pauses, no sense of pace or climax, just brutish frenzy.

It was wonderful anyway. Watching the film was wonderful. But not as wonderful as the acts themselves.

Two major flaws, Dolarhyde felt, were that the film did not actually show the deaths of the Leedses and that his own performance was poor toward the end. He seemed to lose all his values. That was not how the Red Dragon would do it.

Well. He had many films to make and, with experience, he hoped he could maintain some aesthetic distance, even in the most intimate moments.

He must bear down. This was his life's work, a magnificent thing. It would live forever.

He must press on soon. He must select his fellow performers. Already he had copied several films of Fourth of July family outings. The end of summer always brought a rush of business at the film-processing plant as vacation movies came in. Thanksgiving would bring another rush.

Families were mailing their applications to him every day.

CHAPTER 10

THE PLANE from Washington to Birmingham was half-empty. Graham took a window seat with no one beside him.

He declined the tired sandwich the stewardess offered and put his Jacobi file on the tray table. At the front he had listed the similarities between the Jacobis and the Leedses.

Both couples were in their late thirties, both had children—two boys and a girl. Edward Jacobi had another son, by a previous marriage, who was away at college when the family was killed.

Both parents in each case had college degrees, and both families lived in two-story houses in pleasant suburbs. Mrs. Jacobi and Mrs. Leeds were attractive women. The families had some of the same credit cards and they subscribed to some of the same popular magazines.

There the similarities ended. Charles Leeds was a tax attorney, while Edward Jacobi was an engineer and metallurgist. The Atlanta family were Presbyterian; the Jacobis were Catholic. The Leedses were lifelong Atlanta residents, while the Jacobis had lived in Birmingham only three months, transferred there from Detroit.

The word "random" sounded in Graham's head like a dripping faucet. "Random selection of victims," "no apparent motive"—

newspapers used those terms, and detectives spat them out in anger and frustration in homicide squad rooms.

"Random" wasn't accurate, though. Graham knew that mass murderers and serial murderers do not select their victims at random.

The man who killed the Jacobis and the Leedses saw something in them that drew him and drove him to do it. He might have known them well—Graham hoped so—or he might not have known them at all. But Graham was sure the killer saw them at some time before he killed them. He chose them because *something* in them spoke to him, and the women were at the core of it. What was it?

There were some differences in the crimes.

Edward Jacobi was shot as he came down the stairs carrying a flashlight—probably he was awakened by a noise.

Mrs. Jacobi and her children were shot in the head, Mrs. Leeds in the abdomen. The weapon was a nine-millimeter automatic pistol in all the shootings. Traces of steel wool from a homemade silencer were found in the wounds. The cartridge cases bore no fingerprints.

The knife had been used only on Charles Leeds. Dr. Princi believed it was thin-bladed and very keen, possibly a fileting knife.

The methods of entry were different too; a patio door pried open at the Jacobis', the glass cutter at the Leedses'.

Photographs of the crime in Birmingham did not show the quantity of blood found at the Leedses', but there were stains on the bedroom walls about two and one-half feet above the floor. So the killer had an audience in Birmingham too. The Birmingham police checked the bodies for fingerprints, including the fingernails, and found nothing. Burial for a summer month in Birmingham would destroy any prints like the one on the Leeds child.

In both places were the same blond hairs, same spit, same semen.

Graham propped photographs of the two smiling families against the seat back in front of him and stared at them for a long time in the hanging quiet of the airplane.

What could have attracted the murderer specifically to *them?* Graham wanted very much to believe there was a common factor and that he would find it soon.

Otherwise he would have to enter more houses and see what the Tooth Fairy had left for him.

➤

Graham got directions from the Birmingham field office and checked in with the police by telephone from the airport. The compact car he rented spit water from the air-conditioner vents onto his hands and arms.

His first stop was the Geehan Realty office on Dennison Avenue.

Geehan, tall and bald, made haste across his turquoise shag to greet Graham. His smile faded when Graham showed his identification and asked for the key to the Jacobi house.

"Will there be some cops in uniform out there today?" he asked, his hand on the top of his head.

"I don't know."

"I hope to God not. I've got a chance to show it twice this afternoon. It's a nice house. People see it and they forget this other. Last Thursday I had a couple from Duluth, substantial retired people hot on the Sun Belt. I had them down to the short rows—talking mortgages—I mean that man could have fronted a *third,* when the squad car rode up and in they came. Couple asked them questions and, boy, did they get some answers. These good officers gave 'em the whole tour—who was laying where. Then it was Good-bye, Geehan, much oblige for your trouble. I try to show 'em how safe we've fixed it, but they don't listen. There they go, jake-legged through the gravel, climbing back in their Sedan de Ville."

"Have any single men asked to look at it?"

"They haven't asked me. It's a multiple listing. I don't think so, though. Police wouldn't let us start painting until, I don't know, we just got finished inside last Tuesday. Took two coats of interior latex, three in places. We're still working outside. It'll be a genuine showplace."

"How can you sell it before the estate's probated?"

"I can't *close* until probate, but that doesn't mean I can't be ready. People could move in on a memorandum of understanding. I need to do something. A business associate of mine is holding the paper, and that interest just works all day and all night while you're asleep."

"Who is Mr. Jacobi's executor?"

"Byron Metcalf, firm of Metcalf and Barnes. How long you figure on being out there?"

"I don't know. Until I've finished."

"You can drop that key in the mail. You don't have to come back by."

➤

Graham had the flat feeling of a cold trail as he drove out to the Jacobi house. It was barely within the city limits in an area newly annexed. He stopped beside the highway once to check his map before he found the turnoff onto an asphalt secondary road.

More than a month had passed since they were killed. What had he been doing then? Putting a pair of diesels in a sixty-five foot Rybovich hull, signaling to Ariaga in the crane to come down another half-inch. Molly came over in the late afternoon and he and Molly and Ariaga sat under an awning in the cockpit of the half-finished boat and ate the big prawns Molly brought and drank cold Dos Equis beer. Ariaga explained the best way to clean crayfish, drawing the tail fan in sawdust on the deck, and the sunlight, broken on the water, played on the undersides of the wheeling gulls.

Water from the air conditioner squirted on the front of Graham's shirt and he was in Birmingham now and there were no prawns or gulls. He was driving, and pastures and wooded lots were on his right with goats and horses in them, and on his left was Stonebridge, a long-established residential area with a few elegant homes and a number of rich people's houses.

He saw the realtor's sign a hundred yards before he reached it. The Jacobi house was the only one on the right side of the road. Sap from the pecan trees beside the drive had made the gravel sticky, and it rattled inside the fenders of the car. A carpenter on a ladder was installing window guards. The workman raised a hand to Graham as he walked around the house.

A flagged patio at the side was shaded by a large oak tree. At night the tree would block out the floodlight in the side yard as well. This was where the Tooth Fairy had entered, through sliding glass doors. The doors had been replaced with new ones, the aluminum frames still bright and bearing the manufacturer's sticker. Covering the sliding doors was a new wrought-iron security gate. The basement door was new too—flush steel and secured by deadbolts. The components of a hot tub stood in crates on the flagstones.

Graham went inside. Bare floors and dead air. His footsteps echoed in the empty house.

The new mirrors in the bathrooms had never reflected the Jacobis' faces or the killer's. On each was a fuzzy white spot where the price had been torn off. A folded dropcloth lay in a corner of the master bedroom. Graham sat on it long enough for the sunlight through the bare windows to move one board-width across the floor.

There was nothing here. Nothing anymore.

If he had come here immediately after the Jacobis were killed, would the Leedses still be alive? Graham wondered. He tested the weight of that burden.

It did not lift when he was out of the house and under the sky again.

Graham stood in the shade of a pecan tree, shoulders hunched, hands in his pockets, and looked down the long drive to the road that passed in front of the Jacobi house.

How had the Tooth Fairy come to the Jacobi house? He had to drive. Where did he park? The gravel driveway was too noisy for a midnight visit, Graham thought. The Birmingham police did not agree.

He walked down the drive to the roadside. The asphalt road was bordered with ditches as far as he could see. It might be possible to pull across the ditch and hide a vehicle in the brush on the Jacobis' side of the road if the ground were hard and dry.

Facing the Jacobi house across the road was the single entrance to Stonebridge. The sign said that Stonebridge had a private patrol service. A strange vehicle would be noticed there. So would a man walking late at night. Scratch parking in Stonebridge.

Graham went back into the house and was surprised to find the telephone working. He called the Weather Bureau and learned that three inches of rain fell on the day before the Jacobis were killed. The ditches were full, then. The Tooth Fairy did not hide his vehicle beside the asphalt road.

A horse in the pasture beside the yard kept pace with Graham as he walked along the whitewashed fence toward the rear of the property. He gave the horse a Life-Saver and left him at the corner as he turned along the back fence behind the outbuildings.

He stopped when he saw the depression in the ground where the Jacobi children had buried their cat. Thinking about it in the Atlanta police station with Springfield, he had pictured the outbuildings as white. Actually they were dark green.

The children had wrapped the cat in a dish towel and buried it in a shoebox with a flower between its paws.

Graham rested his forearm on top of the fence and leaned his forehead against it.

A pet funeral, solemn rite of childhood. Parents going back into the house, ashamed to pray. The children looking at one another, discovering new nerves in the place loss pierces. One bows her head, then they all do, the shovel taller than any of them. Afterward a discussion of whether or not the cat is in heaven with God and Jesus, and the children don't shout for a while.

A certainty came to Graham as he stood, sun hot on the back of his neck: as surely as the Tooth Fairy killed the cat, he had watched the children bury it. He had to see that if he possibly could.

He did not make two trips out here, one to kill the cat and the second for the Jacobis. He came and killed the cat and waited for the children to find it.

There was no way to determine exactly where the children found the cat. The police had located no one who spoke to the Jacobis after noon, ten hours or so before they died.

How had the Tooth Fairy come, and where had he waited?

Behind the back fence the brush began, running head-high for thirty yards to the trees. Graham dug his wrinkled map out of his back pocket and spread it on the fence. It showed an unbroken strip of woods a quarter-mile deep running across the back of the Jacobi property and continuing in both directions. Beyond the woods, bounding them on the south, was a section line road that paralleled the one in front of the Jacobi house.

Graham drove from the house back to the highway, measuring the distance on his odometer. He went south on the highway and turned onto the section line road he had seen on the map. Measuring again, he drove slowly along it until the odometer showed him he was behind the Jacobi house on the other side of the woods.

Here the pavement ended at a low-income housing project so new it did not show on his map. He pulled into the parking lot. Most of the cars were old and sagging on their springs. Two were up on blocks.

Black children played basketball on the bare earth around a single netless goal. Graham sat on his fender to watch the game for a moment.

He wanted to take off his jacket, but he knew the .44 Special and the flat camera on his belt would attract attention. He always felt a curious embarrassment when people looked at his pistol.

There were eight players on the team wearing shirts. The skins had eleven, all playing at once. Refereeing was by acclamation.

A small skin, shoved down in the rebounding, stalked home mad. He came back fortified with a cookie and dived into the pack again.

The yelling and the thump of the ball lifted Graham's spirits.

One goal, one basketball. It struck him again how many *things* the Leedses had. The Jacobis too, according to the Birmingham police when they ruled out burglary. Boats and sporting equipment, camping equipment, cameras and guns and rods. It was another thing the families had in common.

And with the thought of the Leedses and the Jacobis alive came the thought of how they were afterward, and Graham couldn't watch basketball anymore. He took a deep breath and headed for the dark woods across the road.

The underbrush, heavy at the edge of the pine woods, thinned when Graham reached the deep shade and he had easy going over the pine needles. The air was warm and still. Blue jays in the trees ahead announced his coming.

The ground sloped gently to a dry streambed where a few cypresses grew and the tracks of raccoons and field mice were pressed into the red clay. A number of human footprints marked the streambed, some of them left by children. All were caved in and rounded, left several rains ago.

Past the streambed the land rose again, changing to sandy loam that supported ferns beneath the pines. Graham worked his way uphill in the heat until he saw the light beneath the trees at the edge of the woods.

Between the trunks he could see the upper story of the Jacobi house.

Undergrowth again, head-high from the edge of the woods to the Jacobis' back fence. Graham worked his way through it and stood at the fence looking into the yard.

The Tooth Fairy could have parked at the housing development and come through the woods to the brush behind the house. He could have lured the cat into the brush and choked it, the body limp in one hand as he crawled on his knees and other hand to the fence. Graham could see the cat in the air, never twisting to land on its feet, but hitting on its back with a thump in the yard.

The Tooth Fairy did that in daylight—the children would not have found or buried the cat at night.

And he waited to see them find it. Did he wait for the rest of the day in the heat of the underbrush? At the fence he would be visible through the rails. In order to see the yard from farther back in the brush, he would have to stand and face the windows of the house with the sun beating on him. Clearly he would go back to the trees. So did Graham.

The Birmingham police were not stupid. He could see where they had pushed through the brush, searching the area as a matter of course. But that was before the cat was found. They were looking for clues, dropped objects, tracks—not for a vantage point.

He went a few yards into the forest behind the Jacobi house and worked back and forth in the dappled shade. First he took the high ground that afforded a partial view of the yard and then worked his way down the tree line.

He had searched for more than an hour when a wink of light from the ground caught his eye. He lost it, found it again. It was the ring-pull tab from a soft-drink can half-buried in the leaves beneath an elm tree, one of the few elms among the pines.

He spotted it from eight feet away and went no closer for five minutes while he scanned the ground around the tree. He squatted and brushed the leaves away ahead of him as he approached the tree, duck-walking in the path he made to avoid ruining any impressions. Working slowly, he cleared the leaves all around the trunk. No footprints had pressed through the mat of last year's leaves.

Near the aluminum tab he found a dried apple core eaten thin by ants. Birds had pecked out the seeds. He studied the ground for ten more minutes. Finally he sat on the ground, stretched out his aching legs, and leaned back against the tree.

A cone of gnats swarmed in a column of sunlight. A caterpillar rippled along the underside of a leaf.

There was a wedge of red creek mud from the instep of a boot on the limb above his head.

Graham hung his coat on a branch and began to climb carefully on the opposite side of the tree, peering around the trunk at the limbs above the wedge of mud. At thirty feet he looked around the trunk, and there was the Jacobi house 175 yards away. It looked different from this height, the roof color dominant. He could see the backyard and the ground behind the outbuildings very well. A decent pair of field glasses would pick up the expression on a face easily at this distance.

Graham could hear traffic in the distance, and far away he heard a beagle on a case. A cicada started its numbing bandsaw buzz and drowned out the other sounds.

A thick limb just above him joined the trunk at a right angle to the Jacobi house. He pulled himself up until he could see, and leaned around the trunk to look at it.

Close by his cheek a soft-drink can was wedged between the limb and the trunk.

"I love it," Graham whispered into the bark. "Oh, sweet Jesus, yes. Come on, can."

Still, a child might have left it.

He climbed higher on his side of the tree, dicey work on small branches, and moved around until he could look down on the big limb.

A patch of outer bark on the upper side of the limb was shaved away, leaving a field of green inner bark the size of a playing card. Centered in the green rectangle, carved through to the white wood, Graham saw this:

It was done carefully and cleanly with a very sharp knife. It was not the work of a child.

Graham photographed the mark, carefully bracketing his exposures.

The view from the big limb was good, and it had been improved: the stub of a small branch jutted down from the limb above. It had been clipped off to clear the view. The fibers were compressed and the end slightly flattened in the cutting.

Graham looked for the severed branch. If it had been on the ground, he would have seen it. There, tangled in the limbs below, brown withered leaves amid the green foliage.

The laboratory would need both sides of the cut in order to measure the pitch of the cutting edges. That meant coming back here with a saw. He made several photographs of the stub. All the while he mumbled to himself.

I think that after you killed the cat and threw it into the yard, my man, you climbed up here and waited. I think you watched the children and passed the time whittling and dreaming. When night came, you saw them passing their bright windows and you watched the shades go down, and you saw the lights go out one by one. And after a while you climbed down and went in to them. Didn't you? It wouldn't be too hard a climb straight down from the big limb with a flashlight and the bright moon rising.

It was a hard enough climb for Graham. He stuck a twig into the opening of the soft-drink can, gently lifted it from the crotch of the tree, and descended, holding the twig in his teeth when he had to use both hands.

Back at the housing project, Graham found that someone had written "Levon is a doo-doo head" in the dust on the side of his car. The height of the writing indicated that even the youngest residents were well along in literacy.

He wondered if they had written on the Tooth Fairy's car.

Graham sat for a few minutes looking up at the rows of windows. There appeared to be about a hundred units. It was possible that someone might remember a white stranger in the parking lot late at night. Even though a month had passed, it was well worth trying. To ask every resident, and get it done quickly, he would need the help of the Birmingham police.

He fought the temptation to send the drink can straight to Jimmy Price in Washington. He had to ask the Birmingham police for manpower. It would be better to give them what he had. Dusting the can would be a straightforward job. Trying for fingerprints etched by acid sweat was another matter. Price could still do it after Birmingham dusted, as long as the can wasn't handled with bare fingers. Better give it to the police. He knew the FBI document section would fall on the carving like a rabid mongoose. Pictures of that for everybody, nothing lost there.

He called Birmingham Homicide from the Jacobi house. The detectives arrived just as the realtor, Geehan, was ushering in his prospective buyers.

CHAPTER 11

EILEEN WAS READING a *National Tattler* article called "Filth in Your Bread!" when Dolarhyde came into the cafeteria. She had eaten only the filling in her tuna-salad sandwich.

Behind the red goggles Dolarhyde's eyes zigged down the front page of the *Tattler*. Cover lines in addition to "Filth in Your Bread!" included "Elvis at Secret Love Retreat—Exclusive Pix!!" "Stunning Breakthrough for Cancer Victims!" and the big banner line "Hannibal the Cannibal Helps Lawmen—Cops Consult Fiend in 'Tooth Fairy' Murders."

He stood at the window absently stirring his coffee until he heard Eileen get up. She dumped her tray in the trash container and was about to throw in the *Tattler* when Dolarhyde touched her shoulder.

"May I have that paper, Eileen?"

"Sure, Mr. D. I just get it for the horoscopes."

Dolarhyde read it in his office with the door closed.

Freddy Lounds had two bylines in the same double-page center spread. The main story was a breathless reconstruction of the Jacobi and Leeds murders. Since the police had not divulged many of the specifics, Lounds consulted his imagination for lurid details.

Dolarhyde found them banal.

The sidebar was more interesting:

Insane Fiend Consulted in Mass Murders
by Cop He Tried to Kill
by
Freddy Lounds

BALTIMORE, MD.— Federal manhunters, stymied in their search for the "Tooth Fairy," psychopathic slayer of entire families in Birmingham and Atlanta, have turned to the most savage killer in captivity for help.

Dr. Hannibal Lecter, whose unspeakable practices were reported in these pages three years ago, was consulted this week in his maximum-security-asylum cell by ace investigator William (Will) Graham.

Graham suffered a near-fatal slashing at Lecter's hands when he unmasked the mass murderer.

He was brought back from early retirement to spearhead the hunt for the "Tooth Fairy."

What went on in this bizarre meeting of two mortal enemies? What was Graham after?

"It takes one to catch one," a high federal official told this reporter. He was referring to Lecter, known as "Hannibal the Cannibal," who is both a psychiatrist and a mass murderer.

OR WAS HE REFERRING TO GRAHAM???

The *Tattler* has learned that Graham, former instructor in forensics at the FBI Academy in Quantico, Va., was once confined to a mental institution for a period of four weeks. . . .

Federal officials refused to say why they placed a man with a history of mental instability at the forefront of a desperate manhunt.

The nature of Graham's mental problem was not revealed, but one former psychiatric worker called it "deep depression."

Garmon Evans, a paraprofessional formerly employed at Bethesda Naval Hospital, said Graham was admitted to the psychiatric wing soon after he killed Garrett Jacob Hobbs, the "Minnesota Shrike." Graham shot Hobbs to death in 1975, ending Hobbs's eight-month reign of terror in Minneapolis.

Evans said Graham was withdrawn and refused to eat or speak during the first weeks of his stay.

Graham has never been an FBI agent. Veteran observers attribute this to the Bureau's strict screening procedures, designed to detect instability.

Federal sources would reveal only that Graham originally worked in the FBI crime laboratory and was assigned teaching duties at the FBI Academy after outstanding work both in the laboratory and in the field, where he served as a "special investigator."

The *Tattler* learned that before his federal service, Graham was in the homicide division of the New Orleans police department, a post he left to attend graduate school in forensics at George Washington University.

One New Orleans officer who served with Graham commented, "Well, you can call him retired, but the feds like to know he's around. It's like having a king snake under the house. They may not see him much, but it's nice to know he's there to eat the moccasins."

Dr. Lecter is confined for the rest of his life. If he is ever declared sane, he will have to stand trial on nine counts of first-degree murder.

Lecter's attorney says the mass murderer spends his time writing useful articles for the scientific journals and has an "ongoing dialogue" by mail with some of the most respected figures in psychiatry.

Dolarhyde stopped reading and looked at the pictures. There were two of them above the sidebar. One showed Lecter pinned against the side of a state trooper's car. The other was the picture of Will Graham taken by Freddy Lounds outside the Baltimore State Hospital. A small photograph of Lounds ran beside each of his bylines.

Dolarhyde looked at the pictures for a long time. He ran the tip of his forefinger over them slowly, back and forth, his touch exquisitely sensitive to the rough newsprint. Ink left a smudge on his fingertip. He wet the smudge with his tongue and wiped it off on a Kleenex. Then he cut out the sidebar and put it in his pocket.

➤

On his way home from the plant, Dolarhyde bought toilet paper of the quick-dissolving kind used in boats and campers, and a nasal inhaler.

He felt good despite his hay fever; like many people who have undergone extensive rhinoplasty, Dolarhyde had no hair in his nose and hay fever plagued him. So did upper respiratory infections.

When a stalled truck held him up for ten minutes on the Missouri River bridge to St. Charles, he sat patiently. His black van was carpeted, cool and quiet. Handel's Water Music played on the stereo.

He rippled his fingers on the steering wheel in time with the music and dabbed at his nose.

Two women in a convertible were in the lane beside him. They wore shorts and blouses tied across the midriff. Dolarhyde looked down into the convertible from his van. They seemed tired and bored squinting into the lowering sun. The woman on the passenger side had her head against the seat back and her feet on the dash. Her slumped posture made two creases across her bare stomach. Dolarhyde could see a suck mark on the inside of her thigh. She caught him looking, sat up and crossed her legs. He saw weary distaste in her face.

She said something to the woman at the wheel. Both looked straight ahead. He knew they were talking about him. He was *so* glad it did not make him angry. Few things made him angry anymore. He knew that he was developing a becoming dignity.

The music was very pleasant.

The traffic in front of Dolarhyde began to move. The lane beside him was still stalled. He looked forward to getting home. He tapped the wheel in time with the music and rolled down the window with his other hand.

He hawked and spit a blob of green phlegm into the lap of the woman beside him, hitting her just beside the navel. Her curses sounded high and thin over the Handel as he drove away.

➤

Dolarhyde's great ledger was at least a hundred years old. Bound in black leather with brass corners, it was so heavy a sturdy machine table supported it in the locked closet at the top of the stairs. From the moment he saw it at the bankruptcy sale of an old St. Louis printing company, Dolarhyde knew it should be his.

Now, bathed and in his kimono, he unlocked the closet and rolled it out. When the book was centered beneath the painting of the Great

Red Dragon, he settled himself in a chair and opened it. The smell of foxed paper rose to his face.

Across the first page, in large letters he had illuminated himself, were the words from Revelation: "And There Came a Great Red Dragon Also . . ."

The first item in the book was the only one not neatly mounted. Loose between the pages was a yellowed photograph of Dolarhyde as a small child with his grandmother on the steps of the big house. He is holding to Grandmother's skirt. Her arms are folded and her back is straight.

Dolarhyde turned past it. He ignored it as though it had been left there by mistake.

There were many clippings in the ledger, the earliest ones about the disappearances of elderly women in St. Louis and Toledo. Pages between the clippings were covered with Dolarhyde's writing—black ink in a fine copperplate script not unlike William Blake's own handwriting.

Fastened in the margins, ragged bites of scalp trailed their tails of hair like comets pressed in God's scrapbook.

The Jacobi clippings from Birmingham were there, along with film cartridges and slides set in pockets glued to the pages.

So were stories on the Leedses, with film beside them.

The term "Tooth Fairy" had not appeared in the press until Atlanta. The name was marked out in all the Leeds stories.

Now Dolarhyde did the same with his *Tattler* clipping, obliterating "Tooth Fairy" with angry slashes of a red marker pen.

He turned to a new, blank page in his ledger and trimmed the *Tattler* clipping to fit. Should Graham's picture go in? The words "Criminally Insane" carved in the stone above Graham offended Dolarhyde. He hated the sight of any place of confinement. Graham's face was closed to him. He set it aside for the time being.

But Lecter . . . Lecter. This was not a good picture of the doctor. Dolarhyde had a better one, which he fetched from a box in his closet. It was published upon Lecter's committal and showed the fine eyes. Still, it was not satisfactory. In Dolarhyde's mind, Lecter's likeness should be the dark portrait of a Renaissance prince. For Lecter, alone among all men, might have the sensitivity and experience to understand the glory, the majesty of Dolarhyde's Becoming.

Dolarhyde felt that Lecter knew the unreality of the people who die to help you in these things—understood that they are not flesh, but light and air and color and quick sounds quickly ended when you change them. Like balloons of color bursting. That they are more important for the changing, more important than the lives they scrabble after, pleading.

Dolarhyde bore screams as a sculptor bears dust from the beaten stone.

Lecter was capable of understanding that blood and breath were only elements undergoing change to fuel his Radiance. Just as the source of light is burning.

He would like to meet Lecter, talk and share with him, rejoice with him in their shared vision, be recognized by him as John the Baptist recognized the One who came after, sit on him as the Dragon sat on 666 in Blake's Revelation series, and film his death as, dying, he melded with the strength of the Dragon.

Dolarhyde pulled on a new pair of rubber gloves and went to his desk. He unrolled and discarded the outer layer of the toilet paper he had bought. Then he unrolled a strip of seven sheets and tore it off.

Printing carefully on the tissue with his left hand, he wrote a letter to Lecter.

Speech is never a reliable indicator of how a person writes; you never know. Dolarhyde's speech was bent and pruned by disabilities real and imagined, and the difference between his speech and his writing was startling. Still, he found he could not say the most important things he felt.

He wanted to hear from Lecter. He needed a personal response before he could tell Dr. Lecter the important things.

How could he manage that? He rummaged through his box of Lecter clippings, read them all again.

Finally a simple way occurred to him and he wrote again.

The letter seemed too diffident and shy when he read it over. He had signed it "Avid Fan."

He brooded over the signature for several minutes.

"Avid Fan" indeed. His chin rose an imperious fraction.

He put his gloved thumb in his mouth, removed his dentures, and placed them on the blotter.

The upper plate was unusual. The teeth were normal, straight and white, but the pink acrylic upper part was a tortuous shape cast to fit the twists and fissures of his gums. Attached to the plate was a soft plastic prosthesis with an obturator on top, which helped him close off his soft palate in speech.

He took a small case from his desk. It held another set of teeth. The upper casting was the same, but there was no prosthesis. The crooked teeth had dark stains between them and gave off a faint stench.

They were identical to Grandmother's teeth in the bedside glass downstairs.

Dolarhyde's nostrils flared at the odor. He opened his sunken smile and put them in place and wet them with his tongue.

He folded the letter across the signature and bit down hard on it. When he opened the letter again, the signature was enclosed in an oval bite mark; his notary seal, an imprimatur flecked with old blood.

CHAPTER 12

ATTORNEY BYRON METCALF took off his tie at five o'clock, made himself a drink, and put his feet up on his desk.

"Sure you won't have one?"

"Another time." Graham, picking the cockleburs off his cuffs, was grateful for the air conditioning.

"I didn't know the Jacobis very well," Metcalf said. "They'd only been here three months. My wife and I were there for drinks a couple of times. Ed Jacobi came to me for a new will soon after he was transferred here, that's how I met him."

"But you're his executor."

"Yes. His wife was listed first as executor, then me as alternate in case she was deceased or infirm. He has a brother in Philadelphia, but I gather they weren't close."

"You were an assistant district attorney."

"Yeah, 1968 to '72. I ran for DA in '72. It was close, but I lost. I'm not sorry now."

"How do you see what happened here, Mr. Metcalf?"

"The first thing I thought about was Joseph Yablonski, the labor leader?"

Graham nodded.

"A crime with a motive, power in that case, disguised as an insane attack. We went over Ed Jacobi's papers with a fine-tooth comb—Jerry Estridge from the DA's office and I.

"Nothing. Nobody stood to make much money off Ed Jacobi's death. He made a big salary and he had some patents paying off, but he spent it almost as fast as it came in. Everything was to go to the wife, with a little land in California entailed to the kids and their descendants. He had a small spendthrift trust set up for the surviving son. It'll pay his way through three more years of college. I'm sure he'll still be a freshman by then."

"Niles Jacobi."

"Yeah. The kid gave Ed a big pain in the ass. He lived with his mother in California. Went to Chino for theft. I gather his mother's a flake. Ed went out there to see about him last year. Brought him back to Birmingham and put him in school at Bardwell Community College. Tried to keep him at home, but he dumped on the other kids and made it unpleasant for everybody. Mrs. Jacobi put up with it for a while, but finally they moved him to a dorm."

"Where was he?"

"On the night of June 28?" Metcalf's eyes were hooded as he looked at Graham. "The police wondered about that, and so did I. He went to a movie and then back to school. It's verified. Besides, he has type-O blood. Mr. Graham, I have to pick up my wife in half an hour. We can talk tomorrow if you like. Tell me how I can help you."

"I'd like to see the Jacobis' personal effects. Diaries, pictures, whatever."

"There's not much of that—they lost about everything in a fire in Detroit before they moved down here. Nothing suspicious—Ed was welding in the basement and the sparks got into some paint he had stored down there and the house went up.

"There's some personal correspondence. I have it in the lockboxes with the small valuables. I don't remember any diaries. Everything else is in storage. Niles may have some pictures, but I doubt it. Tell you what—I'm going to court at nine-thirty in the morning, but I could get you into the bank to look at the stuff and come back by for you afterward."

"Fine," Graham said. "One other thing. I could use copies of everything to do with the probate: claims against the estate, any contest of the will, correspondence. I'd like to have all the paper."

"The Atlanta DA's office asked me for that already. They're comparing with the Leeds estate in Atlanta, I know," Metcalf said.

"Still, I'd like copies for myself."

"Okay, copies to you. You don't really think it's money, though, do you?"

"No. I just keep hoping the same name will come up here and in Atlanta."

"So do I."

➤

Student housing at Bardwell Community College was four small dormitory buildings set around a littered quadrangle of beaten earth. A stereo war was in progress when Graham got there.

Opposing sets of speakers on the motel-style balconies blared at each other across the quad. It was Kiss versus the *1812 Overture*. A water balloon arched high in the air and burst on the ground ten feet from Graham.

He ducked under a clothesline and stepped over a bicycle to get through the sitting room of the suite Niles Jacobi shared. The door to Jacobi's bedroom was ajar and music blasted through the crack. Graham knocked.

No response.

He pushed open the door. A tall boy with a spotty face sat on one of the twin beds sucking on a four-foot bong pipe. A girl in dungarees lay on the other bed.

The boy's head jerked around to face Graham. He was struggling to think.

"I'm looking for Niles Jacobi."

The boy appeared stupefied. Graham switched off the stereo.

"I'm looking for Niles Jacobi."

"Just some stuff for my asthma, man. Don't you ever knock?"

"Where's Niles Jacobi?"

"Fuck if I know. What do you want him for?"

Graham showed him the tin. "Try real hard to remember."

"Oh, shit," the girl said.

"Narc, goddammit. I ain't worth it, look, let's talk about this a minute, man."

"Let's talk about where Jacobi is."

"I think I can find out for you," the girl said.

Graham waited while she asked in the other rooms. Everywhere she went, commodes flushed.

There were few traces of Niles Jacobi in the room—one photograph of the Jacobi family lay on a dresser. Graham lifted a glass of melting ice off it and wiped away the wet ring with his sleeve.

The girl returned. "Try the Hateful Snake," she said.

➤

The Hateful Snake bar was in a storefront with the windows painted dark green. The vehicles parked outside were an odd assortment, big trucks looking bobtailed without their trailers, compact cars, a lilac convertible, old Dodges and Chevrolets crippled with high rear ends for the drag-strip look, four full-dress Harley-Davidsons.

An air conditioner, mounted in the transom over the door, dripped steadily onto the sidewalk.

Graham ducked around the dribble and went inside.

The place was crowded and smelled of disinfectant and stale Canoe. The bartender, a husky woman in overalls, reached over heads at the service bar to hand Graham his Coke. She was the only woman there.

Niles Jacobi, dark and razor-thin, was at the jukebox. He put the money in the machine, but the man beside him pushed the buttons.

Jacobi looked like a dissolute schoolboy, but the one selecting the music did not.

Jacobi's companion was a strange mixture; he had a boyish face on a knobby, muscular body. He wore a T-shirt and jeans, worn white over the objects in his pockets. His arms were knotty with muscle, and he had large, ugly hands. One professional tattoo on his left forearm said "Born to Fuck." A crude jailhouse tattoo on his other arm said "Randy." His short jail haircut had grown out unevenly. As he reached for a button on the lighted jukebox, Graham saw a small shaved patch on his forearm.

Graham felt a cold place in his stomach.

He followed Niles Jacobi and "Randy" through the crowd to the back of the room. They sat in a booth.

Graham stopped two feet from the table.

"Niles, my name is Will Graham. I need to talk with you for a few minutes."

Randy looked up with a bright false smile. One of his front teeth was dead. "Do I know you?"

"No. Niles, I want to talk to you."

Niles arched a quizzical eyebrow. Graham wondered what had happened to him in Chino.

"We were having a private conversation here. Butt out," Randy said.

Graham looked thoughtfully at the marred muscular forearms, the dot of adhesive in the crook of the elbow, the shaved patch where Randy had tested the edge of his knife. Knife fighter's mange.

I'm afraid of Randy. Fire or fall back.

"Did you hear me?" Randy said. "Butt out."

Graham unbuttoned his jacket and put his identification on the table.

"Sit still, Randy. If you try to get up, you're gonna have two navels."

"I'm sorry, sir." Instant inmate sincerity.

"Randy, I want you to do something for me. I want you to reach in your left back pocket. Just use two fingers. You'll find a five-inch knife in there with a Flicket clamped to the blade. Put it on the table. . . . Thank you."

Graham dropped the knife into his pocket. It felt greasy.

"Now, in your other pocket is your wallet. Get it out. You sold some blood today, didn't you?"

"So what?"

"So hand me the slip they gave you, the one you show next time at the blood bank. Spread it out on the table."

Randy had type-O blood. Scratch Randy.

"How long have you been out of jail?"

"Three weeks."

"Who's your parole officer?"

"I'm not on parole."

"That's probably a lie." Graham wanted to roust Randy. He could get him for carrying a knife over the legal length. Being in a place with a liquor license was a parole violation. Graham knew he was angry at Randy because he had feared him.

"Randy."

"Yeah."

"Get out."

➤

"I don't know what I can tell you, I didn't know my father very well," Niles Jacobi said as Graham drove him to the school. "He left Mother when I was three, and I didn't see him after that—Mother wouldn't *have* it."

"He came to see you last spring."

"Yes."

"At Chino."

"You know about that."

"I'm just trying to get it straight. What happened?"

"Well, there he was in Visitors, uptight and trying not to look around—so many people treat it like the *zoo*. I'd heard a lot about him from Mother, but he didn't look so bad. He was just a man standing there in a tacky sport coat."

"What did he say?"

"Well, I *expected* him either to jump right in my shit or to be real guilty, that's the way it goes mostly in Visitors. But he just asked me if I thought I could go to school. He said he'd go custody if I'd go to school. And try. 'You have to help *yourself* a little. Try and help yourself, and I'll see you get in school,' and like that."

"How long before you got out?"

"Two weeks."

"Niles, did you ever talk about your family while you were in Chino? To your cellmates or anybody?"

Niles Jacobi looked at Graham quickly. "Oh. Oh, I see. No. Not about my *father*. I hadn't *thought* about him in years, why would I talk about him?"

"How about here? Did you ever take any of your friends over to your parents' house?"

"*Parent*, not parents. She was not my mother."

"Did you ever take anybody over there? School friends or . . ."

"Or rough trade, Officer Graham?"

"That's right."

"No."

"Never?"

"Not once."

"Did he ever mention any kind of threat, was he ever disturbed about anything in the last month or two before it happened?"

"He was disturbed the last time I talked to him, but it was just my grades. I had a lot of cuts. He bought me two alarm clocks. There wasn't anything else that I know of."

"Do you have any personal papers of his, correspondence, photographs, anything?"

"No."

"You have a picture of the family. It's on the dresser in your room. Near the bong."

"That's not my bong. I wouldn't put that filthy thing in my mouth."

"I need the picture. I'll have it copied and send it back to you. What else do you have?"

Jacobi shook a cigarette out of his pack and patted his pockets for matches. "That's all. I can't imagine why they gave *that* to me. My father smiling at *Mrs.* Jacobi and all the little Munchkins. You can have it. He never looked like that to me."

➤

Graham needed to know the Jacobis. Their new acquaintances in Birmingham were little help.

Byron Metcalf gave him the run of the lockboxes. He read the thin stack of letters, mostly business, and poked through the jewelry and the silver.

For three hot days he worked in the warehouse where the Jacobis' household goods were stored. Metcalf helped him at night. Every crate on every pallet was opened and their contents examined. Police photographs helped Graham see where things had been in the house.

Most of the furnishings were new, bought with the insurance from the Detroit fire. The Jacobis hardly had time to leave their marks on their possessions.

One item, a bedside table with traces of fingerprint powder still on it, held Graham's attention. In the center of the tabletop was a blob of green wax.

For the second time he wondered if the killer liked candlelight.

The Birmingham forensics unit was good about sharing.

The blurred print of the end of a nose was the best Birmingham and Jimmy Price in Washington could do with the soft-drink can from the tree.

The FBI laboratory's Firearms and Toolmarks section reported on the severed branch. The blades that clipped it were thick, with a shallow pitch: it had been done with a bolt cutter.

Document section had referred the mark cut in the bark to the Asian Studies department at Langley.

Graham sat on a packing case at the warehouse and read the long report. Asian Studies advised that the mark was a Chinese character which meant "You hit it" or "You hit it on the head"—an expression sometimes used in gambling. It was considered a "positive" or "lucky" sign. The character also appeared on a Mah-Jongg piece, the Asian scholars said. It marked the Red Dragon.

CHAPTER 13

CRAWFORD at FBI headquarters in Washington was on the telephone with Graham at the Birmingham airport when his secretary leaned into the office and flagged his attention.

"Dr. Chilton at Baltimore Hospital on 2706. He says it's urgent."

Crawford nodded. "Hang on, Will." He punched the telephone. "Crawford."

"Frederick Chilton, Mr. Crawford, at the—"

"Yes, Doctor."

"I have a note here, or two pieces of a note, that appears to be from the man who killed those people in Atlanta and—"

"Where did you get it?"

"From Hannibal Lecter's cell. It's written on toilet tissue, of all things, and it has teeth marks pressed in it."

"Can you read it to me without handling it any more?"

Straining to sound calm, Chilton read it:

> My dear Dr. Lecter,
> I wanted to tell you I'm delighted that you have taken an interest in me. And when I learned of your vast correspondence I thought *Dare I?* Of course I do. I don't believe you'd tell them who I am,

even if you knew. Besides, what particular body I currently occupy is trivia.

The important thing is what I am *Becoming*. I know that you alone can understand this. I have some things I'd love to show you. Someday, perhaps, if circumstances permit. I hope we can correspond . . .

"Mr. Crawford, there's a hole torn and punched out. Then it says:

I have admired you for *years* and have a complete collection of your press notices. Actually, I think of them as unfair reviews. As unfair as mine. They like to sling demeaning nicknames, don't they? The *Tooth Fairy*. What could be more inappropriate? It would shame me for you to see that if I didn't know you had suffered the same distortions in the press.

Investigator Graham interests me. Odd-looking for a flatfoot, isn't he? Not very handsome, but purposeful-looking.

You should have taught him not to meddle.

Forgive the stationery. I chose it because it will dissolve very quickly if you should have to swallow it.

"There's a piece missing here, Mr. Crawford. I'll read the bottom part:

If I hear from you, next time I might send you something wet. Until then I remain your

Avid Fan

Silence after Chilton finished reading. "Are you there?"

"Yes. Does Lecter know you have the note?"

"Not yet. This morning he was moved to a holding cell while his quarters were cleaned. Instead of using a proper rag, the cleaning man was pulling handfuls of toilet paper off the roll to wipe down the sink. He found the note wound up in the roll and brought it to me. They bring me anything they find hidden."

"Where's Lecter now?"

"Still in the holding cell."

"Can he see his quarters at all from there?"

"Let me think. . . . No, no, he can't."

"Wait a second, Doctor." Crawford put Chilton on hold. He stared at the two winking buttons on his telephone for several seconds without seeing them. Crawford, fisher of men, was watching his cork move against the current. He got Graham again.

"Will . . . a note, maybe from the Tooth Fairy, hidden in Lecter's cell at Baltimore. Sounds like a fan letter. He wants Lecter's approval, he's curious about you. He's asking questions."

"How was Lecter supposed to answer?"

"Don't know yet. Part's torn out, part's scratched out. Looks like there's a chance of correspondence as long as Lecter's not aware that we know. I want the note for the lab and I want to toss his cell, but it'll be risky. If Lecter gets wise, who knows how he could warn the bastard? We need the link but we need the note too."

Crawford told Graham where Lecter was held, how the note was found. "It's forty miles over to Baltimore. I can't wait for you, buddy. What do you think?"

"Ten people dead in a month—we can't play a long mail game. I say go for it."

"I am," Crawford said.

"See you in two hours."

Crawford hailed his secretary. "Sarah, order a helicopter. I want the next thing smoking and I don't care whose it is—ours, DCPD or Marines. I'll be on the roof in five minutes. Call Documents, tell them to have a document case up there. Tell Herbert to scramble a search team. On the roof. Five minutes."

He picked up Chilton's line.

"Dr. Chilton, we have to search Lecter's cell without his knowledge and we need your help. Have you mentioned this to anybody else?"

"No."

"Where's the cleaning man who found the note?"

"He's here in my office."

"Keep him there, please, and tell him to keep quiet. How long has Lecter been out of his cell?"

"About half an hour."

"Is that unusually long?"

"No, not yet. But it takes only about a half-hour to clean it. Soon he'll begin to wonder what's wrong."

"Okay, do this for me: Call your building superintendent or engineer, whoever's in charge. Tell him to shut off the water in the building and to pull the circuit breakers on Lecter's hall. Have the super walk down the hall past the holding cell carrying tools. He'll be in a hurry, pissed off, too busy to answer any questions—got it? Tell him he'll get an explanation from me. Have the garbage pickup canceled for today if they haven't already come. Don't touch the note, okay? We're coming."

Crawford called the section chief, Scientific Analysis. "Brian, I have a note coming in on the fly, possibly from the Tooth Fairy. Number-one priority. It has to go back where it came from within the hour and unmarked. It'll go to Hair and Fiber, Latent Prints, and Documents, then to you, so coordinate with them, will you? . . . Yes. I'll walk it through. I'll deliver it to you myself."

➤

It was warm—the federally mandated eighty degrees—in the elevator when Crawford came down from the roof with the note, his hair blown silly by the helicopter blast. He was mopping his face by the time he reached the Hair and Fiber section of the laboratory.

Hair and Fiber is a small section, calm and busy. The common room is stacked with boxes of evidence sent by police departments all over the country; swatches of tape that have sealed mouths and bound wrists, torn and stained clothing, deathbed sheets.

Crawford spotted Beverly Katz through the window of an examining room as he wove his way between the boxes. She had a pair of child's coveralls suspended from a hanger over a table covered with white paper. Working under bright lights in the draft-free room, she brushed the overalls with a metal spatula, carefully working with the wale and across it, with the nap and against it. A sprinkle of dirt and sand fell to the paper. With it, falling through the still air more slowly than sand but faster than lint, came a tightly coiled hair. She cocked her head and looked at it with her bright robin's eye.

Crawford could see her lips moving. He knew what she was saying. "Gotcha."

That's what she always said.

Crawford pecked on the glass and she came out fast, stripping off her white gloves.

"It hasn't been printed yet, right?"

"No."

"I'm set up in the next examining room." She put on a fresh pair of gloves while Crawford opened the document case.

The note, in two pieces, was contained gently between two sheets of plastic film. Beverly Katz saw the tooth impressions and glanced up at Crawford, not wasting time with the question.

He nodded: the impressions matched the clear overlay of the killer's bite he had carried with him to Baltimore.

Crawford watched through the window as she lifted the note on a slender dowel and hung it over white paper. She looked it over with a powerful glass, then fanned it gently. She tapped the dowel with the edge of a spatula and went over the paper beneath it with the magnifying glass.

Crawford looked at his watch.

Katz flipped the note over another dowel to get the reverse side up. She removed one tiny object from its surface with tweezers almost as fine as a hair.

She photographed the torn ends of the note under high magnification and returned it to its case. She put a clean pair of white gloves in the case with it. The white gloves—the signal not to touch—would always be beside the evidence until it was checked for fingerprints.

"That's it," she said, handing the case back to Crawford. "One hair, maybe a thirty-second of an inch. A couple of blue grains. I'll work it up. What else have you got?"

Crawford gave her three marked envelopes. "Hair from Lecter's comb. Whiskers from the electric razor they let him use. This is hair from the cleaning man. Gotta go."

"See you later," Katz said. "Love *your* hair."

➤

Jimmy Price in Latent Fingerprints winced at the sight of the porous toilet paper. He squinted fiercely over the shoulder of his technician operating the helium-cadmium laser as they tried to find a fingerprint and make it fluoresce. Glowing smudges appeared on the paper, perspiration stains, nothing.

Crawford started to ask him a question, thought better of it, waited with the blue light reflecting off his glasses.

"We know three guys handled this without gloves, right?" Price said.

"Yeah, the cleanup man, Lecter, and Chilton."

"The fellow scrubbing sinks probably had washed the oil off his fingers. But the others—this stuff is terrible." Price held the paper to the light, forceps steady in his mottled old hand. "I could fume it, Jack, but I couldn't guarantee the iodine stains would fade out in the time you've got."

"Ninhydrin? Boost it with heat?" Ordinarily, Crawford would not have ventured a technical suggestion to Price, but he was floundering for anything. He expected a huffy reply, but the old man sounded rueful and sad.

"No. We couldn't wash it after. I can't get you a print off this, Jack. There isn't one."

"Fuck," Crawford said.

The old man turned away. Crawford put his hand on Price's bony shoulder. "Hell, Jimmy. If there was one, you'd have found it."

Price didn't answer. He was unpacking a pair of hands that had arrived in another matter. Dry ice smoked in his wastebasket. Crawford dropped the white gloves into the smoke.

➤

Disappointment growling in his stomach, Crawford hurried on to Documents where Lloyd Bowman was waiting. Bowman had been called out of court and the abrupt shear in his concentration left him blinking like a man just wakened.

"I congratulate you on your hairstyle. A brave departure," Bowman said, his hands quick and careful as he transferred the note to his work surface. "How long do I have?"

"Twenty minutes max."

The two pieces of the note seemed to glow under Bowman's lights. His blotter showed dark green through a jagged oblong hole in the upper piece.

"The main thing, the first thing, is how Lecter was to reply," Crawford said when Bowman had finished reading.

"Instructions for answering were probably in the part torn out."

Bowman worked steadily with his lights and filters and copy camera as he talked. "Here in the top piece he says 'I hope we can correspond . . .' and then the hole begins. Lecter scratched over that with a felt-tip pen and then folded it and pinched most of it out."

"He doesn't have anything to cut with."

Bowman photographed the tooth impressions and the back of the note under extremely oblique light, his shadow leaping from wall to wall as he moved the light through 360 degrees around the paper and his hands made phantom folding motions in the air.

"Now we can mash just a little." Bowman put the note between two panes of glass to flatten the jagged edges of the hole. The tatters were smeared with vermilion ink. He was chanting under his breath. On the third repetition Crawford made out what he was saying. "You're so sly, but so am I."

Bowman switched filters on his small television camera and focused it on the note. He darkened the room until there was only the dull red glow of a lamp and the blue-green of his monitor screen.

The words "I hope we can correspond" and the jagged hole appeared enlarged on the screen. The ink smear was gone, and on the tattered edges appeared fragments of writing.

"Aniline dyes in colored inks are transparent to infrared," Bowman said. "These could be the tips of T's here and here. On the end is the tail of what could be an M or N, or possibly an R." Bowman took a photograph and turned the lights on. "Jack, there are just two common ways of carrying on a communication that's one-way blind—the phone and publication. Could Lecter take a fast phone call?"

"He can take calls, but it's slow and they have to come in through the hospital switchboard."

"Publication is the only safe way, then."

"We know this sweetheart reads the *Tattler*. The stuff about Graham and Lecter was in the *Tattler*. I don't know of any other paper that carried it."

"Three T's and an R in *Tattler*. Personal column, you think? It's a place to look."

Crawford checked with the FBI library, then telephoned instructions to the Chicago field office.

Bowman handed him the case as he finished.

"The *Tattler* comes out this evening," Crawford said. "It's printed in Chicago on Mondays and Thursdays. We'll get proofs of the classified pages."

"I'll have some more stuff—minor, I think," Bowman said.

"Anything useful, fire it straight to Chicago. Fill me in when I get back from the asylum," Crawford said on his way out the door.

CHAPTER 14

THE TURNSTILE at Washington's Metro Central spit Graham's fare card back to him and he came out into the hot afternoon carrying his flight bag.

The J. Edgar Hoover Building looked like a great concrete cage above the heat shimmer on Tenth Street. The FBI's move to the new headquarters had been under way when Graham left Washington. He had never worked there.

Crawford met him at the escort desk off the underground driveway to augment Graham's hastily issued credentials with his own. Graham looked tired and he was impatient with the signing-in. Crawford wondered how he felt, knowing that the killer was thinking about him.

Graham was issued a magnetically encoded tag like the one on Crawford's vest. He plugged it into the gate and passed into the long white corridors. Crawford carried his flight bag.

"I forgot to tell Sarah to send a car for you."

"Probably quicker this way. Did you get the note back to Lecter all right?"

"Yeah," Crawford said. "I just got back. We poured water on the hall floor. Faked a broken pipe and electrical short. We had Simmons—he's the assistant SAC Baltimore now—we had him

117

mopping when Lecter was brought back to his cell. Simmons thinks he bought it."

"I kept wondering on the plane if Lecter wrote it himself."

"That bothered me too until I looked at it. Bite mark in the paper matches the ones on the women. Also it's ball-point, which Lecter doesn't have. The person who wrote it had read the *Tattler,* and Lecter hasn't had a *Tattler.* Rankin and Willingham tossed the cell. Beautiful job, but they didn't find diddly. They took Polaroids first to get everything back just right. Then the cleaning man went in and did what he always does."

"So what do you think?"

"As far as physical evidence toward an ID, the note is pretty much dreck," Crawford said. "Some way we've got to make the contact work for us, but damn if I know how yet. We'll get the rest of the lab results in a few minutes."

"You've got the mail and phone covered at the hospital?"

"Standing trace-and-tape order for any time Lecter's on the phone. He made a call Saturday afternoon. He told Chilton he was calling his lawyer. It's a damn WATS line, and I can't be sure."

"What did his lawyer say?"

"Nothing. We got a leased line to the hospital switchboard for Lecter's convenience in the future, so that won't get by us again. We'll fiddle with his mail both ways, starting next delivery. No problem with warrants, thank God."

Crawford bellied up to a door and stuck the tag on his vest into the lock slot. "My new office. Come on in. Decorator had some paint left over from a battleship he was doing. Here's the note. This print is exactly the size."

Graham read it twice. Seeing the spidery lines spell his name started a high tone ringing in his head.

"The library confirms the *Tattler* is the only paper that carried a story about Lecter and you," Crawford said, fixing himself an Alka-Seltzer. "Want one of these? Good for you. It was published Monday night a week ago. It was on the stands Tuesday nationwide—some areas not till Wednesday—Alaska and Maine and places. The Tooth Fairy got one—couldn't have done it before Tuesday. He reads it, writes to Lecter. Rankin and Willingham are still sifting the hospital trash for the envelope. Bad job. They don't separate the papers from the diapers at Baltimore.

"All right, Lecter gets the note from the Tooth Fairy no sooner than Wednesday. He tears out the part about how to reply and scratches over and pokes out one earlier reference—I don't know why he didn't tear that out too."

"It was in the middle of a paragraph full of compliments," Graham said. "He couldn't stand to ruin them. That's why he didn't throw the whole thing away." He rubbed his temples with his knuckles.

"Bowman thinks Lecter will use the *Tattler* to answer The Tooth Fairy. He says that's probably the setup. You think he'd answer this thing?"

"Sure. He's a great correspondent. Pen pals all over."

"If they're using the *Tattler,* Lecter would barely have time to get his answer in the issue they'll print tonight, even if he sent it special delivery to the paper the same day he got the Tooth Fairy's note. Chester from the Chicago office is down at the *Tattler* checking the ads. The printers are putting the paper together right now."

"Please God don't stir the *Tattler* up," Graham said.

"The shop foreman thinks Chester's a realtor trying to get a jump on the ads. He's selling him the proof sheets under the table, one by one as they come off. We're getting everything, all the classifieds, just to blow some smoke. All right, say we find out how Lecter was to answer and we can duplicate the method. Then we can fake a message to the Tooth Fairy—but what do we say? How do we use it?"

"The obvious thing is to try to get him to come to a mail drop," Graham said. "Bait him with something he'd like to see. 'Important evidence' that Lecter knows about from talking to me. Some mistake he made that we're waiting for him to repeat."

"He'd be an idiot to go for it."

"I know. Want to hear what the best bait would be?"

"I'm not sure I do."

"Lecter would be the best bait," Graham said.

"Set up how?"

"It would be hell to do, I know that. We'd take Lecter into federal custody—Chilton would never sit still for this at Baltimore—and we stash him in maximum security at a VA psychiatric hospital. We fake an escape."

"Oh, Jesus."

"We send the Tooth Fairy a message in next week's *Tattler,* after the big 'escape.' It would be Lecter asking him for a rendezvous."

"Why in God's name would anybody want to meet Lecter? I mean, even the Tooth Fairy?"

"To kill him, Jack." Graham got up. There was no window to look out of as he talked. He stood in front of the "Ten Most Wanted," Crawford's only wall decoration. "See, the Tooth Fairy could absorb him that way, engulf him, become more than he is."

"You sound pretty sure."

"I'm not sure. Who's sure? What he said in the note was 'I have some things I'd love to show you. Someday, perhaps, if circumstances permit.' Maybe it was a serious invitation. I don't think he was just being polite."

"Wonder what he's got to show? The victims were intact. Nothing missing but a little skin and hair, and that was probably . . . How did Bloom put it?"

"Ingested," Graham said. "God knows what he's got. Tremont, remember Tremont's costumes in Spokane? While he was strapped to a stretcher he was pointing with his chin, still trying to show them to the Spokane PD. I'm not sure Lecter would draw the Tooth Fairy, Jack. I say it's the best shot."

"We'd have a goddamn *stampede* if people thought Lecter was out. Papers all over us screaming. Best shot, maybe, but we'll save it for last."

"He probably wouldn't come near a mail drop, but he might be curious enough to *look* at a mail drop to see if Lecter had sold him. If he could do it from a distance. We could pick a drop that could be watched from only a few places a long way off and stake out the observation points." It sounded weak to Graham even as he said it.

"Secret Service has a setup they've never used. They'd let us have it. But if we don't put an ad in today, we'll have to wait until Monday before the next issue comes out. Presses roll at five our time. That gives Chicago another hour and fifteen minutes to come up with Lecter's ad, if there *is* one."

"What about Lecter's ad *order,* the letter he'd have sent the *Tattler* ordering the ad—could we get to that quicker?"

"Chicago put out some general feelers to the shop foreman," Crawford said. "The mail stays in the classified advertising manager's office. They sell the names and return addresses to mailing lists—outfits that sell products for lonely people, love charms, rooster pills, squack dealers, 'meet beautiful Asian girls,' personality courses, that sort of stuff.

"We might appeal to the ad manager's citizenship and all and get a look, request him to be quiet, but I don't want to chance it and risk the *Tattler* slobbering all over us. It would take a warrant to go in there and Bogart the mail. I'm thinking about it."

"If Chicago turns up nothing, we could put an ad in anyway. If we're wrong about the *Tattler,* we wouldn't lose anything," Graham said.

"And if we're right that the *Tattler* is the medium and we make up a reply based on what we have in this note and screw it up—if it doesn't look right to him—we're down the tubes. I didn't ask you about Birmingham. Anything?"

"Birmingham's shut down and over with. The Jacobi house has been painted and redecorated and it's on the market. Their stuff is in storage waiting for probate. I went through the crates. The people I talked to didn't know the Jacobis very well. The one thing they always mentioned was how affectionate the Jacobis were to each other. Always patting. Nothing left of them now but five pallet loads of stuff in a warehouse. I wish I had—"

"Quit wishing, you're on it now."

"What about the mark on the tree?"

"'You hit it on the head'? Means nothing to me," Crawford said. "The Red Dragon either. Beverly knows Mah-Jongg. She's sharp, and she can't see it. We know from his hair he's not Chinese."

"He cut the limb with a bolt cutter. I don't see—"

Crawford's telephone rang. He spoke into it briefly.

"Lab's ready on the note, Will. Let's go up to Zeller's office. It's bigger and not so gray."

Lloyd Bowman, dry as a document in spite of the heat, caught up with them in the corridor. He was flapping damp photographs in each hand and held a sheaf of Datafax sheets under his arm. "Jack, I have to be in court at four-fifteen," he said as he flapped ahead. "It's that paper hanger Nilton Eskew and his sweetheart, Nan. She could draw a Treasury note freehand. They've been driving me crazy for two years making their own traveler's checks on a color Xerox. Won't leave home without them. Will I make it in time, or should I call the prosecutor?"

"You'll make it," Crawford said. "Here we are."

Beverly Katz smiled at Graham from the couch in Zeller's office, making up for the scowl of Price beside her.

Scientific Analysis Section Chief Brian Zeller was young for his job, but already his hair was thinning and he wore bifocals. On the shelf behind Zeller's desk Graham saw H. J. Walls's forensic science text, Tedeschi's great *Forensic Medicine* in three volumes, and an antique edition of Hopkins' *The Wreck of the Deutschland.*

"Will, we met once at GWU I think," he said. "Do you know everybody? . . . Fine."

Crawford leaned against the corner of Zeller's desk, his arms folded. "Anybody got a blockbuster? Okay, does anything you found indicate the note did *not* come from the Tooth Fairy?"

"No," Bowman said. "I talked to Chicago a few minutes ago to give them some numerals I picked up from an impression on the back of the note. Six-six-six. I'll show you when we get to it. Chicago has over two hundred personal ads so far." He handed Graham a sheaf of Datafax copies. "I've read them and they're all the usual stuff— marriage offers, appeals to runaways. I'm not sure how we'd recognize the ad if it's here."

Crawford shook his head. "I don't know either. Let's break down the physical. Now, Jimmy Price did everything we could do and there was no print. What about you, Bev?"

"I got one whisker. Scale count and core size match samples from Hannibal Lecter. So does color. The color's markedly different from samples taken in Birmingham and Atlanta. Three blue grains and some dark flecks went to Brian's end." She raised her eyebrows at Brian Zeller.

"The grains were commercial granulated cleaner with chlorine," he said. "It must have come off the cleaning man's hands. There were several very minute particles of dried blood. It's definitely blood, but there's not enough to type."

"The tears at the end of the pieces wandered off the perforations," Beverly Katz continued. "If we find the roll in somebody's possession and he hasn't torn it again, we can get a definite match. I recommend issuing an advisory now, so the arresting officers will be sure to search for the roll."

Crawford nodded. "Bowman?"

"Sharon from my office went after the paper and got samples to match. It's toilet tissue for marine heads and motor homes. The texture matches brand name Wedeker manufactured in Minneapolis. It has nationwide distribution."

Bowman set up his photographs on an easel near the windows. His voice was surprisingly deep for his slight stature, and his bow tie moved slightly when he talked. "On the handwriting itself, this is a right-handed person using his left hand and printing in a deliberate block pattern. You can see the unsteadiness in the strokes and varying letter sizes.

"The proportions make me think our man has a touch of uncorrected astigmatism.

"The inks on both pieces of the note look like the same standard ball-point royal blue in natural light, but a slight difference appears under colored filters. He used two pens, changing somewhere in the missing section of the note. You can see where the first one began to skip. The first pen is not used frequently—see the blob it starts with? It might have been stored point-down and uncapped in a pencil jar or canister, which suggests a desk situation. Also the surface the paper lay on was soft enough to be a blotter. A blotter might retain impressions if you find it. I want to add the blotter to Beverly's advisory."

Bowman flipped to a photograph of the back of the note. The extreme enlargement made the paper look fuzzy. It was grooved with shadowed impressions. "He folded the note to write the bottom part, including what was later torn out. In this enlargement of the back side, oblique light reveals a few impressions. We can make out '666 an.' Maybe that's where he had pen trouble and had to bear down and overwrite. I didn't spot it until I had this high-contrast print. There's no 666 in any ad so far.

"The sentence structure is orderly, and there's no rambling. The folds suggest it was delivered in a standard letter-size envelope. These two dark places are printing-ink smudges. The note was probably folded inside some innocuous printed matter in the envelope.

"That's about it," Bowman said. "Unless you have questions, Jack, I'd better go to the courthouse. I'll check in after I testify."

"Sink 'em deep," Crawford said.

Graham studied the *Tattler* personals column. ("Attractive queen-size lady, young 52, seeks Christian Leo nonsmoker 40–70. No children please. Artificial limb welcomed. No phonies. Send photo first letter.")

Lost in the pain and desperation of the ads, he didn't notice that the others were leaving until Beverly Katz spoke to him.

"I'm sorry, Beverly. What did you say?" He looked at her bright eyes and kindly, well-worn face.

"I just said I'm glad to see you back, Champ. You're looking good."

"Thanks, Beverly."

"Saul's going to cooking school. He's still hit-or-miss, but when the dust settles come over and let him practice on you."

"I'll do it."

Zeller went away to prowl his laboratory. Only Crawford and Graham were left, looking at the clock.

"Forty minutes to *Tattler* press time," Crawford said. "I'm going after their mail. What do you say?"

"I think you have to."

Crawford passed the word to Chicago on Zeller's telephone. "Will, we need to be ready with a substitute ad if Chicago bingoes."

"I'll work on it."

"I'll set up the drop." Crawford called the Secret Service and talked at some length. Graham was still scribbling when he finished.

"Okay, the mail drop's a beauty," Crawford said at last. "It's an outside message box on a fire-extinguisher-service outfit in Annapolis. That's Lecter territory. The Tooth Fairy will see that it's something Lecter could know about. Alphabetical pigeonholes. The service people drive up to it and get assignments and mail. Our boy can check it out from a park across the street. Secret Service swears it looks good. They set it up to catch a counterfeiter, but it turned out they didn't need it. Here's the address. What about the message?"

"We have to use two messages in the same edition. The first one warns the Tooth Fairy that his enemies are closer than he thinks. It tells him he made a bad mistake in Atlanta and if he repeats the mistake he's doomed. It tells him Lecter has mailed 'secret information' I showed Lecter about what we're doing, how close we are, the leads we have. It directs the Tooth Fairy to a second message that begins with 'your signature.'

"The second message begins 'Avid Fan . . .' and contains the address of the mail drop. We have to do it that way. Even in roundabout language, the warning in the first message is going to excite some casual nuts. If they can't find out the address, they can't come to the drop and screw things up."

"Good. Damn good. Want to wait it out in my office?"

"I'd rather be doing something. I need to see Brian Zeller."

"Go ahead, I can get you in a hurry if I have to."

Graham found the section chief in Serology.

"Brian, could you show me a couple of things?"

"Sure, what?"

"The samples you used to type the Tooth Fairy."

Zeller looked at Graham through the close-range section of his bifocals. "Was there something in the report you didn't understand?"

"No."

"Was something unclear?"

"No."

"Something *incomplete?*" Zeller mouthed the word as if it had an unpleasant taste.

"Your report was fine, couldn't ask for better. I just want to hold the evidence in my hand."

"*Ah,* certainly. We can do that." Zeller believed that all field men retain the superstitions of the hunt. He was glad to humor Graham. "It's all together down at that end."

Graham followed him between the long counters of apparatus. "You're reading Tedeschi."

"Yes," Zeller said over his shoulder. "We don't do any forensic medicine here, as you know, but Tedeschi has a lot of useful things in there. Graham. Will Graham. You wrote the standard monograph on determining time of death by insect activity, didn't you. Or do I have the right Graham?"

"I did it." A pause. "You're right, Mant and Nuorteva in the Tedeschi are better on insects."

Zeller was surprised to hear his thought spoken. "Well, it does have more pictures and a table of invasion waves. No offense."

"Of course not. They're better. I told them so."

Zeller gathered vials and slides from a cabinet and a refrigerator and set them on the laboratory counter. "If you want to ask me anything, I'll be where you found me. The stage light on this microscope is on the side here."

Graham did not want the microscope. He doubted none of Zeller's findings. He didn't know what he wanted. He raised the vials and slides to the light, and a glassine envelope with two blond hairs found in Birmingham. A second envelope held three hairs found on Mrs. Leeds.

There were spit and hair and semen on the table in front of Graham and empty air where he tried to see an image, a face, something to replace the shapeless dread he carried.

A woman's voice came from a speaker in the ceiling. "Graham, Will Graham, to Special Agent Crawford's office. On Red."

He found Sarah in her headset typing, with Crawford looking over her shoulder.

"Chicago's got an ad order with 666 in it," Crawford said out of the side of his mouth. "They're dictating it to Sarah now. They said part of it looks like code."

The lines were climbing out of Sarah's typewriter.

> *Dear Pilgrim,*
> *You honor me . . .*

"That's it. That's it," Graham said. "Lecter called him a pilgrim when he was talking to me."

> *you're very beautiful . . .*

"Christ," Crawford said.

> *I offer 100 prayers for your safety.*
> *Find help in John 6:22, 8:16, 9:1; Luke 1:7, 3:1; Galatians 6:11,*
> *15:2; Acts 3:3; Revelation 18:7; Jonah 6:8 . . .*

The typing slowed as Sarah read back each pair of numbers to the agent in Chicago. When she had finished, the list of scriptural references covered a quarter of a page. It was signed "Bless you, 666."

"That's it," Sarah said.

Crawford picked up the phone. "Okay, Chester, how did it go down with the ad manager? . . . No, you did right. . . . A complete clam, right. Stand by at that phone, I'll get back to you."

"Code," Graham said.

"Has to be. We've got twenty-two minutes to get a message in if we can break it. Shop foreman needs ten minutes' notice and three hundred dollars to shoehorn one in this edition. Bowman's in his office, he got a recess. If you'll get him cracking, I'll talk to Cryptography at Langley. Sarah, shoot a telex of the ad to CIA cryptography section. I'll tell 'em it's coming."

Bowman put the message on his desk and aligned it precisely with the corners of his blotter. He polished his rimless spectacles for what seemed to Graham a very long time.

Bowman had a reputation for being quick. Even the explosives section forgave him for not being an ex-Marine and granted him that.

"We have twenty minutes," Graham said.

"I understand. You called Langley?"

"Crawford did."

Bowman read the message many times, looked at it upside down and sideways, ran down the margins with his finger. He took a Bible from his shelves. For five minutes the only sounds were the two men breathing and the crackle of onionskin pages.

"No," he said. "We won't make it in time. Better use what's left for whatever else you can do."

Graham showed him an empty hand.

Bowman swiveled around to face Graham and took off his glasses. He had a pink spot on each side of his nose. "Do you feel fairly confident the note to Lecter is the only communication he's had from your Tooth Fairy?"

"Right."

"The code is something simple then. They only needed cover against casual readers. Measuring by the perforations in the note to Lecter only about three inches is missing. That's not much room for instructions. The numbers aren't right for a jailhouse alphabet grid— the tap code. I'm guessing it's a book code."

Crawford joined them. "Book code?"

"Looks like it. The first numeral, that '100 prayers,' could be the page number. The paired numbers in the scriptural references could be line and letter. But what book?"

"Not the Bible?" Crawford said.

"No, not the Bible. I thought it might be at first. Galatians 6:11 threw me off. 'Ye see how large a letter I have written unto you with mine own hand.' That's appropriate, but it's coincidence because next he has Galatians 15:2. Galatians has only six chapters. Same with Jonah 6:8—Jonah has four chapters. He wasn't using a Bible."

"Maybe the book title could be concealed in the clear part of Lecter's message," Crawford said.

Bowman shook his head. "I don't think so."

"Then the Tooth Fairy named the book to use. He specified it in his note to Lecter," Graham said.

"It would appear so," Bowman said. "What about sweating Lecter? In a mental hospital I would think drugs—"

"They tried sodium amytal on him three years ago trying to find out where he buried a Princeton student," Graham said. "He gave them a recipe for dip. Besides, if we sweat him we lose the connection. If the Tooth Fairy picked the book, it's something he knew Lecter would have in his cell."

"I know for sure he didn't order one or borrow one from Chilton," Crawford said.

"What have the papers carried about that, Jack? About Lecter's books."

"That he has medical books, psychology books, cookbooks."

"Then it could be one of the standards in those areas, something so basic the Tooth Fairy knew Lecter would definitely have it," Bowman said. "We need a list of Lecter's books. Do you have one?"

"No." Graham stared at his shoes. "I could get Chilton . . . Wait. Rankin and Willingham, when they tossed his cell, they took Polaroids so they could get everything back in place."

"Would you ask them to meet me with the pictures of the books?" Bowman said, packing his briefcase.

"Where?"

"The Library of Congress."

Crawford checked with the CIA cryptography section one last time. The computer at Langley was trying consistent and progressive number-letter substitutions and a staggering variety of alphabet grids. No progress. The cryptographer agreed with Bowman that it was probably a book code.

Crawford looked at his watch. "Will, we're left with three choices and we've got to decide right now. We can pull Lecter's message out of the paper and run nothing. We can substitute our messages in plain language, inviting the Tooth Fairy to the mail drop. Or we can let Lecter's ad run as is."

"Are you sure we can still get Lecter's message out of the *Tattler?*"

"Chester thinks the shop foreman would chisel it for about five hundred dollars."

"I hate to put in a plain-language message, Jack. Lecter would probably never hear from him again."

"Yeah, but I'm leery of letting Lecter's message run without knowing what it says," Crawford said. "What could Lecter tell him that he doesn't know already? If he found out we have a partial thumbprint and his prints aren't on file anywhere, he could whittle his thumb and pull his teeth and give us a big gummy laugh in court."

"The thumbprint wasn't in the case summary Lecter saw. We better let Lecter's message run. At least it'll encourage the Tooth Fairy to contact him again."

"What if it encourages him to do something besides write?"

"We'll feel sick for a long time," Graham said. "We have to do it."

➤

Fifteen minutes later in Chicago the *Tattler's* big presses rolled, gathering speed until their thunder raised the dust in the pressroom. The FBI agent waiting in the smell of ink and hot newsprint took one of the first ones.

The cover lines included "Head Transplant!" and "Astronomers Glimpse God!"

The agent checked to see that Lecter's personal ad was in place and slipped the paper into an express pouch for Washington. He would see that paper again and remember his thumb smudge on the front page, but it would be years later, when he took his children through the special exhibits on a tour of FBI headquarters.

CHAPTER 15

IN THE HOUR before dawn Crawford woke from a deep sleep. He saw the room dark, felt his wife's ample bottom comfortably settled against the small of his back. He did not know why he had awakened until the telephone rang a second time. He found it with no fumbling.

"Jack, this is Lloyd Bowman. I solved the code. You need to know what it says right now."

"Okay, Lloyd." Crawford's feet searched for his slippers.

"It says: *Graham home Marathon, Florida. Save yourself. Kill them all.*"

"Goddammit. Gotta go."

"I know."

Crawford went to his den without stopping for his robe. He called Florida twice, the airport once, then called Graham at his hotel.

"Will, Bowman just broke the code."

"What did it say?"

"I'll tell you in a second. Now listen to me. Everything is okay. I've taken care of it, so stay on the phone when I tell you."

"Tell me now."

"It's your home address. Lecter gave the bastard your home address. *Wait*, Will. Sheriff's department has two cars on the way to Sugarloaf right now. Customs launch from Marathon is taking the ocean side. The Tooth Fairy couldn't have done anything in this short time. Hold

130

on. You can move faster with me helping you. Now, listen to this.

"The deputies aren't going to scare Molly. The sheriff's cars are just closing the road to the house. Two deputies will move up close enough to watch the house. You can call her when she wakes up. I'll pick you up in half an hour."

"I won't be here."

"The next plane in that direction doesn't go until eight. It'll be quicker to bring them up here. My brother's house on the Chesapeake is available to them. I've got a good plan, Will, wait and hear it. If you don't like it I'll put you on the plane myself."

"I need some things from the armory."

"We'll get it soon as I pick you up."

➤

Molly and Willy were among the first off the plane at National Airport in Washington. She spotted Graham in the crowd, did not smile, but turned to Willy and said something as they walked swiftly ahead of the stream of tourists returning from Florida.

She looked Graham up and down and came to him with a light kiss. Her brown fingers were cold on his cheek.

Graham felt the boy watching. Willy shook hands from a full arm's length away.

Graham made a joke about the weight of Molly's suitcase as they walked to the car.

"I'll carry it," Willy said.

A brown Chevrolet with Maryland plates moved in behind them as they pulled out of the parking lot.

Graham crossed the bridge at Arlington and pointed out the Lincoln and Jefferson memorials and the Washington Monument before heading east toward the Chesapeake Bay. Ten miles outside Washington the brown Chevrolet pulled up beside them in the inside lane. The driver looked across with his hand to his mouth and a voice from nowhere crackled in the car.

"Fox Edward, you're clean as a whistle. Have a nice trip."

Graham reached under the dash for the concealed microphone. "Roger, Bobby. Much obliged."

The Chevrolet dropped behind them and its turn signal came on.

"Just making sure no press cars or anything were following," Graham said.

"I see," Molly said.

They stopped in the late afternoon and ate crabs at a roadside restaurant. Willy went to look at the lobster tank.

"I hate it, Molly. I'm sorry," Graham said.

"Is he after you now?"

"We've had no reason to think so. Lecter just suggested it to him, urged him to do it."

"It's a clammy, sick feeling."

"I know it is. You and Willy are safe at Crawford's brother's house. Nobody in the world knows you're there but me and Crawford."

"I'd just as soon not talk about Crawford."

"It's a nice place, you'll see."

She took a deep breath and when she let it out the anger seemed to go with it, leaving her tired and calm. She gave him a crooked smile. "Hell, I just got mad there for a while. Do we have to put up with any Crawfords?"

"Nope." He moved the cracker basket to take her hand. "How much does Willy know?"

"Plenty. His buddy Tommy's mother had a trash newspaper from the supermarket at their house. Tommy showed it to Willy. It had a lot of stuff about you, apparently pretty distorted. About Hobbs, the place you were after that, Lecter, everything. It upset him. I asked him if he wanted to talk about it. He just asked me if I knew it all along. I said yes, that you and I talked about it once, that you told me everything before we got married. I asked him if he wanted me to tell him about it, the way it really was. He said he'd ask you to your face."

"Damn good. Good for him. What was it, the *Tattler?*"

"I don't know, I think so."

"Thanks a lot, Freddy." A swell of anger at Freddy Lounds lifted him from his seat. He washed his face with cold water in the rest room.

➤

Sarah was saying good night to Crawford in the office when the telephone rang. She put down her purse and umbrella to answer it.

"Special Agent Crawford's office. . . . No, Mr. Graham is not in the office, but let me . . . Wait, I'll be glad to . . . Yes, he'll be in tomorrow afternoon, but let me . . ."

The tone of her voice brought Crawford around his desk.

She held the receiver as though it had died in her hand. "He asked for Will and said he might call back tomorrow afternoon. I tried to hold him."

"Who?"

"He said, 'Just tell Graham it's the Pilgrim.' That's what Dr. Lecter called—"

"The Tooth Fairy," Crawford said.

➤

Graham went to the grocery store while Molly and Willy unpacked. He found canary melons at the market and a ripe cranshaw. He parked across the street from the house and sat for a few minutes, still gripping the wheel. He was ashamed that because of him Molly was rooted out of the house she loved and put among strangers.

Crawford had done his best. This was no faceless federal safe house with chair arms bleached by palm sweat. It was a pleasant cottage, freshly whitewashed, with impatiens blooming around the steps. It was the product of careful hands and a sense of order. The rear yard sloped down to the Chesapeake Bay and there was a swimming raft.

Blue-green television light pulsed behind the curtains. Molly and Willy were watching baseball, Graham knew.

Willy's father had been a baseball player, and a good one. He and Molly met on the school bus, married in college.

They trooped around the Florida State League while he was in the Cardinals' farm system. They took Willy with them and had a terrific time. Spam and spirit. He got a tryout with the Cardinals and hit safely in his first two games. Then he began to have difficulty swallowing. The surgeon tried to get it all, but it metastasized and ate him up. He died five months later, when Willy was six.

Willy still watched baseball whenever he could. Molly watched baseball when she was upset.

Graham had no key. He knocked.

"I'll get it." Willy's voice.

"Wait." Molly's face between the curtains. "All right."

Willy opened the door. In his fist, held close to his leg, was a fish billy.

Graham's eyes stung at the sight. The boy must have brought it in his suitcase.

Molly took the bag from him. "Want some coffee? There's gin, but not the kind you like."

When she was in the kitchen, Willy asked Graham to come outside.

From the back porch they could see the riding lights of boats anchored in the bay.

"Will, is there any stuff I need to know to see about Mom?"

"You're both safe here, Willy. Remember the car that followed us from the airport making sure nobody saw where we went? Nobody can find out where you and your mother are."

"This crazy guy wants to kill you, does he?"

"We don't know that. I just didn't feel easy with him knowing where the house is."

"You gonna kill him?"

Graham closed his eyes for a moment. "No. It's just my job to find him. They'll put him in a mental hospital so they can treat him and keep him from hurting anybody."

"Tommy's mother had this little newspaper, Will. It said you killed a guy in Minnesota and you were in a mental hospital. I never knew that. Is it true?"

"Yes."

"I started to ask Mom, but I figured I'd ask you."

"I appreciate your asking me straight out. It wasn't just a mental hospital; they treat everything." The distinction seemed important. "I was in the psychiatric wing. It bothers you, finding out I was in there. Because I'm married to your mom."

"I told my dad I'd take care of her. I'll do it, too."

Graham felt he had to tell Willy enough. He didn't want to tell him too much.

The lights went out in the kitchen. He could see Molly's dim outline inside the screen door and he felt the weight of her judgment. Dealing with Willy he was handling her heart.

Willy clearly did not know what to ask next. Graham did it for him.

"The hospital part was after the business with Hobbs."

"You shot him?"

"Yes."

"How'd it happen?"

"To begin with, Garrett Hobbs was insane. He was attacking college girls and he . . . killed them."

"How?"

"With a knife; anyway I found a little curly piece of metal in the clothes one of the girls had on. It was the kind of shred a pipe threader makes—remember when we fixed the shower outside?

"I was taking a look at a lot of steamfitters, plumbers and people. It took a long time. Hobbs had left this resignation letter at a construction job I was checking. I saw it and it was . . . peculiar. He wasn't working anywhere, and I had to find him at home.

"I was going up the stairs in Hobbs's apartment house. A uniformed officer was with me. Hobbs must have seen us coming. I was halfway up to his landing when he shoved his wife out the door and she came falling down the stairs dead."

"He had killed her?"

"Yeah. So I asked the officer I was with to call for SWAT, to get some help. But then I could hear kids in there and some screaming. I wanted to wait, but I couldn't."

"You went in the apartment?"

"I did. Hobbs had caught this girl from behind and he had a knife. He was cutting her with it. And I shot him."

"Did the girl die?"

"No."

"She got all right?"

"After a while, yes. She's all right now."

Willy digested this silently. Faint music came from an anchored sailboat.

Graham could leave things out for Willy, but he couldn't help seeing them again himself.

He left out Mrs. Hobbs on the landing clutching at him, stabbed so many times. Seeing she was gone, hearing the screaming from the apartment, prying the slick red fingers off and cracking his shoulder before the door gave in. Hobbs holding his own daughter busy cutting her neck when he could get to it, her struggling with her chin tucked down, the .38 knocking chunks out of him and he still cutting and he wouldn't go down. Hobbs sitting on the floor crying and the girl rasping. Holding her down and seeing Hobbs had gotten through the windpipe, but not the arteries. The daughter looked at him with wide glazed eyes and at her father sitting on the floor crying "See? See?" until he fell over dead.

That was where Graham lost his faith in .38's.

"Willy, the business with Hobbs, it bothered me a lot. You know, I kept it on my mind and I saw it over and over. I got so I couldn't think about much else. I kept thinking there must be some way I could have handled it better. And then I quit feeling anything. I couldn't eat and I stopped talking to anybody. I got really depressed. So a doctor asked me to go into the hospital, and I did. After a while I got some distance on it. The girl that got hurt in Hobbs's apartment came to see me. She was okay and we talked a lot. Finally I put it aside and went back to work."

"Killing somebody, even if you have to do it, it feels that bad?"

"Willy, it's one of the ugliest things in the world."

"Say, I'm going in the kitchen for a minute. You want something, a Coke?" Willy liked to bring Graham things, but he always made it a casual adjunct to something he was going to do anyway. No special trip or anything.

"Sure, a Coke."

"Mom ought to come out and look at the lights."

➤

Late in the night Graham and Molly sat in the back-porch swing. Light rain fell and the boat lights cast grainy halos on the mist. The breeze off the bay raised goose bumps on their arms.

"This could take a while, couldn't it?" Molly said.

"I hope it won't, but it might."

"Will, Evelyn said she could keep the shop for this week and four days next week. But I've got to go back to Marathon, at least for a day or two when my buyers come. I could stay with Evelyn and Sam. I should go to market in Atlanta myself. I need to be ready for September."

"Does Evelyn know where you are?"

"I just told her Washington."

"Good."

"It's hard to have anything, isn't it? Rare to get it, hard to keep it. This is a damn slippery planet."

"Slick as hell."

"We'll be back in Sugarloaf, won't we?"

"Yes we will."

"Don't get in a hurry and hang it out too far. You won't do that?"

"No."

"Are you going back early?"

He had talked to Crawford half an hour on the phone.

"A little before lunch. If you're going to Marathon at all, there's something we need to tend to in the morning. Willy can fish."

"He had to ask you about the other."

"I know, I don't blame him."

"Damn that reporter, what's his name?"

"Lounds. Freddy Lounds."

"I think maybe you hate him. And I wish I hadn't brought it up. Let's go to bed and I'll rub your back."

Resentment raised a minute blister in Graham. He had justified himself to an eleven-year-old. The kid said it was okay that he had been in the rubber Ramada. Now she was going to rub his back. Let's go to bed—it's okay with Willy.

When you feel strain, keep your mouth shut if you can.

"If you want to think awhile, I'll let you alone," she said.

He didn't want to think. He definitely did not. "You rub my back and I'll rub your front," he said.

"Go to it, Buster."

➤

Winds aloft carried the thin rain out over the bay and by nine A.M. the ground steamed. The far targets on the sheriff's department range seemed to flinch in the wavy air.

The rangemaster watched through his binoculars until he was sure the man and woman at the far end of the firing line were observing the safety rules.

The Justice Department credentials the man showed when he asked to use the range said "Investigator." That could be anything. The rangemaster did not approve of anyone other than a qualified instructor teaching pistolcraft.

Still, he had to admit the fed knew what he was doing.

They were only using a .22-caliber revolver but he was teaching the woman combat shooting from the Weaver stance, left foot slightly forward, a good two-handed grip on the revolver with isometric tension in the arms. She was firing at the silhouette target seven yards in front of her. Again and again she brought the weapon up from the outside pocket of her shoulderbag. It went on until the rangemaster was bored with it.

A change in the sound brought the rangemaster's glasses up again. They had the earmuffs on now and she was working with a short, chunky revolver. The rangemaster recognized the pop of the light target loads.

He could see the pistol extended in her hands and it interested him. He strolled along the firing line and stood a few yards behind them.

He wanted to examine the pistol, but this was not a good time to interrupt. He got a good look at it as she shucked out the empties and popped in five from a speedloader.

Odd arm for a fed. It was a Bulldog .44 Special, short and ugly with its startling big bore. It had been extensively modified by Mag Na Port. The barrel was vented near the muzzle to help keep the muzzle down on recoil, the hammer was bobbed and it had a good set of fat grips. He suspected it was throated for the speedloader. One hell of a mean pistol when it was loaded with what the fed had waiting. He wondered how the woman would stand up to it.

The ammunition on the stand beside them was an interesting progression. First there was a box of lightly loaded wadcutters. Then came regular service hardball, and last was something the rangemaster had read much about but had rarely seen. A row of Glaser Safety Slugs. The tips looked like pencil erasers. Behind each tip was a copper jacket containing number-twelve shot suspended in liquid Teflon.

The light projectile was designed to fly at tremendous velocity, smash into the target and release the shot. In meat the results were devastating. The rangemaster even recalled the figures. Ninety Glasers had been fired at men so far. All ninety were instant one-shot stops. In eighty-nine of the cases immediate death resulted. One man survived, surprising the doctors. The Glaser round had a safety advantage, too—no ricochets, and it would not go through a wall and kill someone in the next room.

The man was very gentle with her and encouraging, but he seemed sad about something.

The woman had worked up to the full service loads now and the rangemaster was pleased to see she handled the recoil very well, both eyes open and no flinch. True, it took her maybe four seconds to get the first one off, coming up from the bag, but three were in the X ring. Not bad for a beginner. She had some talent.

He had been back in the tower for some time when he heard the hellish racket of the Glasers going off.

She was pumping all five. It was not standard federal practice.

The rangemaster wondered what in God's name they saw in the silhouette that it would take five Glasers to kill.

Graham came to the tower to turn in the earmuffs, leaving his pupil sitting on a bench, head down, her elbows on her knees.

The rangemaster thought he should be pleased with her, and told him so. She had come a long way in one day. Graham thanked him absently. His expression puzzled the rangemaster. He looked like a man who had witnessed an irrevocable loss.

CHAPTER 16

THE CALLER, "Mr. Pilgrim," had said to Sarah that he might call again on the following afternoon. At FBI headquarters certain arrangements were made to receive the call.

Who was Mr. Pilgrim? Not Lecter—Crawford had made sure of that. Was Mr. Pilgrim the Tooth Fairy? Maybe so, Crawford thought.

The desks and telephones from Crawford's office had been moved overnight to a larger room across the hall.

Graham stood in the open doorway of a soundproof booth. Behind him in the booth was Crawford's telephone. Sarah had cleaned it with Windex. With the voiceprint spectrograph, tape recorders, and stress evaluator taking up most of her desk and another table beside it, and Beverly Katz sitting in her chair, Sarah needed something to do.

The big clock on the wall showed ten minutes before noon.

Dr. Alan Bloom and Crawford stood with Graham. They had adopted a sidelines stance, hands in their pockets.

A technician seated across from Beverly Katz drummed his fingers on the desk until a frown from Crawford stopped him.

Crawford's desk was cluttered with two new telephones, an open line to the Bell System's electronic switching center (ESS) and a hot line to the FBI communications room.

"How much time do you need for a trace?" Dr. Bloom asked.

"With the new switching it's a lot quicker than most people think,"

Crawford said. "Maybe a minute if it comes through all-electronic switching. More if it's from someplace where they have to swarm the frame."

Crawford raised his voice to the room. "If he calls at all, it'll be short, so let's play him perfect. Want to go over the drill, Will?"

"Sure. When we get to the point where I talk, I want to ask you a couple of things, Doctor."

Bloom had arrived after the others. He was scheduled to speak to the behavioral-science section at Quantico later in the day. Bloom could smell cordite on Graham's clothes.

"Okay," Graham said. "The phone rings. The circuit's completed immediately and the trace starts at ESS, but the tone generator continues the ringing noise so he doesn't know we've picked up. That gives us about twenty seconds on him." He pointed to the technician. "Tone generator to 'off' at the end of the fourth ring, got it?"

The technician nodded. "End of the fourth ring."

"Now, Beverly picks up the phone. Her voice is different from the one he heard yesterday. No recognition in the voice. Beverly sounds bored. He asks for me. Bev says, 'I'll have to page him, may I put you on hold?' Ready with that, Bev?" Graham thought it would be better not to rehearse the lines. They might sound flat by rote.

"All right, the line is open to us, dead to him. I think he'll hold longer than he'll talk."

"Sure you don't want to give him the hold music?" the technician asked.

"Hell no," Crawford said.

"We give him about twenty seconds of hold, then Beverly comes back on and tells him, 'Mr. Graham's coming to the phone, I'll connect you now.' I pick up." Graham turned to Dr. Bloom. "How would you play him, Doctor?"

"He'll expect you to be skeptical about it really being him. I'd give him some polite skepticism. I'd make a strong distinction between the nuisance of fake callers and the significance, the importance, of a call from the real person. The fakes are easy to recognize because they lack the *capacity* to understand what has happened, that sort of thing.

"Make him tell something to prove who he is." Dr. Bloom looked at the floor and kneaded the back of his neck.

"You don't know what he wants. Maybe he wants understanding, maybe he's fixed on you as the adversary and wants to gloat—we'll see. Try to pick up his mood and give him what he's after, a little at a time. I'd be very leery of appealing to him to come to us for help, unless you sense he's asking for that.

"If he's paranoid you'll pick it up fast. In that case I'd play into his suspicion or grievance. Let him air it. If he gets rolling on that, he may forget how long he's talked. That's all I know to tell you." Bloom put his hand on Graham's shoulder and spoke quietly. "Listen, this is not a pep talk or any bullshit; you can take him over the jumps. Never mind advice, do what seems right to you."

Waiting. Half an hour of silence was enough.

"Call or no call, we've got to decide where to go from here," Crawford said. "Want to try the mail drop?"

"I can't see anything better," Graham said.

"That would give us two baits, a stakeout at your house in the Keys and the drop."

The telephone was ringing.

Tone generator on. At ESS the trace began. Four rings. The technician hit the switch and Beverly picked up. Sarah was listening.

"Special Agent Crawford's office."

Sarah shook her head. She knew the caller, one of Crawford's cronies at Alcohol, Tobacco, and Firearms. Beverly got him off in a hurry and stopped the trace. Everyone in the FBI building knew to keep the line clear.

Crawford went over the details of the mail drop again. They were bored and tense at the same time. Lloyd Bowman came around to show them how the number pairs in Lecter's Scriptures fit page 100 of the softcover *Joy of Cooking*. Sarah passed around coffee in paper cups.

The telephone was ringing.

The tone generator took over and at ESS the trace began. Four rings. The technician hit the switch. Beverly picked up.

"Special Agent Crawford's office."

Sarah was nodding her head. Big nods.

Graham went into his booth and closed the door. He could see Beverly's lips moving. She punched "Hold" and watched the second hand on the wall clock.

Graham could see his face in the polished receiver. Two bloated faces in the earpiece and mouthpiece. He could smell cordite from the firing range in his shirt. *Don't hang up. Sweet Jesus, don't hang up.* Forty seconds had elapsed. The telephone moved slightly on his table when it rang. *Let it ring. Once more.* Forty-five seconds. *Now.*

"This is Will Graham, can I help you?"

Low laughter. A muffled voice: "I expect you can."

"Could I ask who's calling please?"

"Didn't your secretary tell you?"

"No, but she did call me out of a meeting, sir, and—"

"If you tell me you won't talk to Mr. Pilgrim, I'll hang up right now. Yes or no?"

"Mr. Pilgrim, if you have some problem I'm equipped to deal with, I'll be glad to talk with you."

"I think you have the problem, Mr. Graham."

"I'm sorry, I didn't understand you."

The second hand crawled toward one minute.

"You've been a busy boy, haven't you?" the caller said.

"Too busy to stay on the phone unless you state your business."

"My business is in the same place yours is. Atlanta and Birmingham."

"Do you know something about that?"

Soft laughter. "Know something about it? Are you interested in Mr. Pilgrim? Yes or no. I'll hang up if you lie."

Graham could see Crawford through the glass. He had a telephone receiver in each hand.

"Yes. But, see, I get a lot of calls, and most of them are from people who say they know things." One minute.

Crawford put one receiver down and scrawled on a piece of paper.

"You'd be surprised how many pretenders there are," Graham said. "Talk to them a few minutes and you can tell they don't have the capacity to even understand what's going on. Do you?"

Sarah held a sheet of paper to the glass for Graham to see. It said, "Chicago phone booth. PD scrambling."

"I'll tell you what, you tell me one thing you know about Mr. Pilgrim and maybe I'll tell you whether you're right or not," the muffled voice said.

"Let's get straight who we're talking about," Graham said.

"We're talking about Mr. Pilgrim."

"How do I know Mr. Pilgrim has done anything I'm interested in. Has he?"

"Let's say, yes."

"Are you Mr. Pilgrim?"

"I don't think I'll tell you that."

"Are you his friend?"

"Sort of."

"Well, prove it then. Tell me something that shows me how well you know him."

"You first. You show me yours." A nervous giggle. "First time you're wrong, I hang up."

"All right, Mr. Pilgrim is right-handed."

"That's a safe guess. Most people are."

"Mr. Pilgrim is misunderstood."

"No general crap, please."

"Mr. Pilgrim is really strong physically."

"Yes, you could say that."

Graham looked at the clock. A minute and a half. Crawford nodded encouragement.

Don't tell him anything that he could change.

"Mr. Pilgrim is white and about, say, five-feet-eleven. You haven't told me anything, you know. I'm not so sure you even know him at all."

"Want to stop talking?"

"No, but you said we'd trade. I was just going along with you."

"Do you think Mr. Pilgrim is crazy?"

Bloom was shaking his head.

"I don't think anybody who is as careful as he is could be crazy. I think he's different. I think a lot of people do believe he's crazy, and the reason for that is, he hasn't let people understand much about him."

"Describe exactly what you think he did to Mrs. Leeds and maybe I'll tell you if you're right or not."

"I don't want to do that."

"Good-bye."

Graham's heart jumped, but he could still hear breathing on the other end.

"I can't go into that until I know—"

Graham heard the telephone-booth door slam open in Chicago and the receiver fall with a clang. Faint voices and bangs as the receiver swung on its cord. Everyone in the office heard it on the speaker-phone.

"Freeze. Don't even twitch. Now lock your fingers behind your head and back out of the booth slowly. Slowly. Hands on the glass and spread 'em."

Sweet relief was flooding Graham.

"I'm not armed, Stan. You'll find my ID in my breast pocket. That tickles."

A confused voice loud on the telephone. "Who am I speaking to?"

"Will Graham, FBI."

"This is Sergeant Stanley Riddle, Chicago police department." Irritated now. "Would you tell me what the hell's going on?"

"You tell me. You have a man in custody?"

"Damn right. Freddy Lounds, the reporter. I've known him for ten years. . . . Here's your notebook, Freddy. . . . Are you preferring charges against him?"

Graham's face was pale. Crawford's was red. Dr. Bloom watched the tape reels go around.

"Can you hear me?"

"Yes, I'm preferring charges." Graham's voice was strangled. "Obstruction of justice. Please take him in and hold him for the U.S. attorney."

Suddenly Lounds was on the telephone. He spoke fast and clearly with the cotton wads out of his cheeks.

"Will, listen—"

"Tell it to the U.S. attorney. Put Sergeant Riddle on the phone."

"I know something—"

"Put Riddle on the goddamned telephone."

Crawford's voice came on the line. "Let me have it, Will."

Graham slammed his receiver down with a bang that made everyone in range of the speakerphone flinch. He came out of the booth and left the room without looking at anyone.

"Lounds, you have hubbed hell, my man," Crawford said.

"You want to catch him or not? I can help you. Let me talk one minute." Lounds hurried into Crawford's silence. "Listen, you just showed me how bad you need the *Tattler*. Before, I wasn't sure—now I am. That ad's part of the Tooth Fairy case or you wouldn't have gone balls-out to nail this call. Great. The *Tattler's* here for you. Anything you want."

"How did you find out?"

"The ad manager came to me. Said your Chicago office sent this suit-of-clothes over to check the ads. Your guy took five letters from the incoming ads. Said it was 'pursuant to mail fraud.' Mail fraud nothing. The ad manager made Xerox copies of the letters and envelopes before he let your guy have them.

"I looked them over. I knew he took five letters to smokescreen the one he really wanted. Took a day or two to check them all out. The answer was on the envelope. Baltimore postmark. The postage-meter number was for Baltimore State Hospital. I was over there you know, behind your friend with the wild hair up his ass. What else could it be?"

"I had to be sure, though. That's why I called, to see if you'd come down on 'Mr. Pilgrim' with both feet, and you did."

"You made a large mistake, Freddy."

"You need the *Tattler* and I can open it up for you. Ads, editorial, monitoring incoming mail, anything. You name it. I can be discreet. I can. Cut me in, Crawford."

"There's nothing to cut you in on."

"Okay, then it won't make any difference if somebody happened to put in six personal ads next issue. All to 'Mr. Pilgrim' and signed the same way."

"I'll get an injunction slapped on you and a sealed indictment for obstruction of justice."

"And it might leak to every paper in the country." Lounds knew he was talking on tape. He didn't care anymore. "I swear to God, I'll do it, Crawford. I'll tear up your chance before I lose mine."

"Add interstate transmission of a threatening message to what I just said."

"Let me *help* you, Jack. I can, believe me."

"Run along to the police station, Freddy. Now put the sergeant back on the phone."

➤

Freddy Lounds's Lincoln Versailles smelled of hair tonic and after-shave, socks and cigars, and the police sergeant was glad to get out of it when they reached the station house.

Lounds knew the captain commanding the precinct and many of the patrolmen. The captain gave Lounds coffee and called the U.S. attorney's office to "try and clear this shit up."

No federal marshal came for Lounds. In half an hour he took a call from Crawford in the precinct commander's office. Then he was free to go. The captain walked him to his car.

Lounds was keyed up and his driving was fast and jerky as he crossed the Loop eastward to his apartment overlooking Lake Michigan. There were several things he wanted out of this story and he knew that he could get them. Money was one, and most of that would come from the paperback. He would have an instant paperback on the stands thirty-six hours after the capture. An exclusive story in the daily press would be a news coup. He would have the satisfaction of seeing the straight press—the Chicago *Tribune,* the Los Angeles *Times*, the sanctified Washington *Post* and the holy New York *Times*—run his copyrighted material under his byline with his picture credits.

And then the correspondents of those august journals, who looked down on him, who would not drink with him, could eat their fucking hearts out.

Lounds was a pariah to them because he had taken a different faith. Had he been incompetent, a fool with no other resource, the veterans of the straight press could have forgiven him for working on the *Tattler,* as one forgives a retarded geek. But Lounds was good. He had the qualities of a good reporter—intelligence, guts, and the good eye. He had great energy and patience.

Against him were the fact that he was obnoxious and therefore disliked by news executives, and his inability to keep himself out of his stories.

In Lounds was the lunging need to be noticed that is often miscalled ego. Lounds was lumpy and ugly and small. He had buck teeth and his rat eyes had the sheen of spit on asphalt.

He had worked in straight journalism for ten years when he realized that no one would ever send him to the White House. He saw that his publishers would wear his legs out, use him until it was time for him to become a broken-down old drunk manning a dead-end desk, drifting inevitably toward cirrhosis or a mattress fire.

They wanted the information he could get, but they didn't want Freddy. They paid him top scale, which is not very much money if you have to buy women. They patted his back and told him he had a lot of balls and they refused to put his name on a parking place.

One evening in 1969 while in the office working rewrite, Freddy had an epiphany.

Frank Larkin was seated near him taking dictation on the telephone. Dictation was the glue factory for old reporters on the paper where Freddy worked. Frank Larkin was fifty-five, but he looked seventy. He was oyster-eyed and he went to his locker every half-hour for a drink. Freddy could smell him from where he sat.

Larkin got up and shuffled over to the slot and spoke in a hoarse whisper to the news editor, a woman. Freddy always listened to other people's conversations.

Larkin asked the woman to get him a Kotex from the machine in the ladies' room. He had to use them on his bleeding behind.

Freddy stopped typing. He took the story out of his typewriter, replaced the paper and wrote a letter of resignation.

A week later he was working for the *Tattler.*

He started as cancer editor at a salary nearly double what he had earned before. Management was impressed with his attitude.

The *Tattler* could afford to pay him well because the paper found cancer very lucrative.

One in five Americans dies of it. The relatives of the dying, worn out, prayed out, trying to fight a raging carcinoma with pats and banana pudding and copper-tasting jokes, are desperate for anything hopeful.

Marketing surveys showed that a bold "New Cure for Cancer" or "Cancer Miracle Drug" cover line boosted supermarket sales of any *Tattler* issue by 22.3 percent. There was a six-percentile drop in those sales when the story ran on page one beneath the cover line, as the reader had time to scan the empty text while the groceries were being totaled.

Marketing experts discovered it was better to have the big cover line in color on the front and play the story in the middle pages, where it was difficult to hold the paper open and manage a purse and grocery cart at the same time.

The standard story featured an optimistic five paragraphs in ten-point type, then a drop to eight point, then to six point before mentioning that the "miracle drug" was unavailable or that animal research was just beginning.

Freddy earned his money turning them out, and the stories sold a lot of *Tattlers.*

In addition to increased readership, there were many spinoff sales of miracle medallions and healing cloths. Manufacturers of these paid a premium to get their ads located close to the weekly cancer story.

Many readers wrote to the paper for more information. Some additional revenue was realized by selling their names to a radio "evangelist," a screaming sociopath who wrote to them for money, using envelopes stamped "Someone You Love Will Die Unless . . ."

Freddy Lounds was good for the *Tattler*, and the *Tattler* was good to him. Now, after eleven years with the paper, he earned $72,000 a year. He covered pretty much what he pleased and spent the money trying to have a good time. He lived as well as he knew how to live.

The way things were developing, he believed he could raise the ante on his paperback deal, and there was movie interest. He had heard that Hollywood was a fine place for obnoxious fellows with money.

Freddy felt good. He shot down the ramp to the underground garage in his building and wheeled into his parking place with a spirited squeal of rubber. There on the wall was his name in letters a foot high, marking his private spot. Mr. Frederick Lounds.

Wendy was here already—her Datsun was parked next to his space. Good. He wished he could take her to Washington with him. That would make those flatfeet's eyes pop. He whistled in the elevator on his way upstairs.

➤

Wendy was packing for him. She had lived out of suitcases and she did a good job.

Neat in her jeans and plaid shirt, her brown hair gathered in a chipmunk tail on her neck, she might have been a farm girl except for her pallor and her shape. Wendy's figure was almost a caricature of puberty.

She looked at Lounds with eyes that had not registered surprise in years. She saw that he was trembling.

"You're working too hard, Roscoe." She liked to call him Roscoe, and it pleased him for some reason. "What are you taking, the six-o'clock shuttle?" She brought him a drink and moved her sequined jump suit and wig case off the bed so he could lie down. "I can take you to the airport. I'm not going to the club 'til six."

"Wendy City" was her own topless bar, and she didn't have to dance anymore. Lounds had cosigned the note.

"You sounded like Morocco Mole when you called me," she said.

"Who?"

"You know, on television Saturday morning, he's real mysterious and he helps Secret Squirrel. We watched it when you had the flu. . . . You really pulled one off today, didn't you? You're really pleased with yourself."

"Damn straight. I took a chance today, baby, and it paid off. I've got a chance at something sweet."

"You've got time for a nap before you go. You're running yourself in the ground."

Lounds lit a cigarette. He already had one burning in the ashtray.

"You know what?" she said. "I bet if you drink your drink and get it off, you could go to sleep."

Lounds's face, like a fist pressed against her neck, relaxed at last, became mobile as suddenly as a fist becomes a hand. His trembling stopped. He told her all about it, whispering into the buck jut of her augmented breasts; she tracing eights on the back of his neck with a finger.

"That is some kind of smart, Roscoe," she said. "You go to sleep now. I'll get you up for the plane. It'll be all right, all of it. And then we'll have a high old time."

They whispered about the places they would go. He went to sleep.

CHAPTER 17

DR. ALAN BLOOM and Jack Crawford sat on folding chairs, the only furniture left in Crawford's office.

"The cupboard is bare, Doctor."

Dr. Bloom studied Crawford's simian face and wondered what was coming. Behind Crawford's grousing and his Alka-Seltzers the doctor saw an intelligence as cold as an X-ray table.

"Where did Will go?"

"He'll walk around and cool off," Crawford said. "He hates Lounds."

"Did you think you might lose Will after Lecter published his home address? That he might go back to his family?"

"For a minute, I did. It shook him."

"Understandably," Dr. Bloom said.

"Then I realized—he can't go home, and neither can Molly and Willy, never, until the Tooth Fairy is out of the way."

"You've met Molly?"

"Yeah. She's great, I like her. She'd be glad to see me in hell with my back broken, of course. I'm having to duck her right now."

"She thinks you use Will?"

Crawford looked at Dr. Bloom sharply. "I've got some things I have to talk to him about. We'll need to check with you. When do you have to be at Quantico?"

"Not until Tuesday morning. I put it off." Dr. Bloom was a guest lecturer at the behavioral-science section of the FBI Academy.

"Graham likes you. He doesn't think you run any mind games on him," Crawford said. Bloom's remark about using Graham stuck in his craw.

"I don't. I wouldn't try," Dr. Bloom said. "I'm as honest with him as I'd be with a patient."

"Exactly."

"No, I want to be his friend, and I am. Jack, I owe it to my field of study to observe. Remember, though, when *you* asked me to give you a study on him, I refused."

"That was Petersen, upstairs, wanted the study."

"You were the one who asked for it. No matter, if I ever did anything on Graham, if there were ever anything that might be of therapeutic benefit to others, I'd abstract it in a form that would be totally unrecognizable. If I ever do anything in a scholarly way, it'll only be published posthumously."

"After you or after Graham?"

Dr. Bloom didn't answer.

"One thing I've noticed—I'm curious about this: you're never alone in a room with Graham, are you? You're smooth about it, but you're never one-on-one with him. Why's that? Do you think he's psychic, is that it?"

"No. He's an *eideteker*—he has a remarkable visual memory—but I don't think he's psychic. He wouldn't let Duke test him—that doesn't mean anything, though. He hates to be prodded and poked. So do I."

"But—"

"Will wants to think of this as purely an intellectual exercise, and in the narrow definition of forensics, that's what it is. He's good at that, but there are other people just as good, I imagine."

"Not many," Crawford said.

"What he has in addition is pure empathy and projection," Dr. Bloom said. "He can assume your point of view, or mine—and maybe some other points of view that scare and sicken him. It's an uncomfortable gift, Jack. Perception's a tool that's pointed on both ends."

"Why aren't you ever alone with him?"

"Because I have some professional curiosity about him and he'd pick that up in a hurry. He's fast."

"If he caught you peeking, he'd snatch down the shades."

"An unpleasant analogy, but accurate, yes. You've had sufficient revenge now, Jack. We can get to the point. Let's make it short. I don't feel very well."

"A psychosomatic manifestation, probably," Crawford said.

"Actually it's my gall bladder. What do you want?"

"I have a medium where I can speak to the Tooth Fairy."

"The *Tattler*," Dr. Bloom said.

"Right. Do you think there's any way to push him in a self-destructive way by what we say to him?"

"Push him toward suicide?"

"Suicide would suit me fine."

"I doubt it. In certain kinds of mental illness that might be possible. Here, I doubt it. If he were self-destructive, he wouldn't be so careful. He wouldn't protect himself so well. If he were a classic paranoid schizophrenic, you might be able to influence him to blow up and become visible. You might even get him to hurt himself. I wouldn't help you though." Suicide was Bloom's mortal enemy.

"No, I suppose you wouldn't," Crawford said. "Could we enrage him?"

"Why do you want to know? To what purpose?"

"Let me ask you this: could we enrage him and focus his attention?"

"He's already fixed on Graham as his adversary, and you know it. Don't fool around. You've decided to stick Graham's neck out, haven't you?"

"I think I have to do it. It's that or he gets his feet sticky on the twenty-fifth. Help me."

"I'm not sure you know what you're asking."

"Advice—that's what I'm asking."

"I don't mean from me," Dr. Bloom said. "What you're asking from Graham. I don't want you to misinterpret this, and normally I wouldn't say it, but you ought to know: what do you think one of Will's strongest drives is?"

Crawford shook his head.

"It's fear, Jack. The man deals with a huge amount of fear."

"Because he got hurt?"

"No, not entirely. Fear comes with imagination, it's a penalty, it's the price of imagination."

Crawford stared at his blunt hands folded on his stomach. He reddened. It was embarrassing to talk about it. "Sure. It's what you don't ever mention on the big boys' side of the playground, right? Don't worry about telling me he's afraid. I won't think he's not a 'stand-up guy.' I'm not a total asshole, Doctor."

"I never thought you were, Jack."

"I wouldn't put him out there if I couldn't cover him. Okay, if I couldn't cover him eighty percent. He's not bad himself. Not the best, but he's quick. Will you help us stir up the Tooth Fairy, Doctor? A lot of people are dead."

"Only if Graham knows the entire risk ahead of time and assumes it voluntarily. I have to hear him say that."

"I'm like you, Doctor. I never bullshit him. No more than we all bullshit each other."

➤

Crawford found Graham in the small workroom near Zeller's lab which he had commandeered and filled with photographs and personal papers belonging to the victims.

Crawford waited until Graham put down the *Law Enforcement Bulletin* he was reading.

"Let me fill you in on what's up for the twenty-fifth." He did not have to tell Graham that the twenty-fifth would bring the next full moon.

"When he does it again?"

"Yeah, if we have a problem on the twenty-fifth."

"Not if. When."

"Both times it's been on Saturday night. Birmingham, June 28, a full moon falling on a Saturday night. It was July 26 in Atlanta, that's one day short of a full moon, but also Saturday night. This time the full moon falls on Monday, August 25. He likes the weekend, though, so we're ready from Friday on."

"Ready? We're *ready?*"

"Correct. You know how it is in the textbooks—the ideal way to investigate a homicide?"

"I never saw it done that way," Graham said. "It never works out like that."

"No. Hardly ever. It would be great to be able to do it, though: Send one guy in. Just one. Let him go over the place. He's wired and dictating all the time. He gets the place absolutely cherry for as long as he needs. Just him. . . . just you."

A long pause.

"What are you telling me?"

"Starting the night of Friday, the twenty-second, we have a Grumman Gulfstream standing by at Andrews Air Force Base. I borrowed it from Interior. The basic lab stuff will be on it. We stand by—me, you, Zeller, Jimmy Price, a photographer, and two people to do interrogations. Soon as the call comes in, we're on our way. Anywhere in the East or South, we can be there in an hour and fifteen minutes."

"What about the locals? They don't have to cooperate. They won't wait."

"We're blanketing the chiefs of police and sheriffs' departments. Every one of them. We're asking orders to be posted on the dispatchers' consoles and the duty officers' desks."

Graham shook his head. "Balls. They'd never hold off. They couldn't."

"This is what we're asking—it's not so much. We're asking that when a report comes in, the first officers at the scene go in and look. Medical personnel go in and make sure nobody's left alive. They come back out. Roadblocks, interrogations, go on any way they like, but the *scene,* that's sealed off until we get there. We drive up, you go in. You're wired. You talk it out to us when you feel like it, don't say anything when you don't feel like it. Take as long as you want. Then we'll come in."

"The locals won't wait."

"Of course they won't. They'll send in some guys from Homicide. But the request will have *some* effect. It'll cut down on traffic in there, and you'll get it fresh."

Fresh. Graham tilted his head back against his chair and stared at the ceiling.

"Of course," Crawford said, "we've still got thirteen days before that weekend."

"Aw, Jack."

"'Jack' what?" Crawford said.

"You kill me, you really do."

"I don't follow you."

"Yes you do. What you've done, you've decided to use me for bait because you don't have anything else. So before you pop the question, you pump me up about how bad next time will be. Not bad psychology. To use on a fucking idiot. What did you think I'd say? You worried I don't have the onions for it since that with Lecter?"

"No."

"I wouldn't blame you for wondering. We both know people it happened to. I don't like walking around in a Kevlar vest with my butt puckered up. But hell, I'm in it now. We can't go home as long as he's loose."

"I never doubted you'd do it."

Graham saw that this was true. "It's something more then, isn't it?"

Crawford said nothing.

"No Molly. *No way.*"

"Jesus, Will, even *I* wouldn't ask you that."

Graham stared at him for a moment. "Oh, for Christ's sake, Jack. You've decided to play ball with Freddy Lounds, haven't you? You and little Freddy have cut a deal."

Crawford frowned at a spot on his tie. He looked up at Graham. "You know yourself it's the best way to bait him. The Tooth Fairy's gonna watch the *Tattler.* What else have we got?"

"It has to be Lounds doing it?"

"He's got the corner on the *Tattler.*"

"So I really bad-mouth the Tooth Fairy in the *Tattler* and then we give him a shot. You think it's better than the mail drop? Don't answer that, I know it is. Have you talked to Bloom about it?"

"Just in passing. We'll both get together with him. And Lounds. We'll run the mail drop on him at the same time."

"What about the setup? I think we'll have to give him a pretty good shot at it. Something open. Someplace where he can get close. I don't think he'd snipe. He might fool me, but I can't see him with a rifle."

"We'll have stillwatches on the high places."

They were both thinking the same thing. Kevlar body armor would stop the Tooth Fairy's nine-millimeter and his knife unless Graham got hit in the face. There was no way to protect him against a head shot if a hidden rifleman got the chance to fire.

"You talk to Lounds. I don't have to do that."

"He needs to interview you, Will," Crawford said gently. "He has to take your picture."

Bloom had warned Crawford he'd have trouble on that point.

CHAPTER 18

WHEN THE TIME CAME, Graham surprised both Crawford and Bloom. He seemed willing to meet Lounds halfway and his expression was affable beneath the cold blue eyes.

Being inside FBI headquarters had a salutary effect on Lounds's manners. He was polite when he remembered to be, and he was quick and quiet with his equipment.

Graham balked only once: he flatly refused to let Lounds see Mrs. Leeds's diary or any of the families' private correspondence.

When the interview began, he answered Lounds's questions in a civil tone. Both men consulted notes taken in conference with Dr. Bloom. The questions and answers were often rephrased.

➤

Alan Bloom had found it difficult to scheme toward hurt. In the end, he simply laid out his theories about the Tooth Fairy. The others listened like karate students at an anatomy lecture.

Dr. Bloom said the Tooth Fairy's acts and his letter indicated a projective delusional scheme which compensated for intolerable feelings of inadequacy. Smashing the mirrors tied these feelings to his appearance.

The killer's objection to the name "Tooth Fairy" was grounded in the homosexual implications of the word "fairy." Bloom believed he had an unconscious homosexual conflict, a terrible fear of being gay. Dr. Bloom's opinion was reinforced by one curious observation at the Leeds house: fold marks and covered bloodstains indicated the Tooth Fairy put a pair of shorts on Charles Leeds after he was dead. Dr. Bloom believed he did this to emphasize his lack of interest in Leeds.

The psychiatrist talked about the strong bonding of aggressive and sexual drives that occurs in sadists at a very early age.

The savage attacks aimed primarily at the women and performed in the presence of their families were clearly strikes at a maternal figure. Bloom, pacing, talking half to himself, called his subject "the child of a nightmare." Crawford's eyelids drooped at the compassion in his voice.

➤

In the interview with Lounds, Graham made statements no investigator would make and no straight newspaper would credit.

He speculated that the Tooth Fairy was ugly, impotent with persons of the opposite sex, and he claimed falsely that the killer had sexually molested his male victims. Graham said that the Tooth Fairy doubtless was the laughingstock of his acquaintances and the product of an incestuous home.

He emphasized that the Tooth Fairy obviously was not as intelligent as Hannibal Lecter. He promised to provide the *Tattler* with more observations and insights about the killer as they occurred to him. Many law-enforcement people disagreed with him, he said, but as long as he was heading the investigation, the *Tattler* could count on getting the straight stuff from him.

Lounds took a lot of pictures.

The key shot was taken in Graham's "Washington hideaway," an apartment he had "borrowed to use until he squashed the Fairy." It was the only place where he could "find solitude" in the "carnival atmosphere" of the investigation.

The photograph showed Graham in a bathrobe at a desk, studying late into the night. He was poring over a grotesque "artist's conception" of "the Fairy."

Behind him a slice of the floodlit Capitol dome could be seen through the window. Most importantly, in the lower-left corner of the window, blurred but readable, was the sign of a popular motel across the street.

The Tooth Fairy could find the apartment if he wanted to.

At FBI headquarters, Graham was photographed in front of a mass spectrometer. It had nothing to do with the case, but Lounds thought it looked impressive.

Graham even consented to have his picture taken with Lounds interviewing him. They did it in front of the vast gun racks in Firearms and Toolmarks. Lounds held a nine-millimeter automatic of the same type as the Tooth Fairy's weapon. Graham pointed to the homemade silencer, fashioned from a length of television-antenna mast.

Dr. Bloom was surprised to see Graham put a comradely hand on Lounds's shoulder just before Crawford clicked the shutter.

The interview and pictures were set to appear in the *Tattler* published the next day, Monday, August 11. As soon as he had the material, Lounds left for Chicago. He said he wanted to supervise the layout himself. He made arrangements to meet Crawford on Tuesday afternoon five blocks from the trap.

Starting Tuesday, when the *Tattler* became generally available, two traps would be baited for the monster.

Graham would go each evening to his "temporary residence" shown in the *Tattler* picture.

A coded personal notice in the same issue invited the Tooth Fairy to a mail drop in Annapolis watched around the clock. If he were suspicious of the mail drop, he might think the effort to catch him was concentrated there. Then Graham would be a more appealing target, the FBI reasoned.

Florida authorities provided a stillwatch at Sugarloaf Key.

There was an air of dissatisfaction among the hunters—two major stakeouts took manpower that could be used elsewhere, and Graham's presence at the trap each night would limit his movement to the Washington area.

Though Crawford's judgment told him this was the best move, the whole procedure was too passive for his taste. He felt they were playing games with themselves in the dark of the moon with less than two weeks to go before it rose full again.

Sunday and Monday passed in curiously jerky time. The minutes dragged and the hours flew.

➤

Spurgen, chief SWAT instructor at Quantico, circled the apartment block on Monday afternoon. Graham rode beside him. Crawford was in the back seat.

"The pedestrian traffic falls off around seven-fifteen. Everybody's settled in for dinner," Spurgen said. With his wiry, compact body and his baseball cap tipped back on his head, he looked like an infielder. "Give us a toot on the clear band tomorrow night when you cross the B&O railroad tracks. You ought to try to make it about eight-thirty, eight-forty or so."

He pulled into the apartment parking lot. "This setup ain't heaven, but it could be worse. You'll park here tomorrow night. We'll change the space you use every night after that, but it'll always be on this side. It's seventy-five yards to the apartment entrance. Let's walk it."

Spurgen, short and bandy-legged, went ahead of Graham and Crawford.

He's looking for places where he could get the bad hop, Graham thought.

"The walk is probably where it'll happen, if it happens," the SWAT leader said. "See, from here the direct line from your car to the entrance, the natural route, is across the center of the lot. It's as far as you can get from the line of cars that are here all day. He'll have to come across open asphalt to get close. How well do you hear?"

"Pretty well," Graham said. "Damn well on this parking lot."

Spurgen looked for something in Graham's face, found nothing he could recognize.

He stopped in the middle of the lot. "We're reducing the wattage on these streetlights a little to make it tougher on a rifleman."

"Tougher on your people too," Crawford said.

"Two of ours have Startron night scopes," Spurgen said. "I've got some clear spray I'll ask you to use on your suit jackets, Will. By the way, I don't care how hot it is, you will wear body armor each and every time. Correct?"

"Yes."

"What is it?"

"It's Kevlar—what, Jack?—Second Chance?"

"Second Chance," Crawford said.

"It's pretty likely he'll come up to you, probably from behind, or he may figure on meeting you and then turning around to shoot when he's passed you," Spurgen said. "Seven times he's gone for the head shot, right? He's seen that work. He'll do it with you too if you give him the time. *Don't give him the time.* After I show you a couple of things in the lobby and the flop, let's go to the range. Can you do that?"

"He can do that," Crawford said.

Spurgen was high priest on the range. He made Graham wear earplugs under the earmuffs and flashed targets at him from every angle. He was relieved to see that Graham did not carry the regulation .38, but he worried about the flash from the ported barrel. They worked for two hours. The man insisted on checking the cylinder crane and cylinder latch screws on Graham's .44 when he had finished firing.

Graham showered and changed clothes to get the smell of gunsmoke off him before he drove to the bay for his last free night with Molly and Willy.

He took his wife and stepson to the grocery store after dinner and made a considerable to-do over selecting melons. He made sure they bought plenty of groceries—the old *Tattler* was still on the racks beside the checkout stands and he hoped Molly would not see the new issue coming in the morning. He didn't want to tell her what was happening.

When she asked him what he wanted for dinner in the coming week, he had to say he'd be away, that he was going back to Birmingham. It was the first real lie he had ever told her and telling it made him feel as greasy as old currency.

He watched her in the aisles: Molly, his pretty baseball wife, with her ceaseless vigilance for lumps, her insistence on quarterly medical checkups for him and Willy, her controlled fear of the dark; her hard-bought knowledge that time is luck. She knew the value of their days. She could hold a moment by its stem. She had taught him to relish.

Pachelbel's Canon filled the sun-drowned room where they learned each other and there was the exhilaration too big to hold and even then the fear flickered across him like an osprey's shadow: this is too good to live for long.

Molly switched her bag often from shoulder to shoulder in the grocery aisles, as though the gun in it weighed much more than its nineteen ounces.

Graham would have been offended had he heard the ugly thing he mumbled to the melons: "I have to put that bastard in a rubber sack, that's all. I have to do that."

Variously weighted with lies, guns, and groceries, the three of them were a small and solemn troop.

Molly smelled a rat. She and Graham did not speak after the lights were out. Molly dreamed of heavy crazy footsteps coming in a house of changing rooms.

CHAPTER 19

THERE IS A NEWSSTAND in Lambert St. Louis International Airport which carries many of the major daily newspapers from all over the United States. The New York, Washington, Chicago, and Los Angeles papers come in by air freight and you can buy them on the same day they are published.

Like many newsstands, this one is owned by a chain and, along with the standard magazines and papers, the operator is required to take a certain amount of trash.

When the Chicago *Tribune* was delivered to the stand at ten o'clock on Monday night, a bundle of *Tattlers* thumped to the floor beside it. The bundle was still warm in the center.

The newsstand operator squatted in front of his shelves arranging the *Tribunes*. He had enough else to do. The day guys never did their share of straightening.

A pair of black zippered boots came into the corner of his vision. A browser. No, the boots were pointed at him. Somebody wanted some damn thing. The newsie wanted to finish arranging his *Tribunes* but the insistent attention made the back of his head prickle.

His trade was transient. He didn't have to be nice. "What is it?" he said to the knees.

"A *Tattler*."

"You'll have to wait until I bust the bundle."

164

The boots did not go away. They were too close.

"I said you'll have to wait until I bust the bundle. Understand? See I'm working here?"

A hand and a flash of bright steel and the twine on the bundle beside him parted with a pop. A Susan B. Anthony dollar rang on the floor in front of him. A clean copy of the *Tattler*, jerked from the center of the bundle, spilled the top ones to the floor.

The newsstand operator got to his feet. His cheeks were flushed. The man was leaving with the paper under his arm.

"Hey. Hey, you."

The man turned to face him. "Me?"

"Yeah, you. I told you—"

"You told me what?" He was coming back. He stood too close. "You told me what?"

Usually a rude merchant can fluster his customers. There was something awful in this one's calm.

The newsie looked at the floor. "You got a quarter coming back."

Dolarhyde turned his back and walked out. The newsstand operator's cheeks burned for half an hour. *Yeah, that guy was in here last week too. He comes in here again, I'll tell him where to fuckin' get off. I got somethin' under the counter for wise-asses.*

Dolarhyde did not look at the *Tattler* in the airport. Last Thursday's message from Lecter had left him with mixed feelings. Dr. Lecter had been right, of course, in saying that he was beautiful and it was thrilling to read. He *was* beautiful. He felt some contempt for the doctor's fear of the policeman. Lecter did not understand much better than the public.

Still, he was on fire to know if Lecter had sent him another message. He would wait until he got home to look. Dolarhyde was proud of his self-control.

He mused about the newsstand operator as he drove.

There was a time when he would have apologized for disturbing the man and never come back to the newsstand. For years he had taken shit unlimited from people. Not anymore. The man could have insulted Francis Dolarhyde: he could not face the Dragon. It was all part of Becoming.

➤

At midnight, the light above his desk still burned. The message from the *Tattler* was decoded and wadded on the floor. Pieces of the *Tattler* were scattered where Dolarhyde had clipped it for his journal. The great journal stood open beneath the painting of the Dragon, glue still drying where the new clippings were fastened. Beneath them, freshly attached, was a small plastic bag, empty as yet.

The legend beside the bag said: "With These He Offended Me."

But Dolarhyde had left his desk.

He was sitting on the basement stairs in the cool must of earth and mildew. The beam from his electric lantern moved over draped furniture, the dusty backs of the great mirrors that once hung in the house and now leaned against the walls, the trunk containing his case of dynamite.

The beam stopped on a tall draped shape, one of several in the far corner of the cellar. Cobwebs touched his face as he went to it. Dust made him sneeze when he pulled off the cloth cover.

He blinked back the tears and shone his light on the old oak wheelchair he had uncovered. It was high-backed, heavy, and strong, one of three in the basement. The county had provided them to Grandmother in the 1940's when she ran her nursing home here.

The wheels squeaked as he rolled the chair across the floor. Despite its weight, he carried it easily up the stairs. In the kitchen he oiled the wheels. The small front wheels still squeaked, but the back ones had good bearings and spun freely at a flip of his finger.

The searing anger in him was eased by the wheels' soothing hum. As he spun them, Dolarhyde hummed too.

CHAPTER 20

WHEN FREDDY LOUNDS LEFT the *Tattler* office at noon on Tuesday he was tired and high. He had put together the *Tattler* story on the plane to Chicago and laid it out in the composing room in thirty minutes flat.

The rest of the time he had worked steadily on his paperback, brushing off all callers. He was a good organizer and now he had fifty thousand words of solid background.

When the Tooth Fairy was caught, he'd do a whammo lead and an account of the capture. The background material would fit in neatly. He had arranged to have three of the *Tattler*'s better reporters ready to go on short notice. Within hours of the capture they could be digging for details wherever the Tooth Fairy lived.

His agent talked very big numbers. Discussing the project with the agent ahead of time was, strictly speaking, a violation of his agreement with Crawford. All contracts and memos would be postdated after the capture to cover that up.

Crawford held a big stick—he had Lounds's threat on tape. Interstate transmission of a threatening message was an indictable offense outside any protection Lounds enjoyed under the First Amendment. Lounds also knew that Crawford, with one phone call, could give him a permanent problem with the Internal Revenue Service.

There were polyps of honesty in Lounds; he had few illusions about the nature of his work. But he had developed a near-religious fervor about this project.

He was possessed with a vision of a better life on the other side of the money. Buried under all the dirt he had ever done, his old hopes still faced east. Now they stirred and strained to rise.

Satisfied that his cameras and recording equipment were ready, he drove home to sleep for three hours before the flight to Washington, where he would meet Crawford near the trap.

A damned nuisance in the underground garage. The black van, parked in the space next to his, was over the line. It crowded into the space clearly marked "Mr. Frederick Lounds."

Lounds opened his door hard, banging the side of the van and leaving a dent and a mark. That would teach the inconsiderate bastard.

Lounds was locking his car when the van door opened behind him. He was turning, had half-turned when the flat sap thocked over his ear. He got his hands up, but his knees were going and there was tremendous pressure around his neck and the air was shut off. When his heaving chest could fill again it sucked chloroform.

➤

Dolarhyde parked the van behind his house, climbed out and stretched. He had fought a crosswind all the way from Chicago and his arms were tired. He studied the night sky. The Perseid meteor shower was due soon, and he must not miss it.

Revelation: And his tail drew the third part of the stars of heaven, and did cast them down to the earth . . .

His doing in another time. He must see it and remember.

Dolarhyde unlocked the back door and made his routine search of the house. When he came outside again he wore a stocking mask.

He opened the van and attached a ramp. Then he rolled out Freddy Lounds. Lounds wore nothing but his shorts and a gag and blindfold. Though he was only semiconscious, he did not slump. He sat up very straight, his head against the high back of the old oak wheelchair. From the back of his head to the soles of his feet he was bonded to the chair with epoxy glue.

Dolarhyde rolled him into the house and parked him in a corner of the parlor with his back to the room, as though he had misbehaved.

"Are you too cool? Would you like a blanket?"

Dolarhyde peeled off the sanitary napkins covering Lounds's eyes and mouth. Lounds didn't answer. The odor of chloroform hung on him.

"I'll get you a blanket." Dolarhyde took an afghan from the sofa and tucked it around Lounds up to the chin, then pressed an ammonia bottle under his nose.

Lounds's eyes opened wide on a blurred joining of walls. He coughed and started talking.

"Accident? Am I hurt bad?"

The voice behind him: "No, Mr. Lounds. You'll be just fine."

"My back hurts. My skin. Did I get burned? I hope to God I'm not burned."

"Burned? Burned. No. You just rest here. I'll be with you in a little while."

"Let me lie down. Listen, I want you to call my office. My God, I'm in a Striker frame. My back's broken—tell me the truth!"

Footsteps going away.

"What am I doing here?" The question shrill at the end.

The answer came from far behind him. "Atoning, Mr. Lounds."

Lounds heard footsteps mounting stairs. He heard a shower running. His head was clearer now. He remembered leaving the office and driving, but he couldn't remember after that. The side of his head throbbed and the smell of chloroform made him gag. Held rigidly erect, he was afraid he would vomit and drown. He opened his mouth wide and breathed deep. He could hear his heart.

Lounds hoped he was asleep. He tried to raise his arm from the armrest, increasing the pull deliberately until the pain in his palm and arm was enough to wake him from any dream. He was not asleep. His mind gathered speed.

By straining he could turn his eyes enough to see his arm for seconds at a time. He saw how he was fastened. This was no device to protect broken backs. This was no hospital. Someone had him.

Lounds thought he heard footsteps on the floor above, but they might have been his heartbeats.

He tried to think. Strained to think. *Keep cool and think,* he whispered. Cool and think.

The stairs creaked as Dolarhyde came down.

Lounds felt the weight of him in every step. A presence behind him now.

Lounds spoke several words before he could adjust the volume of his voice.

"I haven't seen your face. I couldn't identify you. I don't know what you look like. The *Tattler*, I work for *The National Tattler*, would pay a reward . . . a big reward for me. Half a million, a million maybe. A million dollars."

Silence behind him. Then a squeak of couch springs. He was sitting down, then.

"What do you think, Mr. Lounds?"

Put the pain and fear away and think. Now. For all time. To have some time. To have years. He hasn't decided to kill me. He hasn't let me see his face.

"What do you think, Mr. Lounds?"

"I don't know what's happened to me."

"Do you know Who I Am, Mr. Lounds?"

"No. I don't want to know, believe me."

"According to you, I'm a vicious, perverted sexual failure. An animal, you said. Probably turned loose from an asylum by a do-good judge." Ordinarily, Dolarhyde would have avoided the sibilant /s/ in "sexual." In the presence of this audience, very far from laughter, he was freed. "You know now, don't you?"

Don't lie. Think fast. "Yes."

"Why do you write lies, Mr. Lounds? Why do you say I'm crazy? Answer now."

"When a person . . . when a person does things that most people can't understand, they call him . . ."

"Crazy."

"They called, like . . . the Wright brothers. All through history—"

"History. Do you understand what I'm doing, Mr. Lounds?"

Understand. There it was. A chance. Swing hard. "No, but I think I've got an opportunity to understand, and then *all my readers could understand too.*"

"Do you feel privileged?"

"It's a privilege. But I have to tell you, man to man, that I'm scared. It's hard to concentrate when you're scared. If you have a great idea, you wouldn't have to scare me for me to really be impressed."

"Man to man. Man to man. You use that expression to imply

frankness, Mr. Lounds, I appreciate that. But you see, I am not a man. I began as one but by the Grace of God and my own Will, I have become Other and More than a man. You say you're frightened. Do you believe that God is in attendance here, Mr. Lounds?"

"I don't know."

"Are you praying to Him now?"

"Sometimes I pray. I have to tell you, I just pray mostly when I'm scared."

"And does God help you?"

"I don't know. I don't think about it after. I ought to."

"You ought to. Um-hmmmm. There are so many things you ought to understand. In a little while I'll help you understand. Will you excuse me now?"

"Certainly."

Footsteps out of the room. The slide and rattle of a kitchen drawer. Lounds had covered many murders committed in kitchens where things are handy. Police reporting can change forever your view of kitchens. Water running now.

Lounds thought it must be night. Crawford and Graham were expecting him. Certainly he had been missed by now. A great, hollow sadness pulsed briefly with his fear.

Breathing behind him, a flash of white caught by his rolling eye. A hand, powerful and pale. It held a cup of tea with honey. Lounds sipped it through a straw.

"I'd do a big story," he said between sips. "Anything you want to say. Describe you any way you want, or no description, no description."

"Shhhh." A single finger tapped the top of his head. The lights brightened. The chair began to turn.

"No. I don't want to see you."

"Oh, but you must, Mr. Lounds. You're a reporter. You're here to report. When I turn you around, open your eyes and look at me. If you won't open them yourself, I'll staple your eyelids to your forehead."

A wet mouth noise, a snapping click and the chair spun. Lounds faced the room, his eyes tight shut. A finger tapped insistently on his chest. A touch on his eyelids. He looked.

To Lounds, seated, he seemed very tall standing in his kimono. A stocking mask was rolled up to his nose. He turned his back to Lounds and dropped the robe. The great back muscles flexed above the brilliant tattoo of the tail that ran down his lower back and wrapped around the leg.

The Dragon turned his head slowly, looked over his shoulder at Lounds and smiled, all jags and stains.

"Oh my dear God Jesus," Lounds said.

Lounds now in the center of the room where he can see the screen. Dolarhyde, behind him, has put on his robe and put in the teeth that allow him to speak.

"Do you want to know What I Am?"

Lounds tried to nod; the chair jerked his scalp. "More than anything. I was afraid to ask."

"Look."

The first slide was Blake's painting, the great Man-Dragon, wings flared and tail lashing, poised above the Woman Clothed with the Sun.

"Do you see now?"

"I see."

Rapidly Dolarhyde ran through his other slides.

Click. Mrs. Jacobi alive. "Do you see?"

"Yes."

Click. Mrs. Leeds alive. "Do you see?"

"Yes."

Click. Dolarhyde, the Dragon rampant, muscles flexed and tail tattoo above the Jacobis' bed. "Do you see?"

"Yes."

Click. Mrs. Jacobi waiting. "Do you see?"

"Yes."

Click. Mrs. Jacobi after. "Do you see?"

"Yes."

Click. The Dragon rampant. "Do you see?"

"Yes."

Click. Mrs. Leeds waiting, her husband slack beside her. "Do you see?"

"Yes."

Click. Mrs. Leeds after, harlequined with blood. "Do you see?"

"Yes."

Click. Freddy Lounds, a copy of a *Tattler* photograph. "Do you see?"

"Oh God."

"Do you see?"

"Oh my God." The words drawn out, as a child speaks crying.

"Do you see?"

"Please no."

"No what?"

"Not me."

"No what? You're a man, Mr. Lounds. Are you a man?"

"Yes."

"Do you imply that I'm some kind of queer?"

"God no."

"Are you a queer, Mr. Lounds?"

"No."

"Are you going to write more lies about me, Mr. Lounds?"

"Oh no, no."

"Why did you write lies, Mr. Lounds?"

"The police told me. It was what they said."

"You quote Will Graham."

"Graham told me the lies. Graham."

"Will you tell the truth now? About Me. My Work. My Becoming. My *Art*, Mr. Lounds. Is this Art?"

"Art."

The fear in Lounds's face freed Dolarhyde to speak and he could fly on sibilants and fricatives; plosives were his great webbed wings.

"You said that I, who see more than you, am insane. I, who pushed the world so much further than you, am insane. I have dared more than you, I have pressed my unique seal so much deeper in the earth, where it will last longer than your dust. Your life to mine is a slug track on stone. A thin silver mucus track in and out of the letters on my monument." The words Dolarhyde had written in his journal swarmed in him now.

"I am the Dragon and you call me *insane?* My movements are followed and recorded as avidly as those of a mighty guest star. Do you know about the guest star in 1054? Of course not. Your readers follow you like a child follows a slug track with his finger, and in the same tired loops of reason. Back to your shallow skull and potato face as a slug follows his own slime back home.

"Before Me you are a slug in the sun. You are privy to a great Becoming and you recognize nothing. You are an ant in the afterbirth.

"It is in your nature to do one thing correctly: before Me you rightly tremble. Fear is not what you owe Me, Lounds, you and the other pismires. *You owe Me awe.*"

Dolarhyde stood with his head down, his thumb and forefinger against the bridge of his nose. Then he left the room.

He didn't take off the mask, Lounds thought. *He didn't take off the mask. If he comes back with it off, I'm dead. God, I'm wet all over.* He rolled his eyes toward the doorway and waited through the sounds from the back of the house.

When Dolarhyde returned, he still wore the mask. He carried a lunch box and two thermoses. "For your trip back home." He held up a thermos. "Ice, we'll need that. Before we go, we'll tape a little while."

He clipped a microphone to the afghan near Lounds's face. "Repeat after me."

They taped for half an hour. Finally, "That's all, Mr. Lounds. You did very well."

"You'll let me go now?"

"I will. There's one way, though, that I can help you better understand and remember." Dolarhyde turned away.

"I want to understand. I want you to know I appreciate you turning me loose. I'm really going to be fair from now on, you know that."

Dolarhyde could not answer. He had changed his teeth.

The tape recorder was running again.

He smiled at Lounds, a brown-stained smile. He placed his hand on Lounds's heart and, leaning to him intimately as though to kiss him, he bit Lounds's lips off and spit them on the floor.

CHAPTER 21

DAWN IN CHICAGO, heavy air and the gray sky low.

A security guard came out of the lobby of the *Tattler* building and stood at the curb smoking a cigarette and rubbing the small of his back. He was alone on the street and in the quiet he could hear the clack of the traffic light changing at the top of the hill, a long block away.

Half a block north of the light, out of the guard's sight, Francis Dolarhyde squatted beside Lounds in the back of the van. He arranged the blanket in a deep cowl that hid Lounds's head.

Lounds was in great pain. He appeared stuporous, but his mind was racing. There were things he must remember. The blindfold was tented across his nose and he could see Dolarhyde's fingers checking the crusted gag.

Dolarhyde put on the white jacket of a medical orderly, laid a thermos in Lounds's lap and rolled him out of the van. When he locked the wheels of the chair and turned to put the ramp back in the van, Lounds could see the end of the van's bumper beneath his blindfold.

Turning now, seeing the bumper guard . . . Yes! the license plate. Only a flash, but Lounds burned it into his mind.

Rolling now. Sidewalk seams. Around a corner and down a curb. Paper crackled under the wheels.

Dolarhyde stopped the wheelchair in a bit of littered shelter between a garbage dumpster and a parked truck. He pulled at the blindfold. Lounds closed his eyes. An ammonia bottle under his nose.

The soft voice close beside him.

"Can you hear me? You're almost there." The blindfold off now. "Blink if you can hear me."

Dolarhyde opened his eye with a thumb and forefinger. Lounds was looking at Dolarhyde's face.

"I told you one fib." Dolarhyde tapped the thermos. "I don't *really* have your lips on ice." He whipped off the blanket and opened the thermos.

Lounds strained hard when he smelled the gasoline, separating the skin from under his forearms and making the stout chair groan. The gas was cold all over him, fumes filling his throat and they were rolling toward the center of the street.

"Do you like being Graham's pet, Freeeeedeeeee?"

Lit with a whump and shoved, sent rolling down on the *Tattler,* eeek, eeek, eeekeeekeeek the wheels.

The guard looked up as a scream blew the burning gag away. He saw the fireball coming, bouncing on the potholes, trailing smoke and sparks and the flames blown back like wings, disjointed reflections leaping along the shop windows.

It veered, struck a parked car and overturned in front of the building, one wheel spinning and flames through the spokes, blazing arms rising in the fighting posture of the burned.

The guard ran back into the lobby. He wondered if it would blow up, if he should get away from the windows. He pulled the fire alarm. What else? He grabbed the fire extinguisher off the wall and looked outside. It hadn't blown up yet.

The guard approached cautiously through the greasy smoke spreading low over the pavement and, at last, sprayed foam on Freddy Lounds.

CHAPTER 22

THE SCHEDULE called for Graham to leave the staked-out apartment in Washington at 5:45 A.M., well ahead of the morning rush.

Crawford called while he was shaving.

"Good morning."

"Not so good," Crawford said. "The Tooth Fairy got Lounds in Chicago."

"Oh hell no."

"He's not dead yet and he's asking for you. He can't wait long."

"I'll go."

"Meet me at the airport. United 245. It leaves in forty minutes. You can be back for the stakeout, if it's still on."

➤

Special Agent Chester from the Chicago FBI office met them at O'Hare in a downpour. Chicago is a city used to sirens. The traffic parted reluctantly in front of them as Chester howled down the expressway, his red light flashing pink on the driving rain.

He raised his voice above the siren. "Chicago PD says he was jumped in his garage. My stuff is secondhand. We're not popular around here today."

"How much is out?" Crawford said.

"The whole thing, trap, all of it."

"Did Lounds get a look at him?"

"I haven't heard a description. Chicago PD put out an all-points bulletin for a license number about six-twenty."

"Did you get hold of Dr. Bloom for me?"

"I got his wife, Jack. Dr. Bloom had his gall bladder taken out this morning."

"Glorious," Crawford said.

Chester pulled under the dripping hospital portico. He turned in his seat. "Jack, Will, before you go up . . . I hear this fruit really trashed Lounds. You ought to be ready for that."

Graham nodded. All the way to Chicago he had tried to choke his hope that Lounds would die before he had to see him.

The corridor of Paege Burn Center was a tube of spotless tile. A tall doctor with a curiously old-young face beckoned Graham and Crawford away from the knot of people at Lounds's door.

"Mr. Lounds's burns are fatal," the doctor said. "I *can* help him with the pain, and I intend to do it. He breathed flames and his throat and lungs are damaged. He may not regain consciousness. In his condition, that would be a blessing.

"In the event that he does regain consciousness, the city police have asked me to take the airway out of his throat so that he might possibly answer questions. I've agreed to try that—briefly.

"At the moment his nerve endings are anesthetized by fire. A lot of pain is coming, if he lives that long. I made this clear to the police and I want to make it clear to you: I'll interrupt any attempted questioning to sedate him if he wants me to. Do you understand me?"

"Yes," Crawford said.

With a nod to the patrolman in front of the door, the doctor clasped his hands behind his white lab coat and moved away like a wading egret.

Crawford glanced at Graham. "You okay?"

"I'm okay. *I* had the SWAT team."

Lounds's head was elevated in the bed. His hair and ears were gone and compresses over his sightless eyes replaced the burned-off lids. His gums were puffed with blisters.

The nurse beside him moved an IV stand so Graham could come close. Lounds smelled like a stable fire.

"Freddy, it's Will Graham."

Lounds arched his neck against the pillow.

"The movement's just reflex, he's not conscious," the nurse said.

The plastic airway holding open his scorched and swollen throat hissed in time with the respirator.

A pale detective sergeant sat in the corner with a tape recorder and a clipboard on his lap. Graham didn't notice him until he spoke.

"Lounds said your name in the emergency room before they put the airway in."

"You were there?"

"Later I was there. But I've got what he said on tape. He gave the firemen a license number when they first got to him. He passed out, and he was out in the ambulance, but he came around for a minute in the emergency room when they gave him a shot in the chest. Some *Tattler* people had followed the ambulance—they were there. I have a copy of their tape."

"Let me hear it."

The detective fiddled with his tape recorder. "I think you want to use the earphone," he said, his face carefully blank. He pushed the button.

Graham heard voices, the rattle of casters, ". . . put him in three," the bump of a litter on a swinging door, a retching cough and a voice croaking, speaking without lips.

"Tooth Hairy."

"Freddy, did you see him? What did he look like, Freddy?"

"Wendy? Hlease Wendy. Grahan set ne uh. The cunt knew it. Grahan set ne uh. Cunt tut his hand on ne in the ticture like a hucking tet. Wendy?"

A noise like a drain sucking. A doctor's voice: "That's it. Let me get there. Get out of the way. *Now.*"

That was all.

Graham stood over Lounds while Crawford listened to the tape.

"We're running down the license number," the detective said. "Could you understand what he was saying?"

"Who's Wendy?" Crawford asked.

"That hooker in the hall. The blonde with the chest. She's been trying to see him. She doesn't know anything."

"Why don't you let her in?" Graham said from the bedside. His back was to them.

"No visitors."

"The man's dying."

"Think I don't know it? I've been here since a quarter to fucking six o'clock—excuse me, Nurse."

"Take a few minutes," Crawford said. "Get some coffee, put some water on your face. He can't say anything. If he does, I'll be here with the recorder."

"Okay, I could use it."

When the detective was gone, Graham left Crawford at the bedside and approached the woman in the hall.

"Wendy?"

"Yeah."

"If you're sure you want to go in there, I'll take you."

"I want to. Maybe I ought to go comb my hair."

"It doesn't matter," Graham said.

When the policeman returned, he didn't try to put her out.

Wendy of Wendy City held Lounds's blackened claw and looked straight at him. He stirred once, a little before noon.

"It's gonna be just fine, Roscoe," she said. "We'll have us some high old times."

Lounds stirred again and died.

CHAPTER 23

CAPTAIN OSBORNE of Chicago Homicide had the gray, pointed face of a stone fox. Copies of the *Tattler* were all over the police station. One was on his desk.

He didn't ask Crawford and Graham to sit down.

"You had nothing at all working with Lounds in the city of Chicago?"

"No, he was coming to Washington," Crawford said. "He had a plane reservation. I'm sure you've checked it."

"Yeah, I got it. He left his office about one-thirty yesterday. Got jumped in the garage of his building, must have been about ten of two."

"Anything in the garage?"

"His keys got kicked under his car. There's no garage attendant— they had a radio-operated door but it came down on a couple of cars and they took it out. Nobody saw it happen. That's getting to be the refrain today. We're working on his car."

"Can we help you there?"

"You can have the results when I get 'em. You haven't said much, Graham. You had plenty to say in the paper."

"I haven't heard much either, listening to you."

"You pissed off, Captain?" Crawford said.

"Me? Why should I be? We run down a phone trace for you and

collar a fucking news reporter. Then you've got no charges against him. You *have* got some deal with him, gets him cooked in front of this scandal sheet. Now the other papers adopt him like he was their own.

"Now we've got our own Tooth Fairy murder right here in Chicago. That's great. 'Tooth Fairy in Chicago,' boy. Before midnight we'll have six accidental domestic shootings, guy trying to sneak in his own house drunk, wife hears him, bang. The Tooth Fairy may like Chicago, decide to stick around, have some fun."

"We can do like this," Crawford said. "Butt heads, get the police commissioner and the U.S. attorney all stirred up, get all the assholes stirred up, yours and mine. Or we can settle down and try to catch the bastard. This was my operation and it went to shit, I know that. You ever have that happen right here in Chicago? I don't want to fight you, Captain. We want to catch him and go home. What do you want?"

Osborne moved a couple of items on his desk, a penholder, a picture of a fox-faced child in band uniform. He leaned back in his chair, pursed his lips and blew out some air.

"Right now I want some coffee. You guys want some?"

"I'd like some," Crawford said.

"So would I," Graham said.

Osborne passed around the Styrofoam cups. He pointed to some chairs.

"The Tooth Fairy had to have a van or a panel truck to move Lounds around in that wheelchair," Graham said.

Osborne nodded. "The license plate Lounds saw was stolen off a TV repair truck in Oak Park. He took a commercial plate, so he was getting it for a truck or a van. He *replaced* the plate on the TV truck with another stolen plate so it wouldn't be noticed so fast. Very sly, this boy. One thing we do know—he got the plate off the TV truck sometime after eight-thirty yesterday morning. The TV repair guy bought gas first thing yesterday and he used a credit card. The attendant copied the correct license number on the slip, so the plate was stolen after that."

"Nobody saw any kind of truck or van?" Crawford said.

"Nothing. The guard at the *Tattler* saw zip. He could referee wrestling he sees so little. The fire department responded first to the *Tattler*. They were just looking for fire. We're canvassing the overnight workers in the *Tattler* neighborhood and the neighborhoods where the TV guy worked Tuesday morning. We hope somebody saw him cop the plate."

"I'd like to see the chair again," Graham said.

"It's in our lab. I'll call them for you." Osborne paused. "Lounds was a ballsy little guy, you have to give him that. Remembering the license number and spitting it out, the shape he was in. You listened to what Lounds said at the hospital?"

Graham nodded.

"I don't mean to rub this in, but I want to know if we heard it the same way. What does it sound like to you?"

Graham quoted in a monotone: "'Tooth Fairy. Graham set me up. The cunt knew it. Graham set me up. Cunt put his hand on me in the picture like a fucking pet.'"

Osborne could not tell how Graham felt about it. He asked another question.

"He was talking about the picture of you and him in the *Tattler?*"

"Had to be."

"Where would he get that idea?"

"Lounds and I had a few run-ins."

"But you looked friendly toward Lounds in the picture. The Tooth Fairy kills the pet first, is that it?"

"That's it." The stone fox was pretty fast, Graham thought.

"Too bad you didn't stake him out."

Graham said nothing.

"Lounds was supposed to be with us by the time the Tooth Fairy saw the *Tattler,*" Crawford said.

"Does what he said mean anything else to you, anything we can use?"

Graham came back from somewhere and had to repeat Osborne's question in his mind before he answered. "We know from what Lounds said that the Tooth Fairy saw the *Tattler* before he hit Lounds, right?"

"Right."

"If you start with the idea that the *Tattler* set him off, does it strike you that he set this up in a hell of a hurry? The thing came off the press Monday night, he's in Chicago stealing license plates sometime Tuesday, probably Tuesday morning, and he's on top of Lounds

Tuesday afternoon. What does that say to you?"

"That he saw it early or he didn't have far to come," Crawford said. "Either he saw it here in Chicago or he saw it someplace else Monday night. Bear in mind, he'd be watching for it to get the personal column."

"Either he was already here, or he came from driving distance," Graham said. "He was on top of Lounds too fast with a big old wheelchair you couldn't carry on a plane—it doesn't even fold. And he didn't fly here, steal a van, steal plates for it, and go around looking for an antique wheelchair to use. He had to have an old wheelchair—a new one wouldn't work for what he did." Graham was up, fiddling with the cord on the venetian blinds, staring at the brick wall across the airshaft. "He already had the wheelchair or he saw it all the time."

Osborne started to ask a question, but Crawford's expression cautioned him to wait.

Graham was tying knots in the blind cord. His hands were not steady.

"He saw it all the time . . ." Crawford prompted.

"Um-hmm," Graham said. "You can see how . . . the idea starts with the wheelchair. From the sight and thought of the wheelchair. That's where the idea would come from when he's thinking what he'll do to those fuckers. Freddy rolling down the street on fire, it must have been quite a sight."

"Do you think he watched it?"

"Maybe. He certainly saw it before he did it, when he was making up his mind what he'd do."

Osborne watched Crawford. Crawford was solid. Osborne knew Crawford was solid, and Crawford was going along with this.

"If he had the chair, or he saw it all the time . . . we can check around the nursing homes, the VA," Osborne said.

"It was perfect to hold Freddy still," Graham said.

"For a long time. He was gone fifteen hours and twenty-five minutes, more or less," Osborne said.

"If he had just wanted to snuff Freddy, he could have done that in the garage," Graham said. "He could have burned him in his car. He wanted to talk to Freddy, or hurt him for a while."

"Either he did it in the back of the van or he took him somewhere," Crawford said. "That length of time, I'd say he took him somewhere."

"It had to be somewhere safe. If he bundled him up good, he

wouldn't attract much notice around a nursing home, going in and out," Osborne said.

"He'd have the racket, though," Crawford said. "A certain amount of cleaning up to do. Assume he had the chair, and he had access to the van, and he had a safe place to take him to work on him. Does that sound like . . . home?"

Osborne's telephone rang. He growled into it.

"What? . . . No, I don't want to talk to the *Tattler* . . . Well, it better not be bullshit. Put her on. . . . Captain Osborne, yes . . . What time? Who answered the phone initially—at the switchboard? Take her off the switchboard, please. Tell me again what he said. . . . I'll have an officer there in five minutes."

Osborne looked at his telephone thoughtfully after he hung up.

"Lounds's secretary got a call about five minutes ago," he said. "She swears it was Lounds's voice. He said something, something she didn't get, '. . . strength of the Great Red Dragon.' That's what she thought he said."

CHAPTER 24

DR. FREDERICK CHILTON stood in the corridor outside Hannibal Lecter's cell. With Chilton were three large orderlies. One carried a straitjacket and leg restraints and another held a can of Mace. The third loaded a tranquilizer dart into his air rifle.

Lecter was reading an actuarial chart at his table and taking notes. He had heard the footsteps coming. He heard the rifle breech close behind him, but he continued to read and gave no sign that he knew Chilton was there.

Chilton had sent him the newspapers at noon and let him wait until night to find out his punishment for helping the Dragon.

"Dr. Lecter," Chilton said.

Lecter turned around. "Good evening, Dr. Chilton." He didn't acknowledge the presence of the guards. He looked only at Chilton.

"I've come for your books. *All* your books."

"I see. May I ask how long you intend to keep them?"

"That depends on your attitude."

"Is this *your* decision?"

"I decide the punitive measures here."

"Of course you do. It's not the sort of thing Will Graham would request."

"Back up to the net and slip these on, Dr. Lecter. I won't ask you twice."

"Certainly, Dr. Chilton. I hope that's a thirty-nine—the thirty-sevens are snug around the chest."

186

Dr. Lecter put on the restraints as though they were dinner clothes. An orderly reached through the barrier and fastened them from the back.

"Help him to his cot," Chilton said.

While the orderlies stripped the bookshelves, Chilton polished his glasses and stirred Lecter's personal papers with a pen.

Lecter watched from the shadowed corner of his cell. There was a curious grace about him, even in restraints.

"Beneath the yellow folder," Lecter said quietly, "you'll find a rejection slip the *Archives* sent you. It was brought to me by mistake with some of my *Archives* mail, and I'm afraid I opened it without looking at the envelope. Sorry."

Chilton reddened. He spoke to an orderly. "I think you'd better take the seat off Dr. Lecter's toilet."

Chilton looked at the actuarial table. Lecter had written his age at the top: forty-one. "And what do you have here?" Chilton asked.

"Time," Dr. Lecter said.

➤

Section Chief Brian Zeller took the courier's case and the wheelchair wheels into Instrumental Analysis, walking at a rate that made his gabardine pants whistle.

The staff, held over from the day shift, knew that whistling sound very well: Zeller in a hurry.

There had been enough delays. The weary courier, his flight from Chicago delayed by weather and then diverted to Philadelphia, had rented a car and driven down to the FBI laboratory in Washington.

The Chicago police laboratory is efficient, but there are things it is not equipped to do. Zeller prepared to do them now.

At the mass spectrometer he dropped off the paint flecks from Lounds's car door.

Beverly Katz in Hair and Fiber got the wheels to share with others in the section.

Zeller's last stop was the small hot room where Liza Lake bent over her gas chromatograph. She was testing ashes from a Florida arson case, watching the stylus trace its spiky line on the moving graph.

"Ace lighter fluid," she said. "That's what he lit it with." She had looked at so many samples that she could distinguish brands without searching through the manual.

Zeller took his eyes off Liza Lake and rebuked himself severely for feeling pleasure in the office. He cleared his throat and held up the two shiny paint cans.

"Chicago?" she said.

Zeller nodded.

She checked the condition of the cans and the seal of the lids. One can contained ashes from the wheelchair; the other, charred material from Lounds.

"How long has it been in the cans?"

"Six hours anyway," Zeller said.

"I'll headspace it."

She pierced the lid with a heavy-duty syringe, extracted air that had been confined with the ashes, and injected the air directly into the gas chromatograph. She made minute adjustments. As the sample moved along the machine's five-hundred-foot column, the stylus jiggled on the wide graph paper.

"Unleaded . . ." she said. "It's gasohol, unleaded gasohol. Don't see much of that." She flipped quickly through a looseleaf file of sample graphs. "I can't give you a brand yet. Let me do it with pentane and I'll get back to you."

"Good," Zeller said. Pentane would dissolve the fluids in the ashes, then fractionate early in the chromatograph, leaving the fluids for fine analysis.

➤

By one A.M. Zeller had all he could get.

Liza Lake succeeded in naming the gasohol: Freddy Lounds was burned with a "Servco Supreme" blend.

Patient brushing in the grooves of the wheelchair treads yielded two kinds of carpet fiber—wool and synthetic. Mold in dirt from the treads indicated the chair had been stored in a cool, dark place.

The other results were less satisfactory. The paint flecks were not original factory paint. Blasted in the mass spectrometer and compared with the national automotive paint file, the paint proved to be high-quality Duco enamel manufactured in a lot of 186,000 gallons during the first quarter of 1978 for sale to several auto-paintshop chains.

Zeller had hoped to pinpoint a make of vehicle and the approximate time of manufacture.

He telexed the results to Chicago.

The Chicago police department wanted its wheels back. The wheels made an awkward package for the courier. Zeller put written lab reports in his pouch along with mail and a package that had come for Graham.

"Federal Express I'm not," the courier said when he was sure Zeller couldn't hear him.

➤

The Justice Department maintains several small apartments near Seventh District Court in Chicago for the use of jurists and favored expert witnesses when court is in session. Graham stayed in one of these, with Crawford across the hall.

He came in at nine P.M., tired and wet. He had not eaten since breakfast on the plane from Washington and the thought of food repelled him.

Rainy Wednesday was over at last. It was as bad a day as he could remember.

With Lounds dead, it seemed likely that he was next and all day Chester had watched his back; while he was in Lounds's garage, while he stood in the rain on the scorched pavement where Lounds was burned. With strobe lights flashing in his face, he told the press he was "grieved at the loss of his friend Frederick Lounds."

He was going to the funeral, too. So were a number of federal agents and police, in the hope that the killer would come to see Graham grieve.

Actually he felt nothing he could name, just cold nausea and an occasional wave of sickly exhilaration that he had not burned to death instead of Lounds.

It seemed to Graham that he had learned nothing in forty years: he had just gotten tired.

He made a big martini and drank it while he undressed. He had another after his shower while he watched the news.

("An FBI trap to catch the Tooth Fairy backfires and a veteran reporter is dead. We'll be back with details on Eyewitness News after this.")

They were referring to the killer as "the Dragon" before the newscast was over. The *Tattler* had spilled it all to the networks. Graham wasn't surprised. Thursday's edition should sell well.

He made a third martini and called Molly.

She had seen the television news at six and ten o'clock and she had seen a *Tattler*. She knew that Graham had been the bait in a trap.

"You should have told me, Will."

"Maybe. I don't think so."

"Will he try to kill you now?"

"Sooner or later. It would be hard for him now, since I'm moving around. I'm covered all the time, Molly, and he knows it. I'll be okay."

"You sound a little slurry, have you been to see your friend in the fridge?"

"I had a couple."

"How do you feel?"

"Fairly rotten."

"The news said the FBI didn't have any protection for the reporter."

"He was supposed to be with Crawford by the time the Tooth Fairy got the paper."

"The news is calling him the Dragon now."

"That's what he calls himself."

"Will, there's something . . . I want to take Willy and leave here."

"And go where?"

"His grandparents'. They haven't seen him in a while, they'd like to see him."

"Oh, um-hmm."

Willy's father's parents had a ranch on the Oregon coast.

"It's creepy here. I know it's supposed to be safe—but we're not sleeping a whole lot. Maybe the shooting lessons spooked me, I don't know."

"I'm sorry, Molly." I wish I could tell you how sorry.

"I'll miss you. We both will."

So she had made up her mind.

"When are you going?"

"In the morning."

"What about the shop?"

"Evelyn wants to take it. I'll underwrite the fall stuff with the wholesalers, just for the interest, and she can keep what she makes."

"The dogs?"

"I asked her to call the county, Will. I'm sorry, but maybe somebody will take some of them."

"Molly, I—"

"If staying here I could keep something bad from happening to you, I'd stay. But you can't save anybody, Will, I'm not helping you here. With us up there, you can just think about taking care of yourself. I'm not carrying this damned pistol the rest of my life, Will."

"Maybe you can get down to Oakland and watch the A's." Didn't mean to say that. Oh boy, this silence is getting pretty long.

"Well, look, I'll call you," she said, "or I guess you'll have to call me up there."

Graham felt something tearing. He felt short of breath.

"Let me get the office to make the arrangements. Have you made a reservation already?"

"I didn't use my name. I thought maybe the newspapers . . ."

"Good. Good. Let me get somebody to see you off. You wouldn't have to board through the gate, and you'd get out of Washington absolutely clean. Can I do that? Let me do that. What time does the plane go?"

"Nine-forty. American 118."

"Okay, eight-thirty . . . behind the Smithsonian. There's a Park-Rite. Leave the car there. Somebody'll meet you. He'll listen to his watch, put it to his ear when he gets out of his car, okay?"

"That's fine."

"Say, do you change at O'Hare? I could come out—"

"No. Change in Minneapolis."

"Oh, Molly. Maybe I could come up there and get you when it's over?"

"That would be very nice."

Very nice.

"Do you have enough money?"

"The bank's wiring me some."

"What?"

"To Barclay's at the airport. Don't worry."

"I'll miss you."

"Me too, but that'll be the same as now. Same distance by phone. Willy says hi."

"Hi to Willy."

"Be careful, darling."

She had never called him darling before. He didn't care for it. He didn't care for new names; darling, Red Dragon.

The night-duty officer in Washington was glad to make the arrangements for Molly. Graham pressed his face to the cool window and watched sheets of rain whip over the muffled traffic below him, the street leaping from gray to sudden color in the lightning flashes. His face left a print of forehead, nose, lips, and chin on the glass.

Molly was gone.

The day was over and there was only the night to face, and the lipless voice accusing him.

Lounds's woman held what was left of his hand until it was over.

"Hello, this is Valerie Leeds. I'm sorry I can't come to the phone right now . . ."

"I'm sorry too," Graham said.

Graham filled his glass again and sat at the table by the window, staring at the empty chair across from him. He stared until the space in the opposite chair assumed a man-shape filled with dark and swarming motes, a presence like a shadow on suspended dust. He tried to make the image coalesce, to see a face. It would not move, had no countenance but, faceless, faced him with palpable attention.

"I know it's tough," Graham said. He was intensely drunk. "You've got to try to stop, just hold off until we find you. If you've got to do something, fuck, come after me. I don't give a shit. It'll be better after that. They've got some things now to help you make it stop. To help you stop *wanting to* so bad. Help me. Help me a little. Molly's gone, old Freddy's dead. It's you and me now, sport." He leaned across the table, his hand extended to touch, and the presence was gone.

Graham put his head down on the table, his cheek on his arm. He could see the print of his forehead, nose, mouth, and chin on the window as the lightning flashed behind it; a face with drops crawling through it down the glass. Eyeless. A face full of rain.

Graham had tried hard to understand the Dragon.

At times, in the breathing silence of the victims' houses, the very spaces the Dragon had moved through tried to speak.

Sometimes Graham felt close to him. A feeling he remembered from other investigations had settled over him in recent days: the taunting sense that he and the Dragon were doing the same things at various times of the day, that there were parallels in the quotidian details of their lives. Somewhere the Dragon was eating, or showering, or sleeping at the same time he did.

Graham tried hard to know him. He tried to see him past the blinding glint of slides and vials, beneath the lines of police reports, tried to see his face through the louvers of print. He tried as hard as he knew how.

But to begin to understand the Dragon, to hear the cold drips in his darkness, to watch the world through his red haze, Graham would have had to see things he could never see, and he would have had to fly through time. . . .

CHAPTER 25

SPRINGFIELD, MISSOURI, June 14, 1938.

Marian Dolarhyde Trevane, tired and in pain, got out of a taxi at City Hospital. Hot wind whipped grit against her ankles as she climbed the steps. The suitcase she lugged was better than her loose wash dress, and so was the mesh evening bag she pressed to her swollen belly. She had two quarters and a dime in her bag. She had Francis Dolarhyde in her belly.

She told the admitting officer her name was Betty Johnson, a lie. She said her husband was a musician, but she did not know his whereabouts, which was true.

They put her in the charity section of the maternity ward. She did not look at the patients on either side of her. She looked across the aisle at the soles of feet.

In four hours she was taken to the delivery room, where Francis Dolarhyde was born. The obstetrician remarked that he looked "more like a leaf-nosed bat than a baby," another truth. He was born with bilateral fissures in his upper lip and in his hard and soft palates. The center section of his mouth was unanchored and protruded. His nose was flat.

The hospital supervisors decided not to show him to his mother immediately. They waited to see if the infant could survive without oxygen. They put him in a bed at the rear of the infant ward and faced

194

him away from the viewing window. He could breathe, but he could not feed. With his palate cleft, he could not suck.

His crying on the first day was not as continuous as that of a heroin-addicted baby, but it was as piercing.

By the afternoon of the second day a thin keening was all he could produce.

When the shifts changed at three P.M., a wide shadow fell across his bed. Prince Easter Mize, 260 pounds, cleaning woman and aide in the maternity ward, stood looking at him, her arms folded on top of her bosom. In twenty-six years in the nursery she had seen about thirty-nine thousand infants. This one would live if he ate.

Prince Easter had received no instructions from the Lord about letting this infant die. She doubted that the hospital had received any either. She took from her pocket a rubber stopper pierced with a curved glass drinking straw. She pushed the stopper into a bottle of milk. She could hold the baby and support his head in one great hand. She held him to her breast until she knew he felt her heartbeat. Then she flipped him over and popped the tube down his throat. He took about two ounces and went to sleep.

"Um-hum," she said. She put him down and went about her assigned duties with the diaper pails.

➤

On the fourth day the nurses moved Marian Dolarhyde Trevane to a private room. Hollyhocks left over from a previous occupant were in an enamel pitcher on the washstand. They had held up pretty well.

Marian was a handsome girl and the puffiness was leaving her face. She looked at the doctor when he started talking to her, his hand on her shoulder. She could smell strong soap on his hand and she thought about the crinkles at the corners of his eyes until she realized what he was saying. Then she closed her eyes and did not open them while they brought the baby in.

Finally she looked. They shut the door when she screamed. Then they gave her a shot.

On the fifth day she left the hospital alone. She didn't know where to go. She could never go home again; her mother had made that clear.

Marian Dolarhyde Trevane counted the steps between the light poles. Each time she passed three poles, she sat on the suitcase to rest. At least she had the suitcase. In every town there was a pawn shop near the bus station. She had learned that traveling with her husband.

➤

Springfield in 1938 was not a center for plastic surgery. In Springfield, you wore your face as it was.

A surgeon at City Hospital did the best he could for Francis Dolarhyde, first retracting the front section of his mouth with an elastic band, then closing the clefts in his lip by a rectangular flap technique that is now outmoded. The cosmetic results were not good.

The surgeon had troubled to read up on the problem and decided, correctly, that repair of the infant's hard palate should wait until he was five. To operate sooner would distort the growth of his face.

A local dentist volunteered to make an obturator, which plugged the baby's palate and permitted him to feed without flooding his nose.

The infant went to the Springfield Foundling Home for a year and a half and then to Morgan Lee Memorial Orphanage.

Reverend S. B. "Buddy" Lomax was head of the orphanage. Brother Buddy called the other boys and girls together and told them that Francis was a harelip but they must be careful never to call him a harelip.

Brother Buddy suggested they pray for him.

➤

Francis Dolarhyde's mother learned to take care of herself in the years following his birth.

Marian Dolarhyde first found a job typing in the office of a ward boss in the St. Louis Democratic machine. With his help she had her marriage to the absent Mr. Trevane annulled.

There was no mention of a child in the annulment proceedings.

She had nothing to do with her mother. ("I didn't raise you to slut for that Irish trash" were Mrs. Dolarhyde's parting words to Marian when she left home with Trevane.)

Marian's ex-husband called her once at the office. Sober and pious, he told her he had been saved and wanted to know if he, Marian, and the child he "never had the joy of knowing" might make a new life together. He sounded broke.

Marian told him the child was born dead and she hung up.

He showed up drunk at her boardinghouse with his suitcase. When she told him to go away, he observed that it was her fault the marriage failed and the child was stillborn. He expressed doubt that the child was his.

In a rage Marian Dolarhyde told Michael Trevane exactly what he had fathered and told him he was welcome to it. She reminded him that there were two cleft palates in the Trevane family.

She put him in the street and told him never to call her again. He didn't. But years later, drunk and brooding over Marian's rich new husband and her fine life, he did call Marian's mother.

He told Mrs. Dolarhyde about the deformed child and said her snag teeth proved the hereditary fault lay with the Dolarhydes.

A week later a Kansas City streetcar cut Michael Trevane in two.

When Trevane told Mrs. Dolarhyde that Marian had a hidden son, she sat up most of the night. Tall and lean in her rocker, Grandmother Dolarhyde stared into the fire. Toward dawn she began a slow and purposeful rocking.

Somewhere upstairs in the big house, a cracked voice called out of sleep. The floor above Grandmother Dolarhyde creaked as someone shuffled toward the bathroom.

A heavy thump on the ceiling—someone falling—and the cracked voice called in pain.

Grandmother Dolarhyde never took her eyes off the fire. She rocked faster and, in time, the calling stopped.

➤

Near the end of his fifth year, Francis Dolarhyde had his first and only visitor at the orphanage.

He was sitting in the thick reek of the cafeteria when an older boy came for him and took him to Brother Buddy's office.

The lady waiting with Brother Buddy was tall and middle-aged, dredged in powder, her hair in a tight bun. Her face was stark white. There were touches of yellow in the gray hair and in the eyes and teeth.

What struck Francis, what he would always remember: she smiled with pleasure when she saw his face. That had never happened before. No one would ever do it again.

"This is your grandmother," Brother Buddy said.

"Hello," she said.

Brother Buddy wiped his own mouth with a long hand. "Say 'hello.' Go ahead."

Francis had learned to say some things by occluding his nostrils with his upper lip, but he did not have much occasion for "hello." "Lhho" was the best he could do.

Grandmother seemed even more pleased with him. "Can you say 'grandmother'?"

"Try to say 'grandmother,'" Brother Buddy said.

The plosive G defeated him. Francis strangled easily on tears.

A red wasp buzzed and tapped against the ceiling.

"Never mind," his grandmother said. "I'll just bet you can say your name. I just know a big boy like you can say his name. Say it for me."

The child's face brightened. The big boys had helped him with this. He wanted to please. He collected himself.

"Cunt Face," he said.

➤

Three days later Grandmother Dolarhyde called for Francis at the orphanage and took him home with her. She began at once to help him with his speech. They concentrated on a single word. It was "Mother."

➤

Within two years of the annulment, Marian Dolarhyde met and married Howard Vogt, a successful lawyer with solid connections to the St. Louis machine and what was left of the old Pendergast machine in Kansas City.

Vogt was a widower with three young children, an affable ambitious man fifteen years older than Marian Dolarhyde. He hated nothing in the world except the St. Louis *Post-Dispatch*, which had singed his feathers in the voter-registration scandal of 1936 and blasted the attempt in 1940 by the St. Louis machine to steal the governorship.

By 1943 Vogt's star was rising again. He was a brewery candidate for the state legislature and was mentioned as a possible delegate to the upcoming state constitutional convention.

Marian was a useful and attractive hostess and Vogt bought her a handsome, half-timbered house on Olive Street that was perfect for entertaining.

Francis Dolarhyde had lived with his grandmother for a week when she took him there.

Grandmother had never seen her daughter's house. The maid who answered the door did not know her.

"I'm Mrs. Dolarhyde," she said, barging past the servant. Her slip was showing three inches in the back. She led Francis into a big living room with a pleasant fire.

"Who is it, Viola?" A woman's voice from upstairs.

Grandmother cupped Francis' face in her hand. He could smell the cold leather glove. An urgent whisper. "Go see Mother, Francis. Go see Mother. Run!"

He shrank from her, twisting on the tines of her eyes.

"Go see Mother. Run!" She gripped his shoulders and marched him toward the stairs. He trotted up to the landing and looked back down at her. She motioned upward with her chin.

Up to the strange hallway toward the open bedroom door.

Mother was seated at her dressing table checking her makeup in a mirror framed with lights. She was getting ready for a political rally, and too much rouge wouldn't do. Her back was to the door.

"Muhner," Francis piped, as he had been taught. He tried hard to get it right. "Muhner."

She saw him in the mirror then. "If you're looking for Ned, he isn't home from . . ."

"Muhner." He came into the heartless light.

Marian heard her mother's voice downstairs demanding tea. Her eyes widened and she sat very still. She did not turn around. She turned out the makeup lights and vanished from the mirror. In the darkened room she gave a single low keening that ended in a sob. It might have been for herself, or it might have been for him.

➤

Grandmother took Francis to all the political rallies after that and explained who he was and where he came from. She had him say hello to everyone. They did not work on "hello" at home.

Mr. Vogt lost the election by eighteen hundred votes.

CHAPTER 26

AT GRANDMOTHER'S HOUSE, Francis Dolarhyde's new world was a forest of blue-veined legs.

Grandmother Dolarhyde had been running her nursing home for three years when he came to live with her. Money had been a problem since her husband's death in 1936; she had been brought up a lady and she had no marketable skills.

What she had was a big house and her late husband's debts. Taking in boarders was out. The place was too isolated to be a successful boardinghouse. She was threatened with eviction.

The announcement in the newspaper of Marian's marriage to the affluent Mr. Howard Vogt had seemed a godsend to Grandmother. She wrote to Marian repeatedly for help, but received no answer. Every time she telephoned, a servant told her Mrs. Vogt was out.

Finally, bitterly, Grandmother Dolarhyde made an arrangement with the county and began to take in elderly indigent persons. For each one she received a sum from the county and erratic payments from such relatives as the county could locate. It was hard until she began to get some private patients from middle-class families.

No help from Marian all this time—and Marian could have helped.

Now Francis Dolarhyde played on the floor in the forest of legs. He played cars with Grandmother's Mah-Jongg pieces, pushing them among feet twisted like gnarled roots.

Mrs. Dolarhyde could keep clean wash dresses on her residents, but she despaired at trying to make them keep on their shoes.

The old people sat all day in the living room listening to the radio. Mrs. Dolarhyde had put in a small aquarium for them to watch as well, and a private contributor had helped her cover her parquet floors with linoleum against the inevitable incontinence.

They sat in a row on the couches and in wheelchairs listening to the radio, their faded eyes fixed on the fish or on nothing or something they saw long ago.

Francis would always remember the shuffle of feet on linoleum in the hot and buzzing day, and the smell of stewed tomatoes and cabbage from the kitchen, the smell of the old people like meat wrappers dried in the sun, and always the radio.

Rinso white, Rinso bright
Happy little washday song.

Francis spent as much time as he could in the kitchen, because his friend was there. The cook, Queen Mother Bailey, had grown up in the service of the late Mr. Dolarhyde's family. She sometimes brought Francis a plum in her apron pocket, and she called him "Little Possum, always dreamin'." The kitchen was warm and safe. But Queen Mother Bailey went home at night. . . .

➤

December 1943.
Francis Dolarhyde, five years old, lay in bed in his upstairs room in Grandmother's house. The room was pitch dark with its blackout curtains against the Japanese. He could not say "Japanese." He needed to pee. He was afraid to get up in the dark.

He called to his grandmother in bed downstairs.

"Aayma. Aayma." He sounded like an infant goat. He called until he was tired. "Mleedse Aayma."

It got away from him then, hot on his legs and under his seat, and then cold, his nightdress sticking to him. He didn't know what to do. He took a deep breath and rolled over to face the door. Nothing happened to him. He put his foot on the floor. He stood up in the dark, nightdress plastered to his legs, face burning. He ran for the door. The doorknob caught him over the eye and he sat down in wetness, jumped up and ran down the stairs, fingers squealing on the banister. To his grandmother's room. Crawling across her in the dark and under the covers, warm against her now.

Grandmother stirred, tensed, her back hardened against his cheek, voice hissing. "I've never sheen . . ." A clatter on the bedside table as she found her teeth, clacket as she put them in. "I've never seen a child as disgusting and dirty as you. Get *out*, get out of this bed."

She turned on the bedside lamp. He stood on the carpet shivering. She wiped her thumb across his eyebrow. Her thumb came away bloody.

"Did you break something?"

He shook his head so fast droplets of blood fell on Grandmother's nightgown.

"Upstairs. Go on."

The dark came down over him as he climbed the stairs. He couldn't turn on the lights because Grandmother had cut the cords off short so only she could reach them. He did not want to get back in the wet bed. He stood in the dark holding on to the footboard for a long time. He thought she wasn't coming. The blackest corners in the room knew she wasn't coming.

She came, snatching the short cord on the ceiling light, her arms full of sheets. She did not speak to him as she changed the bed.

She gripped his upper arm and pulled him down the hall to the bathroom. The light was over the mirror and she had to stand on tiptoe to reach it. She gave him a washcloth, wet and cold.

"Take off your nightshirt and wipe yourself off."

Smell of adhesive tape and the bright sewing scissors clicking. She snipped out a butterfly of tape, stood him on the toilet lid and closed the cut over his eye.

"Now," she said. She held the sewing scissors under his round belly and he felt cold down there.

"Look," she said. She grabbed the back of his head and bent him over to see his little penis lying across the bottom blade of the open scissors. She closed the scissors until they began to pinch him.

"Do you want me to cut it off?"

He tried to look up at her, but she gripped his head. He sobbed and spit fell on his stomach.

"*Do* you?"

"No, Aayma. No, Aayma."

"I pledge you my word, if you ever make your bed dirty again I'll cut it off. Do you understand?"

"Yehn, Aayma."

"You can find the toilet in the dark and you can sit on it like a good boy. You don't have to stand up. Now go back to bed."

➤

At two A.M. the wind rose, gusting warm out of the southeast, clacking together the branches of the dead apple trees, rustling the leaves of the live ones. The wind drove warm rain against the side of the house where Francis Dolarhyde, forty-two years old, lay sleeping.

He lay on his side sucking his thumb, his hair damp and flat on his forehead and his neck.

Now he awakes. He listens to his breathing in the dark and the tiny clicks of his blinking eyes. His fingers smell faintly of gasoline. His bladder is full.

He feels on the bedside table for the glass containing his teeth.

Dolarhyde always puts in his teeth before he rises. Now he walks to the bathroom. He does not turn on the light. He finds the toilet in the dark and sits down on it like a good boy.

CHAPTER 27

THE CHANGE in Grandmother first became apparent in the winter of 1947, when Francis was eight.

She stopped taking meals in her room with Francis. They moved to the common table in the dining room, where she presided over meals with the elderly residents.

Grandmother had been trained as a girl to be a charming hostess, and now she unpacked and polished her silver bell and put it beside her plate.

Keeping a luncheon table going, pacing the service, managing conversation, batting easy conversational lobs to the strong points of the shy ones, turning the best facets of the bright ones in the light of the other guests' attention is a considerable skill and one now sadly in decline.

Grandmother had been good at it in her time. Her efforts at this table did brighten meals initially for the two or three among the residents who were capable of linear conversation.

Francis sat in the host's chair at the other end of the avenue of nodding heads as Grandmother drew out the recollections of those who could remember. She expressed keen interest in Mrs. Floder's honeymoon trip to Kansas City, went through the yellow fever with Mr. Eaton a number of times, and listened brightly to the random unintelligible sounds of the others.

"Isn't that interesting, Francis?" she said, and rang the bell for the next course. The food was a variety of vegetable and meat mushes, but she divided it into courses, greatly inconveniencing the kitchen help.

Mishaps at the table were never mentioned. A ring of the bell and a gesture in mid-sentence took care of those who had spilled or gone to sleep or forgotten why they were at the table. Grandmother always kept as large a staff as she could pay.

As Grandmother's general health declined, she lost weight and was able to wear dresses that had long been packed away. Some of them were elegant. In the cast of her features and her hairstyle, she bore a marked resemblance to George Washington on the dollar bill.

Her manners had slipped somewhat by spring. She ruled the table and permitted no interruptions as she told of her girlhood in St. Charles, even revealing personal matters to inspire and edify Francis and the others.

It was true that Grandmother had enjoyed a season as a belle in 1907 and was invited to some of the better balls across the river in St. Louis.

There was an "object lesson" in this for everyone, she said. She looked pointedly at Francis, who crossed his legs beneath the table.

"I came up at a time when little could be done medically to overcome the little accidents of nature," she said. "I had lovely skin and hair and I took full advantage of them. I overcame my teeth with force of personality and bright spirits—so successfully, in fact, that they became my 'beauty spot.' I think you might even call them my 'charming trademark.' I wouldn't have traded them for the world."

She distrusted doctors, she explained at length, but when it became clear that gum problems would cost her her teeth, she sought out one of the most renowned dentists in the Midwest, Dr. Felix Bertl, a Swiss. Dr. Bertl's "Swiss teeth" were very popular with a certain class of people, Grandmother said, and he had a remarkable practice.

Opera singers fearing that new shapes in their mouths would affect their tone, actors and others in public life came from as far away as San Francisco to be fitted.

Dr. Bertl could reproduce a patient's natural teeth exactly and had experimented with various compounds and their effect on resonance.

When Dr. Bertl had completed her dentures, her teeth appeared just as they had before. She overcame them with personality and lost none of her unique charm, she said with a spiky smile.

If there was an object lesson in all this, Francis did not appreciate it until later; there would be no further surgery for him until he could pay for it himself.

Francis could make it through dinner because there was something he looked forward to afterward.

Queen Mother Bailey's husband came for her each evening in the mule-drawn wagon he used to haul firewood. If Grandmother was occupied upstairs, Francis could ride with them down the lane to the main road.

He waited all day for the evening ride: sitting on the wagon seat beside Queen Mother, her tall flat husband silent and almost invisible in the dark, the iron tires of the wagon loud in the gravel behind the jingle of the bits. Two mules, brown and sometimes muddy, their cropped manes standing up like brushes, swishing their tails across their rumps. The smell of sweat and boiled cotton cloth, snuff and warm harness. There was the smell of woodsmoke when Mr. Bailey had been clearing new ground and sometimes, when he took his shotgun to the new ground, a couple of rabbits or squirrels lay in the wagon box, stretched long as though they were running.

They did not talk on the ride down the lane; Mr. Bailey spoke only to the mules. The wagon motion bumped the boy pleasantly against the Baileys. Dropped off at the end of the lane, he gave his nightly promise to walk straight back to the house and watched the lantern on the wagon move away. He could hear them talking down the road. Sometimes Queen Mother made her husband laugh and she laughed with him. Standing in the dark, it was pleasant to hear them and know they were not laughing at him.

Later he would change his mind about that. . . .

➤

Francis Dolarhyde's occasional playmate was the daughter of a sharecropper who lived three fields away. Grandmother let her come to play because it amused her now and then to dress the child in the clothing Marian had worn when she was small.

She was a red-haired listless child and she was too tired to play much of the time.

One hot June afternoon, bored with fishing for doodlebugs in the chicken yard with straws, she asked to see Francis' private parts.

In a corner between the chicken house and a low hedge that shielded them from the lower windows of the house, he showed her. She reciprocated by showing him her own, standing with her pilled cotton underwear around her ankles. As he squatted on his heels to see, a headless chicken flapped around the corner, traveling on its back, flapping up the dust. The hobbled girl hopped backward as it spattered blood on her feet and legs.

Francis jumped to his feet, his trousers still down, as Queen Mother Bailey came around the corner after the chicken and saw them.

"Look here, boy," she said calmly, "you want to see what's what, well now you see, so go on and find yourselves something else to do. Occupy yourself with children's doings and keep your clothes on. You and that child help me catch that rooster."

The children's embarrassment quickly passed as the rooster eluded them. But Grandmother was watching from the upstairs window. . . .

➤

Grandmother watched Queen Mother come back inside. The children went into the chicken house. Grandmother waited five minutes, then came up on them silently. She flung open the door and found them gathering feathers for headdresses.

She sent the girl home and led Francis into the house.

She told him he was going back to Brother Buddy's orphanage after she had punished him. "Go upstairs. Go to your room and take your trousers off and wait for me while I get my scissors."

He waited for hours in his room, lying on the bed with his trousers off, clutching the bedspread and waiting for the scissors. He waited through the sounds of supper downstairs and he heard the creak and clop of the firewood wagon and the snort of the mules as Queen Mother's husband came for her.

Sometime toward morning he slept, and woke in starts to wait.

Grandmother never came. Perhaps she had forgotten.

He waited through the routine of the days that followed, remembering many times a day in a rush of freezing dread. He would never cease from waiting.

He avoided Queen Mother Bailey, would not speak to her and wouldn't tell her why: he mistakenly believed that she had told

Grandmother what she saw in the chicken yard. Now he was convinced that the laughter he heard while he watched the wagon lantern diminish down the road was about him. Clearly he could trust no one.

➤

It was hard to lie still and go to sleep when it was there to think about. It was hard to lie still on such a bright night.

Francis knew that Grandmother was right. He had hurt her so. He had shamed her. Everyone must know what he had done—even as far away as St. Charles. He was not angry at Grandmother. He was not angry at Grandmother. He knew that he Loved her very much. He wanted to do right.

He imagined that burglars were breaking in and he protected Grandmother and she took back what she said. "You're not a Child of the Devil after all, Francis. You are my good boy."

He thought about a burglar breaking in. Coming in the house determined to show Grandmother his private parts.

How would Francis protect her? He was too small to fight a big burglar.

He thought about it. There was Queen Mother's hatchet in the pantry. She wiped it with newspaper after she killed a chicken. He should see about the hatchet. It was his responsibility. He would fight his fear of the dark. If he really Loved Grandmother, he should be the thing to be afraid of in the dark. The thing for the *burglar* to be afraid of.

He crept downstairs and found the hatchet hanging on its nail. It had a strange smell, like the smell at the sink when they were drawing a chicken. It was sharp and its weight was reassuring in his hand.

He carried the hatchet to Grandmother's room to be sure there were no burglars.

Grandmother was asleep. It was very dark but he knew exactly where she was. If there was a burglar, he would hear him breathing just as he could hear Grandmother breathing. He would know where his neck was just as surely as he knew where Grandmother's neck was. It was just below the breathing.

If there was a burglar, he would come up on him quietly like this. He would raise the hatchet over his head with both hands like this.

Francis stepped on Grandmother's slipper beside the bed. The hatchet swayed in the dizzy dark and pinged against the metal shade of her reading lamp.

Grandmother rolled over and made a wet noise with her mouth. Francis stood still. His arms trembled from the effort of holding up the hatchet. Grandmother began to snore.

The Love Francis felt almost burst him. He crept out of the room. He was frantic to be ready to protect her. He must do something. He did not fear the dark house now, but it was choking him.

He went out the back door and stood in the brilliant night, face upturned, gasping as though he could breathe the light. A tiny disk of moon, distorted on the whites of his rolled-back eyes, rounded as the eyes rolled down and was centered at last in his pupils.

The Love swelled in him unbearably tight and he could not gasp it out. He walked toward the chicken house, hurrying now, the ground cold under his feet, the hatchet bumping cold against his leg, running now before he burst. . . .

➤

Francis, scrubbing himself at the chicken-yard pump, had never felt such sweet and easy peace. He felt his way cautiously into it and found that the peace was endless and all around him.

What Grandmother kindly had not cut off was still there like a prize when he washed the blood off his belly and legs. His mind was clear and calm.

He should do something about the nightshirt. Better hide it under the sacks in the smokehouse.

➤

Discovery of the dead chicken puzzled Grandmother. She said it didn't look like a fox job.

A month later Queen Mother found another one when she went to gather eggs. This time the head had been wrung off.

Grandmother said at the dinner table that she was convinced it was done for spite by some "sorry help I ran off." She said she had called the sheriff about it.

Francis sat silent at his place, opening and closing his hand on the memory of an eye blinking against his palm. Sometimes in bed he held himself to be sure he hadn't been cut. Sometimes when he held himself he thought he felt a blink.

➤

Grandmother was changing rapidly. She was increasingly contentious and could not keep household help. Though she was short of housekeepers, it was the kitchen where she took personal charge, directing Queen Mother Bailey to the detriment of the food. Queen Mother, who had worked for the Dolarhydes all her life, was the only constant on the staff.

Red-faced in the kitchen heat, Grandmother moved restlessly from one task to the next, often leaving dishes half-made, never to be served. She made casseroles of leftovers while vegetables wilted in the pantry.

At the same time, she became fanatical about waste. She reduced the soap and bleach in the wash until the sheets were dingy gray.

In the month of November she hired five different black women to help in the house. They would not stay.

Grandmother was furious the evening the last one left. She went through the house yelling. She came into the kitchen and saw that Queen Mother Bailey had left a teaspoonful of flour on the board after rolling out some dough.

In the steam and heat of the kitchen a half-hour before dinner she walked up to Queen Mother and slapped her face.

Queen Mother dropped her ladle, shocked. Tears sprang into her eyes. Grandmother drew back her hand again. A big pink palm pushed her away.

"Don't you *ever* do that. You're not yourself, Mrs. Dolarhyde, but don't you *ever* do that."

Screaming insults, Grandmother with her bare hand shoved over a kettle of soup to slop and hiss down through the stove. She went to her room and slammed the door. Francis heard her cursing in her room and objects thrown against the walls. She didn't come out again all evening.

Queen Mother cleaned up the soup and fed the old people. She got her few things together in a basket and put on her old sweater and stocking cap. She looked for Francis but couldn't find him.

She was in the wagon when she saw the boy sitting in the corner of the porch. He watched her climb down heavily and come back to him.

"Possum, I'm going now. I won't be back here. Sironia at the feed store, she'll call your mama for me. You need me before your mama get here, you come to my house."

He twisted away from the touch on his cheek.

Mr. Bailey clucked to the mules. Francis watched the wagon lantern move away. He had watched it before, with a sad and empty feeling since he understood that Queen Mother betrayed him. Now he didn't care. He was glad. A feeble kerosene wagon light fading down the road. It was nothing to the moon.

He wondered how it feels to kill a mule.

➤

Marian Dolarhyde Vogt did not come when Queen Mother Bailey called her.

She came two weeks later after a call from the sheriff in St. Charles. She arrived in midafternoon, driving herself in a prewar Packard. She wore gloves and a hat.

A deputy sheriff met her at the end of the lane and stooped to the car window.

"Mrs. Vogt, your mother called our office around noon, saying something about the help stealing. When I come out here, you'll excuse me but she was talking out of her head and it looked like things wasn't tended to. Sheriff thought he ought to get ahold of y'all first, if you understand me. Mr. Vogt being before the public and all."

Marian understood him. Mr. Vogt was commissioner of public works in St. Louis now and was not in the party's best graces.

"To my knowledge, nobody else has saw the place," the deputy said.

Marian found her mother asleep. Two of the old people were still sitting at the table waiting for lunch. One woman was out in the backyard in her slip.

Marian telephoned her husband. "How often do they inspect these places? . . . They must not have seen anything. . . . I don't *know* if any relatives have complained, I don't think these people have any relatives. . . . No. You stay away. I need some Negroes. Get me some Negroes . . . and Dr. Waters. I'll take care of it."

The doctor with an orderly in white arrived in forty-five minutes, followed by a panel truck bringing Marian's maid and five other domestics.

Marian, the doctor, and the orderly were in Grandmother's room when Francis came home from school. Francis could hear his grandmother cursing. When they rolled her out in one of the nursing-home wheelchairs, she was glassy-eyed and a piece of cotton was taped to her arm. Her face looked sunken and strange without her teeth. Marian's arm was bandaged too; she had been bitten.

Grandmother rode away in the doctor's car, sitting in the backseat with the orderly. Francis watched her go. He started to wave, but let his hand fall back to his side.

Marian's cleaning crew scrubbed and aired the house, did a tremendous wash, and bathed the old people. Marian worked alongside them and supervised a sketchy meal.

She spoke to Francis only to ask where things were.

Then she sent the crew away and called the county authorities. Mrs. Dolarhyde had suffered a stroke, she explained.

It was dark when the welfare workers came for the patients in a school bus. Francis thought they would take him too. He was not discussed.

Only Marian and Francis remained at the house. She sat at the dining-room table with her head in her hands. He went outside and climbed a crabapple tree.

Finally Marian called him. She had packed a small suitcase with his clothes.

"You'll have to come with me," she said, walking to the car. "Get in. Don't put your feet on the seat."

They drove away in the Packard and left the empty wheelchair standing in the yard.

There was no scandal. The county authorities said it was sure a shame about Mrs. Dolarhyde, she sure kept things nice. The Vogts remained untarnished.

Grandmother was confined to a private nerve sanatorium. It would be fourteen years before Francis went home to her again.

➤

"Francis, here are your stepsisters and stepbrother," his mother said. They were in the Vogts' library.

Ned Vogt was twelve, Victoria thirteen, and Margaret nine. Ned and Victoria looked at each other. Margaret looked at the floor.

Francis was given a room at the top of the servants' stairs. Since the disastrous election of 1944 the Vogts no longer employed an upstairs maid.

He was enrolled in Potter Gerard Elementary School, within walking distance of the house and far from the Episcopal private school the other children attended.

The Vogt children ignored him as much as possible during the first few days, but at the end of the first week Ned and Victoria came up the servants' stairs to call.

Francis heard them whispering for minutes before the knob turned on his door. When they found it bolted, they didn't knock. Ned said, "Open this door."

Francis opened it. They did not speak to him again while they looked through his clothes in the wardrobe. Ned Vogt opened the drawer in the small dressing table and picked up the things he found with two fingers: birthday handkerchiefs with F.D. embroidered on them, a capo for a guitar, a bright beetle in a pill bottle, a copy of *Baseball Joe in the World Series* which had once been wet, and a get-well card signed "Your classmate, Sarah Hughes."

"What's this?" Ned asked.

"A capo."

"What's it for?"

"A guitar."

"Do you have a guitar?"

"No."

"What do you have it for?" Victoria asked.

"My father used it."

"I can't understand you. What did you say? Make him say it again, Ned."

"He said it belonged to his father." Ned blew his nose on one of the handkerchiefs and dropped it back in the drawer.

"They came for the ponies today," Victoria said. She sat on the narrow bed. Ned joined her, his back against the wall, his feet on the quilt.

"No more ponies," Ned said. "No more lake house for the

summer. Do you know why? Speak up, you little bastard."

"Father is sick a lot and doesn't make as much money," Victoria said. "Some days he doesn't go to the office at all."

"Know why he's sick, you little bastard?" Ned asked. "Talk where I can understand you."

"Grandmother said he's a drunk. Understand that all right?"

"He's sick because of your ugly face," Ned said.

"That's why people didn't vote for him, too," Victoria said.

"Get out," Francis said. When he turned to open the door, Ned kicked him in the back. Francis tried to reach his kidney with both hands, which saved his fingers as Ned kicked him in the stomach.

"Oh, Ned," Victoria said. "Oh, Ned."

Ned grabbed Francis by the ears and held him close to the mirror over the dressing table.

"That's why he's sick!" Ned slammed his face into the mirror. "That's why he's sick!" Slam. "That's why he's sick!" Slam. The mirror was smeared with blood and mucus. Ned let him go and he sat on the floor. Victoria looked at him, her eyes wide, holding her lower lip between her teeth. They left him there. His face was wet with blood and spit. His eyes watered from the pain, but he did not cry.

CHAPTER 28

RAIN IN CHICAGO drums through the night on the canopy over the open grave of Freddy Lounds.

Thunder jars Will Graham's pounding head as he weaves from the table to a bed where dreams coil beneath the pillow.

The old house above St. Charles, shouldering the wind, repeats its long sigh over the hiss of rain against the windows and the bump of thunder.

The stairs are creaking in the dark. Mr. Dolarhyde is coming down them, his kimono whispering over the treads, his eyes wide with recent sleep.

His hair is wet and neatly combed. He has brushed his nails. He moves smoothly and slowly, carrying his concentration like a brimming cup.

Film beside his projector. Two subjects. Other reels are piled in the wastebasket for burning. Two left, chosen from the dozens of home movies he has copied at the plant and brought home to audition.

Comfortable in his reclining chair with a tray of cheese and fruit beside him, Dolarhyde settles in to watch.

The first film is a picnic from the Fourth of July weekend. A handsome family; three children, the father bull-necked, dipping into the pickle jar with his thick fingers. And the mother.

The best view of her is in the softball game with the neighbors' children. Only about fifteen seconds of her; she takes a lead off second base, faces the pitcher and the plate, feet apart ready to dash either way, her breasts swaying beneath her pullover as she leans forward from the waist. An annoying interruption as a child swings a bat. The woman again, walking back to tag up. She puts one foot on the boat cushion they use for a base and stands hip-shot, the thigh muscle tightening in her locked leg.

Over and over Dolarhyde watches the frames of the woman. Foot on the base, pelvis tilts, thigh muscle tightens under the cutoff jeans.

He freezes the last frame. The woman and her children. They are dirty and tired. They hug, and a dog wags among their legs.

A terrific crash of thunder clinks the cut crystal in Grandmother's tall cabinet. Dolarhyde reaches for a pear.

The second film is in several segments. The title, *The New House*, is spelled out in pennies on a shirt cardboard above a broken piggy bank. It opens with Father pulling up the "For Sale" sign in the yard. He holds it up and faces the camera with an embarrassed grin. His pockets are turned out.

An unsteady long shot of Mother and three children on the front steps. It is a handsome house. A cut to the swimming pool. A child, sleek-headed and small, pads around to the diving board, leaving wet footprints on the tile. Heads bob in the water. A small dog paddles toward a daughter, his ears back, chin high, and the whites of his eyes showing.

Mother in the water holds to the ladder and looks up at the camera. Her curly black hair has the gloss of pelt, her bosom swelling shining wet above her suit, her legs wavy below the surface, scissoring.

Night. A badly exposed shot across the pool to the lighted house, the lights reflected in the water.

Indoors and family fun. Boxes everywhere, and packing materials. An old trunk, not yet stored in the attic.

A small daughter is trying on Grandmother's clothes. She has on a big garden-party hat. Father is on the sofa. He looks a little drunk. Now Father must have the camera. It is not quite level. Mother is at the mirror in the hat.

The children jostle around her, the boys laughing and plucking at the old finery. The girl watches her mother coolly, appraising herself in time to come.

A close-up. Mother turns and strikes a pose for the camera with an arch smile, her hand at the back of her neck. She is quite lovely. There is a cameo at her throat.

Dolarhyde freezes the frame. He backs up the film. Again and again she turns from the mirror and smiles.

Absently Dolarhyde picks up the film of the softball game and drops it in the wastebasket.

He takes the reel from the projector and looks at the Gateway label on the box: *Bob Sherman, Star Route 7, Box 603, Tulsa, Okla.*

An easy drive, too.

Dolarhyde holds the film in his palm and covers it with his other hand as though it were a small living thing that might struggle to escape. It seems to jump against his palm like a cricket.

He remembers the jerkiness, the haste at the Leeds house when the lights came on. He had to deal with Mr. Leeds before turning on his movie lights.

This time he wants a smoother progression. It would be wonderful to crawl in between the sleepers with the camera going and snuggle up a little while. Then he could strike in the dark and sit up between them happily getting wet.

He can do that with infrared film, and he knows where to get some.

The projector is still on. Dolarhyde sits holding the film between his hands while on the bright blank screen other images move for him to the long sigh of the wind.

There is no sense of vengeance in him, only Love and thoughts of the Glory to come; hearts becoming faint and fast, like footsteps fleeing into silence.

Him rampant. Him rampant, filled with Love, the Shermans opening to him.

The past does not occur to him at all; only the Glory to come. He does not think of his mother's house. In fact, his conscious memories of that time are remarkably few and indistinct.

Sometime in his twenties Dolarhyde's memories of his mother's house sank out of sight, leaving a slick on the surface of his mind.

He knew that he had lived there only a month. He did not recall that he was sent away at the age of nine for hanging Victoria's cat.

One of the few images he retained was the house itself, lighted, viewed from the street in winter twilight as he passed it going from

Potter Gerard Elementary School to the house where he was boarded a mile away.

He could remember the smell of the Vogt library, like a piano just opened, when his mother received him there to give him holiday things. He did not remember the faces at the upstairs windows as he walked away, down the frozen sidewalk, the practical gifts burning hateful under his arm; hurrying home to a place inside his head that was quite different from St. Louis.

At the age of eleven his fantasy life was active and intense and when the pressure of his Love grew too great, he relieved it. He preyed on pets, carefully, with a cool eye to consequence. They were so tame that it was easy. The authorities never linked him with the sad little bloodstains soaked into the dirt floors of garages.

At forty-two he did not remember that. Nor did he ever think about the people in his mother's house—his mother, stepsisters, or stepbrother.

Sometimes he saw them in his sleep, in the brilliant fragments of a fever dream; altered and tall, faces and bodies in bright parrot colors, they poised over him in a mantis stance.

When he chose to reflect, which was seldom, he had many satisfactory memories. They were of his military service.

Caught at seventeen entering the window of a woman's house for a purpose never established, he was given the choice of enlisting in the Army or facing criminal charges. He took the Army.

After basic training he was sent to specialist school in darkroom operation and shipped to San Antonio, where he worked on medical-corps training films at Brooke Army Hospital.

Surgeons at Brooke took an interest in him and decided to improve his face.

They performed a Z-plasty on his nose, using ear cartilage to lengthen the columella, and repaired his lip with an interesting Abbé flap procedure that drew an audience of doctors to the operating theater.

The surgeons were proud of the result. Dolarhyde declined the mirror and looked out the window.

Records at the film library show Dolarhyde checked out many films, mainly on trauma, and kept them overnight.

He reenlisted in 1958 and in his second hitch he found Hong Kong. Stationed at Seoul, Korea, developing film from the tiny spotter planes the Army floated over the thirty-eighth parallel in the late 1950's, he was able to go to Hong Kong twice on leave. Hong Kong and Kowloon could satisfy any appetite in 1959.

➤

Grandmother was released from the sanatorium in 1961 in a vague Thorazine peace. Dolarhyde asked for and received a hardship discharge two months before his scheduled separation date and went home to take care of her.

It was a curiously peaceful time for him as well. With his new job at Gateway, Dolarhyde could hire a woman to stay with Grandmother in the daytime. At night they sat in the parlor together, not speaking. The tick of the old clock and its chimes were all that broke the silence.

He saw his mother once, at Grandmother's funeral in 1970. He looked through her, past her, with his yellow eyes so startlingly like her own. She might have been a stranger.

His appearance surprised his mother. He was deep-chested and sleek, with her fine coloring and a neat mustache which she suspected was hair transplanted from his head.

She called him once in the next week and heard the receiver slowly replaced.

➤

For nine years after Grandmother's death Dolarhyde was untroubled and he troubled no one. His forehead was as smooth as a seed. He knew that he was waiting. For what, he didn't know.

One small event, which occurs to everyone, told the seed in his skull it was Time: standing by a north window, examining some film, he noticed aging in his hands. It was as though his hands, holding the film, had suddenly appeared before him and he saw in that good north light that the skin had slackened over the bones and tendons and his hands were creased in diamonds as small as lizard scales.

As he turned them in the light, an intense odor of cabbage and stewed tomatoes washed over him. He shivered though the room was warm. That evening he worked out harder than usual.

A full-length mirror was mounted on the wall of Dolarhyde's attic gym beside his barbells and weight bench. It was the only mirror hanging in his house, and he could admire his body in it comfortably because he always worked out in a mask.

He examined himself carefully while his muscles were pumped up. At forty, he could have competed successfully in regional body-building competition. He was not satisfied.

Within the week he came upon the Blake painting. It seized him instantly.

He saw it in a large, full-color photograph in *Time* magazine illustrating a report on the Blake retrospective at the Tate Museum in London. The Brooklyn Museum had sent *The Great Red Dragon and the Woman Clothed with the Sun* to London for the show.

Time's critic said: "Few demonic images in Western art radiate such a nightmarish charge of sexual energy. . . ." Dolarhyde didn't have to read the text to find that out.

He carried the picture with him for days, photographed and enlarged it in the darkroom late at night. He was agitated much of the time. He posted the painting beside his mirror in the weight room and stared at it while he pumped. He could sleep only when he had worked out to exhaustion and watched his medical films to aid him in sexual relief.

He had known since the age of nine that essentially he was alone and that he would always be alone, a conclusion more common to the forties.

Now, in his forties, he was seized by a fantasy life with the brilliance and freshness and immediacy of childhood. It took him a step beyond Alone.

At a time when other men first see and fear their isolation, Dolarhyde's became understandable to him: he was alone because he was Unique. With the fervor of conversion he saw that if he worked at it, if he followed the true urges he had kept down for so long— cultivated them as the inspirations they truly were—he could Become.

The Dragon's face is not visible in the painting, but increasingly Dolarhyde came to know how it looked.

Watching his medical films in the parlor, pumped up from lifting, he stretched his jaw wide to hold in Grandmother's teeth. They did not fit his distorted gums and his jaw cramped quickly.

He worked on his jaw in private moments, biting on a hard rubber block until the muscles stood out in his cheeks like walnuts.

In the fall of 1979, Francis Dolarhyde withdrew part of his considerable savings and took a three-month leave of absence from Gateway. He went to Hong Kong and he took with him his grandmother's teeth.

When he returned, red-haired Eileen and his other fellow workers agreed that the vacation had done him good. He was calm. They hardly noticed that he never used the employees' locker room or shower anymore—he had never done that often anyway.

His grandmother's teeth were back in the glass beside her bed. His own new ones were locked in his desk upstairs.

If Eileen could have seen him before his mirror, teeth in place, new tattoo brilliant in the harsh gym light, she would have screamed. Once.

There was time now; he did not have to hurry now. He had forever. It was five months before he selected the Jacobis.

The Jacobis were the first to help him, the first to lift him into the Glory of his Becoming. The Jacobis were better than anything, better than anything he ever knew.

Until the Leedses.

And now, as he grew in strength and Glory, there were the Shermans to come and the new intimacy of infrared. Most promising.

CHAPTER 29

FRANCIS DOLARHYDE had to leave his own territory at Gateway Film Processing to get what he needed.

Dolarhyde was production chief of Gateway's largest division—home-movie processing—but there were four other divisions.

The recessions of the 1970's cut deeply into home moviemaking, and there was increasing competition from home video recorders. Gateway had to diversify.

The company added departments which transferred film to videotape, printed aerial survery maps, and offered custom services to small-format commercial filmmakers.

In 1979 a plum fell to Gateway. The company contracted jointly with the Department of Defense and the Department of Energy to develop and test new emulsions for infrared photography.

The Department of Energy wanted sensitivie infrared film for its heat-conservation studies. Defense wanted it for night reconnaissance.

Gateway bought a small company next door, Baeder Chemical, in late 1979 and set up the project there.

Dolarhyde walked across to Baeder on his lunch hour under a scrubbed blue sky, carefully avoiding the reflecting puddles on the asphalt. Lounds's death had put him in an excellent humor.

Everyone at Baeder seemed to be out for lunch.

He found the door he wanted at the end of a labyrinth of halls. The sign beside the door said "Infrared Sensitive Materials in Use. NO Safelights, NO Smoking, NO hot beverages." The red light was on above the sign.

Dolarhyde pushed a button and, in a moment, the light turned green. He entered the light trap and rapped on the inner door.

"Come." A woman's voice.

Cool, absolute darkness. The gurgle of water, the familiar smell of D-76 developer, and a trace of perfume.

"I'm Francis Dolarhyde. I came about the dryer."

"Oh, good. Excuse me, my mouth's full. I was just finishing lunch."

He heard papers wadded and dropped in a wastebasket.

"Actually, Ferguson wanted the dryer," said the voice in the dark. "He's on vacation, but I know where it goes. You have one over at Gateway?"

"I have two. One is larger. He didn't say how much room he has." Dolarhyde had seen a memo about the dryer problem weeks ago.

"I'll show you, if you don't mind a short wait."

"All right."

"Put your back against the door"—her voice took on a touch of the lecturer's practiced tone—"come forward three steps, until you feel the tile under your feet, and there'll be a stool just to your left."

He found it. He was closer to her now. He could hear the rustle of her lab apron.

"Thanks for coming down," she said. Her voice was clear, with a faint ring of iron in it. "You're head of processing over in the big building, right?"

"Um-humm."

"The same 'Mr. D.' who sends the rockets when the requisitions are filed wrong?"

"The very one."

"I'm Reba McClane. Hope there's nothing wrong over here."

"Not my project anymore. I just planned the darkroom construction when we bought this place. I haven't been over here in six months." A long speech for him, easier in the dark.

"Just a minute more and we'll get you some light. Do you need a tape measure?"

"I have one."

Dolarhyde found it rather pleasant, talking to the woman in the dark. He heard the rattle of a purse being rummaged, the click of a compact.

He was sorry when the timer rang.

"There we go. I'll put this stuff in the Black Hole," she said.

He felt a breath of cold air, heard a cabinet close on rubber seals and the hiss of a vacuum lock. A puff of air, and fragrance touched him as she passed.

Dolarhyde pressed his knuckle under his nose, put on his thoughtful expression and waited for the light.

The lights came on. She stood by the door smiling in his approximate direction. Her eyes made small random movements behind the closed lids.

He saw her white cane propped in the corner. He took his hand away from his face and smiled.

"Do you think I could have a plum?" he said. There were several on the counter where she had been sitting.

"Sure, they're really good."

Reba McClane was about thirty, with a handsome prairie face shaped by good bones and resolution. She had a small star-shaped scar on the bridge of her nose. Her hair was a mixture of wheat and red-gold, cut in a pageboy that looked slightly out-of-date, and her face and hands were pleasantly freckled by the sun. Against the tile and stainless steel of the darkroom she was as bright as Fall.

He was free to look at her. His gaze could move over her as freely as the air. She had no way to parry eyes.

Dolarhyde often felt warm spots, stinging spots on his skin when he talked to a woman. They moved over him to wherever he thought the woman was looking. Even when a woman looked away from him, he suspected that she saw his reflection. He was always aware of reflective surfaces, knew the angles of reflection as a pool shark knows the banks.

His skin now was cool. Hers was freckled, pearly on her throat and the insides of her wrists.

"I'll show you the room where he wants to put it," she said. "We can get the measuring done."

They measured.

"Now, I want to ask a favor," Dolarhyde said.

"Okay."

"I need some infrared movie film. Hot film, sensitive up around one thousand nanometers."

"You'll have to keep it in the freezer and put it back in the cold after you shoot."

"I know."

"Could you give me an idea of the conditions, maybe I—"

"Shooting at maybe eight feet, with a pair of Wratten filters over the lights." It sounded too much like a surveillance rig. "At the zoo," he said. "In the World of Darkness. They want to photograph the nocturnal animals."

"They must really be spooky if you can't use commercial infrared."

"Ummm-hmmmm."

"I'm sure we can fix you up. One thing, though. You know a lot of our stuff is under the DD contract. Anything that goes out of here, you have to sign for."

"Right."

"When do you need it?"

"About the twentieth. No later."

"I don't have to tell you—the more sensitive it is, the meaner it is to handle. You get into coolers, dry ice, all that. They're screening some samples about four o'clock, if you want to look. You can pick the tamest emulsion that'll do what you want."

"I'll come."

Reba McClane counted her plums after Dolarhyde left. He had taken one.

Strange man, Mr. Dolarhyde. There had been no awkward pause of sympathy and concern in his voice when she turned on the lights. Maybe he already knew she was blind. Better yet, maybe he didn't give a damn.

That would be refreshing.

CHAPTER 30

IN CHICAGO, Freddy Lounds's funeral was under way. *The National Tattler* paid for the elaborate service, rushing the arrangements so that it could be held on Thursday, the day after his death. Then the pictures would be available for the *Tattler* edition published Thursday night.

The funeral was long in the chapel and it was long at the graveside.

A radio evangelist went on and on in fulsome eulogy. Graham rode the greasy swells of his hangover and tried to study the crowd.

The hired choir at graveside gave full measure for the money while the *Tattler* photographers' motor-driven cameras whizzed. Two TV crews were present with fixed cameras and creepy-peepies. Police photographers with press credentials photographed the crowd.

Graham recognized several plainclothes officers from Chicago Homicide. Theirs were the only faces that meant anything to him.

And there was Wendy of Wendy City, Lounds's girlfriend. She was seated beneath the canopy, nearest the coffin. Graham hardly recognized her. Her blonde wig was drawn back in a bun and she wore a black tailored suit.

During the last hymn she rose, went forward unsteadily, knelt and laid her head on the casket, her arms outstretched in the pall of chrysanthemums as the strobe lights flashed.

The crowd made little noise moving over the spongy grass to the cemetery gates.

Graham walked beside Wendy. A crowd of the uninvited stared at them through the bars of the high iron fence.

"Are you all right?" Graham asked.

They stopped among the tombstones. Her eyes were dry, her gaze level.

"Better than you," she said. "Got drunk, didn't you?"

"Yep. Is somebody keeping an eye on you?"

"The precinct sent some people over. They've got plainclothes in the club. Lot of business now. More weirdos than usual."

"I'm sorry you had this. You did . . . I thought you were fine at the hospital. I admired that."

She nodded. "Freddy was a sport. He shouldn't have to go out that hard. Thanks for getting me in the room." She looked into the distance, blinking, thinking, eye shadow like stone dust on her lids. She faced Graham. "Look, the *Tattler's* giving me some money, you figured that, right? For an interview and the dive at the graveside. I don't think Freddy would mind."

"He'd have been mad if you passed it up."

"That's what I thought. They're jerks, but they pay. What it is, they tried to get me to say that I think you deliberately turned this freak on to Freddy, chumming with him in that picture. I didn't say it. If they print that I did say it, well that's bullshit."

Graham said nothing as she scanned his face.

"You didn't like him, maybe—it doesn't matter. But if you thought this could happen, you wouldn't have missed the shot at the Fairy, right?"

"Yeah, Wendy, I'd have staked him out."

"Do you have anything at all? I hear noise from these people and that's about it."

"We don't have much. A few things from the lab we're following up. It was a clean job and he's lucky."

"Are you?"

"What?"

"Lucky."

"Off and on."

"Freddy was never lucky. He told me he'd clean up on this. Big deals everywhere."

"He probably would have, too."

"Well look, Graham, if you ever, you know, feel like a drink, I've got one."

"Thanks."

"But stay sober on the street."

"Oh yes."

Two policemen cleared a path for Wendy through the crowd of curiosity-seekers outside the gate. One of the gawkers wore a printed T-shirt reading "The Tooth Fairy Is a One-Night Stand." He whistled at Wendy. The woman beside him slapped his face.

A big policeman squeezed into the 280ZX beside Wendy and she pulled into the traffic. A second policeman followed in an unmarked car.

Chicago smelled like a spent skyrocket in the hot afternoon.

Graham was lonely, and he knew why; funerals often make us want sex—it's one in the eye for death.

The wind rattled the dry stalks of a funeral arrangement near his feet. For a hard second he remembered palm fronds rustling in the sea wind. He wanted very much to go home, knowing that he would not, could not, until the Dragon was dead.

CHAPTER 31

THE PROJECTION ROOM at Baeder Chemical was small—five rows of folding chairs with an aisle in the middle.

Dolarhyde arrived late. He stood at the back with his arms folded while they screened gray cards, color cards, and cubes variously lighted, filmed on a variety of infrared emulsions.

His presence disturbed Dandridge, the young man in charge. Dolarhyde carried an air of authority at work. He was the recognized darkroom expert from the parent company next door, and he was known to be a perfectionist.

Dandridge had not consulted him in months, a petty rivalry that had gone on since Gateway bought Baeder Chemical.

"Reba, give us the development dope on sample . . . eight," Dandridge said.

Reba McClane sat at the end of a row, a clipboard in her lap. Speaking in a clear voice, her fingers moving over the clipboard in the semidarkness, she outlined the mechanics of the development—chemicals, temperature and time, and storage procedures before and after filming.

Infrared-sensitive film must be handled in total darkness. She had done all the darkroom work, keeping the many samples straight by touch code and keeping a running record in the dark. It was easy to see her value to Baeder.

230

The screening ran through quitting time.

Reba McClane kept her seat as the others were filing out. Dolarhyde approached her carefully. He spoke to her at a distance while there were others in the room. He didn't want her to feel watched.

"I thought you hadn't made it," she said.

"I had a machine down. It made me late."

The lights were on. Her clean scalp glistened in the part of her hair as he stood over her.

"Did you get to see the 1000C sample?"

"I did."

"They said it looked all right. It's a lot easier to handle than the 1200 series. Think it'll do?"

"It will."

She had her purse with her, and a light raincoat. He stood back when she came into the aisle behind her searching cane. She didn't seem to expect any help. He didn't offer any.

Dandridge stuck his head back into the room.

"Reba, dear, Marcia had to fly. Can you manage?"

Spots of color appeared in her cheeks. "I can manage very well, thank you, Danny."

"I'd drop you, love, but I'm late already. Say, Mr. Dolarhyde, if it wouldn't be too much trouble, could you—"

"Danny, I have a ride home." She held in her anger. The nuances of expression were denied her, so she kept her face relaxed. She couldn't control her color, though.

Watching with his cold yellow eyes, Dolarhyde understood her anger perfectly; he knew that Dandridge's limp sympathy felt like spit on her cheek.

"I'll take you," he said, rather late.

"No, but thank you." She had thought he might offer and had intended to accept. She wouldn't have anybody forced into it. Damn Dandridge, damn his fumbling, she'd ride the damned bus, dammit. She had the fare and she knew the way and she could go anywhere she fucking pleased.

She stayed in the women's room long enough for the others to leave the building. The janitor let her out.

She followed the edge of a dividing strip across the parking lot toward the bus stop, her raincoat over her shoulders, tapping the edge with her cane and feeling for the slight resistance of the puddles when the cane swished through them.

Dolarhyde watched her from his van. His feelings made him uneasy; they were dangerous in daylight.

For a moment under the lowering sun, windshields, puddles, high steel wires splintered the sunlight into the glint of scissors.

Her white cane comforted him. It swept the light of scissors, swept scissors away, and the memory of her harmlessness eased him. He was starting the engine.

Reba McClane heard the van behind her. It was beside her now.

"Thank you for inviting me."

She nodded, smiled, tapped along.

"Ride with me."

"Thanks, but I take the bus all the time."

"Dandridge is a fool. Ride with me . . ."—*what would someone say?*—"for my pleasure."

She stopped. She heard him get out of the van.

People usually grasped her upper arm, not knowing what else to do. Blind people do not like to have their balance disturbed by a firm hold on their triceps. It is as unpleasant for them as standing on wiggly scales to weigh. Like anyone else, they don't like to be propelled.

He didn't touch her. In a moment she said, "It's better if *I* take *your* arm."

She had wide experience of forearms, but his surprised her fingers. It was as hard as an oak banister.

She could not know the amount of nerve he summoned to let her touch him.

The van felt big and high. Surrounded by resonances and echoes unlike those of a car, she held to the edges of the bucket seat until Dolarhyde fastened her safety belt. The diagonal shoulder belt pressed one of her breasts. She moved it until it lay between them.

They said little during the drive. Waiting at the red lights, he could look at her.

She lived in the left side of a duplex on a quiet street near Washington University.

"Come in and I'll give you a drink."

In his life, Dolarhyde had been in fewer than a dozen private homes. In the past ten years he had been in four; his own, Eileen's briefly, the Leedses', and the Jacobis'. Other people's houses were exotic to him.

She felt the van rock as he got out. Her door opened. It was a long step down from the van. She bumped into him lightly. It was like bumping into a tree. He was much heavier, more solid than she would have judged from his voice and his footfalls. Solid and light on his feet. She had known a Bronco linebacker once in Denver who came out to film a United Way appeal with some blind kids . . .

Once inside her front door, Reba McClane stood her cane in the corner and was suddenly free. She moved effortlessly, turning on music, hanging up her coat.

Dolarhyde had to reassure himself that she was blind. Being in a home excited him.

"How about a gin and tonic?"

"Tonic will be fine."

"Would you rather have juice?"

"Tonic."

"You're not a drinker, are you?"

"No."

"Come on in the kitchen." She opened the refrigerator. "How about . . ."—she made a quick inventory with her hands—"a piece of pie, then? Karo pecan, it's dynamite."

"Fine."

She took a whole pie from the icebox and put it on the counter.

Hands pointing straight down, she spread her fingers along the edge of the pie tin until its circumference told her that her middle fingers were at nine and three o'clock. Then she touched her thumbtips together and brought them down to the surface of the pie to locate its exact center. She marked the center with a toothpick.

Dolarhyde tried to make conversation to keep her from feeling his stare. "How long have you been at Baeder?" No S's in that one.

"Three months. Didn't you know?"

"They tell me the minimum."

She grinned. "You probably stepped on some toes when you laid out the darkrooms. Listen, the techs love you for it. The plumbing works and there are plenty of outlets. Two-twenty wherever you need it."

She put the middle finger of her left hand on the toothpick, her thumb on the edge of the tin and cut him a slice of pie, guiding the knife with her left index finger.

He watched her handle the bright knife. Strange to look at the front of a woman as much as he liked. How often in company can one look where he wants to look?

She made herself a stiff gin and tonic and they went into the living room. She passed her hand over a floor lamp, felt no heat, switched it on.

Dolarhyde ate his pie in three bites and sat stiffly on the couch, his sleek hair shining under the lamp, his powerful hands on his knees.

She put her head back in her chair and propped her feet on an ottoman.

"When will they film at the zoo?"

"Maybe next week." He was glad he had called the zoo and offered the infrared film: Dandridge might check.

"It's a great zoo. I went with my sister and my niece when they came to help me move in. They have the contact area, you know. I hugged this llama. It felt nice, but talk about *aroma,* boy . . . I thought I was being followed by a llama until I changed my shirt."

This was Having a Conversation. He had to say something or leave. "How did you come to Baeder?"

"They advertised at the Reiker Institute in Denver where I was working. I was checking the bulletin board one day and just happened to come across this job. Actually, what happened, Baeder had to shape up their employment practices to keep this Defense contract. They managed to pack six women, two blacks, two chicanos, an oriental, a paraplegic, and me into a total of eight hirings. We all count in at least two categories, you see."

"You worked out well for Baeder."

"The others did too. Baeder's not giving anything away."

"Before that?" He was sweating a little. Conversation was hard. Looking was good, though. She had good legs. She had nicked an ankle shaving. Along his arms a sense of the weight of her legs, limp.

"I trained newly blind people at the Reiker Institute in Denver for ten years after I finished school. This is my first job on the outside."

"Outside of what?"

"Out in the big world. It was really insular at Reiker. I mean, we were training people to live in the sighted world and we didn't live in it ourselves. We talked to each other too much. I thought I'd get out and knock around a little. Actually, I had intended to go into speech therapy, for speech-and-hearing-impaired children. I expect I'll go back to that, one of these days." She drained her glass. "Say, I've got some Mrs. Paul's crab-ball miniatures in here. They're pretty good. I shouldn't have served dessert first. Want some?"

"Um-hmmm."

"Do you cook?"

"Um-hmmm."

A tiny crease appeared in her forehead. She went into the kitchen. "How about coffee?" she called.

"Uh-huh."

She made small talk about grocery prices and got no reply. She came back into the living room and sat on the ottoman, her elbows on her knees.

"Let's talk about something for a minute and get it out of the way, okay?"

Silence.

"You haven't said anything lately. In fact, you haven't said anything since I mentioned speech therapy." Her voice was kind, but firm. It carried no taint of sympathy. "I understand you fine because you speak very well and because I listen. People don't pay attention. They ask me *what? what?* all the time. If you don't want to talk, okay. But I hope you will talk. Because you can, and I'm interested in what you have to say."

"Ummm. That's good," Dolarhyde said softly. Clearly this little speech was very important to her. Was she inviting him into the two-category club with her and the Chinese paraplegic? He wondered what his second category was.

Her next statement was incredible to him.

"May I touch your face? I want to know if you're smiling or frowning." Wryly, now. "I want to know whether to just shut up or not."

She raised her hand and waited.

How well would she get around with her fingers bitten off? Dolarhyde mused. Even in street teeth he could do it as easily as biting off breadsticks. If he braced his heels on the floor, his weight back on the couch, and locked both hands on her wrist, she could never pull away from him in time. Crunch, crunch, crunch, crunch, maybe leave the thumb. For measuring pies.

He took her wrist between his thumb and forefinger and turned her shapely, hard-used hand in the light. There were many small scars on it, and several new nicks and abrasions. A smooth scar on the back might have been a burn.

Too close to home. Too early in his Becoming. She wouldn't be there to look at anymore.

To ask this incredible thing, she could know nothing personal about him. She had not gossiped.

"Take my word that I'm smiling," he said. Okay on the S. It was true that he had a sort of smile which exposed his handsome public teeth.

He held her wrist above her lap and released it. Her hand settled to her thigh and half-closed, fingers trailing on the cloth like an averted glance.

"I think the coffee's ready," she said.

"I'm going." Had to go. Home for relief.

She nodded. "If I offended you, I didn't mean to."

"No."

She stayed on the ottoman, listened to be sure the lock clicked as he left.

Reba McClane made herself another gin and tonic. She put on some Segovia records and curled up on the couch. Dolarhyde had left a warm dent in the cushion. Traces of him remained in the air—shoe polish, a new leather belt, good shaving lotion.

What an intensely private man. She had heard only a few references to him at the office—Dandridge saying "that son of a bitch Dolarhyde" to one of his toadies.

Privacy was important to Reba. As a child, learning to cope after she lost her sight, she had had no privacy at all.

Now, in public, she could never be sure that she was not watched. So Francis Dolarhyde's sense of privacy appealed to her. She had not felt one ion of sympathy from him, and that was good.

So was this gin.

Suddenly the Segovia sounded busy. She put on her whale songs.

Three tough months in a new town. The winter to face, finding curbs in the snow. Reba McClane, leggy and brave, damned self-pity.

She would not have it. She was aware of a deep vein of cripple's anger in her and, while she could not get rid of it, she made it work for her, fueling her drive for independence, strengthening her determination to wring all she could from every day.

In her way, she was a hard one. Faith in any sort of natural justice was nothing but a night-light; she knew that. Whatever she did, she would end the same way everyone does: flat on her back with a tube in her nose, wondering "Is this all?"

She knew that she would never have the light, but there were things she *could* have. There were things to enjoy. She had gotten pleasure from helping her students, and the pleasure was oddly intensified by the knowledge that she would be neither rewarded nor punished for helping them.

In making friends she was ever wary of people who foster dependency and feed on it. She had been involved with a few—the blind attract them, and they are the enemy.

Involved. Reba knew that she was physically attractive to men— God knows enough of them copped a feel with their knuckles when they grabbed her upper arm.

She liked sex very much, but years ago she had learned something basic about men; most of them are terrified of entailing a burden. Their fear was augmented in her case.

She did not like for a man to creep in and out of her bed as though he were stealing chickens.

Ralph Mandy was coming to take her to dinner. He had a particularly cowardly mew about being so scarred by life that he was incapable of love. Careful Ralph told her that too often, and it scalded her. Ralph was amusing, but she didn't want to own him.

She didn't want to see Ralph. She didn't feel like making conversation and hearing the hitches in conversations around them as people watched her eat.

It would be so nice to be wanted by someone with the courage to get his hat or stay as he damn pleased, and who gave her credit for the same. Someone who didn't *worry* about her.

Francis Dolarhyde—shy, with a linebacker's body and no bullshit.

She had never seen or touched a cleft lip and had no visual associations with the sound. She wondered if Dolarhyde thought she understood him easily because "blind people hear so much better than we do." That was a common myth. Maybe she should have explained to him that it was not true, that blind people simply pay more attention to what they hear.

There were so many misconceptions about the blind. She wondered if Dolarhyde shared the popular belief that the blind are "purer in spirit" than most people, that they are somehow sanctified by their affliction. She smiled to herself. That one wasn't true either.

CHAPTER 32

THE CHICAGO POLICE worked under a media blitz, a nightly news "countdown" to the next full moon. Eleven days were left.

Chicago families were frightened.

At the same time, attendance rose at horror movies that should have died at the drive-ins in a week. Fascination and horror. The entrepreneur who hit the punk-rock market with "Tooth Fairy" T-shirts came out with an alternate line that said "The Red Dragon Is a One-Night Stand." Sales were divided about equally between the two.

Jack Crawford himself had to appear at a news conference with police officials after the funeral. He had received orders from Above to make the federal presence more visible; he did not make it more audible, as he said nothing.

When heavily manned investigations have little to feed on, they tend to turn upon themselves, covering the same ground over and over, beating it flat. They take on the circular shape of a hurricane or a zero.

Everywhere Graham went he found detectives, cameras, a rush of uniformed men and the incessant crackle of radios. He needed to be still.

Crawford, ruffled from his news conference, found Graham at nightfall in the quiet of an unused jury room on the floor above the U.S. prosecutor's office.

Good lights hung low over the green felt jury table where Graham spread out his papers and photographs. He had taken off his coat and tie and he was slumped in a chair staring at two photographs. The Leedses' framed picture stood before him and beside it, on a clipboard propped against a carafe, was a picture of the Jacobis.

Graham's pictures reminded Crawford of a bullfighter's folding shrine, ready to be set up in any hotel room. There was no photograph of Lounds. He suspected that Graham had not been thinking about the Lounds case at all. He didn't need trouble with Graham.

"Looks like a poolroom in here," Crawford said.

"Did you knock 'em dead?" Graham was pale but sober. He had a quart of orange juice in his fist.

"Jesus." Crawford collapsed in a chair. "You try to think out there, it's like trying to take a piss on the train."

"Any news?"

"The commissioner was popping sweat over a question and scratched his balls on television, that's the only notable thing I saw. Watch at six and eleven if you don't believe it."

"Want some orange juice?"

"I'd just as soon swallow barbed wire."

"Good. More for me." Graham's face was drawn. His eyes were too bright. "How about the gas?"

"God bless Liza Lake. There're forty-one Servco Supreme franchise stations in greater Chicago. Captain Osborne's boys swarmed those, checking sales in containers to people driving vans and trucks. Nothing yet, but they haven't seen all shifts. Servco has 186 other stations—they're scattered over eight states. We've asked for help from the local jurisdictions. It'll take a while. If God loves me, he used a credit card. There's a chance."

"Not if he can suck a siphon hose, there isn't."

"I asked the commissioner not to say anything about the Tooth Fairy maybe living in this area. These people are spooked enough. If he told them that, this place would sound like Korea tonight when the drunks come home."

"You still think he's close?"

"Don't you? It figures, Will." Crawford picked up the Lounds autopsy report and peered at it through his half-glasses.

"The bruise on his head was older than the mouth injuries. Five to eight hours older, they're not sure. Now, the mouth injuries were hours old when they got Lounds to the hospital. They were burned over too, but inside his mouth they could tell. He retained some chloroform in his . . . hell, someplace in his wheeze. You think he was unconscious when the Tooth Fairy bit him?"

"No. He'd want him awake."

"That's what I figure. All right, he takes him out with a lick on the head—that's in the garage. He has to keep him quiet with chloroform until he gets him someplace where the noise won't matter. Brings him back and gets here hours after the bite."

"He could have done it all in the back of the van, parked way out somewhere," Graham said.

Crawford massaged the sides of his nose with his fingers, giving his voice a megaphone effect. "You're forgetting about the wheels on the chair. Bev got two kinds of carpet fuzz, wool and synthetic. Synthetic's from a van, maybe, but when have you ever seen a wool rug in a van? How many wool rugs have you seen in someplace you can rent? Damn few. Wool rug is a house, Will. And the dirt and mold were from a dark place where the chair was stored, a dirt-floored cellar."

"Maybe."

"Now, look at this." Crawford pulled a Rand McNally road atlas out of his briefcase. He had drawn a circle on the "United States mileage and driving time" map. "Freddy was gone a little over fifteen hours, and his injuries are spaced over that time. I'm going to make a couple of assumptions. I don't like to do that, but here goes. . . . What are you laughing at?"

"I just remembered when you ran those field exercises at Quantico—when that trainee told you he *assumed* something."

"I don't remember that. Here's—"

"You made him write 'assume' on the blackboard. You took the chalk and started underlining and yelling in his face. 'When you assume, you make an *ASS* out of *U* and *ME* both,' that's what you told him, as I recall."

"He needed a boot in the ass to shape up. Now, look at this. Figure he had Chicago traffic on Tuesday afternoon, going out of town with Lounds. Allow a couple of hours to fool with Lounds at the location where he took him, and then the time driving back. He couldn't have gone much farther than six hours' driving time out of Chicago. Okay, this circle around Chicago is six hours' driving time. See, it's wavy because some roads are faster than others."

"Maybe he just stayed here."

"Sure, but this is the farthest away he *could* be."

"So you've narrowed it down to Chicago, or inside a circle covering Milwaukee, Madison, Dubuque, Peoria, St. Louis, Indianapolis, Cincinnati, Toledo, and Detroit, to name a few."

"Better than that. We know he got a *Tattler* very fast. Monday night, probably."

"He could have done that in Chicago."

"I know it, but once you get out of town the *Tattlers* aren't available on Monday night in a lot of locations. Here's a list from the *Tattler* circulation department—places *Tattlers* are air-freighted or trucked inside the circle on Monday night. See, that leaves Milwaukee, St. Louis, Cincinnati, Indianapolis, and Detroit. They go to the airports and maybe ninety newsstands that stay open all night, not counting the ones in Chicago. I'm using the field offices to check them. Some newsie might remember an odd customer on Monday night."

"Maybe. That's a good move, Jack."

Clearly Graham's mind was elsewhere.

If Graham were a regular agent, Crawford would have threatened him with a lifetime appointment to the Aleutians. Instead he said, "My brother called this afternoon. Molly left his house, he said."

"Yeah."

"Someplace safe, I guess?"

Graham was confident Crawford knew exactly where she went.

"Willy's grandparents.'"

"Well, they'll be glad to see the kid." Crawford waited.

No comment from Graham.

"Everything's okay, I hope."

"I'm working, Jack. Don't worry about it. No, look, it's just that she got jumpy over there."

Graham pulled a flat package tied with string from beneath a stack of funeral pictures and began to pick at the knot.

"What's that?"

"It's from Byron Metcalf, the Jacobis' lawyer. Brian Zeller sent it on. It's okay."

"Wait a minute, let me see." Crawford turned the package in his hairy fingers until he found the stamp and signature of S. F. "Semper

Fidelis" Aynesworth, head of the FBI's explosives section, certifying that the package had been fluoroscoped.

"Always check. Always check."

"I always check, Jack."

"Did Chester bring you this?"

"Yes."

"Did he show you the stamp before he handed it to you?"

"He checked it and showed me."

Graham cut the string. "It's copies of all the probate business in the Jacobi estate. I asked Metcalf to send it to me—we can compare with the Leeds stuff when it comes in."

"We have a lawyer doing that."

"*I* need it. I don't know the Jacobis, Jack. They were new in town. I got to Birmingham a month late, and their stuff was scattered to shit and gone. I've got a feel for the Leedses. I don't for the Jacobis. I need to know them. I want to talk to people they knew in Detroit, and I want a couple of days more in Birmingham."

"I need you here."

"Listen, Lounds was a straight snuff. We made him mad at Lounds. The only connection to Lounds is one *we* made. There's a little hard evidence with Lounds, and the police are handling it. Lounds was just an annoyance to him, but the Leedses and the Jacobis are *what he needs*. We've got to have the connection between them. If we ever get him, that's how we'll do it."

"So you have the Jacobi paper to use here," Crawford said. "What are you looking for? What kind of thing?"

"Any damn thing, Jack. Right now, a medical deduction." Graham pulled the IRS estate-tax form from the package. "Lounds was in a wheelchair. Medical. Valerie Leeds had surgery about six weeks before she died—remember in her diary? A small cyst in her breast. Medical again. I was wondering if Mrs. Jacobi had surgery too."

"I don't remember anything about surgery in the autopsy report."

"No, but it might have been something that didn't show. Her medical history was split between Detroit and Birmingham. Something might have gotten lost there. If she had anything done, there'll be a deduction claimed and maybe an insurance claim."

"Some itinerant orderly, you're thinking? Worked both places—Detroit or Birmingham and Atlanta?"

"If you spend time in a mental hospital you pick up the drill. You could pass as an orderly, get a job doing it when you got out," Graham said.

"Want some dinner?"

"I'll wait till later. I get dumb after I eat."

Leaving, Crawford looked back at Graham from the gloom of the doorway. He didn't care for what he saw. The hanging lights deepened the hollows in Graham's face as he studied with the victims staring at him from the photographs. The room smelled of desperation.

Would it be better for the case to put Graham back on the street? Crawford couldn't afford to let him burn himself out in here for nothing. But for something?

Crawford's excellent administrative instincts were not tempered by mercy. They told him to leave Graham alone.

CHAPTER 33

BY TEN P.M. Dolarhyde had worked out to near-exhaustion with the weights, had watched his films and tried to satisfy himself. Still he was restless.

Excitement bumped his chest like a cold medallion when he thought of Reba McClane. He should not think of Reba McClane.

Stretched out in his recliner, his torso pumped up and reddened by the workout, he watched the television news to see how the police were coming along with Freddy Lounds.

There was Will Graham standing near the casket with the choir howling away. Graham was slender. It would be easy to break his back. Better than killing him. Break his back and twist it just to be sure. They could roll him to the next investigation.

There was no hurry. Let Graham dread it.

Dolarhyde felt a quiet sense of power all the time now.

The Chicago police department made some noise at a news conference. Behind the racket about how hard they were working, the essence was: no progress on Freddy. Jack Crawford was in the group behind the microphones. Dolarhyde recognized him from a *Tattler* picture.

A spokesman from the *Tattler*, flanked by two bodyguards, said, "This savage and senseless act will only make the *Tattler's* voice ring louder."

Dolarhyde snorted. Maybe so. It had certainly shut Freddy up.

The news readers were calling him "the Dragon" now. His acts were "what the police *had* termed the 'Tooth Fairy murders.'"

Definite progress.

Nothing but local news left. Some prognathous lout was reporting from the zoo. Clearly they'd send him anywhere to keep him out of the office.

Dolarhyde had reached for his remote control when he saw on the screen someone he had talked with only hours ago on the telephone: Zoo Director Dr. Frank Warfield, who had been so pleased to have the film Dolarhyde offered.

Dr. Warfield and a dentist were working on a tiger with a broken tooth. Dolarhyde wanted to see the tiger, but the reporter was in the way. Finally the newsman moved.

Rocked back in his recliner, looking along his own powerful torso at the screen, Dolarhyde saw the great tiger stretched unconscious on a heavy work table.

Today they were preparing the tooth. In a few days they would cap it, the oaf reported.

Dolarhyde watched them calmly working between the jaws of the tiger's terrible striped face.

"May I touch your face?" said Miss Reba McClane.

He wanted to tell Reba McClane something. He wished she had one inkling of what she had almost done. He wished she had one flash of his Glory. But she could not have that and live. She must live: he had been seen with her and she was too close to home.

He had tried to share with Lecter, and Lecter had betrayed him.

Still, he would like to share. He would like to share with her a little, in a way she could survive.

CHAPTER 34

"*I* KNOW IT'S POLITICAL, *you* know it's political, but it's pretty much what you're doing anyway," Crawford told Graham. They were walking down the State Street Mall toward the federal office building in the late afternoon. "Do what you're doing, just write out the parallels and I'll do the rest."

The Chicago police department had asked the FBI's Behavioral Science section for a detailed victim profile. Police officials said they would use it in planning disposition of extra patrols during the period of the full moon.

"Covering their ass is what they're doing," Crawford said, waving his bag of Tater Tots. "The victims have been affluent people, they need to stack the patrols in affluent neighborhoods. They know there'll be a squawk about that—the ward bosses have been fighting over the extra manpower ever since Freddy lit off. If they patrol the upper-middle-class neighborhoods and he hits the South Side, God help the city fathers. But if it happens, they can point at the damned feds. I can hear it now—'They told us to do it that way. That's what *they* said do.'"

"I don't think he's any more likely to hit Chicago than anywhere else," Graham said. "There's no reason to think so. It's a jerkoff. Why can't Bloom do the profile? He's a consultant to Behavioral Science."

"They don't want it from Bloom, they want it from us. It wouldn't

247

do them any good to blame Bloom. Besides, he's still in the hospital. I'm instructed to do this. Somebody on the Hill has been on the phone with Justice. Above says do it. Will you just do it?"

"I'll do it. It's what I'm doing anyway."

"That's what I know," Crawford said. "Just keep doing it."

"I'd rather go back to Birmingham."

"No," Crawford said. "Stay with me on this."

The last of Friday burned down the west.

Ten days to go.

CHAPTER 35

"READY TO TELL ME what kind of an 'outing' this is?" Reba McClane asked Dolarhyde on Saturday morning when they had ridden in silence for ten minutes. She hoped it was a picnic.

The van stopped. She heard Dolarhyde roll down his window.

"Dolarhyde," he said. "Dr. Warfield left my name."

"Yes, sir. Would you put this under your wiper when you leave the vehicle?"

They moved forward slowly. Reba felt a gentle curve in the road. Strange and heavy odors on the wind. An elephant trumpeted.

"The zoo," she said. "Terrific." She would have preferred a picnic. What the hell, this was okay. "Who's Dr. Warfield?"

"The zoo director."

"Is he a friend of yours?"

"No. We did the zoo a favor with the film. They're paying back."

"How?"

"You get to touch the tiger."

"Don't surprise me too much!"

"Did you ever look at a tiger?"

She was glad he could ask the question. "No. I remember a puma when I was little. That's all they had at the zoo in Red Deer. I think we better talk about this."

"They're working on the tiger's tooth. They have to put him to . . . sleep. If you want to, you can touch him."

"Will there be a crowd, people waiting?"

"No. No audience. Warfield, me, a couple of people. TV's coming in after we leave. Want to do it?" An odd urgency in the question.

"Hell fuzzy yes, I do! Thank you . . . that's a fine surprise."

The van stopped.

"Uh, how do I know he's sound asleep?"

"Tickle him. If he laughs, run for it."

The floor of the treatment room felt like linoleum under Reba's shoes. The room was cool with large echoes. Radiant heat was coming from the far side.

A rhythmic shuffling of burdened feet and Dolarhyde guided her to one side until she felt the forked pressure of a corner.

It was in here now, she could smell it.

A voice. "Up, now. Easy. Down. Can we leave the sling under him, Dr. Warfield?"

"Yeah, wrap that cushion in one of the green towels and put it under his head. I'll send John for you when we've finished."

Footsteps leaving.

She waited for Dolarhyde to tell her something. He didn't.

"It's in here," she said.

"Ten men carried it in on a sling. It's big. Ten feet. Dr. Warfield's listening to its heart. Now he's looking under one eyelid. Here he comes."

A body damped the noise in front of her.

"Dr. Warfield, Reba McClane," Dolarhyde said.

She held out her hand. A large, soft hand took it.

"Thanks for letting me come," she said. "It's a treat."

"Glad you *could* come. Enlivens my day. We appreciate the film, by the way."

Dr. Warfield's voice was middle-aged, deep, cultured, black. Virginia, she guessed.

"We're waiting to be sure his respiration and heartbeat are strong and steady before Dr. Hassler starts. Hassler's over there adjusting his head mirror. Just between us, he only wears it to hold down his toupee. Come meet him. Mr. Dolarhyde?"

"You go ahead."

She put out her hand to Dolarhyde. The pat was slow in coming, light when it came. His palm left sweat on her knuckles.

Dr. Warfield placed her hand on his arm and they walked forward slowly.

"He's sound asleep. Do you have a general impression . . . ? I'll describe as much as you like." He stopped, uncertain how to put it.

"I remember pictures in books when I was a child, and I saw a puma once in the zoo near home."

"This tiger is like a super puma," he said. "Deeper chest, more massive head, and a heavier frame and musculature. He's a four-year-old male Bengal. He's about ten feet long, from his nose to the tip of his tail, and he weighs eight hundred and fifteen pounds. He's lying on his right side under bright lights."

"I can feel the lights."

"He's striking, orange and black stripes, the orange is so bright it seems almost to bleed into the air around him." Suddenly Dr. Warfield feared that it was cruel to talk of colors. A glance at her face reassured him.

"He's six feet away, can you smell him?"

"Yes."

"Mr. Dolarhyde may have told you, some dimwit poked at him through the barrier with one of our gardener's spades. He snapped off the long fang on the upper left side on the blade. Okay, Dr. Hassler?"

"He's fine. We'll give it another minute or two."

Warfield introduced the dentist to Reba.

"My dear, you're the first *pleasant* surprise I've ever had from Frank Warfield," Hassler said. "You might like to examine this. It's a gold tooth, fang actually." He put it in her hand. "Heavy, isn't it? I cleaned up the broken tooth and took an impression several days ago, and today I'll cap it with this one. I could have done it in white of course, but I thought this would be more fun. Dr. Warfield will tell you I never pass up an opportunity to show off. He's too inconsiderate to let me put an advertisement on the cage."

She felt the taper, curve, and point with her sensitive battered fingers. "What a nice piece of work!" She heard deep, slow breathing nearby.

"It'll give the kids a start when he yawns," Hassler said. "And I don't think it'll tempt any thieves. Now for the fun. You're not apprehensive, are you? Your muscular gentleman over there is watching us like a ferret. He's not making you do this?"

"No! No, I want to."

"We're facing his back," Dr. Warfield said. "He's just sleeping away about two and a half feet from you, waist-high on a work table. Tell you what: I'll put your left hand—you're right-handed aren't you?—I'll put your left hand on the edge of the table and you can explore with your right. Take your time. I'll be right here beside you."

"So will I," Dr. Hassler said. They were enjoying this. Under the hot lights her hair smelled like fresh sawdust in the sun.

Reba could feel the heat on the top of her head. It made her scalp tingle. She could smell her warm hair, Warfield's soap, alcohol and disinfectant, and the cat. She felt a touch of faintness, quickly over.

She gripped the edge of the table and reached out tentatively until her fingers touched tips of fur, warm from the lights, a cooler layer and then a deep steady warmth from below. She flattened her hand on the thick coat and moved it gently, feeling the fur slide across her palm, with and against the lay, felt the hide slide over the wide ribs as they rose and fell.

She gripped the pelt and fur sprang between her fingers. In the very presence of the tiger her face grew pink and she lapsed into blindisms, inappropriate facial movements she had schooled herself against.

Warfield and Hassler saw her forget herself and were glad. They saw her through a wavy window, a pane of new sensation she pressed her face against.

As he watched from the shadows, the great muscles in Dolarhyde's back quivered. A drop of sweat bounced down his ribs.

"The other side's all business," Dr. Warfield said close to her ear.

He led her around the table, her hand trailing down the tail.

A sudden constriction in Dolarhyde's chest as her fingers trailed over the furry testicles. She cupped them and moved on.

Warfield lifted a great paw and put it in her hand. She felt the roughness of the pads and smelled faintly the cage floor. He pressed a toe to make the claw slide out. The heavy, supple muscles of the shoulders filled her hands.

She felt the tiger's ears, the width of its head and, carefully, the veterinarian guiding her, touched the roughness of its tongue. Hot breath stirred the hair on her forearms.

Last, Dr. Warfield put the stethoscope in her ears. Her hands on the rhythmic chest, her face upturned, she was filled with the tiger heart's bright thunder.

➤

Reba McClane was quiet, flushed, elated as they drove away. She turned to Dolarhyde once and said slowly, "Thank you . . . very much. If you don't mind, I would dearly love a martini."

➤

"Wait here a minute," Dolarhyde said as he parked in his yard.

She was glad they hadn't gone back to her apartment. It was stale and safe. "Don't tidy up. Take me in and tell me it's neat."

"Wait here."

He carried in the sack from the liquor store and made a fast inspection tour. He stopped in the kitchen and stood for a moment with his hands over his face. He wasn't sure what he was doing. He felt danger, but not from the woman. He couldn't look up the stairs. He had to do something and he didn't know how. He should take her back home.

Before his Becoming, he would not have dared any of this.

Now he realized he could do anything. Anything. Anything.

He came outside, into the sunset, into the long blue shadow of the van. Reba McClane held on to his shoulders until her foot touched the ground.

She felt the loom of the house. She sensed its height in the echo of the van door closing.

"Four steps on the grass. Then there's a ramp," he said.

She took his arm. A tremor through him. Clean perspiration in cotton.

"You *do* have a ramp. What for?"

"Old people were here."

"Not now, though."

"No."

"It feels cool and tall," she said in the parlor. Museum air. And was that incense? A clock ticked far away. "It's a big house, isn't it? How many rooms?"

"Fourteen."

"It's old. The things in here are old." She brushed against a fringed lampshade and touched it with her fingers.

Shy Mr. Dolarhyde. She was perfectly aware that it had excited him to see her with the tiger; he had shuddered like a horse when she took his arm leaving the treatment room.

An elegant gesture, his arranging that. Maybe eloquent as well, she wasn't sure.

"Martini?"

"Let me go with you and do it," she said, taking off her shoes.

She flicked vermouth from her finger into the glass. Two and a half ounces of gin on top, and two olives. She picked up points of reference quickly in the house—the ticking clock, the hum of a window air conditioner. There was a warm place on the floor near the kitchen door where the sunlight had fallen through the afternoon.

He took her to his big chair. He sat on the couch.

There was a charge in the air. Like fluorescence in the sea, it limned movement; she found a place for her drink on the stand beside her, he put on music.

To Dolarhyde the room seemed changed. She was the first voluntary company he ever had in the house, and now the room was divided into her part and his.

There was the music, Debussy as the light failed.

He asked her about Denver and she told him a little, absently, as though she thought of something else. He described the house and the big hedged yard. There wasn't much need to talk.

In the silence while he changed records, she said, "That wonderful tiger, this house, you're just full of surprises, D. I don't think anybody knows you at all."

"Did you ask them?"

"Who?"

"Anybody."

"No."

"Then how do you know that nobody knows me?" His concentration on the tongue-twister kept the tone of the question neutral.

"Oh, some of the women from Gateway saw us getting into your van the other day. Boy, were they curious. All of a sudden I have company at the Coke machine."

"What do they want to know?"

"They just wanted some juicy gossip. When they found out there isn't any, they went away. They were just fishing."

"And what did they say?"

She had meant to make the women's avid curiosity into humor directed at herself. It was not working out that way.

"They wonder about everything," she said. "They find you very mysterious and interesting. Come on, it's a compliment."

"Did they tell you how I look?"

The question was spoken lightly, very well done, but Reba knew that nobody is ever kidding. She met it head-on.

"I didn't ask them. But, yes, they told me how they think you look. Want to hear it? Verbatim? Don't ask if you don't." She was sure he would ask.

No reply.

Suddenly Reba felt that she was alone in the room, that the place where he had stood was emptier than empty, a black hole swallowing everything and emanating nothing. She knew he could not have left without her hearing him.

"I think I'll tell you," she said. "You have a kind of hard clean neatness that they like. They said you have a remarkable body." Clearly she couldn't leave it at that. "They say you're very sensitive about your face and that you shouldn't be. Okay, here's the dippy one with the Dentine, is it Eileen?"

"Eileen."

Ah, a return signal. She felt like a radio astronomer.

Reba was an excellent mimic. She could have reproduced Eileen's speech with startling fidelity, but she was too wise to mimic anyone's speech for Dolarhyde. She quoted Eileen as though she read from a transcript.

"'He's not a bad-looking guy. Honest to God I've gone out with lots of guys didn't look that good. I went out with a hockey player one time—played for the Blues?—had a little dip in his lip where his gum shrank back from his bridge? They all have that, hockey players. It's kind of, you know, *macho*, I think. Mr. D.'s got the nicest skin, and what I wouldn't give for his hair.' Satisfied? Oh, and she asked me if you're as strong as you look."

"And?"

"I said I didn't know." She drained her glass and got up. "Where the hell are you anyway, D.?" She knew when he moved between her and a stereo speaker. "Aha. Here you are. Do you want to know what I think about it?"

She found his mouth with her fingers and kissed it, lightly pressing his lips against his clenched teeth. She registered instantly that it was shyness and not distaste that held him rigid.

He was astonished.

"Now, would you show me where the bathroom is?"

She took his arm and went with him down the hall.

"I can find my own way back."

In the bathroom she patted her hair and ran her fingers along the top of the basin, hunting toothpaste or mouthwash. She tried to find the door of the medicine cabinet and found there was no door, only hinges and exposed shelves. She touched the objects on them carefully, leery of a razor, until she found a bottle. She took off the cap, smelled to verify mouthwash, and swished some around.

When she returned to the parlor, she heard a familiar sound—the whir of a projector rewinding.

"I have to do a little homework," Dolarhyde said, handing her a fresh martini.

"Sure," she said. She didn't know how to take it. "If I'm keeping you from working, I'll go. Will a cab come up here?"

"No. I want you to be here. I do. It's just some film I need to check. It won't take long."

He started to take her to the big chair. She knew where the couch was. She went to it instead.

"Does it have a soundtrack?"

"No."

"May I keep the music?"

"Um-hmmm."

She felt his attention. He wanted her to stay, he was just frightened. He shouldn't be. All right. She sat down.

The martini was wonderfully cold and crisp.

He sat on the other end of the couch, his weight clinking the ice in her glass. The projector was still rewinding.

"I think I'll stretch out for a few minutes if you don't mind," she said. "No, don't move, I have plenty of room. Wake me up if I drop off, okay?"

She lay on the couch, holding the glass on her stomach; the tips of her hair just touched his hand beside his thigh.

He flicked the remote switch and the film began.

Dolarhyde had wanted to watch his Leeds film or his Jacobi film with this woman in the room. He wanted to look back and forth from the screen to Reba. He knew she would never survive that. The women saw her getting into his van. Don't even think about that. The women saw her getting into his van.

He would watch his film of the Shermans, the people he would visit next. He would see the promise of relief to come, and do it in Reba's presence, looking at her all he liked.

On the screen, *The New House* spelled in pennies on a shirt cardboard. A long shot of Mrs. Sherman and the children. Fun in the pool. Mrs. Sherman holds to the ladder and looks up at the camera, bosom swelling shining wet above her suit, pale legs scissoring.

Dolarhyde was proud of his self-control. He would think of this film, not the other one. But in his mind he began to speak to Mrs. Sherman as he had spoken to Valerie Leeds in Atlanta.

You see me now, yes

That's how you feel to see me, yes

Fun with old clothes. Mrs. Sherman has the wide hat on. She is before the mirror. She turns with an arch smile and strikes a pose for the camera, her hand at the back of her neck. There is a cameo at her throat.

Reba McClane stirs on the couch. She sets her glass on the floor. Dolarhyde feels a weight and warmth. She has rested her head on his thigh. The nape of her neck is pale and the movie light plays on it.

He sits very still, moves only his thumb to stop the film, back it up. On the screen, Mrs. Sherman poses before the mirror in the hat. She turns to the camera and smiles.

You see me now, yes

That's how you feel to see me, yes

Do you feel me now? yes

Dolarhyde is trembling. His trousers are mashing him so hard. He feels heat. He feels warm breath through the cloth. Reba has made a discovery.

Convulsively his thumb works the switch.

You see me now, yes

That's how you feel to see me, yes

Do you feel this? yes

Reba has unzipped his trousers.

A stab of fear in him; he has never been erect before in the presence of a living woman. He is the Dragon, he doesn't have to be afraid.

Busy fingers spring him free.

OH.

Do you feel me now? yes

Do you feel this yes

You do I know it yes

Your heart is loud yes

He must keep his hands off Reba's neck. Keep them off. The women saw them in the van. His hand is squeezing the arm of the couch. His fingers pop through the upholstery.

Your heart is loud yes

And fluttering now

It's fluttering now

It's trying to get out yes

And now it's quick and light and quicker and light and . . .

Gone.

Oh, gone.

Reba rests her head on his thigh and turns her gleaming cheek to him. She runs her hand inside his shirt and rests it warm on his chest.

"I hope I didn't shock you," she said.

It was the sound of her living voice that shocked him, and he felt to see if her heart was going and it was. She held his hand there gently.

"My goodness, you're not through yet, are you?"

A living woman. How bizarre. Filled with power, the Dragon's or his own, he lifted her from the couch easily. She weighed nothing, so much easier to carry because she wasn't limp. Not upstairs. Not upstairs. Hurrying now. Somewhere. Quick. Grandmother's bed, the satin comforter sliding under them.

"Oh, wait, I'll get them off. Oh, now it's torn. I don't care. Come on. My God, man. That's so sweeeet. Don't please hold me down, let me come up to you and take it."

➤

With Reba, his only living woman, held with her in this one bubbleskin of time, he felt for the first time that it was all right: it was his life he was releasing, himself past all mortality that he was sending into her starry darkness, away from this pain planet, ringing harmonic distances away to peace and the promise of rest.

Beside her in the dark, he put his hand on her and pressed her together gently to seal the way back. As she slept, Dolarhyde, damned murderer of eleven, listened time and again to her heart.

Images. Baroque pearls flying through the friendly dark. A Very pistol he had fired at the moon. A great firework he saw in Hong Kong called "The Dragon Sows His Pearls."

The Dragon.

He felt stunned, cloven. And all the long night beside her he listened, fearful, for himself coming down the stairs in the kimono.

She stirred once in the night, searching sleepily until she found the bedside glass. Grandmother's teeth rattled in it.

Dolarhyde brought her water. She held him in the dark. When she slept again, he took her hand off his great tattoo and put it on his face.

➤

He slept hard at dawn.

Reba McClane woke at nine and heard his steady breathing. She stretched lazily in the big bed. He didn't stir. She reviewed the layout of the house, the order of rugs and floor, the direction of the ticking clock. When she had it straight, she rose quietly and found the bathroom.

After her long shower, he was still asleep. Her torn underclothes were on the floor. She found them with her feet and stuffed them in her purse. She pulled her cotton dress on over her head, picked up her cane and walked outside.

He had told her the yard was large and level, bounded by hedges grown wild, but she was cautious at first.

The morning breeze was cool, the sun warm. She stood in the yard and let the wind toss the seed heads of the elderberry through her hands. The wind found the creases of her body, fresh from the shower. She raised her arms to it and the wind blew cool beneath her breasts and arms and between her legs. Bees went by. She was not afraid of them and they left her alone.

Dolarhyde woke, puzzled for an instant because he was not in his room upstairs. His yellow eyes grew wide as he remembered. An owlish turn of his head to the other pillow. Empty.

Was she wandering around the house? What might she find? Or had something happened in the night? Something to clean up. He would be suspected. He might have to run.

He looked in the bathroom, in the kitchen. Down in the basement where his other wheelchair stood. The upper floor. He didn't want to go upstairs. He had to look. His tattoo flexed as he climbed the stairs. The Dragon glowed at him from the picture in his bedroom. He could not stay in the room with the Dragon.

From an upstairs window he spotted her in the yard.

"FRANCIS." He knew the voice came from his room. He knew it was the voice of the Dragon. This new twoness with the Dragon disoriented him. He first felt it when he put his hand on Reba's heart.

The Dragon had never spoken *to* him before. It was frightening.

"FRANCIS, COME HERE."

He tried to shut out the voice calling him, calling him as he hurried down the stairs.

What could she have found? Grandmother's teeth had rattled in the glass, but he put them away when he brought her water. She couldn't see anything.

Freddy's tape. It was in a cassette recorder in the parlor. He checked it. The cassette was rewound to the beginning. He couldn't remember if he had rewound it after he played it on the telephone to the *Tattler*.

She must not come back in the house. He didn't know what might happen in the house. She might get a surprise. The Dragon might come down. He knew how easily she would tear.

The women saw her getting in his van. Warfield would remember them together. Hurriedly he dressed.

Reba McClane felt the cool bar of a tree trunk's shadow, and then the sun again as she wandered across the yard. She could always tell where she was by the heat of the sun and the hum of the window air conditioner. Navigation, her life's discipline, was easy here. She turned around and around, trailing her hands on the shrubs and overgrown flowers.

A cloud blocked the sun and she stopped, not knowing in which direction she faced. She listened for the air conditioner. It was off. She felt a moment of uneasiness, then clapped her hands and heard the reassuring echo from the house. Reba flipped up her watch crystal and felt the time. She'd have to wake D. soon. She needed to go home.

The screen door slammed.

"Good morning," she said.

His keys tinkled as he came across the grass.

He approached her cautiously, as though the wind of his coming might blow her down, and saw that she was not afraid of him.

She didn't seem embarrassed or ashamed of what they had done in the night. She didn't seem angry. She didn't run from him or threaten him. He wondered if it was because she had not seen his private parts.

Reba put her arms around him and laid her head on his hard chest. His heart was going fast.

He managed to say good morning.

"I've had a really terrific time, D."

Really? What would someone say back? "Good. Me too." *That seemed all right. Get her away from here.*

"But I need to go home now," she was saying. "My sister's coming by to pick me up for lunch. You could come too if you like."

"I have to go to the plant," he said, modifying the lie he had ready.

"I'll get my purse."

Oh no. "I'll get it."

Almost blind to his own true feelings, no more able to express them than a scar can blush, Dolarhyde did not know what had happened to him with Reba McClane, or why. He was confused, spiked with new fright at being Two.

She threatened him, she did not threaten him.

There was the matter of her startling live movements of acceptance in Grandmother's bed.

Often Dolarhyde did not find out what he felt until he acted. He didn't know how he felt toward Reba McClane.

An ugly incident as he drove her home enlightened him a little.

Just past the Lindbergh Boulevard exit off Interstate 70, Dolarhyde pulled into a Servco Supreme station to fill his van.

The attendant was a heavyset, sullen man with muscatel on his breath. He made a face when Dolarhyde asked him to check the oil.

The van was a quart low. The attendant jammed the oil spout into the can and stuck the spout into the engine.

Dolarhyde climbed out to pay.

The attendant seemed enthusiastic about wiping the windshield; the passenger side of the windshield. He wiped and wiped.

Reba McClane sat in the high bucket seat, her legs crossed, her skirt riding up over her knee. Her white cane lay between the seats.

The attendant started over on the windshield. He was looking up her dress.

Dolarhyde glanced up from his wallet and caught him. He reached in through the window of the van and turned the wipers on high speed, batting the attendant's fingers.

"Hey, watch that." The attendant got busy removing the oil can from the engine compartment. He knew he was caught and he wore a sly grin until Dolarhyde came around the van to him.

"You son of a bitch." Fast over the /s/.

"What the hell's the matter with you?" The attendant was about Dolarhyde's height and weight, but he had nowhere near the muscle. He was young to have dentures, and he didn't take care of them.

Their greenness disgusted Dolarhyde. "What happened to your teeth?" he asked softly.

"What's it to you?"

"Did you pull them for your boyfriend, you rotten prick?" Dolarhyde stood too close.

"Get the hell away from me."

Quietly, "Pig. Idiot. Trash. Fool."

With a one-hand shove Dolarhyde sent him flying back to slam against the van. The oil can and spout clattered on the asphalt.

Dolarhyde picked it up.

"Don't run. I can catch you." He pulled the spout from the can and looked at its sharp end.

The attendant was pale. There was something in Dolarhyde's face that he had never seen before, anywhere.

For a red instant Dolarhyde saw the spout jammed in the man's chest, draining his heart. He saw Reba's face through the windshield. She was shaking her head, saying something. She was trying to find the handle to roll her window down.

"Ever had anything broken, ass-eyes?"

The attendant shook his head fast. "I didn't mean no offense, now. Honest to God."

Dolarhyde held the curved metal spout in front of the man's face.

He held it in both hands and his chest muscles bunched as he bent it double. He pulled out the man's waistband and dropped the spout down the front of his pants.

"Keep your pig eyes to yourself." He stuffed money for the gas in the man's shirt pocket. "You can run now," he said. "But I could catch you anytime."

CHAPTER 36

THE TAPE CAME ON SATURDAY in a small package addressed to Will Graham, c/o FBI Headquarters, Washington. It had been mailed in Chicago on the day Lounds was killed.

The laboratory and Latent Prints found nothing useful on the cassette case or the wrapper.

A copy of the tape went to Chicago in the afternoon pouch. Special Agent Chester brought it to Graham in the jury room at midafternoon. A memo from Lloyd Bowman was attached:

> Voiceprints verify this is Lounds. Obviously he was repeating dictation. It's a new tape, manufactured in the last three months and never used before. Behavioral Science is picking at the content. Dr. Bloom should hear it when he's well enough—you decide about that.
>
> Clearly the killer's trying to rattle you.
>
> He'll do that once too often, I think.

A dry vote of confidence, much appreciated.

Graham knew he had to listen to the tape. He waited until Chester left.

He didn't want to be closed up in the jury room with it. The empty courtroom was better—some sun came in the tall windows. The cleaning women had been in and dust still hung in the sunlight.

The tape recorder was small and gray. Graham put it on a counsel table and pushed the button.

A technician's monotone: "Case number 426238, item 814, tagged and logged, a tape cassette. This is a rerecording."

A shift in the quality of the sound.

Graham held on to the railing of the jury box with both hands.

Freddy Lounds sounded tired and frightened.

"I have had a great privilege. I have seen . . . I have seen with wonder . . . wonder and awe . . . awe . . . the strength of the Great Red Dragon."

The original recording had been interrupted frequently as it was made. The machine caught the clack of the stop key each time. Graham saw the finger on the key. Dragon finger.

"I lied about Him. All I wrote was lies from Will Graham. He made me write them. I have . . . I have blasphemed against the Dragon. Even so . . . the Dragon is merciful. Now I want to serve Him. He . . . has helped me understand . . . His Splendor and I will praise Him. Newspapers, when you print this, always capitalize the H in 'Him.'

"He knows you made me lie, Will Graham. Because I was forced to lie, He will be more . . . more merciful to me than to you, Will Graham.

"Reach behind you, Will Graham . . . and feel for the small . . . knobs on the top of your pelvis. Feel your spine between them . . . that is the precise spot . . . where the Dragon will snap your spine."

Graham kept his hands on the railing. Damn if I'll feel. Did the Dragon not know the nomenclature of the iliac spine, or did he choose not to use it?

"There's much . . . for you to dread. From . . . from my own lips you'll learn a little more to dread."

A pause before the awful screaming. Worse, the blubbering lipless cry, "You goddanned astard you romised."

Graham put his head between his knees until the bright spots stopped dancing in front of his eyes. He opened his mouth and breathed deep.

An hour passed before he could listen to it again.

He took the recorder into the jury room and tried to listen there.

Too close. He left the tape recorder turning and went back into the courtroom. He could hear through the open door.

"I have had a great privilege . . ."

Someone was at the courtroom door. Graham recognized the young clerk from the Chicago FBI office and motioned for him to come in.

"A letter came for you," the clerk said. "Mr. Chester sent me with it. He told me to be sure and say the postal inspector fluoroscoped it."

The clerk pulled the letter out of his breast pocket. Heavy mauve stationery. Graham hoped it was from Molly.

"It's stamped, see?"

"Thank you."

"Also it's payday." The clerk handed him his check.

On the tape, Freddy screamed.

The young man flinched.

"Sorry," Graham said.

"I don't see how you stand it," the young man said.

"Go home," Graham said.

He sat in the jury box to read his letter. He wanted some relief. The letter was from Dr. Hannibal Lecter.

Dear Will,

A brief note of congratulations for the job you did on Mr. Lounds. I admired it enormously. What a cunning boy you are!

Mr. Lounds often offended me with his ignorant drivel, but he did enlighten me on one thing—your confinement in the mental hospital. My inept attorney should have brought that out in court, but never mind.

You know, Will, you worry too much. You'd be so much more comfortable if you relaxed with yourself.

We don't invent our natures, Will; they're issued to us along with our lungs and pancreas and everything else. Why fight it?

I want to help you, Will, and I'd like to start by asking you this: When you were so depressed after you shot Mr. Garrett Jacob Hobbs to death, it wasn't the *act* that got you down, was it? Really, didn't you feel so bad *because killing him felt so good?*

Think about it, but don't worry about it. Why shouldn't it feel good? It must feel good to God—He does it all the time, and are we not made in His image?

You may have noticed in the paper yesterday, God dropped a church roof on thirty-four of His worshipers in Texas Wednesday night—just as they were groveling through a hymn. Don't you think that felt good?

Thirty-four. He'd let you have Hobbs.

He got 160 Filipinos in one plane crash last week—He'll let you have measly Hobbs. He won't begrudge you one measly murder. Two now. That's all right.

Watch the papers. God always stays ahead.

Best,

Hannibal Lecter, M.D.

Graham knew that Lecter was dead wrong about Hobbs, but for a half-second he wondered if Lecter might be a little bit right in the case of Freddy Lounds. The enemy inside Graham agreed with any accusation.

He had put his hand on Freddy's shoulder in the *Tattler* photograph to establish that he really had told Freddy those insulting things about the Dragon. Or had he wanted to put Freddy at risk, just a little? He wondered.

The certain knowledge that he would not knowingly miss a chance at the Dragon reprieved him.

"I'm just about worn out with you crazy sons of bitches," Graham said aloud.

He wanted a break. He called Molly, but no one answered the telephone at Willy's grandparents' house. "Probably out in their damned motorhome," he mumbled.

He went out for coffee, partly to assure himself that he was not hiding in the jury room.

In the window of a jewelry store he saw a delicate antique gold bracelet. It cost him most of his paycheck. He had it wrapped and stamped for mailing. Only when he was sure he was alone at the mail drop did he address it to Molly in Oregon. Graham did not realize, as Molly did, that he gave presents when he was angry.

He didn't want to go back to his jury room and work, but he had to. The thought of Valerie Leeds spurred him.

I'm sorry I can't come to the phone right now, Valerie Leeds had said.

He wished that he had known her. He wished . . . Useless, childish thought.

Graham was tired, selfish, resentful, fatigued to a child-minded state in which his standards of measurement were the first ones he learned; where the direction "north" was Highway 61 and "six feet" was forever the length of his father.

He made himself settle down to the minutely detailed victim profile he was putting together from a fan of reports and his own observations.

Affluence. That was one parallel. Both families were affluent. Odd that Valerie Leeds saved money on panty hose.

Graham wondered if she had been a poor child. He thought so; her own children were a little too well turned out.

Graham had been a poor child, following his father from the boatyards in Biloxi and Greenville to the lake boats on Erie. Always the new boy at school, always the stranger. He had a half-buried grudge against the rich.

Valerie Leeds might have been a poor child. He was tempted to watch his film of her again. He could do it in the courtroom. No. The Leedses were not his immediate problem. He knew the Leedses. He did not know the Jacobis.

His lack of intimate knowledge about the Jacobis plagued him. The house fire in Detroit had taken everything—family albums, probably diaries too.

Graham tried to know them through the objects they wanted, bought and used. That was all he had.

The Jacobi probate file was three inches thick, and a lot of it was lists of possessions—a new household outfitted since the move to Birmingham. *Look at all this shit.* It was all insured, listed with serial numbers as the insurance companies required. Trust a man who has been burned out to buy plenty of insurance for the next time.

The attorney, Byron Metcalf, had sent him carbons instead of Xerox copies of the insurance declarations. The carbons were fuzzy and hard to read.

Jacobi had a ski boat, Leeds had a ski boat. Jacobi had a three-wheeler, Leeds had a trail bike. Graham licked his thumb and turned the page.

The fourth item on the second page was a Chinon Pacific movie projector.

Graham stopped. How had he missed it? He had looked through every crate on every pallet in the Birmingham warehouse, alert for anything that would give him an intimate view of the Jacobis.

Where was the projector? He could cross-check this insurance declaration against the inventory Byron Metcalf had prepared as executor when he stored the Jacobis' things. The items had been checked off by the warehouse supervisor who signed the storage contract.

It took fifteen minutes to go down the list of stored items. No projector, no camera, no film.

Graham leaned back in his chair and stared at the Jacobis smiling from the picture propped before him.

What the hell did you do with it?

Was it stolen?

Did the killer steal it?

If the killer stole it, did he fence it?

Dear God, give me a traceable fence.

Graham wasn't tired anymore. He wanted to know if anything else was missing. He looked for an hour, comparing the warehouse storage inventory with the insurance declarations. Everything was accounted for except the small precious items. They should all be on Byron Metcalf's own lockbox list of things he had put in the bank vault in Birmingham.

All of them were on the list. Except two.

"Crystal oddment box, 4″ × 3″, sterling silver lid" appeared on the insurance declaration, but was not in the lockbox. "Sterling picture frame, 9 × 11 inches, worked with vines and flowers" wasn't in the vault either.

Stolen? Mislaid? They were small items, easily concealed. Usually fenced silver is melted down immediately. It would be hard to trace. But movie equipment had serial numbers inside and out. It could be traced.

Was the killer the thief?

As he stared at his stained photograph of the Jacobis, Graham felt the sweet jolt of a new connection. But when he saw the answer whole it was seedy and disappointing and small.

There was a telephone in the jury room. Graham called Birmingham Homicide. He got the three-to-eleven watch commander.

"In the Jacobi case I noticed you kept an in-and-out log at the house after it was sealed off, right?"

"Let me get somebody to look," the watch commander said.

Graham knew they kept one. It was good procedure to record every person entering or leaving a murder scene, and Graham had been pleased to see that Birmingham did it. He waited five minutes before a clerk picked up the telephone.

"Okay, in-and-out, what do you want to know?"

"Is Niles Jacobi, son of the deceased—is he on it?"

"Umm-hmmm, yep. July 2, seven P.M. He had permission to get personal items."

"Did he have a suitcase, does it say?"

"Nope. Sorry."

Byron Metcalf's voice was husky and his breathing heavy when he answered the telephone. Graham wondered what he was doing.

"Hope I didn't disturb you."

"What can I do for you, Will?"

"I need a little help with Niles Jacobi."

"What's he done now?"

"I think he lifted a few things out of the Jacobi house after they were killed."

"Ummm."

"There's a sterling picture frame missing from your lockbox inventory. When I was in Birmingham I picked up a loose photograph of the family in Niles's dormitory room. It used to be in a frame—I can see the impression the mat left on it."

"The little bastard. I gave permission for him to get his clothes and some books he needed," Metcalf said.

"Niles has expensive friendships. This is mainly what I'm after, though—a movie projector and a movie camera are missing too. I want to know if he got them. Probably he did, but if he *didn't*, maybe the killer got them. In that case we need to get the serial numbers out to the hock shops. We need to put 'em on the national hot sheet. The frame's probably melted down by now."

"He'll think 'frame' when I get through with him."

"One thing—if Niles took the projector, he might have kept the film. He couldn't get anything for it. I want the film. I need to see it. If you come at him from the front, he'll deny everything and flush the film if he has any."

"Okay," Metcalf said. "His car title reverted to the estate. I'm executor, so I can search it without a warrant. My friend the judge won't mind papering his room for me. I'll call you."

Graham went back to work.

Affluence. Put affluence in the profile the police would use.

Graham wondered if Mrs. Leeds and Mrs. Jacobi ever did their marketing in tennis clothes. That was a fashionable thing to do in some areas. It was a dumb thing to do in some areas because it was doubly provocative—arousing class resentment and lust at the same time.

Graham imagined them pushing grocery carts, short pleated skirts brushing the brown thighs, the little balls on their sweat socks winking—passing the husky man with the barracuda eyes who was buying cold lunch meat to gnaw in his car.

How many families were there with three children and a pet, and only common locks between them and the Dragon as they slept?

When Graham pictured possible victims, he saw clever, successful people in graceful houses.

But the next person to confront the Dragon did not have children or a pet, and there was no grace in his house. The next person to confront the Dragon was Francis Dolarhyde.

CHAPTER 37

THE THUMP OF WEIGHTS on the attic floor carried through the old house.

Dolarhyde was lifting, straining, pumping more weight than he had ever lifted. His costume was different; sweatpants covered his tattoo. The sweatshirt hung over *The Great Red Dragon and the Woman Clothed with the Sun*. The kimono hung on the wall like the shed skin of a tree snake. It covered the mirror.

Dolarhyde wore no mask.

Up. Two hundred and eighty pounds from the floor to his chest in one heave. Now over his head.

"WHOM ARE YOU THINKING ABOUT?"

Startled by the voice, he nearly dropped the weight, swayed beneath it. Down. The plates thudded and clanked on the floor.

He turned, his great arms hanging, and stared in the direction of the voice.

"WHOM ARE YOU THINKING ABOUT?"

It seemed to come from behind the sweatshirt, but its rasp and volume hurt his throat.

"WHOM ARE YOU THINKING ABOUT?"

He knew who spoke and he was frightened. From the beginning, he and the Dragon had been one. He was Becoming and the Dragon was his higher self. Their bodies, voices, wills were one.

272

Not now. Not since Reba. Don't think Reba.

"WHO IS ACCEPTABLE?" the Dragon asked.

"Mrs. . . . erhman—Sherman." It was hard for Dolarhyde to say.

"SPEAK UP. I CAN'T UNDERSTAND YOU. WHOM ARE YOU THINKING ABOUT?"

Dolarhyde, his face set, turned to the barbell. Up. Over his head. Much harder this time.

"Mrs. . . . erhman wet in the water."

"YOU THINK ABOUT YOUR LITTLE BUDDY, DON'T YOU? YOU WANT HER TO BE YOUR LITTLE BUDDY, DON'T YOU?"

The weight came down with a thud.

"I on't have a li'l . . . huddy." With the fear his speech was failing. He had to occlude his nostrils with his upper lip.

"A STUPID LIE." The Dragon's voice was strong and clear. He said the /s/ without effort. "YOU FORGET THE BECOMING. PREPARE FOR THE SHERMANS. LIFT THE WEIGHT."

Dolarhyde seized the barbell and strained. His mind strained with his body. Desperately he tried to think of the Shermans. He forced himself to think of the weight of Mrs. Sherman in his arms. Mrs. Sherman was next. It was Mrs. Sherman. He was fighting Mr. Sherman in the dark. Holding him down until loss of blood made Sherman's heart quiver like a bird. It was the only heart he heard. He didn't hear Reba's heart. He didn't.

Fear leeched his strength. He got the weight up to his thighs, could not make the turn up to his chest. He thought of the Shermans ranged around him, eyes wide, as he took the Dragon's due. It was no good. It was hollow, empty. The weight thudded down.

"NOT ACCEPTABLE."

"Mrs. . . ."

"YOU CAN'T EVEN SAY 'MRS. SHERMAN.' YOU NEVER INTEND TO TAKE THE SHERMANS. YOU WANT REBA MCCLANE. YOU WANT HER TO BE YOUR LITTLE BUDDY, DON'T YOU? YOU WANT TO BE 'FRIENDS.'"

"No."

"LIE!"

"Nyus mhor a niddow wyow."

"JUST FOR A LITTLE WHILE? YOU SNIVELING HARELIP, WHO WOULD BE FRIENDS WITH YOU? COME HERE. I'LL SHOW YOU WHAT YOU ARE."

Dolarhyde did not move.

"I'VE NEVER SEEN A CHILD AS DISGUSTING AND DIRTY AS YOU. COME HERE."

He went.

"TAKE DOWN THE SWEATSHIRT."

He took it down.

"LOOK AT ME."

The Dragon glowed from the wall.

"TAKE DOWN THE KIMONO. LOOK IN THE MIRROR."

He looked. He could not help himself or turn his face from the scalding light. He saw himself drool.

"LOOK AT YOURSELF. I'M GOING TO GIVE YOU A SURPRISE FOR YOUR LITTLE BUDDY. TAKE OFF THAT RAG."

Dolarhyde's hands fought each other at the waistband of the sweatpants. The sweatpants tore. He stripped them away from him with his right hand, held the rags to him with his left.

His right hand snatched the rags away from his trembling, failing left. He threw them into the corner and fell back on the mat, curling on himself like a lobster split live. He hugged himself and groaned, breathing hard, his tattoo brilliant in the harsh gym lights.

"I'VE NEVER SEEN A CHILD AS DISGUSTING AND DIRTY AS YOU. GO GET THEM."

"aaaymah."

"GET THEM."

He padded from the room and returned with the Dragon's teeth.

"PUT THEM IN YOUR PALMS. LOCK YOUR FINGERS AND SQUEEZE MY TEETH TOGETHER."

Dolarhyde's pectoral muscles bunched.

"YOU KNOW HOW THEY CAN SNAP. NOW HOLD THEM UNDER YOUR BELLY. HOLD YOURSELF BETWEEN THE TEETH."

"no."

"DO IT. . . . NOW LOOK."

The teeth were beginning to hurt him. Spit and tears fell on his chest.

"mleadse."

"YOU ARE OFFAL LEFT BEHIND IN THE BECOMING. YOU ARE OFFAL AND I WILL NAME YOU. YOU ARE CUNT FACE. SAY IT."

"i am cunt face." He occluded his nostrils with his lip to say the words.

"SOON I WILL BE CLEANSED OF YOU," the Dragon said effortlessly. "WILL THAT BE GOOD?"

"good."

"WHO WILL BE NEXT WHEN IT IS TIME?"

"mrs. . . . ehrman . . ."

Sharp pain shot through Dolarhyde, pain and terrible fear.

"I'LL TEAR IT OFF."

"reba. reba. i'll give you reba." Already his speech was improving.

"YOU'LL GIVE ME NOTHING. SHE IS MINE. THEY ARE ALL MINE. REBA MCCLANE AND THEN THE SHERMANS."

"reba and then the shermans. the law will know."

"I HAVE PROVIDED FOR THAT DAY. DO YOU DOUBT IT?"

"no."

"WHO ARE YOU?"

"cunt face."

"YOU MAY PUT AWAY MY TEETH. YOU PITIFUL WEAK HARELIP, YOU'D KEEP YOUR LITTLE BUDDY FROM ME, WOULD YOU? I'LL TEAR HER APART AND RUB THE PIECES IN YOUR UGLY FACE. I'LL HANG YOU WITH HER LARGE INTESTINE IF YOU OPPOSE ME. YOU KNOW I CAN. PUT THREE HUNDRED POUNDS ON THE BAR."

Dolarhyde added the plates to the bar. He had never lifted as much as 280 until today.

"LIFT IT."

If he were not as strong as the Dragon, Reba would die. He knew it. He strained until the room turned red before his bulging eyes.

"i can't."

"NO YOU CAN'T. BUT I CAN."

Dolarhyde gripped the bar. It bowed as the weight rose to his shoulders. UP. Above his head easily. "GOOD-BYE, CUNT FACE," he said, proud Dragon, quivering in the light.

CHAPTER 38

FRANCIS DOLARHYDE never got to work on Monday morning.

He started from his house exactly on time, as he always did. His appearance was impeccable, his driving precise. He put on his dark glasses when he made the turn at the Missouri River bridge and drove into the morning sun.

His Styrofoam cooler squeaked as it jiggled against the passenger seat. He leaned across and set it on the floor, remembering that he must pick up the dry ice and get the film from . . .

Crossing the Missouri channel now, moving water under him. He looked at the whitecaps on the sliding river and suddenly felt that he was sliding and the river was still. A strange, disjointed, collapsing feeling flooded him. He let up on the accelerator.

The van slowed in the outside lane and stopped. Traffic behind him was stacking up, honking. He didn't hear it.

He sat, sliding slowly northward over the still river, facing the morning sun. Tears leaked from beneath his sunglasses and fell hot on his forearms.

Someone was pecking on the window. A driver, face early-morning pale and puffed with sleep, had gotten out of a car behind him. The driver was yelling something through the window.

Dolarhyde looked at the man. Flashing blue lights were coming from the other end of the bridge. He knew he should drive. He asked his body to step on the gas, and it did. The man beside the van skipped backward to save his feet.

Dolarhyde pulled into the parking lot of a big motel near the U.S. 270 interchange. A school bus was parked in the lot, the bell of a tuba leaning against its back window.

Dolarhyde wondered if he was supposed to get on the bus with the old people.

No, that wasn't it. He looked around for his mother's Packard.

"Get in. Don't put your feet on the seat," his mother said.

That wasn't it either.

He was in a motel parking lot on the west side of St. Louis and he wanted to be able to Choose and he couldn't.

In six days, if he could wait that long, he would kill Reba McClane. He made a sudden high sound through his nose.

Maybe the Dragon would be willing to take the Shermans first and wait another moon.

No. He wouldn't.

Reba McClane didn't know about the Dragon. She thought she was with Francis Dolarhyde. She wanted to put her body on Francis Dolarhyde. She welcomed Francis Dolarhyde in Grandmother's bed.

"I've had a really terrific time, D.," Reba McClane said in the yard.

Maybe she liked Francis Dolarhyde. That was a perverted, despicable thing for a woman to do. He understood that he should despise her for it, but oh God it was good.

Reba McClane was guilty of liking Francis Dolarhyde. Demonstrably guilty.

If it weren't for the power of his Becoming, if it weren't for the Dragon, he could never have taken her to his house. He would not have been capable of sex. Or would he?

"My God, man. That's so sweeeet."

That's what she said. She said "man."

The breakfast crowd was coming out of the motel, passing his van. Their idle glances walked on him with many tiny feet.

He needed to think. He couldn't go home. He checked into the motel, called his office and reported himself sick. The room he got was bland and quiet. The only decorations were bad steamboat prints. Nothing glowed from the walls.

Dolarhyde lay down in his clothes. The ceiling had sparkling flecks in the plaster. Every few minutes he had to get up and urinate. He shivered, then he sweated. An hour passed.

He did not want to give Reba McClane to the Dragon. He thought about what the Dragon would do to him if he didn't serve her up.

Intense fear comes in waves; the body can't stand it for long at a time. In the heavy calm between the waves, Dolarhyde could think.

How could he keep from giving her to the Dragon? One way kept nudging him. He got up.

The light switch clacked loud in the tiled bathroom. Dolarhyde looked at the shower-curtain rod, a solid piece of one-inch pipe bolted to the bathroom walls. He took down the shower curtain and hung it over the mirror.

Grasping the pipe, he chinned himself with one arm, his toes dragging up the side of the bathtub. It was stout enough. His belt was stout enough too. He could make himself do it. He wasn't afraid of *that*.

He tied the end of his belt around the pipe in a bowline knot. The buckle end formed a noose. The thick belt didn't swing, it hung down in a stiff noose.

He sat on the toilet lid and looked at it. He wouldn't get any drop, but he could stand it. He could keep his hands off the noose until he was too weak to raise his arms.

But how could he be positive that his death would affect the Dragon, now that he and the Dragon were Two? Maybe it wouldn't. How could he be sure the Dragon then would leave her alone?

It might be days before they found his body. She would wonder where he was. In that time would she go to his house and feel around for him? Go upstairs and feel around for him and get a surprise?

The Great Red Dragon would take an hour spitting her down the stairs.

Should he call her and warn her? What could she do against Him, even warned? Nothing. She could hope to die quickly, hope that in His rage He would quickly bite deep enough.

Upstairs in Dolarhyde's house, the Dragon waited in pictures he had framed with his own hands. The Dragon waited in art books and magazines beyond number, reborn every time a photographer . . . did what?

Dolarhyde could hear in his mind the Dragon's powerful voice cursing Reba. He would curse her first, before he bit. He would curse Dolarhyde too—tell her he was nothing.

"Don't do that. Don't . . . do that," Dolarhyde said to the echoing tile. He listened to his voice, the voice of Francis Dolarhyde, the voice that Reba McClane understood easily, his own voice. He had been ashamed of it all his life, had said bitter and vicious things to others with it.

But he had never heard the voice of Francis Dolarhyde curse him. "Don't do that."

The voice he heard now had never, ever cursed him. It had repeated the Dragon's abuse. The memory shamed him.

He probably was not much of a man, he thought. It occurred to him that he had never really found out about that, and now he was curious.

He had one rag of pride that Reba McClane had given him. It told him dying in a bathroom was a sorry end.

What else? What other way was there?

There was a way and when it came to him it was blasphemy, he knew. But it was a way.

He paced the motel room, paced between the beds and from the door to the windows. As he walked he practiced speaking. The words came out all right if he breathed deep between the sentences and didn't hurry.

He could talk very well between the rushes of fear. Now he had a bad one, he had one that made him retch. A calm was coming after. He waited for it and when it came he hurried to the telephone and placed a call to Brooklyn.

➤

A junior high school band was getting on the bus in the motel parking lot. The children saw Dolarhyde coming. He had to go through them to get to his van.

A fat, round-faced boy with his Sam Browne belt all crooked put on a scowl, puffed up his chest and flexed his biceps after Dolarhyde passed. Two girls giggled. The tuba blatted out the bus window as Dolarhyde went by, and he never heard the laughter behind him.

In twenty minutes he stopped the van in the lane three hundred yards from Grandmother's house.

He mopped his face, inhaled deeply three or four times. He gripped his house key in his left hand, the steering wheel with his right.

A high keening sounded through his nose. And again, louder. Louder, louder again. Go.

Gravel showered behind the van as it shot forward, the house bouncing bigger in the windshield. The van slid sideways into the yard and Dolarhyde was out of it, running.

Inside, not looking left or right, pounding down the basement stairs, fumbling at the padlocked trunk in the basement, looking at his keys.

The trunk keys were upstairs. He didn't give himself time to think. A high humming through his nose as loud as he could to numb thought, drown out voices as he climbed the stairs at a run.

At the bureau now, fumbling in the drawer for the keys, not looking at the picture of the Dragon at the foot of the bed.

"WHAT ARE YOU DOING?"

Where were the keys, where were the keys?

"WHAT ARE YOU DOING? STOP. I'VE NEVER SEEN A CHILD AS DISGUSTING AND DIRTY AS YOU. STOP."

His searching hands slowed.

"LOOK . . . LOOK AT ME."

He gripped the edge of the bureau—tried not to turn to the wall. He cut his eyes painfully away as his head turned in spite of him.

"WHAT ARE YOU DOING?"

"nothing."

The telephone was ringing, telephone ringing, telephone ringing. He picked it up, his back to the picture.

"Hey, D., how are you feeling?" Reba McClane's voice.

He cleared his throat. "Okay"—hardly a whisper.

"I tried to call you down here. Your office said you were sick—you sound terrible."

"Talk to me."

"Of course I'll talk to you. What do you think I called you for? What's wrong?"

"Flu," he said.

"Are you going to the doctor? . . . Hello? I said, are you going to the doctor?"

"Talk loud." He scrabbled in the drawer, tried the drawer next to it.

"Have we got a bad connection? D., you shouldn't be there sick by yourself."

"TELL HER TO COME OVER TONIGHT AND TAKE CARE OF YOU."

Dolarhyde almost got his hand over the mouthpiece in time.

"My God, what was that? Is somebody with you?"

"The radio, I grabbed the wrong knob."

"Hey, D., do you want me to send somebody? You don't sound so hot. I'll come myself. I'll get Marcia to bring me at lunch."

"No." The keys were under a belt coiled in the drawer. He had them now. He backed into the hall, carrying the telephone. "I'm okay. I'll see you soon." The /s/s nearly foundered him. He ran down the stairs. The phone cord jerked out of the wall and the telephone tumbled down the stairs behind him.

A scream of savage rage. "COME HERE CUNT FACE."

Down to the basement. In the trunk beside his case of dynamite was a small valise packed with cash, credit cards and driver's licenses in various names, his pistol, knife, and blackjack.

He grabbed the valise and ran up to the ground floor, quickly past the stairs, ready to fight if the Dragon came down them. Into the van and driving hard, fishtailing in the gravel lane.

He slowed on the highway and pulled over to the shoulder to heave yellow bile. Some of the fear went away.

Proceeding at legal speed, using his flashers well ahead of turns, carefully he drove to the airport.

CHAPTER 39

DOLARHYDE PAID his taxi fare in front of an apartment house on Eastern Parkway two blocks from the Brooklyn Museum. He walked the rest of the way. Joggers passed him, heading for Prospect Park.

Standing on the traffic island near the IRT subway station, he got a good view of the Greek Revival building. He had never seen the Brooklyn Museum before, though he had read its guidebook—he had ordered the book when he first saw "Brooklyn Museum" in tiny letters beneath photographs of *The Great Red Dragon and the Woman Clothed with the Sun.*

The names of the great thinkers from Confucius to Demosthenes were carved in stone above the entrance. It was an imposing building with botanical gardens beside it, a fitting house for the Dragon.

The subway rumbled beneath the street, tingling the soles of his feet. Stale air puffed from the gratings and mixed with the smell of the dye in his mustache.

Only an hour left before closing time. He crossed the street and went inside. The checkroom attendant took his valise.

"Will the checkroom be open tomorrow?" he asked.

"The museum's closed tomorrow." The attendant was a wizened woman in a blue smock. She turned away from him.

"The people who come in tomorrow, do they use the checkroom?"

"No. The museum's closed, the checkroom's closed."

Good. "Thank you."

"Don't mention it."

Dolarhyde cruised among the great glass cases in the Oceanic Hall and the Hall of the Americas on the ground floor—Andes pottery, primitive edged weapons, artifacts and powerful masks from the Indians of the Northwest coast.

Now there were only forty minutes left before the museum closed. There was no more time to learn the ground floor. He knew where the exits and the public elevators were.

He rode up to the fifth floor. He could feel that he was closer to the Dragon now, but it was all right—he wouldn't turn a corner and run into Him.

The Dragon was not on public display; the painting had been locked away in the dark since its return from the Tate Gallery in London.

Dolarhyde had learned on the telephone that *The Great Red Dragon and the Woman Clothed with the Sun* was rarely displayed. It was almost two hundred years old and a watercolor—light would fade it.

Dolarhyde stopped in front of Albert Bierstadt's *A Storm in the Rocky Mountains—Mt. Rosalie 1866.* From there he could see the locked doors of the Painting Study and Storage Department. That's where the Dragon was. Not a copy, not a photograph: the Dragon. This is where he would come tomorrow when he had his appointment.

He walked around the perimeter of the fifth floor, past the corridor of portraits, seeing nothing of the paintings. The exits were what interested him. He found the fire exits and the main stairs, and marked the location of the public elevators.

The guards were polite middle-aged men in thick-soled shoes, years of standing in the set of their legs. None was armed, Dolarhyde noted; one of the guards in the lobby was armed. Maybe he was a moonlighting cop.

The announcement of closing time came over the public-address system.

Dolarhyde stood on the pavement under the allegorical figure of

Brooklyn and watched the crowd come out into the pleasant summer evening.

Joggers ran in place, waiting while the stream of people crossed the sidewalk toward the subway.

Dolarhyde spent a few minutes in the botanical gardens. Then he flagged a taxi and gave the driver the address of a store he had found in the Yellow Pages.

CHAPTER 40

AT NINE P.M. MONDAY Graham set his briefcase on the floor outside the Chicago apartment he was using and rooted in his pocket for the keys.

He had spent a long day in Detroit interviewing staff and checking employment records at a hospital where Mrs. Jacobi did volunteer work before the family moved to Birmingham. He was looking for a drifter, someone who might have worked in both Detroit and Atlanta or in Birmingham and Atlanta; someone with access to a van and a wheelchair who saw Mrs. Jacobi and Mrs. Leeds before he broke into their houses.

Crawford thought the trip was a waste of time, but humored him. Crawford had been right. Damn Crawford. He was right too much.

Graham could hear the telephone ringing in the apartment. The keys caught in the lining of his pocket. When he jerked them out, a long thread came with them. Change spilled down the inside of his trouser leg and scattered on the floor.

"Son of a bitch."

He made it halfway across the room before the phone stopped ringing. Maybe that was Molly trying to reach him.

He called her in Oregon.

Willy's grandfather answered the telephone with his mouth full. It was suppertime in Oregon.

"Just ask Molly to call me when she's finished," Graham told him.

He was in the shower with shampoo in his eyes when the telephone rang again. He sluiced his head and went dripping to grab the receiver. "Hello, Hotlips."

"You silver-tongued devil, this is Byron Metcalf in Birmingham."

"Sorry."

"I've got good news and bad news. You were right about Niles Jacobi. He took the stuff out of the house. He'd gotten rid of it, but I squeezed him with some hash that was in his room and he owned up. That's the bad news—I know you hoped the Tooth Fairy stole it and fenced it.

"The good news is there's some film. I don't have it yet. Niles says there are two reels stuffed under the seat in his car. You still want it, right?"

"Sure, sure I do."

"Well, his intimate friend Randy's using the car and we haven't caught up with him yet, but it won't be long. Want me to put the film on the first plane to Chicago and call you when it's coming?"

"Please do. That's good, Byron, thanks."

"Nothing to it."

Molly called just as Graham was drifting off to sleep. After they assured each other that they were all right, there didn't seem to be much to say.

Willy was having a real good time, Molly said. She let Willy say good night.

Willy had plenty more to say than just good night—he told Will the exciting news: Grandpa bought him a pony.

Molly hadn't mentioned it.

CHAPTER 41

THE BROOKLYN MUSEUM is closed to the general public on Tuesdays, but art classes and researchers are admitted.

The museum is an excellent facility for serious scholarship. The staff members are knowledgeable and accommodating; often they allow researchers to come by appointment on Tuesdays to see items not on public display.

Francis Dolarhyde came out of the IRT subway station shortly after 2 P.M. on Tuesday carrying his scholarly materials. He had a notebook, a Tate Gallery catalog, and a biography of William Blake under his arm.

He had a flat 9-mm pistol, a leather sap and his razor-edged fileting knife under his shirt. An elastic bandage held the weapons against his flat belly. His sport coat would button over them. A cloth soaked in chloroform and sealed in a plastic bag was in his coat pocket.

In his hand he carried a new guitar case.

Three pay telephones stand near the subway exit in the center of Eastern Parkway. One of the telephones has been ripped out. One of the others works.

Dolarhyde fed it quarters until Reba said, "Hello."

He could hear darkroom noises over her voice.

"Hello, Reba," he said.

"Hey, D. How're you feeling?"

Traffic passing on both sides made it hard for him to hear. "Okay."

"Sounds like you're at a pay phone. I thought you were home sick."

"I want to talk to you later."

"Okay. Call me late, all right?"

"I need to . . . see you."

"I want you to see me, but I can't tonight. I have to work. Will you call me?"

"Yeah. If nothing . . ."

"Excuse me?"

"I'll call."

"I do want you to come soon, D."

"Yeah. Good-bye . . . Reba."

All right. Fear trickled from his breastbone to his belly. He squeezed it and crossed the street.

Entrance to the Brooklyn Museum on Tuesdays is through a single door on the extreme right. Dolarhyde went in behind four art students. The students piled their knapsacks and satchels against the wall and got out their passes. The guard behind the desk checked them.

He came to Dolarhyde.

"Do you have an appointment?"

Dolarhyde nodded. "Painting Study, Miss Harper."

"Sign the register, please." The guard offered a pen.

Dolarhyde had his own pen ready. He signed "Paul Crane."

The guard dialed an upstairs extension. Dolarhyde turned his back to the desk and studied Robert Blum's *Vintage Festival* over the entrance while the guard confirmed his appointment. From the corner of his eye he could see one more security guard in the lobby. Yes, that was the one with the gun.

"Back of the lobby by the shop there's a bench next to the main elevators," the desk officer said. "Wait there. Miss Harper's coming down for you." He handed Dolarhyde a pink-on-white plastic badge.

"Okay if I leave my guitar here?"

"I'll keep an eye on it."

The museum was different with the lights turned down. There was twilight among the great glass cases.

Dolarhyde waited on the bench for three minutes before Miss Harper got off the public elevator.

"Mr. Crane? I'm Paula Harper."

She was younger than she had sounded on the telephone when he called from St. Louis; a sensible-looking woman, severely pretty. She wore her blouse and skirt like a uniform.

"You called about the Blake watercolor," she said. "Let's go upstairs and I'll show it to you. We'll take the staff elevator—this way."

She led him past the dark museum shop and through a small room lined with primitive weapons. He looked around fast to keep his bearings. In the corner of the Americas section was a corridor which led to the small elevator.

Miss Harper pushed the button. She hugged her elbows and waited. The clear blue eyes fell on the pass, pink on white, clipped to Dolarhyde's lapel.

"That's a sixth-floor pass he gave you," she said. "It doesn't matter—there aren't any guards on five today. What kind of research are you doing?"

Dolarhyde had made it on smiles and nods until now. "A paper on Butts," he said.

"On Thomas Butts?"

He nodded.

"I've never read much on him. You only see him in footnotes as a patron of Blake's. Is he interesting?"

"I'm just beginning. I'll have to go to England."

"I think the National Gallery has two watercolors he did for Butts. Have you seen them yet?"

"Not yet."

"Better write ahead of time."

He nodded. The elevator came.

Fifth floor. He was tingling a little, but he had blood in his arms and legs. Soon it would be just yes or no. If it went wrong, he wouldn't let them take him.

She led him down the corridor of American portraits. This wasn't the way he came before. He could tell where he was. It was all right.

But something waited in the corridor for him, and when he saw it he stopped dead still.

Paula Harper realized he wasn't following and turned around.

He was rigid before a niche in the wall of portraits.

She came back to him and saw what he was staring at.

"That's a Gilbert Stuart portrait of George Washington," she said.

No it wasn't.

"You see a similar one on the dollar bill. They call it a Lansdowne portrait because Stuart did one for the Marquis of Lansdowne to thank him for his support in the American Revolution . . . Are you all right, Mr. Crane?"

Dolarhyde was pale. This was worse than all the dollar bills he had ever seen. Washington with his hooded eyes and bad false teeth stared out of the frame. My God he looked like Grandmother. Dolarhyde felt like a child with a rubber knife.

"Mr. Crane, are you okay?"

Answer or blow it all. Get past this. *My God, man, that's so sweeeet.* YOU'RE THE DIRTIEST . . . No.

Say something.

"I'm taking cobalt," he said.

"Would you like to sit down for a few minutes?" There *was* a faint medicinal smell about him.

"No. Go ahead. I'm coming."

And you are not going to cut me, Grandmother. God damn you, I'd kill you if you weren't already dead. Already dead. Already dead. Grandmother was already dead! Dead now, dead for always. My God, man, that's so sweeeet.

The other wasn't dead though, and Dolarhyde knew it.

He followed Miss Harper through thickets of fear.

They went through double doors into the Painting Study and Storage Department. Dolarhyde looked around quickly. It was a long, peaceful room, well-lighted and filled with carousel racks of draped paintings. A row of small office cubicles was partitioned off along the wall. The door to the cubicle on the far end was ajar, and he heard typing.

He saw no one but Paula Harper.

She took him to a counter-height work table and brought him a stool.

"Wait here. I'll bring the painting to you."

She disappeared behind the racks.

Dolarhyde undid a button at his belly.

Miss Harper was coming. She carried a flat black case no bigger than a briefcase. It was in there. How did she have the strength to carry the picture? He had never thought of it as flat. He had seen the dimensions in the catalogs—17⅛ by 13½ inches—but he had paid no attention to them. He expected it to be immense. But it was small. It was small and it was *here* in a quiet room. He had never realized how much strength the Dragon drew from the old house in the orchard.

Miss Harper was saying something ". . . have to keep it in this solander box because light will fade it. That's why it's not on display very often."

She put the case on the table and unclasped it. A noise at the double doors. "Excuse me, I have to get the door for Julio." She refastened the case and carried it with her to the glass doors. A man with a wheeled dolly waited outside. She held the doors open while he rolled it in.

"Over here okay?"

"Yes, thank you, Julio."

The man went out.

Here came Miss Harper with the solander box.

"I'm sorry, Mr. Crane. Julio's dusting today and getting the tarnish off some frames." She opened the case and took out a white cardboard folder. "You understand that you aren't allowed to touch it. I'll display it for you—that's the rule. Okay?"

Dolarhyde nodded. He couldn't speak.

She opened the folder and removed the covering plastic sheet and mat.

There it was. *The Great Red Dragon and the Woman Clothed with the Sun*—the Man-Dragon rampant over the prostrate pleading woman caught in a coil of his tail.

It was small all right, but it was powerful. Stunning. The best reproductions didn't do justice to the details and the colors.

Dolarhyde saw it clear, saw it all in an instant—Blake's handwriting on the borders, two brown spots at the right edge of the paper. It seized him hard. It was too much . . . the colors were so much stronger.

Look at the woman wrapped in the Dragon's tail. Look.

He saw that her hair was the exact color of Reba McClane's. He saw that he was twenty feet from the door. He held in voices.

I hope I didn't shock you, said Reba McClane.

"It appears that he used chalk as well as watercolor," Paula Harper was saying. She stood at an angle so that she could see what he was doing. Her eyes never left the painting.

Dolarhyde put his hand inside his shirt.

Somewhere a telephone was ringing. The typing stopped. A woman stuck her head out of the far cubicle.

"Paula, telephone for you. It's your mother."

Miss Harper did not turn her head. Her eyes never left Dolarhyde or the painting. "Would you take a message?" she said. "Tell her I'll call her back."

The woman disappeared into the office. In a moment the typing started again.

Dolarhyde couldn't hold it anymore. Play for it all, right now.

But the Dragon moved first. "I'VE NEVER SEEN—"

"What?" Miss Harper's eyes were wide.

"—a rat that big!" Dolarhyde said, pointing. "Climbing that frame!"

Miss Harper was turning. "Where?"

The blackjack slid out of his shirt. With his wrist more than his arm, he tapped the back of her skull. She sagged as Dolarhyde grabbed a handful of her blouse and clapped the chloroform rag over her face. She made a high sound once, not overloud, and went limp.

He eased her to the floor between the table and the racks of paintings, pulled the folder with the watercolor to the floor, and squatted over her. Rustling, wadding, hoarse breathing and a telephone ringing.

The woman came out of the far office.

"Paula?" She looked around the room. "It's your mother," she called. "She needs to talk to you *now.*"

She walked behind the table. "I'll take care of the visitor if you . . ." She saw them then. Paula Harper on the floor, her hair across her face, and squatting over her, his pistol in his hand, Dolarhyde stuffing the last bite of the watercolor in his mouth. Rising, chewing, running. Toward her.

She ran for her office, slammed the flimsy door, grabbed at the phone and knocked it to the floor, scrambled for it on her hands and knees and tried to dial on the busy line as her door caved in. The lighted dial burst in bright colors at the impact behind her ear. The receiver fell quacking to the floor.

Dolarhyde in the staff elevator watched the indicator lights blink down, his gun held flat across his stomach, covered by his books.

First floor.

Out into the deserted galleries. He walked fast, his running shoes whispering on the terrazzo. A wrong turn and he was passing the whale masks, the great mask of Sisuit, losing seconds, running now into the presence of the Haida high totems and lost. He ran to the totems, looked left, saw the primitive edged weapons and knew where he was.

He peered around the corner at the lobby.

The desk officer stood at the bulletin board, thirty feet from the reception desk.

The armed guard was closer to the door. His holster creaked as he bent to rub a spot on the toe of his shoe.

If they fight, drop him first. Dolarhyde put the gun under his belt and buttoned his coat over it. He walked across the lobby, unclipping his pass.

The desk officer turned when he heard the footsteps.

"Thank you," Dolarhyde said. He held up his pass by the edges, then dropped it on the desk.

The guard nodded. "Would you put it through the slot there, please?"

The reception desk telephone rang.

The pass was hard to pick up off the glass top.

The telephone rang again. Hurry.

Dolarhyde got hold of the pass, dropped it through the slot. He picked up his guitar case from the pile of knapsacks.

The guard was coming to the telephone.

Out the door now, walking fast for the botanical gardens, he was ready to turn and fire if he heard pursuit.

Inside the gardens and to the left, Dolarhyde ducked into a space between a small shed and a hedge. He opened the guitar case and dumped out a tennis racket, a tennis ball, a towel, a folded grocery sack and a big bunch of leafy celery.

Buttons flew as he tore off his coat and shirt in one move and stepped out of his trousers. Underneath he wore a Brooklyn College T-shirt and warm-up pants. He stuffed his books and clothing into the grocery bag, then the weapons. The celery stuck out the top. He wiped the handle and clasps of the case and shoved it under the hedge.

Cutting across the gardens now toward Prospect Park, the towel around his neck, he came out onto Empire Boulevard. Joggers were ahead of him. As he followed the joggers into the park, the first police cruisers screamed past. None of the joggers paid any attention to them. Neither did Dolarhyde.

He alternated jogging and walking, carrying his grocery bag and racket and bouncing his tennis ball, a man cooling off from a hard workout who had stopped by the store on the way home.

He made himself slow down; he shouldn't run on a full stomach. He could choose his pace now.

He could choose anything.

CHAPTER 42

CRAWFORD sat in the back row of the jury box eating Redskin peanuts while Graham closed the courtroom blinds.

"You'll have the profile for me later this afternoon, I take it," Crawford said. "You told me Tuesday; this is Tuesday."

"I'll finish it. I want to watch this first."

Graham opened the express envelope from Byron Metcalf and dumped out the contents—two dusty rolls of home-movie film, each in plastic sandwich bag.

"Is Metcalf pressing charges against Niles Jacobi?"

"Not for theft—he'll probably inherit anyway—he and Jacobi's brother," Graham said. "On the hash, I don't know. Birmingham DA's inclined to break his chops."

"Good," Crawford said.

The movie screen swung down from the courtroom ceiling to face the jury box, an arrangement which made it easy to show jurors filmed evidence.

Graham threaded the projector.

"On checking the newsstands where the Tooth Fairy could have gotten a *Tattler* so fast—I've had reports back from Cincinnati, Detroit, and a bunch from Chicago," Crawford said. "Various weirdos to run down."

Graham started the film. It was a fishing movie.

The Jacobi children hunkered on the bank of a pond with cane poles and bobbers.

Graham tried not to think of them in their small boxes in the ground. He tried to think of them just fishing.

The girl's cork bobbed and disappeared. She had a bite.

Crawford crackled his peanut sack. "Indianapolis is dragging ass on questioning newsies and checking the Servco Supreme stations," he said.

"Do you want to watch this or what?" Graham said.

Crawford was silent until the end of the two-minute film. "Terrific, she caught a perch," he said. "Now the profile—"

"Jack, you were in Birmingham right after it happened. I didn't get there for a month. You saw the house while it was still their house—I didn't. It was stripped and remodeled when I got there. Now, for Christ's sake let me look at these people and then I'll finish the profile."

He started the second film.

A birthday party appeared on the screen in the courtroom. The Jacobis were seated around a dining table. They were singing.

Graham lip-read "Haaappy Birth-day to you."

Eleven-year-old Donald Jacobi faced the camera. He was seated at the end of the table with the cake in front of him. The candles reflected in his glasses.

Around the corner of the table, his brother and sister were side by side watching him as he blew out the candles.

Graham shifted in his seat.

Mrs. Jacobi leaned over, her dark hair swinging, to catch the cat and dump it off the table.

Now Mrs. Jacobi brought a large envelope to her son. A long ribbon trailed from it. Donald Jacobi opened the envelope and took out a big birthday card. He looked up at the camera and turned the card around. It said "Happy Birthday—follow the ribbon."

Bouncing progress as the camera followed the procession to the kitchen. A door there, fastened with a hook. Down the basement stairs, Donald first, then the others, following the ribbon down the steps. The end of the ribbon was tied around the handlebars of a ten-speed bicycle.

Graham wondered why they hadn't given him the bike outdoors.

A jumpy cut to the next scene, and his question was answered.

Outdoors now, and clearly it had been raining hard. Water stood in the yard. The house looked different. Realtor Geehan had changed the color when he did it over after the murders. The outside basement door opened and Mr. Jacobi emerged carrying the bicycle. This was the first view of him in the movie. A breeze lifted the hair combed across his bald spot. He set the bicycle ceremoniously on the ground.

The film ended with Donald's cautious first ride.

"Sad damn thing," Crawford said, "but we already knew that."

Graham started the birthday film over.

Crawford shook his head and began to read something from his briefcase with the aid of a penlight.

On the screen Mr. Jacobi brought the bicycle out of the basement. The basement door swung closed behind him. A padlock hung from it.

Graham froze the frame.

"There. That's what he wanted the bolt cutter for, Jack—to cut that padlock and go in through the basement. Why didn't he go in that way?"

Crawford clicked off his penlight and looked over his glasses at the screen. "What's that?"

"I know he had a bolt cutter—he used it to trim that branch out of his way when he was watching from the woods. Why didn't he use it and go in through the basement door?"

"He couldn't." With a small crocodile smile, Crawford waited. He loved to catch people in assumptions.

"Did he try? Did he mark it up? I never even saw that door— Geehan had put in a steel one with deadbolts by the time I got there."

Crawford opened his jaws. "You *assume* Geehan put it in. Geehan didn't put it in. The steel door was there when they were killed. Jacobi must have put it in—he was a Detroit guy, he'd favor deadbolts."

"*When* did Jacobi put it in?"

"I don't know. Obviously it was after the kid's birthday—when was that? It'll be in the autopsy if you've got it here."

"His birthday was April 14, a Monday," Graham said, staring at the screen, his chin in his hand. "I want to know when Jacobi changed the door."

Crawford's scalp wrinkled. It smoothed out again as he saw the point. "You think the Tooth Fairy cased the Jacobi house while the old door with the padlock was still there," he said.

"He brought a bolt cutter, didn't he? How do you break in someplace with a bolt cutter?" Graham said. "You cut padlocks, bars, or chain. Jacobi didn't have any bars or chained gates, did he?"

"No."

"Then he went there expecting a padlock. A bolt cutter's fairly heavy and it's long. He was moving in daylight, and from where he parked he had to hike a long way to the Jacobi house. For all he knew, he might be coming back in one hell of a hurry if something went wrong. He wouldn't have carried a bolt cutter unless he knew he'd need it. He was expecting a padlock."

"You figure he cased the place *before* Jacobi changed the door. Then he shows up to kill them, waits in the woods—"

"You can't see this side of the house from the woods."

Crawford nodded. "He waits in the woods. They go to bed and he moves in with his bolt cutter and finds the new door with the deadbolts."

"Say he finds the new door. He had it all worked out, and now this," Graham said, throwing up his hands. "He's really pissed off, frustrated, he's hot to get in there. So he does a fast, loud pry job on the patio door. It was messy the way he went in—he woke Jacobi up and had to blow him away on the stairs. That's not like the Dragon. He's not messy that way. He's careful and he leaves nothing behind. He did a neat job at the Leedses' going in."

"Okay, all right," Crawford said. "If we find out when Jacobi changed his door, maybe we'll establish the interval between when he cased it and when he killed them. The *minimum* time that elapsed, anyway. That seems like a useful thing to know. Maybe it'll match some interval the Birmingham convention and visitors bureau could show us. We can check car rentals again. This time we'll do vans too. I'll have a word with the Birmingham field office."

Crawford's word must have been emphatic: in forty minutes flat a Birmingham FBI agent, with realtor Geehan in tow, was shouting to a carpenter working in the rafters of a new house. The carpenter's information was relayed in a radio patch to Chicago.

"Last week in April," Crawford said, putting down the telephone. "That's when they put in the new door. My God, that's two months before the Jacobis were hit. Why would he case it two months in advance?"

"I don't know, but I promise you he saw Mrs. Jacobi or saw the whole family before he checked out their house. Unless he followed them down there from Detroit, he spotted Mrs. Jacobi sometime between April 10, when they moved to Birmingham, and the end of April, when the door was changed. Sometime in that period he was in Birmingham. The bureau's going on with it down there?"

"Cops too," Crawford said. "Tell me this: how did he know there was an inside door from the basement into the house? You couldn't count on that—not in the South."

"He saw the inside of the house, no question."

"Has your buddy Metcalf got the Jacobi bank statements?"

"I'm sure he does."

"Let's see what service calls they paid for between April 10 and the end of the month. I know the service calls have been checked for a couple of weeks back from the killings, but maybe we aren't looking back far enough. Same for the Leedses."

"We always figured he looked around inside the *Leeds* house," Graham said. "From the alley he couldn't have seen the glass in the kitchen door. There's a latticed porch back there. But he was ready with his glass cutter. And they didn't have any service calls for three months before they were killed."

"If he's casing this far ahead, maybe we didn't check back far enough. We will now. At the Leedses' though—when he was in the alley reading meters behind the Leeds house two days before he killed them—maybe he saw them going in the house. He could have looked in there while the porch door was open."

"No, the doors don't line up—remember? Look here."

Graham threaded the projector with the Leeds home movie.

The Leedses' gray Scotty perked up his ears and ran to the kitchen door. Valerie Leeds and the children came in carrying groceries. Through the kitchen door nothing but lattice was visible.

"All right, you want to get Byron Metcalf busy on the bank statement for April? Any kind of service call or purchase that a door-to-door salesman might handle. No—I'll do that while you wind up the profile. Have you got Metcalf's number?"

Seeing the Leedses preoccupied Graham. Absently he told Crawford three numbers for Byron Metcalf.

He ran the films again while Crawford used the phone in the jury room.

The Leeds film first.

There was the Leedses' dog. It wore no collar, and the neighborhood was full of dogs, but the Dragon knew which dog was theirs.

Here was Valerie Leeds. The sight of her tugged at Graham. There was the door behind her, vulnerable with its big glass pane. Her children played on the courtroom screen.

Graham had never felt as close to the Jacobis as he did to the Leedses. Their movie disturbed him now. It bothered him that he had thought of the Jacobis as chalk marks on a bloody floor.

There were the Jacobi children, ranged around the corner of the table, the birthday candles flickering on their faces.

For a flash Graham saw the blob of candle wax on the Jacobis' bedside table, the bloodstains around the corner of the bedroom at the Leedses'. Something . . .

Crawford was coming back. "Metcalf said to ask you—"

"Don't talk to me!"

Crawford wasn't offended. He waited stock-still and his little eyes grew narrow and bright.

The film ran on, its light and shadows playing over Graham's face.

There was the Jacobis' cat. The Dragon knew it was the Jacobis' cat.

There was the inside basement door.

There was the outside basement door with its padlock. The Dragon had brought a bolt cutter.

The film ended. Finally it came off the reel and the end flapped around and around.

Everything the Dragon needed to know was on the two films.

They hadn't been shown in public, there wasn't any film club, film festi . . .

Graham looked at the familiar green box the Leeds movie came in. Their name and address were on it. And Gateway Film Laboratory, St. Louis, Mo. 63102.

His mind retrieved "St. Louis" just as it would retrieve any telephone number he had ever seen. What about St. Louis? It was one of the places where the *Tattler* was available on Monday night, the same day it was printed—the day before Lounds was abducted.

"Oh me," Graham said. "Oh Jesus."

He clamped his hands on the sides of his head to keep the thought from getting away.

"Do you still have Metcalf on the phone?"

Crawford handed him the receiver.

"Byron, it's Graham. Listen, did those reels of Jacobi film you sent—were they in any containers? . . . Sure, sure I know you would have sent 'em along. I need help bad on something. Do you have the Jacobi bank statements there? Okay, I want to know where they got movie film developed. Probably a store sent it off for them. If there're any checks to pharmacies or camera stores, we can find out where they did business. It's urgent, Byron. I'll tell you about it first chance. Birmingham FBI will start now checking the stores. If you find something, shoot it straight to them, then to us. Will you do that? Great. What? *No,* I will *not* introduce you to Hotlips."

Birmingham FBI agents checked four camera stores before they found the one where the Jacobis traded. The manager said all customers' film was sent to one place for processing.

Crawford had watched the films twelve times before Birmingham called back. He took the message.

Curiously formal, he held out his hand to Graham. "It's Gateway," he said.

CHAPTER 43

CRAWFORD was stirring an Alka-Seltzer in a plastic glass when the stewardess's voice came over the 727's public-address system.

"Passenger Crawford, please?"

When he waved from his aisle seat, she came aft to him. "Mr. Crawford, would you go to the cockpit, please?"

Crawford was gone for four minutes. He slid back into the seat beside Graham.

"Tooth Fairy was in New York today."

Graham winced and his teeth clicked together.

"No. He just tapped a couple of women on the head at the Brooklyn Museum and, listen to this, he *ate* a painting."

"Ate it?"

"Ate it. The Art Squad in New York snapped to it when they found out what he ate. They got two partial prints off the plastic pass he used and they flashed them down to Price a little while ago. When Price put 'em together on the screen, he rang the cherries. No ID, but it's the same thumb that was on the Leeds kid's eye."

"New York," Graham said.

"Means nothing, he was in New York today. He could still work at Gateway. If he does, he was off the job today. Makes it easier."

"What did he eat?"

"It was a thing called *The Great Red Dragon and the Woman Clothed with the Sun.* William Blake drew it, they said."

"What about the women?"

"He's got a sweet touch with the sap. Younger one's just at the hospital for observation. The older one had to have four stitches. Mild concussion."

"Could they give a description?"

"The younger one did. Quiet, husky, dark mustache and hair—a wig, I think. The guard at the door said the same thing. The older woman—he could've been in a rabbit suit for all she saw."

"But he didn't kill anybody."

"Odd," Crawford said. "He'd have been better off to wax 'em both—he could have been sure of his lead time leaving and saved himself a description or two. Behavioral Science called Bloom in the hospital about it. You know what he said? Bloom said maybe he's trying to stop."

CHAPTER 44

DOLARHYDE heard the flaps moan down. The lights of St. Louis wheeled slowly beneath the black wing. Under his feet the landing gear rumbled into a rush of air and locked down with a thud.

He rolled his head on his shoulders to ease the stiffness in his powerful neck.

Coming home.

He had taken a great risk, and the prize he brought back was the power to choose. He could choose to have Reba McClane alive. He could have her to talk to, and he could have her startling and harmless mobility in his bed.

He did not have to dread his house. He had the Dragon in his belly now. He could go into his house, walk up to a copy Dragon on the wall and wad him up if he wanted to.

He did not have to worry about feeling Love for Reba. If he felt Love for her, he could toss the Shermans to the Dragon and ease it that way, go back to Reba calm and easy, and treat her well.

From the terminal Dolarhyde telephoned her apartment. Not home yet. He tried Baeder Chemical. The night line was busy. He thought of Reba walking toward the bus stop after work, tapping along with her cane, her raincoat over her shoulders.

He drove to the film laboratory through the light evening traffic in less than fifteen minutes.

She wasn't at the bus stop. He parked on the street behind Baeder Chemical, near the entrance closest to the darkrooms. He'd tell her he was here, wait until she had finished working, and drive her home. He was proud of his new power to choose. He wanted to use it.

There were things he could catch up on in his office while he waited.

Only a few lights were on in Baeder Chemical.

Reba's darkroom was locked. The light above the door was neither red nor green. It was off. He pressed the buzzer. No response.

Maybe she had left a message in his office.

He heard footsteps in the corridor.

The Baeder supervisor, Dandridge, passed the darkroom area and never looked up. He was walking fast and carrying a thick bundle of buff personnel files under his arm.

A small crease appeared in Dolarhyde's forehead.

Dandridge was halfway across the parking lot, heading for the Gateway building, when Dolarhyde came out of Baeder behind him.

Two delivery vans and half a dozen cars were on the lot. That Buick belonged to Fisk, Gateway's personnel director. What were they doing?

There was no night shift at Gateway. Much of the building was dark. Dolarhyde could see by the red exit signs in the corridor as he went toward his office. The lights were on behind the frosted glass door of the personnel department. Dolarhyde heard voices in there, Dandridge's for one, and Fisk's.

A woman's footsteps coming. Fisk's secretary turned the corner into the corridor ahead of Dolarhyde. She had a scarf tied over her curlers and she carried ledgers from Accounting. She was in a hurry. The ledgers were heavy, a big armload. She pecked on Fisk's office door with her toe.

Will Graham opened it for her.

Dolarhyde froze in the dark hall. His gun was in his van.

The office door closed again.

Dolarhyde moved fast, his running shoes quiet on the smooth floor. He put his face close to the glass of the exit door and scanned the parking lot. Movement now under the floodlights. A man moving. He was beside one of the delivery vans and he had a flashlight. Flicking something. He was dusting the outside mirror for fingerprints.

Behind Dolarhyde, somewhere in the corridors, a man was walking. Get away from the door. He ducked around the corner and down the stairs to the basement and the furnace room on the opposite side of the building.

By standing on a workbench he could reach the high windows that opened at ground level behind the shrubbery. He rolled over the sill and came up on his hands and knees in the bushes, ready to run or fight.

Nothing moved on this side of the building. He stood up, put a hand in his pocket and strolled across the street. Running when the sidewalk was dark, walking as cars went by, he made a long loop around Gateway and Baeder Chemical.

His van stood at the curb behind Baeder. There was no place to hide close to it. All right. He sprinted across the street and leaped in, clawing at his valise.

Full clip in the automatic. He jacked a round into the chamber and laid the pistol on the console, covering it with a T-shirt.

Slowly he drove away—don't catch the light red—slowly around the corner and into the scattered traffic.

He had to think now and it was hard to think.

It had to be the films. Graham knew about the films somehow. Graham knew *where*. He didn't know *who*. If he knew who, he wouldn't need personnel records. Why accounting records too? Absences, that's why. Match absences against the dates when the Dragon struck. No, those were Saturdays, except for Lounds. Absences on the days before those Saturdays; he'd look for those. Fool him there—no workmen's compensation slips were kept for management.

Dolarhyde drove slowly up Lindbergh Boulevard, gesturing with his free hand as he ticked off the points.

They were looking for fingerprints. He'd given them no chance for fingerprints—except maybe on the plastic pass at Brooklyn Museum. He'd picked it up in a hurry, mostly by the edges.

They must have a print. Why fingerprint if they didn't have something to match it to?

They were checking that van for prints. No time to see if they were checking cars too.

Van. Carrying the wheelchair with Lounds in it—that tipped them. Or maybe somebody in Chicago saw the van. There were a lot of vans at Gateway, private vans, delivery vans.

No, Graham just knew he had a van. Graham knew because he knew. Graham knew. Graham knew. The son of a bitch was a monster.

They'd fingerprint everyone at Gateway and Baeder too. If they didn't spot him tonight, they'd do it tomorrow. He had to run forever with his *face* on every bulletin board in every post office and police station. It was all coming to pieces. He was puny and small before them.

"Reba," he said aloud. Reba couldn't save him now. They were closing in on him, and he was nothing but a puny hareli—

"ARE YOU SORRY NOW THAT YOU BETRAYED ME?"

The Dragon's voice rumbled from deep within him, deep as the shredded painting in his bowels.

"I didn't. I just wanted to choose. You called me—"

"GIVE ME WHAT I WANT AND I'LL SAVE YOU."

"No. I'll run."

"GIVE ME WHAT I WANT AND YOU'LL HEAR GRAHAM'S SPINE SNAP."

"No."

"NOW ADMIRE WHAT YOU DID TODAY. WE'RE CLOSE NOW. WE CAN BE ONE AGAIN. DO YOU FEEL ME INSIDE YOU? YOU DO, DON'T YOU?"

"Yes."

"AND YOU KNOW I CAN SAVE YOU. YOU KNOW THEY'LL SEND YOU TO A PLACE WORSE THAN BROTHER BUDDY'S. GIVE ME WHAT I WANT AND YOU'LL BE FREE."

"No."

"THEY'LL KILL YOU. YOU'LL JERK ON THE GROUND."

"No."

"WHEN YOU'RE GONE SHE'LL FUCK OTHER PEOPLE, SHE'LL—"

"No! Shut up."

"SHE'LL FUCK OTHER PEOPLE, PRETTY PEOPLE, SHE'LL PUT THEIR—"

"Stop it. Shut up."

"SLOW DOWN AND I WON'T SAY IT."

Dolarhyde's foot lifted on the accelerator.

"THAT'S GOOD. GIVE ME WHAT I WANT AND IT CAN'T HAPPEN. GIVE IT TO ME AND THEN I'LL ALWAYS LET YOU CHOOSE, YOU CAN ALWAYS CHOOSE, AND YOU'LL SPEAK WELL, I WANT YOU TO SPEAK WELL, SLOW DOWN, THAT'S RIGHT, SEE THE SERVICE STATION? PULL OVER THERE AND LET ME TALK TO YOU. . . ."

CHAPTER 45

GRAHAM came out of the office suite and rested his eyes for a moment in the dim hallway. He was restive, uneasy. This was taking too long.

Crawford was sifting the 380 Gateway and Baeder employees as fast and well as it could be done—the man was a marvel at this kind of job—but time was passing and secrecy could be maintained only so long.

Crawford had kept the working group at Gateway to a minimum. ("We want to find him, not spook him," Crawford had told them. "If we can spot him tonight, we can take him outside the plant, maybe at his house or on the lot.")

The St. Louis police department was cooperating. Lieutenant Fogel of St. Louis homicide and one sergeant came quietly in an unmarked car, bringing a Datafax.

Wired to a Gateway telephone, in minutes the Datafax was transmitting the employment roll simultaneously to the FBI identification section in Washington and the Missouri Department of Motor Vehicles.

In Washington, the names would be checked against both the civil and criminal fingerprint records. Names of Baeder employees with security clearances were flagged for faster handling.

The Department of Motor Vehicles would check for ownership of vans.

Only four employees were brought in—the personnel manager, Fisk; Fisk's secretary; Dandridge from Baeder Chemical; and Gateway's chief accountant.

No telephones were used to summon the employees to this late-night meeting at the plant. Agents called at their houses and stated their business privately. ("Look 'em over before you tell 'em why you want 'em," Crawford said. "And don't let them use the telephone after. This kind of news travels fast.")

They had hoped for a quick identification from the teeth. None of the four employees recognized them.

Graham looked down the long corridors lit with red exit signs. Damn it felt right.

What else could they do tonight?

Crawford had requested that the woman from the Brooklyn Museum—Miss Harper—be flown out as soon as she could travel. Probably that would be in the morning. The St. Louis police department had a good surveillance van. She could sit in it and watch the employees go in.

If they didn't hit it tonight, all traces of the operation would be removed from Gateway before work started in the morning. Graham didn't kid himself—they'd be lucky to have a whole day to work before the word got out at Gateway. The Dragon would be watching for anything suspicious. He would fly.

CHAPTER 46

A LATE SUPPER with Ralph Mandy had seemed all right. Reba McClane knew she had to tell him sometime, and she didn't believe in leaving things hanging.

Actually, she thought Mandy knew what was coming when she insisted on going dutch.

She told him in the car as he took her home; that it was no big deal, she'd had a lot of fun with him and wanted to be his friend, but she was involved with somebody now.

Maybe he was hurt a little, but she knew he was relieved a little too. He was pretty good about it, she thought.

At her door he didn't ask to come in. He did ask to kiss her good-bye, and she responded gladly. He opened her door and gave her the keys. He waited until she was inside and had closed the door and locked it.

When he turned around Dolarhyde shot him in the throat and twice in the chest. Three putts from the silenced pistol. A scooter is louder.

Dolarhyde lifted Mandy's body easily, laid him between the shrubs and the house and left him there.

Seeing Reba kiss Mandy had stabbed Dolarhyde deep. Then the pain left him for good.

He still looked and sounded like Francis Dolarhyde—the Dragon was a very good actor; he played Dolarhyde well.

Reba was washing her face when she heard the doorbell. It rang four times before she got there. She touched the chain, but didn't take it off.

"Who is it?"

"Francis Dolarhyde."

She eased the door open, still on the chain. "Tell me again."

"Dolarhyde. It's me."

She knew it was. She took off the chain.

Reba did not like surprises. "I thought you said you'd call me, D."

"I would have. But this is an emergency, really," he said, clapping the chloroformed cloth over her face as he stepped inside.

The street was empty. Most of the houses were dark. He carried her to the van. Ralph Mandy's feet stuck out of the shrubbery into the yard. Dolarhyde didn't bother with him anymore.

She woke on the ride. She was on her side, her cheek in the dusty carpet of the van, transmission whine loud in her ear.

She tried to bring her hands to her face. The movement mashed her bosom. Her forearms were stuck together.

She felt them with her face. They were bound together from her elbows to her wrists with what felt like soft strips of cloth. Her legs were tied the same way from knees to ankles. Something was across her mouth.

What . . . what . . . ? D. was at the door, and then . . . She remembered twisting her face away and the terrible strength of him. Oh Lord . . . what was it . . . ? D. was at the door and then she was choking something cold and she tried to twist her face away but there was a terrible grip on her head.

She was in D.'s van now. She recognized the resonances. The van was going. Fear ballooned in her. Her instinct said be quiet, but the fumes were in her throat, chloroform and gasoline. She retched against the gag.

D.'s voice. "It won't be long now."

She felt a turn and they were on gravel now, rocks pinging under the fenders and floorboard.

He's crazy. All right. That's it: Crazy.

"Crazy" is a fearsome word.

What was it? Ralph Mandy. He must have seen them at her house. It set him off.

Christ Jesus, get it all ready. A man had tried to slap her once at Reiker Institute. She was quiet and he couldn't find her—he couldn't see either. This one could fucking well see. Get it all ready. Get ready to talk. God he could kill me with this gag in my mouth. God he could be killing me and not understand what I was saying.

Be ready. Have it all ready and don't say "Huh?" Tell him he can back out, no damage. I won't tell. Be passive as long as you can. If you can't be passive, wait until you can find his eyes.

The van stopped. The van rocked as he got out. Side door sliding open. Grass and hot tires on the air. Crickets. He came in the van.

In spite of herself she squealed into the gag and twisted her face away from him when he touched her.

Soft pats on the shoulder didn't stop her writhing. A stinging slap across the face did.

She tried to talk into the gag. She was lifted, carried. His footsteps hollow on the ramp. She was sure where she was now. His house. Where in his house? Clock ticking to the right. Rug, then floor. The bedroom where they did it. She was sinking in his arms, felt the bed under her.

She tried to talk into the gag. He was leaving. Noise outside. Van door slammed. Here he comes. Setting something on the floor—metal cans.

She smelled gasoline.

"Reba." D.'s voice all right, but so calm. So terribly calm and strange. "Reba, I don't know what to . . . say to you. You felt so good, and you don't know what I did for you. And I was wrong, Reba. You made me weak and then you hurt me."

She tried to talk into the gag.

"If I untie you and let you sit up, will you be good? Don't try to run. I can catch you. Will you be good?"

She twisted her head toward the voice to nod.

A touch of cold steel against her skin, whisper of a knife through cloth and her arms were free. Now her legs. Her cheeks were wet where the gag came off.

Carefully and slowly she sat up in the bed. Take your best shot.

"D.," she said, "I didn't know you cared this much about me. I'm glad you feel that way but, see, you scared me with this."

No answer. She knew he was there.

"D., was it old dumb Ralph Mandy that made you mad? Did you see him at my house? That's it, isn't it? I was telling him I don't want to see him anymore. Because I want to see you. I'm never going to see Ralph again."

"Ralph died," Dolarhyde said. "I don't think he liked it very much."

Fantasy. He's making it up Jesus do I hope. "I've never hurt you, D. I never wanted to. Let's just be friends and fuck and have a good time and forget about this."

"Shut up," he said calmly. "I'll tell you something. The most important thing you'll ever hear. Sermon-on-the-Mount important. Ten-Commandments important. Got it?"

"Yes, D. I—"

"Shut up. Reba, some remarkable events have happened in Birmingham and Atlanta. Do you know what I'm talking about?"

She shook her head.

"It's been on the news a lot. Two groups of people were changed. Leeds. And Jacobi. The police think they were murdered. Do you know now?"

She started to shake her head. Then she did know and slowly she nodded.

"Do you know what they call the Being that visited those people? You can say."

"The Tooth—"

A hand gripped her face, shutting off the sound.

"Think carefully and answer correctly."

"It's Dragon something. Dragon . . . Red Dragon."

He was close to her. She could feel his breath on her face.

"I AM THE DRAGON."

Leaping back, driven by the volume and terrible timbre of the voice, she slammed against the headboard.

"The Dragon wants you, Reba. He always has. I didn't want to give you to Him. I did a thing for you today so He couldn't have you. And I was wrong."

This was D., she could talk to D. "Please. Please don't let him have me. You won't, please don't, you wouldn't—I'm for *you*. Keep me with you. You like me, I know you do."

"I haven't made up my mind yet. Maybe I can't help giving you to Him. I don't know. I'm going to see if you do as I tell you. Will you? Can I depend on you?"

"I'll try. I will try. Don't scare me too much or I can't."

"Get up, Reba. Stand by the bed. Do you know where you are in the room?"

She nodded.

"You know where you are in the house, don't you? You wandered around in the house while I was asleep, didn't you?"

"Asleep?"

"Don't be stupid. When we spent the night here. You went through the house, didn't you? Did you find something odd? Did you take it and show it to somebody? Did you do that, Reba?"

"I just went outside. You were asleep and I went outside. I promise."

"Then you know where the front door is, don't you?"

She nodded.

"Reba, feel on my chest. Bring your hands up slowly."

Try for his eyes?

His thumb and fingers touched lightly on each side of her windpipe. "Don't do what you're thinking, or I'll squeeze. Just feel on my chest. Just at my throat. Feel the key on the chain? Take it off over my head. Careful . . . that's right. Now I'm going to see if I can trust you. Go close the front door and lock it and bring me back the key. Go ahead. I'll wait right here. Don't try to run. I can catch you."

She held the key in her hand, the chain tapping against her thigh. It was harder navigating in her shoes, but she kept them on. The ticking clock helped.

Rug, then floor, rug again. Loom of the sofa. Go to the right.

What's my best shot? Which? Fool along with him or go for it? Did the others fool along with him? She felt dizzy from deep breathing. Don't be dizzy. Don't be dead.

It depends on whether the door is open. Find out where he is.

"Am I going right?" She knew she was.

"It's about five more steps." The voice was from the bedroom all right.

She felt air on her face. The door was half-open. She kept her body between the door and the voice behind her. She slipped the key in the keyhole below the knob. On the outside.

Now. Through the door fast making herself pull it to and turn the key. Down the ramp, no cane, trying to remember where the van was, running. Running. Into what—a bush—screaming now. Screaming "Help me. Help me. Help me, help me." On gravel running. A truck horn far away. Highway that way, a fast walk and trot and run, fast as she could, veering when she felt grass instead of gravel, zigging down the lane.

Behind her footsteps coming fast and hard, running in the gravel. She stooped and picked up a handful of rocks, waited until he was close and flung them, heard them thump on him.

A shove on the shoulder spun her, a big arm under her chin, around her neck, squeezing, squeezing, blood roared in her ears. She kicked backward, hit a shin as it

became   increasingly   quiet.

CHAPTER 47

IN TWO HOURS, the list of white male employees twenty to fifty years old who owned vans was completed. There were twenty-six names on it.

Missouri DMV provided hair color from driver's-license information, but it was not used as an exclusionary factor; the Dragon might wear a wig.

Fisk's secretary, Miss Trillman, made copies of the list and passed them around.

Lieutenant Fogel was going down the list of names when his beeper went off.

Fogel spoke to his headquarters briefly on the telephone, then put his hand over the receiver. "Mr. Crawford . . . Jack, one Ralph Mandy, white male, thirty-eight, was found shot to death a few minutes ago in University City—that's in the middle of town, close to Washington University—he was in the front yard of a house occupied by a woman named Reba McClane. The neighbors said she works for Baeder. Her door's unlocked, she's not home."

"Dandridge!" Crawford called. "Reba McClane, what about her?"

"She works in the darkroom. She's blind. She's from someplace in Colorado—"

"You know a Ralph Mandy?"

"Mandy?" Dandridge said. "Randy Mandy?"

"*Ralph* Mandy, he work here?"

A check of the roll showed he didn't.

"Coincidence maybe," Fogel said.

"Maybe," Crawford said.

"I hope nothing's happened to Reba," Miss Trillman said.

"You know her?" Graham said.

"I've talked with her several times."

"What about Mandy?"

"I don't know him. The only man I've seen her with, I saw her getting into Mr. Dolarhyde's van."

"Mr. Dolarhyde's van, Miss Trillman? What color is Mr. Dolarhyde's van?"

"Let's see. Dark brown, or maybe black."

"Where does Mr. Dolarhyde work?" Crawford asked.

"He's production supervisor," Fisk said.

"Where's his office?"

"Right down the hall."

Crawford turned to speak to Graham, but he was already moving.

Mr. Dolarhyde's office was locked. A passkey from Maintenance worked.

Graham reached in and flipped on the light. He stood still in the doorway while his eyes went over the room. It was extremely neat. No personal items were anywhere in sight. The bookshelf held only technical manuals.

The desk lamp was on the left side of the chair, so he was right-handed. Need a left thumbprint fast off a right-handed man.

"Let's toss it for a clipboard," he said to Crawford, behind him in the hall. "He'll use his left thumb on the clip."

They had started on the drawers when the desk appointment calendar caught Graham's eye. He flipped back through the scribbled pages to Saturday, June 28, the date of the Jacobi killings.

The calendar was unmarked on the Thursday and Friday before that weekend.

He flipped forward to the last week in July. The Thursday and Friday were blank. There was a note on Wednesday. It said: "Am 552 3:45–6:15."

Graham copied the entry. "I want to find out where this flight goes."

"Let me do it, you go ahead here," Crawford said. He went to a telephone across the hall.

Graham was looking at a tube of denture adhesive in the bottom desk drawer when Crawford called from the door.

"It goes to Atlanta, Will. Let's take him out."

CHAPTER 48

WATER COLD on Reba's face, running in her hair. Dizzy. Something hard under her, sloping. She turned her head. Wood under her. A cold wet towel wiped her face.

"Are you all right, Reba?" Dolarhyde's calm voice.

She shied from the sound. "Uhhhh."

"Breathe deeply."

A minute passed.

"Do you think you can stand up? Try to stand up."

She could stand with his arm around her. Her stomach heaved. He waited until the spasm passed.

"Up the ramp. Do you remember where you are?"

She nodded.

"Take the key out of the door, Reba. Come inside. Now lock it and put the key around my neck. Hang it around my neck. Good. Let's just be sure it's locked."

She heard the knob rattle.

"That's good. Now go in the bedroom, you know the way."

She stumbled and went down on her knees, her head bowed. He lifted her by the arms and supported her into the bedroom.

"Sit in this chair."

She sat.

"GIVE HER TO ME NOW."

She struggled to rise; big hands on her shoulders held her down.

"Sit still or I can't keep Him off you," Dolarhyde said.

Her mind was coming back. It didn't want to.

"Please try," she said.

"Reba, it's all over for me."

He was up, doing something. The odor of gasoline was very strong.

"Put out your hand. Feel this. Don't grab it, feel it."

She felt something like steel nostrils, slick inside. The muzzle of a gun.

"That's a shotgun, Reba. A twelve-gauge magnum. Do you know what it will do?"

She nodded.

"Take your hand down." The cold muzzle rested in the hollow of her throat.

"Reba, I wish I could have trusted you. I wanted to trust you."

He sounded like he was crying.

"You felt so good."

He *was* crying.

"So did you, D. I love it. Please don't hurt me now."

"It's all over for me. I can't leave you to Him. You know what He'll do?"

Bawling now.

"Do you know what He'll do? He'll bite you to death. Better you go with me."

She heard a match struck, smelled sulfur, heard a whoosh. Heat in the room. Smoke. Fire. The thing she feared most in the world. Fire. Anything was better than that. She hoped the first shot killed her. She tensed her legs to run.

Blubbering.

"Oh, Reba, I can't stand to watch you burn."

The muzzle left her throat.

Both barrels of the shotgun went off at once as she came to her feet.

Ears numbed, she thought she was shot, thought she was dead, felt the heavy thump on the floor more than she heard it.

Smoke now and the crackle of flames. Fire. Fire brought her to herself. She felt heat on her arms and face. Out. She stepped on legs, stumbled choking into the foot of the bed.

Stoop low, they said, under the smoke. Don't run, you'll bump into things and die.

She was locked in. Locked in. Walking, stooping low, fingers trailing on the floor, she found legs—other end—she found hair, a hairy flap, put her hand in something soft below the hair. Only pulp, sharp bone splinters and a loose eye in it.

Key around his neck . . . hurry. Both hands on the chain, legs under her, snatch. The chain broke and she fell backward, scrambling up again. Turned around, confused. Trying to feel, trying to listen with her numbed ears over the crackle of the flames. Side of the bed . . . which side? She stumbled on the body, tried to listen.

BONG, BONG, the clock striking. BONG, BONG, into the living room, BONG, BONG, take a right.

Throat seared with smoke. BONG BONG. Door here. Under the knob. Don't drop it. Click the lock. Snatch it open. Air. Down the ramp. Air. Collapsed in the grass. Up again on hands and knees, crawling.

She came up on her knees to clap, picked up the house echo and crawled away from it, breathing deep until she could stand, walk, run until she hit something, run again.

CHAPTER 49

LOCATING FRANCIS DOLARHYDE'S HOUSE was not so easy. The address listed at Gateway was a post-office box in St. Charles.

Even the St. Charles sheriff's department had to check a service map at the power-company office to be sure.

The sheriff's department welcomed St. Louis SWAT to the other side of the river, and the caravan moved quietly up State Highway 94. A deputy beside Graham in the lead car showed the way. Crawford leaned between them from the back seat and sucked at something in his teeth. They met light traffic at the north end of St. Charles, a pickup full of children, a Greyhound bus, a tow truck.

They saw the glow as they cleared the northern city limits.

"That's *it!*" the deputy said. "That's where it is!"

Graham put his foot down. The glow brightened and swelled as they roared up the highway.

Crawford snapped his fingers for the microphone.

"All units, that's his house burning. Watch it now. He may be coming out. Sheriff, let us have a roadblock here, if you will."

A thick column of sparks and smoke leaned southeast over the fields, hanging over them now.

"Here," the deputy said, "turn in on this gravel."

They saw the woman then, silhouetted black against the fire, saw her as she heard them and raised her arms to them.

And then the great fire blasted upward, outward, burning beams and window frames describing slow high arcs into the night sky, the blazing van rocked over on its side, orange tracery of the burning trees suddenly blown out and dark. The ground shuddered as the explosion whump rocked the police cars.

The woman was face down in the road. Crawford and Graham and the deputies out, running to her as fire rained in the road, some running past her with their weapons drawn.

Crawford took Reba from a deputy batting sparks from her hair.

He held her arms, face close to hers, red in the firelight.

"Francis Dolarhyde," he said. He shook her gently. "Francis Dolarhyde, where is he?"

"He's in there," she said, raising her stained hand toward the heat, letting it fall. "He's dead in there."

"You *know* that?" Crawford peered into her sightless eyes.

"I was with him."

"Tell me, please."

"He shot himself in the face. I put my hand in it. He set fire to the house. He shot himself. I put my hand in it. He was on the floor. I put my hand in it can I sit down?"

"Yes," Crawford said. He got into the back of a police car with her. He put his arms around her and let her cry into his jowl.

Graham stood in the road and watched the flames until his face was red and sore.

The winds aloft whipped smoke across the moon.

CHAPTER 50

THE WIND IN THE MORNING was warm and wet. It blew wisps of cloud over the blackened chimneys where Dolarhyde's house had stood. Thin smoke blew flat across the fields.

A few raindrops struck coals and exploded in tiny puffs of steam and ashes.

A fire truck stood by, its light revolving.

S. F. Aynesworth, FBI section chief, Explosives, stood with Graham upwind of the ruins, pouring coffee from a thermos.

Aynesworth winced as the local fire marshal reached into the ashes with a rake.

"Thank God it's still too hot for him in there," he said out of the side of his mouth. He had been carefully cordial to the local authorities. To Graham, he spoke his mind. "I got to wade it, hell. This place'll look like a fucking turkey farm soon as all the special deputies and constables finish their pancakes and take a crap. They'll be right on down to help."

Until Aynesworth's beloved bomb van arrived from Washington, he had to make do with what he could bring on the plane. He pulled a faded Marine Corps duffel bag out of the trunk of a patrol car and unpacked his Nomex underwear and asbestos boots and coveralls.

"What did it look like when it went up, Will?"

"A flash of intense light that died down. Then it looked darker at the base. A lot of stuff was going up, window frames, flat pieces of the roof, and chunks flying sideways, tumbling in the fields. There was a shock wave, and the wind after. It blew out and sucked back in again. It looked like it almost blew the fire out."

"The fire was going good when it blew?"

"Yeah, it was through the roof and out the windows upstairs and down. The trees were burning."

Aynesworth recruited two local firemen to stand by with a hose, and a third dressed in asbestos stood by with a winch line in case something fell on him.

He cleared the basement steps, now open to the sky, and went down into the tangle of black timbers. He could stay only a few minutes at a time. He made eight trips.

All he got for his effort was one flat piece of torn metal, but it seemed to make him happy.

Red-faced and wet with sweat, he stripped off his asbestos clothing and sat on the running board of the fire truck with a fireman's raincoat over his shoulders.

He laid the flat piece of metal on the ground and blew away a film of ash.

"Dynamite," he told Graham. "Look here, see the fern pattern in the metal? This stuff's the right gauge for a trunk or a footlocker. That's probably it. Dynamite in a footlocker. It didn't go off in the basement, though. Looks like the ground floor to me. See where the tree's cut there where that marble tabletop hit it? Blown out sideways. The dynamite was in something that kept the fire off of it for a while."

"How about remains?"

"There may not be a lot, but there's always something. We've got a lot of sifting to do. We'll find him. I'll give him to you in a small sack."

➤

A sedative had finally put Reba McClane to sleep at DePaul Hospital shortly after dawn. She wanted the policewoman to sit close beside her bed. Several times through the morning she woke and reached out for the officer's hand.

When she asked for breakfast, Graham brought it in.

Which way to go? Sometimes it was easier for them if you were impersonal. With Reba McClane, he didn't think so.

He told her who he was.

"Do you know him?" she asked the policewoman.

Graham passed the officer his credentials. She didn't need them.

"I know he's a federal officer, Miss McClane."

She told him everything, finally. All about her time with Francis Dolarhyde. Her throat was sore, and she stopped frequently to suck cracked ice.

He asked her the unpleasant questions and she took him through it, once waving him out the door while the policewoman held the basin to catch her breakfast.

She was pale and her face was scrubbed and shiny when he came back into the room.

He asked the last of it and closed his notebook.

"I won't put you through this again," he said, "but I'd like to come back by. Just to say hi and see how you're doing."

"How could you help it?—a charmer like me."

For the first time he saw tears and realized where it ate her.

"Would you excuse us for a minute, officer?" Graham said. He took Reba's hand.

"Look here. There was plenty wrong with Dolarhyde, but there's nothing wrong with you. You said he was kind and thoughtful to you. I believe it. That's what you brought out in him. At the end, he couldn't kill you and he couldn't watch you die. People who study this kind of thing say he was trying to stop. Why? Because you helped him. That probably saved some lives. You didn't draw a freak. You drew a man with a freak on his back. Nothing wrong with you, kid. If you let yourself believe there is, you're a sap. I'm coming back to see you in a day or so. I have to look at cops all the time, and I need relief—try to do something about your hair there."

She shook her head and waved him toward the door. Maybe she grinned a little, he couldn't be sure.

➤

Graham called Molly from the St. Louis FBI office. Willy's grandfather answered the telephone.

"It's Will Graham, Mama," he said. "Hello, Mr. Graham."

Willy's grandparents always called him "Mr. Graham."

"Mama said he killed himself. She was looking at Donahue and they broke in with it. Damn lucky thing. Saved you fellows a lot of trouble catching him. Saves us taxpayers footing any more bills for this thing too. Was he really white?"

"Yes sir. Blond. Looked Scandinavian."

Willy's grandparents were Scandinavian.

"May I speak to Molly, please?"

"Are you going back down to Florida now?"

"Soon. Is Molly there?"

"Mama, he wants to speak to Molly. She's in the bathroom, Mr. Graham. My grandboy's eating breakfast again. Been out riding in that good air. You ought to see that little booger eat. I bet he's gained ten pounds. Here she is."

"Hello."

"Hi, hotshot."

"Good news, huh?"

"Looks like it."

"I was out in the garden. Mamamma came out and told me when she saw it on TV. When did you find out?"

"Late last night."

"Why didn't you call me?"

"Mamamma was probably asleep."

"No, she was watching Johnny Carson. I can't tell you, Will. I'm so glad you didn't have to catch him."

"I'll be here a little longer."

"Four or five days?"

"I'm not sure. Maybe not that long. I want to see you, kid."

"I want to see you too, when you get through with everything you need to do."

"Today's Wednesday. By Friday I ought to—"

"Will, Mamamma has all Willy's uncles and aunts coming down from Seattle next week, and—"

"Fuck Mamamma. What is this 'Mamamma' anyway?"

"When Willy was real little, he couldn't say—"

"Come home with me."

"Will, *I've* waited for *you*. They never get to see Willy and a few more days—"

"Come yourself. Leave Willy there, and your ex-mother-in-law can stick him on a plane next week. Tell you what—let's stop in New Orleans. There's a place called—"

"I don't think so. I've been working—just part-time—at this western store in town, and I have to give them a little notice."

"What's wrong, Molly?"

"Nothing. Nothing's wrong. . . . I got so sad, Will. You know I came up here after Willy's father died." She always said "Willy's father" as though it were an office. She never used his name. "And we were all together—I got myself together, I got calm. I've gotten myself together now, too, and I—"

"Small difference: I'm not dead."

"Don't be that way."

"What way? Don't be what way?"

"You're mad."

Graham closed his eyes for a moment.

"Hello."

"I'm not mad, Molly. You do what you want to. I'll call you when things wind up here."

"You could come up here."

"I don't think so."

"Why not? There's plenty of room. Mamamma would—"

"Molly, they don't like me and you know why. Every time they look at me, I remind them."

"That's not fair and it's not true either."

Graham was very tired.

"Okay. They're full of shit and they make me sick—try that one."

"Don't say that."

"They want the boy. Maybe they like you all right, probably they do, if they ever think about it. But they want the boy and they'll take you. They don't want me and I could care less. *I* want *you*. In Florida. Willy too, when he gets tired of his pony."

"You'll feel better when you get some sleep."

"I doubt it. Look, I'll call you when I know something here."

"Sure." She hung up.

"*Ape* shit," Graham said. "*Ape* shit."

Crawford stuck his head in the door. "Did I hear you say 'ape shit'?"

"You did."

"Well, cheer up. Aynesworth called in from the site. He has something for you. He said we ought to come on out, he's got some static from the locals."

CHAPTER 51

AYNESWORTH was pouring ashes carefully into new paint cans when Graham and Crawford got to the black ruin where Dolarhyde's house had stood.

He was covered with soot and a large blister puffed under his ear. Special Agent Janowitz from Explosives was working down in the cellar.

A tall sack of a man fidgeted beside a dusty Oldsmobile in the drive. He intercepted Crawford and Graham as they crossed the yard.

"Are you Crawford?"

"That's right."

"I'm Robert L. Dulaney. I'm the coroner and this is my jurisdiction." He showed them his card. It said "Vote for Robert L. Dulaney."

Crawford waited.

"Your man here has some evidence that should have been turned over to me. He's kept me waiting for nearly an hour."

"Sorry for the inconvenience, Mr. Dulaney. He was following my instructions. Why don't you have a seat in your car and I'll clear this up."

Dulaney started after them.

Crawford turned around. "You'll excuse us, Mr. Dulaney. Have a seat in your car."

Section Chief Aynesworth was grinning, his teeth white in his sooty face. He had been sieving ashes all morning.

"As section chief, it gives me great pleasure—"

"To pull your prong, we all know that," Janowitz said, climbing from the black tangle of the cellar.

"Silence in the ranks, Indian Janowitz. Fetch the items of interest." He tossed Janowitz a set of car keys.

From the trunk of an FBI sedan Janowitz brought a long cardboard box. A shotgun, the stock burned off and barrels twisted by the heat, was wired to the bottom of the box. A smaller box contained a blackened automatic pistol.

"The pistol came out better," Aynesworth said. "Ballistics may be able to make a match with it. Come on, Janowitz, get to it."

Aynesworth took three plastic freezer bags from him.

"Front and center, Graham." For a moment the humor left Aynesworth's face. This was a hunter's ritual, like smearing Graham's forehead with blood.

"That was a real sly show, podna." Aynesworth put the bags in Graham's hands.

One bag contained five inches of a charred human femur and the ball of a hip. Another contained a wristwatch. The third held the teeth.

The plate was black and broken and only half was there, but that half contained the unmistakable pegged lateral incisor.

Graham supposed he should say something. "Thanks. Thanks a lot."

His head swam briefly and he relaxed all over.

". . . museum piece," Aynesworth was saying. "We have to turn it over to the turkey, don't we, Jack?"

"Yeah. But there're some pros in the St. Louis coroner's office. They'll come over and make good impressions. We'll have those."

Crawford and the others huddled with the coroner beside his car.

Graham was alone with the house. He listened to the wind in the chimneys. He hoped Bloom would come here when he was well. Probably he would.

Graham wanted to know about Dolarhyde. He wanted to know

what happened here, what bred the Dragon. But he had had enough
for now.

A mockingbird lit on the top of a chimney and whistled.

Graham whistled back.

He was going home.

CHAPTER 52

GRAHAM smiled when he felt the jet's big push rocket him up and away from St. Louis, turning across the sun's path south and east at last toward home.

Molly and Willy would be there.

"Let's don't jack around about who's sorry for what. I'll pick you up in Marathon, kiddo," she said on the phone.

In time he hoped he would remember the few good moments—the satisfaction of seeing people at work who were deeply committed to their skills. He supposed you could find that anywhere if you knew enough about what you were watching.

It would have been presumptuous to thank Lloyd Bowman and Beverly Katz, so he just told them on the telephone that he was glad to have worked with them again.

One thing bothered him a little: the way he felt when Crawford turned from the telephone in Chicago and said, "It's Gateway."

Possibly that was the most intense and savage joy that had ever burst in him. It was unsettling to know that the happiest moment of his life had come then, in that stuffy jury room in the city of Chicago. *When even before he knew, he knew.*

He didn't tell Lloyd Bowman how it felt; he didn't have to.

"You know, when his theorem rang the cherries, Pythagoras gave one hundred oxen to the Muse," Bowman said. "Nothing sweeter, is there? Don't answer—it lasts better if you don't spend it talking."

Graham grew more impatient the closer he got to home and to Molly. In Miami he had to go out on the apron to board *Aunt Lula*, the old DC-3 that flew to Marathon.

He liked DC-3's. He liked everything today.

Aunt Lula was built when Graham was five years old and her wings were always dirty with a film of oil that blew back from the engines. He had great confidence in her. He ran to her as though she had landed in a jungle clearing to rescue him.

Islamorada's lights were coming on as the island passed under the wing. Graham could still see whitecaps on the Atlantic side. In minutes they were descending to Marathon.

It was like the first time he came to Marathon. He had come aboard *Aunt Lula* that time too, and often afterward he went to the airfield at dusk to watch her coming in, slow and steady, flaps down, fire flickering out her exhausts and all the passengers safe behind their lighted windows.

The takeoffs were good to watch as well, but when the old airplane made her great arc to the north it left him sad and empty and the air was acrid with good-byes. He learned to watch only the landings and hellos.

That was before Molly.

With a final grunt, the airplane swung onto the apron. Graham saw Molly and Willy standing behind the fence, under the floodlights.

Willy was solidly planted in front of her. He'd stay there until Graham joined them. Only then would he wander along, examining whatever interested him. Graham liked him for that.

Molly was the same height as Graham, five feet ten inches. A level kiss in public carries a pleasant jolt, possibly because level kisses usually are exchanged in bed.

Willy offered to carry his suitcase. Graham gave him the suit bag instead.

Riding home to Sugarloaf Key, Molly driving, Graham remembered the things picked out by the headlights, imagined the rest.

When he opened the car door in the yard, he could hear the sea.

Willy went into the house, holding the suit bag on top of his head, the bottom flapping against the backs of his legs.

Graham stood in the yard absently brushing mosquitoes away from his face.

Molly put her hand on his cheek. "What you ought to do is come on in the house before you get eaten up."

He nodded. His eyes were wet.

She waited a moment longer, tucked her head and peered up at him, wiggling her eyebrows. "Tanqueray martinis, steaks, hugging and stuff. Right this way . . . and the light bill and the water bill and lengthy conversations with my child," she added out of the side of her mouth.

CHAPTER 53

GRAHAM AND MOLLY wanted very much for it to be the same again between them, to go on as they had before.

When they saw that it was not the same, the unspoken knowledge lived with them like unwanted company in the house. The mutual assurances they tried to exchange in the dark and in the day passed through some refraction that made them miss the mark.

Molly had never looked better to him. From a painful distance, he admired her unconscious grace.

She tried to be good to him, but she had been to Oregon and she had raised the dead.

Willy felt it and he was cool to Graham, maddeningly polite.

A letter came from Crawford. Molly brought it in the mail and did not mention it.

It contained a picture of the Sherman family, printed from movie film. Not everything had burned, Crawford's note explained. A search of the fields around the house had turned this picture up, along with a few other things the explosion had blown far from the fire.

"These people were probably on his itinerary," Crawford wrote. "Safe now. Thought you'd like to know."

Graham showed it to Molly.

"See? That's why," he said. "That's why it was worth it."

"I know," she said. "I understand that, really I do."

The bluefish were running under the moon. Molly packed suppers and they fished and they built fires, and none of it was any good.

Grandpa and Mamamma sent Willy a picture of his pony and he tacked it to the wall in his room.

The fifth day home was the last day before Graham and Molly would go back to work in Marathon. They fished in the surf, walking a quarter-mile around the curving beach to a place where they had luck before.

Graham had decided to talk to both of them together.

The expedition did not begin well. Willy pointedly put aside the rod Graham had rigged for him and brought the new surf-casting rod his grandfather sent home with him.

They fished for three hours in silence. Graham opened his mouth to speak several times, but it didn't seem right.

He was tired of being disliked.

Graham caught four snappers, using sand fleas for bait. Willy caught nothing. He was casting a big Rapala with three treble hooks which his grandfather had given him. He was fishing too fast, casting again and again, retrieving too fast, until he was red-faced and his T-shirt stuck to him.

Graham waded into the water, scooped sand in the backwash of a wave, and came up with two sand fleas, their legs waving from their shells.

"How about one of these, partner?" He held out a sand flea to Willy.

"I'll use the Rapala. It was my father's, did you know that?"

"No," Graham said. He glanced at Molly.

She hugged her knees and looked far off at a frigate bird sailing high.

She got up and brushed off the sand. "I'll go fix some sandwiches," she said.

When Molly had gone, Graham was tempted to talk to the boy by himself. No. Willy would feel whatever his mother felt. He'd wait and get them both together when she came back. He'd do it this time.

She wasn't gone long and she came back without the sandwiches, walking swiftly on the packed sand above the surf.

"Jack Crawford's on the phone. I told him you'd call him back, but he said it's urgent," she said, examining a fingernail. "Better hurry."

Graham blushed. He stuck the butt of his rod in the sand and trotted toward the dunes. It was quicker than going around the beach if you carried nothing to catch in the brush.

He heard a low whirring sound carried on the wind and, wary of a rattler, he scanned the ground as he went into the scrub cedar.

He saw boots beneath the brush, the glint of a lens and a flash of khaki rising.

He looked into the yellow eyes of Francis Dolarhyde and fear raised the hammers of his heart.

Snick of a pistol action working, an automatic coming up and Graham kicked at it, struck it as the muzzle bloomed pale yellow in the sun, and the pistol flew into the brush. Graham on his back, something burning in the left side of his chest, slid headfirst down the dune onto the beach.

Dolarhyde leaped high to land on Graham's stomach with both feet and he had the knife out now and never looked up at the thin screaming from the water's edge. He pinned Graham with his knees, raised the knife high and grunted as he brought it down. The blade missed Graham's eye and crunched deep into his cheek.

Dolarhyde rocked forward and put his weight on the handle of the knife to shove it through Graham's head.

The rod whistled as Molly swung it hard at Dolarhyde's face. The big Rapala's hooks sank solidly in his cheek and the reel screamed, paying out line as she drew back to strike again.

He growled, grabbed at his face as she hit him, and the treble hooks jammed into his hand as well. One hand free, one hand hooked to his face, he tugged the knife out and started after her.

Graham rolled over, got to his knees, then his feet, eyes wild and choking blood he ran, ran from Dolarhyde, ran until he collapsed.

Molly ran for the dunes, Willy ahead of her. Dolarhyde was coming, dragging the rod. It caught on a bush and pulled him howling to a stop before he thought to cut the line.

"Run baby, run baby, run baby! Don't look back," she gasped. Her legs were long and she shoved the boy ahead of her, the crashing ever closer in the brush behind them.

They had one hundred yards on him when they left the dunes, seventy yards when they reached the house. Scrambling up the stairs. Clawing in Will's closet.

To Willy, "Stay here."

Down again to meet him. Down to the kitchen, not ready, fumbling with the speedloader.

She forgot the stance and she forgot the front sight but she got a good two-handed grip on the pistol and as the door exploded inward she blew a rat hole through his thigh—"Muhner!"—and she shot him in the face as he slid down the door facing and she shot him in the face as he sat on the floor and she ran to him and shot him twice in the face as he sprawled against the wall, scalp down to his chin and his hair on fire.

➤

Willy tore up a sheet and went to look for Will. His legs were shaking and he fell several times crossing the yard.

The sheriff's deputies and ambulances came before Molly ever thought to call them. She was taking a shower when they came in the house behind their pistols. She was scrubbing hard at the flecks of blood and bone on her face and hair and she couldn't answer when a deputy tried to talk to her through the shower curtain.

One of the deputies finally picked up the dangling telephone receiver and talked to Crawford in Washington, who had heard the shots and summoned them.

"I don't know, they're bringing him in now," the deputy said. He looked out the window as the litter passed. "It don't look good to me," he said.   .

CHAPTER 54

ON THE WALL at the foot of the bed there was a clock with numbers large enough to read through the drugs and the pain.

When Will Graham could open his right eye, he saw the clock and knew where he was—an intensive-care unit. He knew to watch the clock. Its movement assured him that this was passing, would pass.

That's what it was there for.

It said four o'clock. He had no idea which four o'clock and he didn't care, as long as the hands were moving. He drifted away.

The clock said eight when he opened his eye again.

Someone was to the side of him. Cautiously he turned his eye. It was Molly, looking out the window. She was thin. He tried to speak, but a great ache filled the left side of his head when he moved his jaw. His head and his chest did not throb together. It was more of a syncopation. He made a noise as she left the room.

The window was light when they pulled and tugged at him and did things that made the cords in his neck stand out.

Yellow light when he saw Crawford's face over him.

Graham managed to wink. When Crawford grinned, Graham could see a piece of spinach between his teeth.

Odd. Crawford eschewed most vegetables.

Graham made writing motions on the sheet beneath his hand.

Crawford slid his notebook under Graham's hand and put a pen between his fingers.

"Willy OK," he wrote.

"Yeah, he's fine," Crawford said. "Molly too. She's been in here while you were asleep. Dolarhyde's dead, Will. I promise you, he's dead. I took the prints myself and had Price match them. There's no question. He's dead."

Graham drew a question mark on the pad.

"We'll get into it. I'll be here, I can tell you the whole thing when you feel good. They only give me five minutes."

"Now," Graham wrote.

"Has the doctor talked to you? No? About you first—you'll be okay. Your eye's just swollen shut from a deep stab wound in the face. They've got it fixed, but it'll take time. They took out your spleen. But who needs a spleen? Price left his in Burma in '41."

A nurse pecked on the glass.

"I've got to go. They don't respect credentials, nothing, around here. They just throw you out when the time's up. See you later."

Molly was in the ICU waiting room. A lot of tired people were.

Crawford went to her. "Molly . . ."

"Hello, Jack," she said. "*You're* looking really well. Want to give him a face transplant?"

"Don't, Molly."

"Did you look at him?"

"Yes."

"I didn't think I could look at him, but I did."

"They'll fix him up. The doctor told me. They can do it. You want somebody to stay with you, Molly? I brought Phyllis down, she—"

"No. Don't do anything else for me."

She turned away, fumbling for a tissue. He saw the letter when she opened her purse: expensive mauve stationery that he had seen before.

Crawford hated this. He had to do it.

"Molly."

"What is it?"

"Will got a letter?"

"Yes."

"Did the nurse give it to you?"

"Yes, she *gave* it to me. They're holding some flowers from all his *friends* in Washington, too."

"May I see the letter?"

"I'll give it to him when he feels like it."

"Please let me see it."

"Why?"

"Because he doesn't need to hear from . . . that particular person."

Something was wrong with the expression on his face and she looked down at the letter and dropped it, purse and all. A lipstick rolled across the floor.

Stooping to pick up Molly's things, Crawford heard her heels tap fast as she left him, abandoning her purse.

He gave the purse to the charge nurse.

Crawford knew it would be nearly impossible for Lecter to get what he would need, but with Lecter he took no chances.

He had an intern fluoroscope the letter in the X-ray department. Crawford slit the envelope on all sides with a penknife and examined its inside surface and the note for any stain or dust—they would have lye for scrubbing at Baltimore Hospital, and there was a pharmacy.

Satisfied at last, he read it:

Dear Will,

Here we are, you and I, languishing in our hospitals. You have your pain and I am without my books—the learned Dr. Chilton has seen to that.

We live in a primitive time—don't we, Will?—neither savage nor wise. Half measures are the curse of it. Any rational society would either kill me or give me my books.

I wish you a speedy convalescence and hope you won't be very ugly.

I think of you often.

Hannibal Lecter

The intern looked at his watch, "Do you need me anymore?"

"No," Crawford said. "Where's the incinerator?"

When Crawford returned in four hours for the next visiting period, Molly wasn't in the waiting room and she wasn't in the intensive-care unit.

Graham was awake. He drew a question mark on the pad at once. "D. dead how?" he wrote under it.

Crawford told him. Graham lay still for a full minute. Then he wrote, "Lammed how?"

"Okay," Crawford said. "St. Louis. Dolarhyde must have been looking for Reba McClane. He came in the lab while we were there and spotted us. His prints were on an open furnace-room window—it wasn't reported until yesterday."

Graham tapped the pad. "Body?"

"We think it was a guy named Arnold Lang—he's missing. His car was found in Memphis. It had been wiped down. They'll run me out in a minute. Let me give it to you in order.

"Dolarhyde knew we were there. He gave us the slip at the plant and drove to a Servco Supreme station at Lindbergh and U.S. 270. Arnold Lang worked there.

"Reba McClane said Dolarhyde had a tiff with a service-station attendant on Saturday before last. We think it was Lang.

"He snuffed Lang and took his body to the house. Then he went by Reba McClane's. She was in a clinch with Ralph Mandy at the door. He shot Mandy and dragged him into the hedge."

The nurse came in.

"For God's sake, it's police business," Crawford said. He talked fast as she pulled him by the coat sleeve to the door. "He chloroformed Reba McClane and took her to the house. The body was there," Crawford said from the hall.

Graham had to wait four hours to find out the rest.

"He gave her this and that, you know, 'Will I kill you or not?'" Crawford said as he came in the door.

"You know the routine about the key hanging around his neck— that was to make sure she felt the body. So she could tell *us* she certainly did feel a body. All right, it's this way and that way. 'I can't stand to see you burn,' he says, and blows Lang's head off with a twelve-gauge.

"Lang was perfect. He didn't have any teeth anyway. Maybe Dolarhyde knew the maxillary arch survives fires a lot of times—who knows what he knew? Anyway, Lang didn't have any maxillary arch after Dolarhyde got through with him. He shot the head off Lang's body and he must have tipped a chair or something for the thud of the body falling. He'd hung the key around Lang's neck.

"Now Reba's scrambling around looking for the key. Dolarhyde's in the corner watching. Her ears are ringing from the shotgun. She won't hear his little noises.

"He's started a fire, but he hasn't put the gas to it yet. He's got gas in the room. She got out of the house okay. If she had panicked too much, run into a wall or something or frozen, I guess he'd have sapped her and dragged her outside. She wouldn't have known how she got out. But she had to get out for it to work. Oh hell, here comes that nurse."

Graham wrote fast. "How vehicle?"

"You have to admire this," Crawford said. "He knew he'd have to leave his van at the house. He couldn't drive two vehicles out there, and he needed a getaway piece.

"This is what he did: he made *Lang* hook up the service-station tow truck to his van. He snuffed Lang, locked the station, and towed his van out to his house. Then he left the tow truck on a dirt road back in the fields behind the house, got back in his van and went after Reba. When she got out of the house all right, he dragged out his dynamite, put the gasoline around the fire, and lammed out the back. He drove the tow truck *back* to the service station, left it and got Lang's car. No loose ends.

"It drove me crazy until we figured it out. I know it's right because he left a couple of prints on the tow bar.

"We probably met him in the road when we were going up there to the house . . . Yes, ma'am. I'm coming. Yes, ma'am."

Graham wanted to ask a question, but it was too late.

Molly took the next five-minute visit.

Graham wrote "I love you" on Crawford's pad.

She nodded and held his hand.

A minute later he wrote again. "Willy okay?"

She nodded.

"Here?"

She looked up at him too quickly from the pad. She made a kiss with her mouth and pointed to the approaching nurse.

He tugged her thumb.

"*Where?*" he insisted, underlining twice.

"Oregon," she said.

Crawford came a final time.

Graham was ready with his note. It said, "Teeth?"

"His grandmother's," Crawford said. "The ones we found in the house were his grandmother's. St. Louis PD located one Ned Vogt— Dolarhyde's mother was Vogt's stepmother. Vogt saw Mrs. Dolarhyde when he was a kid, and he never forgot the teeth.

"That's what I was calling you about when you ran into Dolarhyde. The Smithsonian had just called me. They finally had gotten the teeth from the Missouri authorities, just to examine for their own satisfaction. They noticed the upper part was made of vulcanite instead of acrylic like they use now. Nobody's made vulcanite plates in thirty-five years.

"Dolarhyde had a new acrylic pair just like them made to fit him. The new ones were on his body. Smithsonian looked at some features on them—the fluting, they said, and rugae. Chinese manufacture. The old ones were Swiss.

"He had a key on him too, for a locker in Miami. Big book in there. Kind of a diary—hell of a thing. I'll have it when you want to see it.

"Look, sport, I have to go back to Washington. I'll get back down here the weekend, if I can. You gonna be okay?"

Graham drew a question mark, then scratched it out and wrote "sure."

The nurse came after Crawford left. She shot some Demerol into his intravenous line and the clock grew fuzzy. He couldn't keep up with the second hand.

He wondered if Demerol would work on your feelings. He could hold Molly a while with his face. Until they finished fixing it anyway. That would be a cheap shot. Hold her for what? He was drifting off and he hoped he wouldn't dream.

He did drift between memory and dream, but it wasn't so bad. He didn't dream of Molly leaving, or of Dolarhyde. It was a long memory-dream of Shiloh, interrupted by lights shone in his face and the gasp and hiss of the blood-pressure cuff. . . .

It was spring, soon after he shot Garrett Jacob Hobbs, when Graham visited Shiloh.

On a soft April day he walked across the asphalt road to Bloody Pond. The new grass, still light green, grew down the slope to the water. The clear water had risen into the grass, and the grass was visible in the water, growing down, down, as though it covered the bottom of the pond.

Graham knew what had happened there in April 1862.

He sat down in the grass, felt the damp ground through his trousers.

A tourist's automobile went by and after it had passed, Graham saw movement behind it in the road. The car had broken a chicken snake's back. It slid in endless figure eights across itself in the center of the asphalt road, sometimes showing its black back, sometimes its pale belly.

Shiloh's awesome presence hooded him with cold, though he was sweating in the mild spring sun.

Graham got up off the grass, his trousers damp behind. He was light-headed.

The snake looped on itself. He stood over it, picked it up by the end of its smooth dry tail, and with a long fluid motion cracked it like a whip.

Its brains zinged into the pond. A bream rose to them.

He had thought Shiloh haunted, its beauty sinister like flags.

Now, drifting between memory and narcotic sleep, he saw that Shiloh was not sinister; it was indifferent. Beautiful Shiloh could witness anything. Its unforgivable beauty simply underscored the indifference of nature, the Green Machine. The loveliness of Shiloh mocked our plight.

He roused and watched the mindless clock, but he couldn't stop thinking:

In the Green Machine there is no mercy; we make mercy, manufacture it in the parts that have overgrown our basic reptile brain.

There is no murder. We make murder, and it matters only to us.

Graham knew too well that he contained all the elements to make murder; perhaps mercy too.

He understood murder uncomfortably well, though.

He wondered if, in the great body of humankind, in the minds of men set on civilization, the vicious urges we control in ourselves and the dark instinctive knowledge of those urges function like the crippled virus the body arms against.

He wondered if old, awful urges are the virus that makes vaccine.

Yes, he had been wrong about Shiloh. Shiloh isn't haunted—men are haunted.

Shiloh doesn't care.

And I gave my heart to know wisdom, and to know madness and folly:
I perceived that this also is vexation of spirit.
                                                    —ECCLESIASTES